I0742410

THE LAST SAFE PLACE

ANDY GORMAN

For those who seek adventure and dream of better days.

For those who see things from a cosmic perspective, and those who don't yet.

For those who have lost a loved one or have seen their heroes fall.

For those who have felt trapped in a cycle of self-abuse.

You are not alone.

We are all citizens of Earth.

And better days are ahead.

Andy Gorman's biography is a work in progress. The best way to learn more about him is to visit his website:

www.AuthorAndyGorman.com

"Weightless, unhinged,
Eons from even our own moon, we'll drift
In the haze of space, which will be, once
And for all, scrutable and safe."
- Tracy K. Smith

1

LIQUID CONFIDENCE

Kapp Adams spent his last night on Earth the same way he spent many nights—drunk and daydreaming in a Las Vegas dive bar. Slouched over an empty coaster, tired eyes drifting from tap to tap, he silently waited his turn in a long row of thirsty men. Looking up, he let his mind wander. Decorative doors hung from the ceiling of the bar, painted in various colors. Kapp's thoughts drifted far beyond the confines of the doors as he imagined opening one and floating through it.

His attention bounced between the ceiling and a holographic display above the bar, which showed a press-conference gathered around a small stage. A large, ornate building filled the background of the shot, and behind a podium stood a man in a suit. He had a bald head, but a youthful face that Kapp recognized. The camera zoomed in on a cake-faced reporter. Kapp tapped a tiny earbud in his right ear until he found the correct audio feed.

"Doctor Cage," the reporter said, *"what's the success rate for the treatment?"*

Doctor Cage looked around, pausing on each segment of the crowd. *"I'm pleased to say that a hundred percent of our test subjects have gone into remission."*

A wave of shock and excitement swept over the crowd portrayed in the hologram. Kapp watched with lazy intrigue as before-and-after pictures of cancer patients flashed across the projection screen set up behind Doctor Cage. He thought about commercials he had seen for weight loss treatments, in which he was certain the before pictures were really the after pictures—an easy swap. The crowd calmed, and then a different reporter stood to address Doctor Cage.

"That's amazing," he said, *"but the cost must be extremely high for such results. How long will it take to get the nano-therapy to market, and how much can the consumer expect to pay?"*

"You're right," Doctor Cage said, straightening his jacket. *"The treatment took years to develop, and the cost was great. However, Cage Industries is prepared to begin large-scale production of the drug. It will take several months, but once it reaches the American market, each nano-injection will cost no more than a common flu shot."*

The crowd released a collective gasp, and the man addressing Doctor Cage went pale. *"I just—I don't see how that's possible, sir."*

"Son." He paused for a few seconds. *"Possibility is only limited by what one can imagine. I've imagined a world—"*

Kapp looked away from the screen, and the sound from his earbud automatically muted with his lost interest. His eyes returned to the ceiling, his thoughts to the void. The smell of hot wings—vinegar and cayenne pepper—poked at his nostrils, a scent that would usually be overbearing, but his mind continued to wander until the sounds of the room became a dull drone. This happened often.

Eventually, something woke Kapp from his reverie, igniting something primal within…the one thing that could always pull him out of a daydream. His stare, drawn away from the ceiling, locked onto the subtle bounce of incoming cleavage.

"Sorry about the wait." The bartender, a curvy blonde with several visible tattoos, leaned over the counter. "What can I get you, sweetie?"

Kapp's gaze lingered on the low cut neckline of her crop top before he caught himself and looked up at the woman's smiling face.

"Stone IPA," he said, running a hand through his short, dark undercut—disheveling it just enough. He straightened his black blazer.

The bartender grabbed a pair of mugs from behind the bar and held them up. "Sixteen or twenty-four ounce, babe?"

Kapp pointed at the larger glass, a step he could usually skip, but this bartender was apparently new.

"I just need to scan your ID, babe."

Of course, Kapp thought. He already had his left wrist turned over in preparation. He was used to people assuming his age, but it still annoyed him. The scan gun beeped in approval as it passed over the smooth bump created by his identity implant—a tiny microchip embedded under his skin.

"Wow," she said, "you don't look thirty-five, Mr. Adams!"

"It's Kapp," he said, smirking. With a beer on the way, his mood had already improved. "I'm guessing the hops keep me preserved."

"Could be," she said, tucking her hair behind her ear. Kapp lost count at five piercings as she turned away.

The Porch—Kapp's second watering hole of the night—was crowded for a Tuesday. Spring had come to Vegas about a week early, and the tourists came with it. A pleasant breeze blew through the open garage doors that made up the wall behind Kapp.

When the bartender brought his beer, it never hit the coaster. He took generous sips, one after another, each swallow a calming meditation. Sip. *Ahh.* Repeat.

"Kapp!" a voice called out from across the room. Asher West, Kapp's best friend, approached the nearest bar stool. He stood shorter than Kapp by several inches and had his long, brown hair tied back in a messy bun. A vintage Coldplay tee shirt hung loosely over his lean frame.

"What's up, buddy?" he said, flashing a crooked smile.

Kapp inclined his head. "Not much, man."

Asher settled in and looked at the display. "Theo Cage. Isn't that the guy who installed your cyborg arm?"

"Yeah," Kapp said. "But stop calling it a cyborg arm. It's a bionic prosthetic. Mass-market now."

"*Right,*" Asher said. "What's he up to these days?"

"Cage Industries just cured cancer." Kapp ended each sentence with a sip of beer. "And some other diseases. Says the treatments will be as cheap as a flu shot."

Asher shook his head. "No way."

"Yep," Kapp said. He didn't understand the Theo Cage hype. Though brilliant, the man had strange ideas and stranger tendencies.

Kapp's metal fingers clinked against his empty beer mug, gaining the attention of the bartender, who was busy filling a tall cup with machine-blended margarita mix. She looked at the duo, held up a single finger, and smiled as if to say, "I'll be there in a minute, sweetie."

"Haven't seen her before," Asher said, honing in on either her name tag or the chest it was attached to. "Emily, huh? She looks talented."

Kapp chuckled. "She does seem to have her virtues," he said. As she approached, he pretended to stifle a yawn.

"Hey, nice shirt," she said to Asher, offering a quick smile. "What can I get for you guys?"

Asher beamed at the compliment, and Kapp held up his empty mug. "Another Stone, please."

"Make that two," Asher added, struggling to keep his eyes on her face.

"Coming right up," she said.

"Hold on!" Kapp feigned disgust, and the bartender turned back. "Aren't you going to ID my friend?"

"I don't think so." She looked from one man to the other. "He looks old enough."

"Ha!" Asher said.

"Unbelievable," Kapp said to Asher as the bartender bounced away.

Asher's eyes followed her across the bar until she turned and winked at Kapp.

"Man, you *have* to hit that," Asher said.

"Women aren't usually fans of the cyborg arm." Kapp's voice held a hint of sarcasm.

"Come on, it makes you look—I don't know—heroic or something."

"It scares them."

"Wait just a goddamn minute!" Asher turned to Kapp dramatically. "Are you saying that thing's worth a million credits, and it *doesn't* have a vibrate setting?"

Kapp grinned. "I never said that."

Asher snickered. "I guess that would be kind of scary. Look, all I'm saying—"

The bartender dropped off their drinks, stopping the conversation for just a moment. Asher waited for her to leave.

"All I'm saying is that this is your last night on Earth for a while, and—"

"Possibly forever," Kapp said, taking a break from a long chug. "Space travel is not for the faint of heart."

"Quit the doom and gloom shit, Kapp. This girl is fine with a capital F." Asher shook his head. "And she's clearly into you. I just know what I would do if this was my last night."

"If you like her so much, then why don't you try?"

Asher's eagerness for Kapp to score never came as a surprise. Asher had a constant desire to live vicariously through his less socially-awkward friend, so Kapp knew he wouldn't try. Though he didn't usually indulge in carnal pursuits for his friend's amusement, he sat there and humored Asher's long list of reasons to consummate the night. As if on cue, the bartender came back when Kapp finished his drink—maybe his third, but he couldn't remember. Asher still had half a mug of beer left.

"Anything else, boys?" the bartender asked.

"I'll take one more and close out," Kapp said.

"Okay, babe." She smiled and headed back to the row of taps. As she walked away, Kapp's and Asher's eyes drifted from the back of her head to the tattoo just above her nearly non-existent shorts. Their jaws stayed open until she left their sight.

"Capital F," Asher said, shaking his head.

"You know," Kapp said, patting his friend on the back with his bionic arm, still looking forward. "You're right, Ash. I could live a little before I go."

Ash grunted from the impact of Kapp's strong touch. "Dude, be gentle."

"Sorry." Kapp laughed. "I need to have Jesse recalibrate this thing before we leave."

"Yeah, good idea," Asher said. "Hey, you want my beer? I only ordered it so I wouldn't look like a bitch. I should've had the usual."

"You have a man bun and a Coldplay tee, and you're worried about a mojito making you look like a bitch?"

Kapp reached for his friend's mug and downed the rest of it in three quick gulps, relishing the burn of carbonation and bitter hops. He looked around the bar, starry-eyed. Asher played with his phone, ignoring the insult. They sat in silence until the bartender came back.

"Your total is…28 credits. Would you like to add a tip?" she suggested, leaning seductively across the bar to hand Kapp his final drink. Her false lashes flickered as she reached for the scan gun. Asher stared.

"Charge me a hundred," Kapp said as the scanner passed over his wrist. "Keep the rest."

"That's very generous, Mr. Ad—"

"It's Kapp," he said.

"Well, thank you, Kapp," she said, already beginning to process the transaction. "If there's anything else you need before you go, please let me know."

Kapp made eye contact with Asher, who was already getting up to leave, and they shared a knowing smile.

"I've got an earlier morning than you. See you tomorrow." Asher nodded to the bartender. "Good night, beautiful."

Kapp grinned at Asher's feigned confidence, a recent development in his friend's personality. Once Asher exited, Kapp and the bartender looked back at each other.

"I just have two questions." He took her hand, liquid confidence guiding his actions. "If you were leaving Earth tomorrow, what would you do tonight?"

She opened her mouth to speak, but hesitated for a moment, her blue eyes twinkling in the bar light. Pretty. "Well, I sure as hell wouldn't sleep."

"That's a good answer." Kapp felt a living buzz. "Really good."

"What's the other question, Kapp?"

"When do you get off?" he asked, still holding her hand.

She bit her lip.

•|•

Faint light spilled into the window of Kapp's bedroom as he untangled himself from blankets and tattooed limbs. He stepped over a pile of clothes and crept into the master bathroom. His mouth felt like the Mojave as he stood over the toilet. *How much did I drink?* Almost in response to his internal question, he took a neon piss. He closed his eyes for a moment, pressing his thumbs against his throbbing temples, then he noticed the time blinking in the upper right corner of the floor to ceiling mirror: *12:14 p.m.*

"Shit," he said just above a whisper, organic face colliding with metallic palm. "Jax, what time does Oliver get here?"

The mirror pinged, and a map appeared in the top left quadrant of the display, a blue line drawn between a helicopter icon and Kapp's condo. Jax's voice came from speakers set in the ceiling.

"Oliver is scheduled to pick you up at 12:30, sir," he said in a posh British accent.

"Okay, shit. Uhhh…start some coffee. Get a Ryde for my friend."

"Of course, sir." Jax paused. "Although, her level of undress would suggest she is more than a friend."

Kapp fumbled for his toothbrush. He couldn't believe the sense of humor his A.I. assistant had developed over the years. Jax was like an omnipresent roommate, but he didn't pay rent, and he left no trace. A message flashed across the mirror from Asher: *How was last night? ;)*

Shaking his head, Kapp squeezed the last drop of toothpaste out of the tube. In the reflection below Asher's message, he saw the bartender beginning to stir.

What was her name again?

Beneath the headache, he felt toxic, empty, like the joy had been sucked out of him. He could blame it on the impending mission or the alcohol leaving his blood, but he knew the feeling ran deeper than that. He looked at the woman sprawled across his bed. She was beautiful, and they had a good time as far as he could remember, but that was all. In all his memory, Kapp's life had been a struggle to connect with the people around him. Part of him wanted to blame it on the father he never knew and the mother he could barely remember, but he brushed away such thoughts. He sometimes thought that his tendency to seek isolation was what drove him to become an astronaut, to constantly crave the emptiness of space. Just as his thoughts drifted into the void, the vacancy in Kapp's mind was filled by the gargle of a coffee pot finishing its job.

"You seem to have a latte on your mind, sir," Jax said.

"Really?" Kapp rolled his eyes. "Coffee puns?"

"All a part of the daily grind, sir."

Despite his annoyance, Kapp laughed. While waiting for his coffee to reach the perfect chugging temperature, he stood by his dresser and started to pull on his pants, but his progress was halted by tattooed arms around his waist.

"I had fun last night," the bartender said, lips pressed against the back of his neck. "Ready for round two?"

He could feel her nipple piercings grazing his bare back, but the goosebumps forming on his skin weren't enough to stop him from focusing on the task at hand.

"I have to go to work," he said bluntly.

"Well, when are you done? I can be patient"—her hands drifted from his abs down to the pockets of his jeans—"sometimes."

"Not for a while." He shrugged, reaching for his shirt, breaking contact with the woman. "Jax, how far away is the Ryde?" He turned around. By the look on the woman's face, he could tell she wasn't used to being turned down.

"Look." He faced her. "I'm sorry, but last night all that 'leaving Earth' shit wasn't just a trick to get you naked. I'm actually leaving—today—and I'm running late."

"What do you mean?" she asked.

"I'm an IES Astronaut, and I fly out tonight."

"Oh." She avoided eye contact. "I see."

"Your ride is here, miss," Jax said, his voice always near. "And yours, sir."

Kapp started downing his coffee. By the time he finished, the woman was already dressed and walking toward the door of the loft. She turned to Kapp.

"I don't usually do this kind of thing, you know?" A muted wrath replaced the service industry sweetness from the night before. "I'm not a one-night-stand kinda girl."

Kapp doubted that. He tried to soothe her with a smile.

"Listen, I'll look you up when I get back. Remind me of your name." The words left Kapp's mouth before his hungover brain could filter them.

"Fuck you," she said and slammed the door.

2

FORGET RETIREMENT

3 Months Earlier

Kapp stepped into the bright office of Bryce Holden, The Director of the Interplanetary Explorers Society. Director Holden smiled from behind his oakwood desk, waiting for Kapp to take a seat. A buzzcut of salt and pepper hair combined with a rigid jawline completed his rectangular face. He had a thick neck and ruddy skin. On his tie, he wore a gold pin with the IES logo on it, a mini solar system with a web of lines connecting the planets.

"Commander Adams," he said, "can I get you something to drink? Water, coffee—"

"Scotch," Kapp said. Holden's voice was far too loud for Kapp to listen to sober.

Holden looked at his watch. "It's 11 a.m., Kapp."

"Hey," Kapp said, shrugging. "You offered."

Holden chuckled, a deep boom that resonated in his chest. He poured two generous doses of 18-year Glenlivet from a bottle behind his desk and handed one to Kapp.

"I'll get straight to the point, Adams." Holden took a sip; Kapp took a bigger one. "We need to send you back to Mars orbit."

The light coming through the glass wall behind Holden's desk made Kapp's head hurt, but he stared ahead anyway, waiting for Holden to continue.

"I know we promised you retirement after your injury, but you're the best we've got, and there's not enough time to train someone new. It's urgent."

Kapp felt a twinge in his lower back that radiated down his right leg, remnants of the nerve damage he suffered from a rough landing on his last mission. Beneath the pain hid a much stronger emotion, though: excitement. It had been almost three years since he felt the rush of leaving the atmosphere, an incomparable high.

"Forget retirement," Kapp said, eager to take a long vacation away from Earth. "When do I leave?"

A massive grin came to Holden's face. "The launch window for Starling II is in three months, but Adams, I have to tell you"— Holden glanced at the door and lowered his voice—"it's different this time."

Kapp raised his eyebrows. "Meaning?"

The director took a deep breath. He pressed a button on his desk, which turned the glass behind him opaque. "A few months ago, the Wisdom rover detected an anomaly, a spike in the albedo of Phobos."

Kapp finished his drink. "That doesn't make sense."

"Further inspection showed a large reflective object on the surface—"

"Are you fucking with me?" Kapp asked. "Damn it, Holden, why am I here? If this is some kind of—"

"This is serious, Adams," Holden said. "I'll show you."

Holden tapped a button on the edge of the double-sided monitor between him and Kapp. The side facing Kapp lit up, and two images appeared next to each other.

"On the left is the last photo taken of Phobos before we detected the anomaly, and on the right is the latest photo—taken yesterday."

Kapp saw the vague outline of a long symmetrical shape in the photo on the right. Inside the almond-shaped outline, the color shone a brighter gray than the surrounding area.

"What is it?" he asked.

"We're not sure, but the symmetry suggests intelligent design. We've attempted communication with it, but we can't detect any response."

Deep in thought, Kapp sat with a face void of emotion.

"The object is in the middle of Stickney, the—"

"The big crater," Kapp said, still staring at the screen. "Go on."

"It's nearly 2 kilometers long and half as wide."

"Jesus!" Kapp said.

He peered into his empty glass, fingers tapping as he contemplated what all of this meant. His mind revolved around a single word: *Aliens.* He couldn't believe the words coming from Holden's mouth. This was deep, historical shit, and Kapp was wading in the middle of it. The spacefaring community loved talking about extraterrestrial life—a joke to most, but a dream to some. Curious eyes constantly searched the skies for signs of life, but no one, certainly not Kapp, expected evidence to appear so close to home.

"Who knows about this?" he asked.

"The team that discovered the anomaly, of course, the engineers building Starling II, The President, the Secretary of Defense." Holden looked at Adams seriously. "And now you."

Kapp pondered the severity of the situation. He hadn't been stressed coming into the meeting, but suddenly he felt tense. "What's the objective?" he asked.

"First," Holden said, "attempt communication with whatever this thing is."

"And how am I supposed to do that?"

"Your four-person crew will include a linguist—Mara Stone. She's truly brilliant! Top of her class at—"

"Wait, why is the crew so small?"

Starling I had an eight-person crew.

"With the new design, the crew module only has a four-person capacity." Director Holden took another sip of his scotch, then, after a slow breath, he looked deep into Kapp's green eyes. "We had to make room for the failsafe."

Kapp sighed. "Cut the vague shit."

"There are a few weapon systems on board," Holden said. "Just in case."

If Kapp had any scotch left, he would have spit it out. Never before in history had a spacecraft been weaponized. Spaceflight had enough dangers without the added risk of blowing yourself up. Plus, weaponizing a spacecraft would break the Outer Space Treaty—not that Kapp cared much about obeying the law.

"You want me to kill whatever's up there?" he asked with more surprise than disgust.

"No. I want you to have the option to defend yourself if it ends up being hostile."

"And if it's not?"

"Then let them know we welcome them to Earth with open arms." Holden spread his hands apart in gesture while his elbows rested on the desk. Kapp reached for the bottle between them and poured himself another glass, shaking his head.

"I don't know about this."

"You wouldn't be the one pulling the trigger, Kapp—if that's your concern."

"That's not it," he said, unable to process what actually concerned him.

"You'll have a weapons specialist on board. Jesse McCall will be there too. We need you, Kapp." Holden looked desperate. "This is important."

The mention of Jesse, the flight engineer from his last mission, reassured Kapp. Jesse had become a good friend, a mentor even. After another long sip, Kapp inhaled sharply. "Fine. I'll do it—but I have two conditions."

"Of course."

"Hire my friend Asher for Mission Control. He's more than qualified."

"Consider it done," Director Holden said, scribbling a note on his tablet. "What else?"

Kapp finished his drink in one more gulp and smiled. "Make sure there's a case of this scotch in the cargo hold."

Holden laughed, and Kapp stood to leave.

"Wait," Holden said. "You accepted the mission so quickly, I nearly forgot. The IES has a gift for you, something to sweeten the deal."

Kapp liked the sound of that. "Yeah?"

"I've made you an appointment with Doctor Theo Cage." Holden began tapping on his tablet. "I'm sending you the details now."

•|•

A day later, Kapp sat in the lobby of Doctor Cage's office, a room with high ceilings and white walls decorated with minimalist art. A synthetic female voice came from the intercom.

"Doctor Cage will see you now."

Frosted glass pocket doors opened and disappeared into the walls, revealing a wide corridor beyond.

"Just follow the blue lights," the voice said.

Kapp stood and followed the illuminated path, swaying slightly. Doctors made him nervous, and nerves made him drink. He still had a nice buzz from the cocktails he drank at the airport, on the plane, and then at lunch in Los Angeles. When he arrived at the designated door, it opened automatically.

"Please take a seat. The doctor will be here shortly."

The examination room looked much like the lobby, but instead of art, monitors adorned the sterile walls. A polished concrete surface filled one side of the room, beneath a spinning hologram of a bionic arm projected from the ceiling. Instead of sitting, Kapp stood in front of the display, comparing the 3D model to his own prosthetic. Unlike the skin-tone of his false arm, the prosthetic portrayed in the hologram had a metallic sheen to it.

"I've always valued power and functionality over lifelike design, but there is a synthetic skin we can stretch over the prosthetic if you want."

The voice startled Kapp, not because of its proximity but because it seemed to respond directly to his thoughts. He turned and saw a man in a white lab coat approaching, his bald head reflecting fluorescent light.

"You know," Kapp said, "I kind of like the chrome."

"Theo Cage," the man said, reaching out to shake Kapp's hand. "Good choice."

Theo's eyes—the only thing about him that looked old—found Kapp's current prosthetic, and his hands followed. "May I?" he asked.

Kapp nodded, and Theo proceeded to examine him, whispering things to himself. Then he gently loosened the prosthetic with a twist, revealing a threaded metal rod protruding from Kapp's residual limb—a stump halfway between his shoulder and where his elbow had once been.

"Titanium osseointegrated implant," Theo said under his breath. "Subdermal electrodes."

Kapp understood that neural signals could communicate with his prosthetic through this interface, an incredible feat of science, but one that he didn't enjoy looking at. With his stump exposed, he felt naked.

"Bionic technology has come a long way," Theo said, walking away with Kapp's prosthetic. "Direct neural sensory feedback. Polymers that mimic white blood cells. Retinal prostheses to restore sight."

Theo dropped Kapp's prosthetic arm into a trash receptacle.

"Hey," Kapp said. "What if I wanted to keep that?"

Theo turned toward Kapp and smiled, revealing a set of shining white teeth. "It was garbage compared to what you're getting."

"It was expensive," Kapp said.

"Believe me, son," Theo said, "this upgrade will make your old arm look like a plastic robot claw. Please take a seat."

Kapp settled into the reclining exam chair. "How long is this gonna take?" he asked.

Doctor Cage sat down on a rolling stool. "Do you have a history of mental illness in the family?"

Kapp's eyebrows lowered. "What does that have to do with my arm?"

"Delusions?" Theo cleared his throat. "Hallucinations? Night terrors?"

"I—" Kapp paused. He knew nothing about his family's history, but he did suffer from occasional nightmares. "I don't know."

"I only ask to keep you safe," Theo said. "This prosthetic packs a much bigger punch than your last. Literally."

"Everyone gets bad dreams," Kapp said.

"I suppose," Theo said. "Either way, I don't recommend sleeping with the arm attached. You could hurt yourself."

"Noted," Kapp said.

"You're a lucky man, you know?" Theo went to the work surface beneath the hologram and opened a drawer. "The first on Earth to be augmented by such a powerful modular prosthetic limb. You see, this is not just a replacement for a lost arm. It's an upgrade."

Theo returned to the side of the recliner with Kapp's new prosthetic, which glistened in the light, even brighter than Theo's scalp.

"Looks shinier in person," Kapp said. He really did like the chrome.

"The amazing thing about technology is that it never ceases to improve." Theo turned the arm to show every angle. "Soon, this too will look like a toy."

"Well," Kapp said, ready to get the appointment over with so he could get back to Vegas, "let's play with it."

Theo sat down. "This may feel strange at first," he warned. "The direct neural interface provides an extremely lifelike sensation."

"Wait," Kapp said, "I'll be able to feel it?"

"Yes, quite well," Theo said. "The technology isn't new, but it's never been done to this extent before. You won't feel any pain, only pressure, a foreign sensation for someone who has been an amputee as long as you."

Over thirty years, Kapp thought.

Theo sat down again, then he gripped Kapp's residual limb in one hand. "Are you ready?"

Kapp nodded. "I guess so."

Theo twisted the new arm onto the threads, then pressed a small button. Kapp felt nothing at first, only the dead weight now hanging at his side.

"Try lifting your forearm."

Kapp imagined the motion, and the prosthetic obeyed—just like his old model.

"Good," Theo said. "Now turn it over."

The motors barely made a sound as Kapp rotated his wrist, revealing an open palm.

"Close your eyes." Theo reached into the pocket of his lab coat. "I want you to pinch your forefinger and thumb together, but stop when you feel pressure."

"How?" Kapp asked. "I've never—"

"I know," Theo said, "just give it a try."

Kapp took a deep breath and tried to concentrate on the task. He didn't know what sensation to watch out for. He imagined his new fingers closing, heard the faint sound of the motors doing their job. When his fingertips found the object, he knew it instantly and nearly jerked his arm away in alarm. It felt like he had a phantom hand floating a foot away from his body, disconnected but somehow still part of him.

"Weird," Kapp said.

"Open your eyes."

He did so and saw an egg pinched between his new thumb and forefinger.

"Motor control will become more natural with practice, once the machine learning picks up on your movements."

Kapp brought the egg closer to his face, observing the way he could twist and turn it at will.

"We're nearly done here," Theo said, pulling a stainless steel bowl from under the seat. "Just one more test."

"What is it?"

"Your new prosthetic has a built-in safety limit, but it can be surpassed." Theo held out the bowl. "Break the egg into this."

"Easy enough." Kapp let it roll into his palm, tightened his fingers around it, and squeezed as hard as he could. But the egg, designed by nature to withstand even pressure, held its shape.

Theo snickered. "It helps to think of something that angers you."

Kapp had plenty of options to choose from, but he settled on his most recent irritant—having to sit next to a chatty tourist on the plane. He thought about her small-talking, gum-smacking ways, and tightened his fist once again. The shell cracked, and its contents spilled into the bowl. Kapp looked at it, expecting to see a pure yellow yolk, but instead, he saw a yolk marbled by red veins, enclosing a half-formed chicken embryo. The sight nearly made him gag.

"Life," Theo said, tilting his head slightly. His throat made a short humming sound. "How fragile."

3

HAPPY THOUGHTS

The chopper flew north, from Kapp's home in the southern foothills of the Las Vegas valley, over the vast urban sprawl surrounding the Strip, to the emptiness of the desert beyond. He couldn't stop dozing off during the ride, but at least he had a long nap to look forward to: 240 days of stasis on Starling II.

Kapp looked back at the disappearing city skyline. Three months living in Vegas had been fun—almost too much fun. After receiving the direct deposit for the mission, he lived like a king in Sin City. The IES required him to train in the simulator four days a week, but he had the other three to spend with Asher in drunken revelry—just like in college, only this time they weren't broke.

When they arrived, dust flew in an omnidirectional pattern from the center of the helipad as the pilot touched down.

"Thanks again, Oli," Kapp said into his headset microphone.

Oliver replied in a thick New Zealand accent. "Any time, Kapp."

The helicopter pilot had been Kapp's personal chauffeur for months.

"What are you gonna do while I'm gone?" he asked.

"Short vacation then heaps of contract work." Kapp rarely saw Oliver without his aviator sunglasses, but knew that the man had fierce eyes and a thirst for adventure. His idea of vacation probably meant scuba diving with sharks.

"Maybe find a client that tips better," Oliver added.

"I'll get you next time," Kapp said.

"You're spinning yarns, mate," Oliver said.

"Huh?"

"Means I think you're lying." The doors sprung open. "See ya next year, mate."

Kapp stepped out of the helicopter onto the asphalt and looked ahead at the towering height of Starling II. Below the trapezoidal shape of the crew module stood the service module, which would provide water, oxygen, and nitrogen, as well as course-adjusting thrust once the ship detached from the launch vehicle, a massive multi-stage rocket that sat below everything else. From the edge of the complex, Kapp could see the simulation hangar where he spent most of his time, warehouses he didn't have clearance for, and the most modern building in the complex: mission control. A dusty sign above the entrance to mission control read **Groom Lake Launch Facility**. Kapp scanned his ID chip at the front door. A pair of bulletproof glass doors slid open to reveal an empty lobby, then he walked down a long, sterile hallway to the crew lounge.

"Kapp?" a small voice said from behind big glasses. Mara Stone sat on a black loveseat, which looked more like a couch for someone her size. Framed by shoulder-length pink curls, her pale face glowed in contrast to her dark red lipstick. Between delicate hands, she held a leather-bound notebook and a pen. To Kapp, she always looked nervous as hell.

"Hey, Mars." Kapp smiled and tilted his head down a few degrees. "Ready for tonight?"

"I will be," she said. She didn't usually talk much, but every once in a while—when the subject interested her—those floodgates would open. Whenever she didn't have her face buried in a book, she spent her time solving intricate puzzles, the kind that made a Rubix Cube look like a baby's rattle. Before Kapp could respond, Mara's attention returned to her notebook, which she began to scribble in furiously.

"What are you working on?" Kapp asked.

"I'm constructing my own language." Mara kept writing while she talked. "It has similar grammatical structures to the romance languages, but with more standardized conjugations."

"That's good, Mara," Kapp said, his headache making him wish he hadn't asked.

"I borrowed some verb stems from my favorite South Asian dialects, but most of the morphemes—"

"I'll see you on the bridge," Kapp said, continuing onward.

Mara, who continued to speak out loud while she wrote, either didn't notice or didn't care about Kapp's departure. The floodgates had opened.

•|•

In the kitchenette attached to the crew lounge, Kapp found flight engineer Jesse McCall, a sizable man with a mop of dirty blonde hair tucked behind his ears. He stood in front of the microwave with a slight smile on his face—something he always seemed to wear for no reason at all, even when no one was around. When Jesse saw Kapp, his gray-stubbled cheeks wrinkled into a massive grin, and his blue eyes lit up behind a pair of reading glasses.

"I heard a rumor about you," he said in a low voice.

"Oh yeah?"

"Word on the street"—Jesse's suppressed Alabama twang began to surface—"is that you knocked boots with that new bartender from The Porch last night."

Kapp sighed. He'd have to deal with Asher's loud mouth later. The microwave beeped, and Jesse pulled out a plate of pizza rolls, half of them oozing melted cheese.

"Your last meal on Earth, and you're eating that shit?" Kapp asked. He reached for one of the pizza rolls anyway, realizing he hadn't eaten since dinner the night before.

"Don't change the subject," Jesse said, nudging Kapp with his elbow. "You know I like a good story."

After a long sigh, Kapp obliged, recounting what he could remember from the night before between long sips of water. He really needed a Bloody Mary, but drinking before spaceflight was generally frowned upon.

"Wow," Jesse said at the end of Kapp's tale. "You know, Kapp, it wouldn't hurt to remember a young lady's name now and then? You'll never settle down acting like that."

"How's that working for you?" Kapp nudged Jesse with his bionic elbow.

Jesse had eight years on Kapp and still hadn't settled down.

"Long distance relationships break down on interplanetary missions," Jesse said, still grinning. "I'm fixin' to find a wife after this one. Buy some more land. Retire in the country."

The conversation dwindled as both men focused on filling their mouths. Two water bottles and a black coffee later, Kapp felt almost human again. He peered through the glass door of the crew lounge at Eli Morgan—the weapons specialist—who paced in the hallway, his figure like a shadow on the stark walls. His phone looked like a toy in his massive hands. Well over six feet tall and bulky, Eli didn't seem to Kapp like he would fit in the close quarters of the crew module simulator, but somehow he did. A single crystalline tear rolled down the giant's cheek, and Kapp realized that he was probably saying goodbye to his family.

Kapp didn't have to worry about anything like that. Asher was the closest thing to family that he had, and they'd still be in communication during the mission. Kapp looked at the tear streaked-face of Eli and thought that he might be better off than the big man. He found comfort in caring for few. He had less to lose than the rest of his crew, less to lose than most people—but a sense of sadness always blanketed that comfort.

•|•

Before the launch, the crew walked to Mission Control. The staff there stood and applauded, electrifying the air with their excited yells. Kapp wondered how many of them knew the truth about the mission. The launch would not be televised, so no camera crew worked the room. Holden had decided to spin the launch as a standard research mission, the kind that often happened in this new age of affordable rockets.

When the crowd settled down, Holden gave a quick speech, and the crew members said a few words of gratitude. With the pleasantries done, Kapp found Asher and pulled him aside.

"First of all." Kapp punched Asher's arm, just hard enough to cause him some pain. "That's for telling everyone about last night."

"I only told Jesse," Asher said, "and Eli, and Mara. Holden might have overheard it too."

"That's just great." Kapp shook his head, considering one more punch but ultimately deciding against it. "Anyway, I have something for you."

"Yeah?"

Kapp pulled out his phone, opened the permissions and access settings, and held it up to Asher's wrist.

"Use my condo while I'm gone," Kapp said, the phone scanning his face to verify the transfer. "You might have better luck with the ladies if they think you're rich."

"I have more money than you, man," Asher said. "I've been investing in cryptocurrencies since I was twelve."

"Yeah, but your place looks like a dorm room compared to mine."

"Ouch," Asher said. "But you're not wrong. Thanks for the crash course on how to win hearts and forget names."

Kapp scoffed. "I left you something, too. Check it out when you get there."

"I hope it's weed."

Someone in Mission Control yelled out the time, one hour to launch. Almost time to head to the bridge.

"Thanks," Asher said, stepping closer to Kapp. "And thanks again for getting me this job. It's been great."

"No problem," Kapp said. "Just try not to destroy the place while I'm gone."

•|•

Just after sunset, Kapp, Jesse, Mara, and Eli walked across the skybridge in suits tailored for a different world. An engineer stood by the hatch of the crew module. Kapp took a good look at the young man's face, perhaps the last earthbound face he would see. Starry eyes, full of hope, peered back at him.

"Good luck, commander," the engineer said, unsealing the hatch. "I'll see you when you return."

Kapp had doubts about that, but he nodded anyway. "Thank you."

He took a breath of dry desert air, twisted on his helmet, and climbed down the ladder. The rest of the crew followed, and then the engineer shut and sealed the hatch. Inside the capsule, everything was arranged in launch configuration, the backs of seats laid horizontally across the floor. Kapp strapped himself in next to Jesse, beneath three vertical displays surrounded by controls. Mara and Eli settled in on the opposite side of the capsule, the latter struggling to buckle himself in. He looked even bigger next to Mara. Everyone stayed silent as they waited. Kapp knew they were doing something historic, but it felt routine after countless hours spent in the simulator. Finally, Asher's voice broke through the static into their headsets.

"T minus three minutes to the launch of Starling II. Close and lock your visors at this time."

The crew pulled their dome-shaped visors down and clicked them into place. Mara, her hands fidgety, looked like she could vomit at any minute. Kapp and Jesse waited for the next steps. This wasn't their first rodeo, as Jesse often said.

"T minus two minutes to launch." Asher's voice dropped an octave when he worked.

Both Kapp's real hand and his metallic hand rested on his lap. Jesse tapped through pre-launch procedures with the razor-sharp precision he had developed as a NASA engineer before joining the privately funded IES.

"T minus one minute to launch. Onboard computers now have primary control of all the vehicle's critical functions."

"Roger that"—Kapp flipped a switch on the left side of display one—"Starling II is ready for ascent."

"T Minus fifteen seconds. All systems go for launch. TEN—NINE—EIGHT—SEVEN—"

Beneath his cool demeanor, Kapp always got shit-your-pants nervous during the final countdown—even in the simulator. He forced himself to think happy thoughts.

"—SIX—FIVE—FOUR—"

On the opposite side of the capsule, Mara mouthed along to the countdown with her eyes closed.

Happy thoughts.

"—THREE—TWO—ONE—BLAST OFF!"

Kapp's meditation worked. The last thought on his mind before the initial G-force acceleration deprived his brain of oxygen was indeed a happy one. Before his vision began to gray out, Commander Kapp Adams thought about two of the few things he would miss about Earth: liquor in his blood and the soft skin of a stranger in his bed.

4

THE LONG NAP

Kapp's initial adrenaline rush wore off just as Starling II reached escape velocity. The crew breathed a collective sigh of relief. They had freed themselves from the gravitational pull of Earth to enter an orbit around the sun. The third and final rocket of the launch vehicle gave them the change in velocity needed to push them into an elliptical orbit, the path of least resistance between Earth and Mars.

"Detaching stage three of the launch vehicle," Jesse said, tapping away at his controls.

A small explosive detached the last rocket from the undercarriage of the service module. The spent rocket would orbit Earth as irretrievable space debris for the foreseeable future.

"Let's get rid of this spin," Kapp said, initiating thrusters that stabilized the craft. "That's better."

"Cabin pressure is stable," Jesse said through the comm. "Atmosphere is now standard. You can lift your visors."

Mara lifted the dome from her face. She unwrapped a specially-designed plastic bag velcroed to the wall and vomited into it.

"It'll get better, Mars," Kapp said.

If he could have reached her, he would have patted her on the back. Kapp was no stranger to the woes of space sickness. It took time for the body to adapt to the forces necessary to leave Earth—and none of the crew had been given more than three months to prepare. Mara pulled out a disinfectant wipe and began to clean herself up.

"Ugh, I haven't felt this dizzy since initiation week."

"You were in a sorority?" Kapp asked.

Mara's voice bubbled. "Zeta Theta Psi."

"I didn't take you for a party girl."

Mara shrugged inside her space suit. "It was mostly about making connections that helped me get into my master's program. The parties were just a bonus."

"Any of your sisters single?" Kapp asked.

Continuing to clean herself up, she ignored him.

"Y'all see this?" Jesse asked, inclining his head toward a porthole.

The crew peered out at the world they left behind—a spinning orb of blue and green and white. Kapp had always thought that Earth looked better from a distance. High above it all, he couldn't see violence or illness or death. Blind to the stains of humanity, he savored the feeling of true freedom that always accompanied his release from the shackles of gravity—a feeling he often craved.

"It's so"—Eli looked like he could weep. His unfinished sentence hung in the air as he took in the beauty, his massive arms floating in the relaxed awe of zero Gs.

Eli continued to stare out of porthole while Kapp and Jesse checked and double-checked their trajectory. The two of them would be doing most if not all of the work until they reached the red planet and the mysterious object on the Martian moon Phobos.

•|•

Three days later, the crew finally adjusted to the odd sensations of outer space. With help from Mission Control, they had locked in the final trajectory. They rearranged the gear in the cockpit for comfort. Floors became ceilings, walls became floors, up became down, and all of that became irrelevant without gravity. Jesse opened the tunnel to the lower deck, and the crew floated around the craft like so many bubbles, pushing off surfaces with their arms and legs instead of walking from place to place. Kapp found his stash of scotch and decided to raise a toast.

"To Holden," he said, "the man who brought us together."

Kapp had already snuck a few shots, and he could feel the effects. Drinking in space wasn't easy. After taking the lid off the Glenlivet bottle, he had to insert a special stopper with a straw pierced through it. The straw had a valve to prevent liquids from floating out while not in use.

For the toast, he had to get extra creative. After taking the cork out, he used a long straw to pull out a good amount of scotch. Blowing through one end of the straw created an orb of alcohol held together by surface tension. Kapp did this until four imperfect spheres floated in the middle of the cabin.

"To Holden."

The crew laughed and sucked their drinks out of the air.

•|•

After a short night of sleep following their celebration, Kapp's eyes opened slowly. He tried to roll over, but his sleeping bag was strapped to the wall, or floor—or whatever it was. After trying for several minutes to sleep through the pressure building in his bladder, he knew he would have to get up. Resigning to his fate, he unzipped his sleeping bag and pushed his way to the small closet across the hall. He dropped his sweatpants, flipped a switch, and pissed into a funnel attached to a vacuum tube. His shoulder twitched in relief. Deciding that more sleep probably wouldn't come, he kicked off the surface of the lower level and shot up the tube.

In the cockpit, he found Eli hovering in front of one of the computers, clumsy fingers typing slowly. His massive torso blocked the monitor from Kapp's view.

"You're up early," Kapp said.

Eli's flinched, and his head jerked to the side.

"I never went to sleep," he said in a deep voice, hitting the keys more rapidly.

"What're you doing?" Kapp asked.

"I'm trying to record a message for my son."

Eli talked about his son often, the one thing that could soften the big man's rough exterior. Kapp thought he might be a single dad, but he had never asked. Former military, Eli had the kind of face you didn't want to question. His stature alone looked crafted to intimidate.

"It's easier on the tablets." Kapp pulled one off the wall. "Here."

"Thanks," Eli said, turning around to accept the rectangle of glass.

"How old is your son, again?"

"Almost eleven," Eli said, shaking his head and smiling.

"Wow." The word turned into a yawn. "He'll be a teenager when we get back."

Eli sucked in a giant breath. "If we get back," he said.

With a vacant expression, Kapp just stared at Eli. He had similar thoughts, but hearing them from someone else made those worries real.

"Sorry," Eli said after an awkward pause. "I just want to focus on the mission. If my mind is on Earth, I don't think I can do that."

Kapp understood.

•|•

From the ladder on the lower deck, Kapp saw Mara crawling out of her sleeping chamber. She couldn't see him without her glasses, so Kapp kicked off the ladder and sent himself flying behind her. When he got close enough, he clapped his hands together right by her ear. She crumpled into the fetal position and squealed.

"Ughhh, why do you always do that?" Mara punched his arm, which only sent her flying in the opposite direction. Kapp managed to grab her foot with his bionic prosthetic before she could get too far away.

"Because it's easy," he said, helping her get back into an upright position. "You should probably invest in contacts."

"Once they put screens in contacts, I will."

Mara popped open her Adderall prescription, swallowed an orange and white capsule, and chased it with bagged coffee sipped through a straw. Behind pink locks, her face contorted from the bitterness.

"You can heat that stuff up, you know?" Kapp said, done with the teasing. "It's no Starbucks, but it's better hot."

"Starbucks coffee is subpar," she said, letting him pull her into a hug. "But thanks."

"Any time, Mars," he said. Throughout training, they had gotten along well. Sibling-like quarrels aside, they had each other's back.

Jesse appeared from the adjacent room as the embrace ended. "Where's mine?" he asked with his usual smirk. Kapp thought he detected a hint of jealousy from the older man, but he ignored it.

"You're next," Mara said, sipping her cold coffee, already fidgeting from the rush.

"Anyway," Jesse said, "the stasis pods are prepped. Y'all ready for a long nap?"

•|•

Dressed in sterile long johns, Kapp, Jesse, Mara, and Eli entered the stasis room. Four coffin-like metal tubes lined the surface opposite of the door. Windows at head-height revealed straps, nodes, and an IV feeding tube floating inside each pod. Kapp moved toward the cave he'd be hibernating in for the next eight months. Hungry from the necessary pre-sleep fast and shivering from the cold, he typed his pin into the keypad, and the door slid open. He stayed still for a moment, observing his crew.

In front of his pod, Jesse McCall grinned at himself, lost in some amusing thought. Mara Stone looked anxious as ever as she velcroed her glasses case to the wall and felt her way to the keypad. Eli Morgan taped a photo of his son to his pod's window, facing in, then he shimmied his big shoulders into the pod.

Kapp looked at the display above his keypad, which showed two lines of data. The date on top amused him, one of his favorite holidays.

He turned to the crew and said, "Happy St. Patrick's Day, everyone."

Jesse's smile tripled. "I'd kill for some shepherd's pie right now," he said, scratching at his grayish stubble. "And the freeze-dried kind don't count."

The crew laughed away the fear, thinking of warm meals as they pulled themselves into the ice-cold pods. Kapp stayed outside for a moment, looking at the second line of data, the date they were scheduled to wake up on. When he lowered himself into the freezing chamber and strapped in, the door swung shut automatically. A small robotic arm placed nodes on his head and chest and stuck an IV needle into the vein inside his left elbow. He barely felt it. As the sedative started to dull his mind, Kapp wondered if Asher had plans for St. Patrick's Day, and whether his condo would be trashed. He thought about the length and severity of their mission, and how much might change back home between that moment and November 12th, 2040.

5

LIES ON LIES

Earth, 6 Months Later

A pre-storm haze descended on the valley, blurring the Sierra Nevada mountain range into a vague and jagged outline. Asher West sat on the balcony of Kapp's condo, taking in the view. The setting sun before him painted the western sky with brilliant orange and pink hues. Besides the aesthetic pleasure of his surroundings, his vision was filtered even further by the smoke in front of his face and the THC hitting his brain after another paranoid day. Puffing on his pre-rolled joint, he looked skyward. It felt good to relax, but the weed couldn't numb the worry in his heart. It couldn't fix the all-encompassing anxiety of losing contact with Starling II.

Asher tried to sleep that night, but his brain wouldn't shut down. After taking out his hair tie and climbing into bed, he tossed and turned for hours—like a glitch-riddled application caught in a loop. *How the hell do you lose a billion credit spacecraft?* It made no sense. Everything had run smoothly for six months, and then… radio silence. Like mission control was getting the cold shoulder from a disgruntled lover. He recalled the press conference from earlier in the day.

"We're doing everything in our power to reestablish contact with Starling II," Holden had said to the crowd. *"And if we fail, we have full faith in the abilities of Commander Adams and flight engineer*

Jesse McCall. Once the crew wakes from stasis, we're sure they'll resolve the communication issues and return safely after mission completion."

Lies on lies, Asher thought. Nobody was doing shit. After two sleepless days of pounding on keyboards, trying to find the issue, Asher and everyone else in his small team at mission control had been sent home "until further notice." It had been over a week since then. In Asher's opinion, the IES had given up on Starling II far too soon. The paranoia churned his mind into a frenzy. That night he stared at the ceiling, filled with a strange mixture of fear and anger, until sleep pulled him under a warm blanket of darkness.

•|•

The thunder crept into Asher's waking dreams, adding turbulence to his chaotic mind. The storm neared, and a flash of lightning opened his eyes.

He decided to skip the shower again, pulling his greasy hair into a bun and putting on a hat to hide his lack of hygiene. The patchy stubble on his face didn't look good, but he didn't care. He grabbed his phone from the nightstand and slipped his tablet into his backpack.

"Call Lana," he said to his phone. It began to ring. He waved his hand over the screen, and the video call moved to the upper left quadrant of the smart mirror.

Lana answered on the third ring, and her round face appeared on the screen. She sported a navy blue suit and a blonde pixie cut.

"You look like shit, dude," she said.

"And you just look like a dude," he said, annoyed.

"Damn, you're salty today," she said, glancing at her watch. "Did you just wake up? It's almost two."

"Yeah, I'm a hot mess. I get it." He scratched the back of his head. "Lana, listen. I have a story for you."

"Okay?" she said. "I'm listening."

"I can't talk about it now." Asher looked both ways. "Can you meet me at The Porch in a few hours?"

"I guess," Lana said hesitantly. "I'm leaving the office at five."

"Perfect," he said, reaching toward the mirror to hang up. "I'll see you then!"

"This better be—"

The video call ended.

"Oh, it'll be good," Asher said to no one.

•|•

Hours later, Asher sat in the front seat of a driverless Ryde, peering through the glass and the storm at the world around him.

After leaving the vast residential sprawl at the south end of the valley, he rode past chain restaurants, pawn shops, and charging stations. He passed a clinic with a marquee that read **NOW OFFERING NANO-THERAPY**. A long line wrapped around the building, people waiting to procure Doctor Cage's new preventative therapy, a nano-vaccine against a long list of common illnesses and pains. A side effect of the drug even gave those injected a youthful glow, reason enough for many to line up. Health insurance companies hated Cage Industries, but they could do nothing to hinder this new age of medicine. The cat was out of the bag, and everyone wanted to pet the cat.

Asher's Ryde got onto the I-15 and drove north, past the neon lights of the Las Vegas Strip. A high powered beam from the Luxor shone like a beacon through the rain. Without the traffic of human error, Asher arrived downtown too early. Waiting for Lana, he let his mind drift to thoughts of the past—and his concern for the only person who ever stood up for him.

•|•

After skipping a couple grades at a young age, Asher had been continuously picked on by the larger, less intelligent children. As a teenager he moved far from home to pursue an Aerospace Engineering Program at Stanford, hoping to one day float above Earth, far from the ignorance fostered by humanity. The bullying didn't stop in college, though. It only changed forms. During finals week of Freshman year, one student, fed up with Asher wrecking the grading curve, approached him on his way to class.

"Nice backpack," he said, taking it away. "Can I take a look?"

Asher cowered, his voice feeble. "Give it back."

"Don't worry, I will," the bully said through gritted teeth, unzipping the bag. He pulled out a stack of papers and combed through them. Without looking up, he held out the bag but dropped it before Asher could get to it. Something inside shattered. "Oops," he said.

The people in the hall walked along, eyes on their phones as they either avoided or failed to notice the incident. Eyes turned down, Asher didn't respond.

"This looks like a good term paper," the bully said, holding the pages horizontally between two hands. His beady eyes darted from the paper to Asher. "Shame if it ripped minutes before it's due."

"Please," Asher begged, drawing in a quick breath. "Don't."

Asher continued to stare at the floor as the bully laughed. "I really need a good grade in this class, Asher, but you've been ruining that. This is just survival of the—"

"Drop it," a voice said from behind, calm and confident. Asher looked up to see that the bully hadn't been silenced by the interruption, but by a one-armed choke hold. "Okay man, you're about to go to sleep—that much is given. What happens after that depends on your cooperation."

The bully struggled against the embrace, still gripping the term paper between his hands. Asher's savior continued. "I said—drop it."

The bully's eyes bulged, and his face turned red, but, unrelenting, he held on to the paper until the last bit of oxygen in his brain left him. He collapsed to the marble floor, and the essay floated down beside him.

"You should have listened." The man directed a swift kick to the ribs of the sleeping bully, then offered Asher a handshake. The boy's jaw dropped when he realized that his savior had only one arm. "Hey man, I'm Kapp."

•|•

Asher sat next to his backpack in a dark booth while he waited for Lana to arrive. Sipping on a mojito, he looked over at the tattooed bartender that Kapp had spent his last night on Earth with. She looked sexy as ever, even considering the pregnancy.

Asher wondered when she would take maternity leave: it had to be soon. Barely smiling, he closed his eyes and projected his thoughts through the high ceiling to the space beyond.

I hope you wrapped it, Kapp.

"What are you smiling at?" Lana slid into the booth. In her suit, she looked out of place in the casual bar, though there were barely any patrons there to judge her.

"Nothing," he said. "Come sit next to me."

"What?"

"I don't want anyone to hear us." His voice dropped lower after she scooted around to his side of the booth.

"You're being weird," Lana said, straightening her coat. "Like more than usual."

"You know about Starling II?" he asked.

"I'm a reporter"—she flashed a sarcastic smile—"Of course I watched the press conference."

"Lies," Asher said. "All of it. Director Holden is full of shit. They're not—the IES—we're not doing everything in our power to fix the communication issue." Asher spoke faster, pulling at his own hair. "We're not doing anything, Lana."

"And why not?" she asked, her thin eyebrows lowering in concern.

"Because Holden won't even let us try. He gave me a big fat check and told me to go home until I hear from him. He won't return my calls."

She let out a long breath. "Ash, I know your friend is out there, and that's hard, but it's not in your power—I mean—there's nothing more *you* can really do, right?"

"There's always more you can do," Asher said, vexed. He paused for a moment, collecting himself. There would be no undoing what he planned to do. "Do you know the purpose of the Starling II mission?"

Lana tilted her head to the side. "Umm…research right? One of the moons."

"That's what we were told"—Asher pulled the tablet out of his backpack and put it on the table between them. A few gestures later, a design diagram appeared. He tilted the screen toward

Lana—"But I think your readers might want to know why a research vessel is carrying a nuclear weapon."

Lana's jaw dropped a notch, her eyes scanning over the blueprints for a long time. Asher knew he looked and sounded like a crazy person. He could only hope she would believe him.

"Is this real?" she asked.

Asher nodded firmly, his hand still squeezing his hair. "I downloaded it directly from the IES network."

"And you want me to leak classified documents?"

Asher took a deep breath. "I want you to leak the truth, Lana."

She looked up from the screen, the important questions forming behind her eyes. "Why are they carrying a missile, Ash?"

Asher didn't say a word. He just swiped to the next picture on his tablet, the image he had hunted down in secret months earlier, the one Kapp left breadcrumbs for before he left Earth. He handed Lana the tablet, and she saw what few had seen before: a strange object on a distant moon.

"Just warn me before you release the article, please."

6

CONNECTION ERROR

She screams, but a bright flash of light and a loud boom quickly silences her. He sees nothing, but he hears a high-pitched ringing, smells blood and smoke. His right arm is numb. When his vision returns, a wall of fire threatens to swallow him. He squeezes his eyes shut, hoping it's just a bad dream. He can sense the flames coming closer, but only wonders why it's so cold. Slowly, the darkness tunnels until it becomes fluorescent light.

Passing out in a nightmare and waking up in a frozen box, Kapp's eyes shot open. Like in the dream, he tried to move but couldn't. He felt the pins and needles of three and a half sleeping limbs coming to life. Fear gripped his brain and squeezed it into a single instinctual thought—escape. Something clicked, releasing the tension built up inside him. Kapp's stasis pod exploded open from the force of a bionic punch. A few breaths of warm air later, his senses still foggy, he finally realized his location.

"Kapp!" he heard, as if from far away—but the voice came from the shattered opening. He pointed at his ears.

Mara opened the pod and pulled two earplugs out of Kapp's ears. He didn't know what looked more broken, the door or her pale and tear-streaked face.

"Kapp"—she gulped—"something's wrong with Jesse."

"What?" he asked with a rasp, still in a daze.

"I don't know. He started seizing and then—"

"Mara, what happened?"

"He—Jesse won't wake up," she said, pulling on Kapp's left arm.

As fast as their tense limbs would allow, the two of them pulled themselves to the other side of the room where Jesse lay, still strapped into his pod. His chest rose and fell, but barely. Transparent foam clung to his whiskers, and his face lacked that constant smile.

"How long ago did he get the stimulant?" Kapp asked.

"I don't know—an hour?"

"Help me take him out of here. Where's Eli?" Kapp asked, regaining composure in the face of emergency. He stretched his back and could tell it would hurt later.

"I'm here, commander," Eli said, pulling himself into the room.

"Get me a saline IV kit and a sleeping bag," he said as he and Mara pulled Jesse out of the stasis pod.

"On it," Eli said.

"And heating pads!" he yelled as Eli exited.

Once they removed Jesse from the pod and strapped him into a sleeping bag, hydration pumping into his blood, Mara took his vitals and Kapp had time to think. Still foggy, he had trouble focusing on his thoughts. After having no mental stimulation for eighth months, he felt hyper-aware of his surroundings. With every movement, he noticed his clothes rubbing against his skin, could almost feel each individual thread. He could see upside-down reflections of himself in Mara's tears. When Eli shaved his face, Kapp swore he could hear the cutting of each and every hair.

"Why is he so sick, Kapp?" Mara asked, her bottom lip quivering.

"I'm sure we'll figure it out," he said. "Keep an eye on him. I'm going up to call Mission Control."

•|•

On the upper deck, Kapp grabbed a comm tablet and tapped the icon for Mission Control. In blinking red, the screen displayed *Connection Error*. He hovered in a state of disbelief. There was always a chance of radioactive interference, but a quick glance at the nav charts showed that it was unlikely in their current position. Starling II would soon enter the same orbit around Mars as Phobos, where it would follow the moon at a safe distance and attempt to make contact. With interference out of the question, *Connection Error* could mean nothing good. Kapp eagerly found one of his bottles of scotch and took a long draw. He thought about the shit storm howling around him and the crew, and how much harder it would make their mission.

His hyper-awareness still not dulled by the liquor, Kapp gathered Mara and Eli to share the bad news. Mara's face appeared dry, her eyes swollen. Kapp could hear the skin of her fingers rubbing together as they twitched.

"What did they say?" she asked.

Kapp hesitated, sucking applesauce out of a bag. "Well"—he paused, overwhelmed by the first taste of food after being fed through a tube for many months—"They didn't say anything."

Mara just stared at him.

"What?" Eli asked.

"Communications are down," Kapp said. He avoided Mara's gaze, and his eyes focused on a single drop of dried blood leftover from Eli's shave. He felt his own face, still smooth from pre-stasis grooming.

"Can you fix it?" Mara asked, leaning in and widening the swollen skin that held her eyes. Kapp snapped out of his wandering thoughts and pointed to the motionless sleeping bag that held Jesse.

"He can."

•|•

Kapp couldn't sleep that night, or what the clock called night—day and night were subjective in empty space. His lower back ached, but the inflamed injury wasn't what stole his sleep. Concerned about Jesse, he went to check on him. He found Mara asleep by the man's side, exhausted from crying. Jesse looked no better than before, but he looked no worse. Kapp searched through the medicine cabinet in the dark, looking for the pain pills his back so desperately craved. Unable to find them, he cursed. He swore they had been there before stasis. Giving up, he ascended to the command module where he stored his booze. He drank enough to take the edge off before turning on his tablet. When the device booted up, an alert read:

Connection Error

"Fuck," Kapp whisper-yelled, slamming his palm against his head. "Fuckin' shit."

With a three finger gesture, he switched from the live comm app to his personal inbox. He had a few dozen unread messages, weekly updates from Asher. He opened one up randomly, and a video began to play.

"Hey buddy," Asher said, looking disheveled as ever. *"I finally tracked down"*—he looked over his shoulder—*"I tracked down that picture you told me about. And, well—I'm so jealous right now."*

Asher shook his head and then said, *"Anyway, that bartender that hates you is pregnant."*

It took a moment for Kapp to recall which bartender Asher spoke of.

"Emily. She's still hot, but yeah—definitely pregnant."

Kapp didn't remember much about that night.

"I'm thinking of asking her out, but it might be weird to take her home to your condo. I don't know yet. I would ask what you think, but you're asleep right now."

Asher's nervous rambling made Kapp smile.

"Anyway," Asher said. *"Vegas isn't as fun without you. Call me when you wake up."*

Kapp swiped to the next video.

"Hey man," Asher said, a massive grin on his face. *"Guess who just got season tickets for the Golden Knights? I guess I'll sell half of them since you're—"*

Kapp stopped the video. Too upset about the connection issue, he rushed through the rest, only watching the first ten seconds of each. When he reached the end, he realized that the newest message had come in over two months before. He swallowed the strangeness with another swig of Glenlivet and felt his way back to bed.

•|•

The connection to Mission Control was still down in the morning, and Jesse was still asleep. Mara took the covers and heating pads off to stop his sweating, plopped a thermometer in his mouth. Her eyes widened.

"Jesus," she gasped. "He's at 103°."

"It's probably a side effect of the stimulant," Kapp said, keeping his cool. In truth, his body began to tense up. "Give him another bag of saline. We need to strap in for orbital entry."

"I'll do it," Eli said.

Kapp nodded his consent. "Meet us in the cockpit in ten."

In the command module, Kapp effortlessly ran through the procedure he had practiced a hundred times on Earth. Without a flight engineer, any hiccup in the system could become deadly. Eli arrived late, but everyone still had time to strap in for orbital entry. They completed the drop into orbit around Mars in relative silence. Kapp looked down at the familiar red planet, then ahead at the object of their pursuit, an irregularly shaped moon hosting a mysterious ship. The possibilities rattled his brain. The ship could mean anything from enlightenment to destruction. Kapp's excitement came to a halt when he remembered that communication with the craft would be impossible if Jesse didn't wake up—if it was even possible to begin with.

•|•

Later that day, Kapp tried to drink himself to clarity. Looking over the unconscious body of Jesse, he took long sips from the bottle as he contemplated what could've caused the problem. They had all followed procedure. Jesse's pod appeared undamaged—pristine, even. With each sip of liquor, Kapp imagined a new scenario to explain the dilemma. *Where did we go wrong?* When both Kapp and the bottle were nearly drained, Mara floated down into the room.

"Kapp, what are you doing?!"

"Thinking," he muttered.

She took the bottle from him and put it in a trash receptacle.

"Hey, give that back," he said, suddenly angry.

"Stop!" she yelled. "We have to get Jesse to wake up! If he doesn't fix this, our attempts at communication fail, and if they fail—"

"Eli pulls the trigger. I know the mission." He laughed, but he knew it wasn't funny. "Kaboom," he said, adding gas to the flame.

Mara's disgust became even more evident as Kapp reached into the trash for his bottle.

"You're a fucking drunk," she said, disappointment turning her mouth to a scowl.

He ignored her and took out the scotch bottle, but something caught his eye before he could take a sip. Above some empty food containers, a razor dirtied with black hair floated near the top of the receptacle, right next to an empty medicine bottle. He pulled the container out and felt the day-old stubble on his face. He recalled his fruitless search for pain pills, the too-loud sound of Eli shaving.

"Take out Jesse's IV," he said, the grip of his metal hand tightening around the glass bottle, threatening to destroy it.

"Wha—Why?"

Kapp finished the alcohol, but his face became sober. He stared into Mara's tired and worried eyes, and after a serious pause, he continued.

"Who came out of stasis first?" Kapp asked. "Was it you?"

"I don't—"

"Was it you, Mara?"

"No." Mara shook her head. "No, it was Eli—he woke up first."

"This"—Kapp held up the empty pill bottle—"This was full before we went down for the long nap."

"What are you—"

"And Eli just shaved his beard. He shaved it yesterday, remember?"

Mara put a small hand on Kapp's shoulder. "You're not making any sense, Kapp."

"Mara," Kapp said, bobbing his head in affirmation. "Hair doesn't grow while you're in stasis. I think—no I don't think. I feel like I know."

"Know what?"

Kapp looked down at Jesse's fading form. "Eli did this."

His grip tightened, and the empty scotch bottle in his bionic hand shattered, sending shards of glass in every direction.

Kapp never would have expected such a betrayal to occur on a spacecraft, especially one under his command. Moments after the glass-shattering revelation of Eli's treachery, he heard the slam of metal on metal and the hiss of a sealing hatch. He shot up the tube to the command module while Mara pulled the tainted IV out of Jesse's arm.

"What the fuck!?" Kapp yelled.

"Kapp, what's going on?" Mara's voice echoed up the tube as Kapp pushed himself toward the room below.

"It's locked," he said, feet hitting the floor not so gently.

"Why—why would he do this?" Mara asked. She looked over her shoulder at Jesse.

Kapp just shook his head. With glass floating around him in the room where Jesse still slept, his anger inspired action. He pulled a handheld microphone from its designated spot and held down the button.

"Eli!" His voice boomed with rage as it filled the chambers of Starling II. "I command you to open the hatch."

The room remained silent like the emptiness of space.

"Open it!" he screamed into the handheld. "I know you can hear—"

Kapp and Mara fell to the floor, showered in broken glass. The acceleration of Starling II had given them a moment of artificial gravity that quickly passed. Once everything stabilized, Kapp made his way back to the radio.

"Why?" he asked, more calm than angry this time. "Just tell me why, Eli."

A minute passed before a burst of static marked Eli's response. The voice of the giant sounded small through the intercom. *"I'm sorry,"* he said, *"I have to destroy that ship. My son. If I don't—If I don't do it, they'll"*—he was crying—*"they'll hurt him."*

Kapp heard the click of a finished transmission. "Who will? Eli, who told you this? Who's going to be hurt? Your son?"

They waited for answers that never came. Kapp tried getting through to Eli every few minutes. He pled and begged and yelled for what seemed like hours before he gave up trying altogether. Mara searched the cabin for anything they might use to break into the command module, but she came up empty-handed. Starling II seemed cold and hopeless. Defeated, Kapp and Mara strapped in next to Jesse and shared hot bagged coffee and crackers. Mara popped an Adderall to augment the caffeine. Jesse had been stirring for over an hour, and he seemed to be getting increasingly restless.

"Jesse? Can you hear me?" Mara asked, looking hopeful for the first time. She held his hand in hers. He squeezed gently, and she smiled. "The drugs must be wearing off."

Not long after the first sign of life, Jesse's eyes opened to the chaos around him. He coughed dryly, and Mara got him to choke down a few sips of water.

"Where am I?" he asked in a drowsy whisper.

Mara and Kapp let him rest for a few hours before they expressed anything but relief at his recovery. He drifted in and out of consciousness as the drugs coursing through his blood dwindled beyond their half-life to a safe level. When he grew strong enough to communicate, the two of them explained the treacherous situation unfolding around them. Jesse looked hurt, but otherwise calm.

"Take me"—he coughed—"Take me to the aux command station."

"Can you open the cockpit from there?" Mara asked, shivering.

"Not if he bolted it from the inside," Jesse said, still struggling to speak.

That scenario seemed likely to Kapp, but unable to come up with an alternative plan, he agreed to it. "We have to try," he said.

Kapp pulled Jesse, still wrapped in a sleeping bag, to the display of the computer in the adjacent room that housed backup system controls. The engineer fumbled at rows of buttons, but he instantly found a problem.

"Screen won't turn on," he said.

Kapp unscrewed the wingnuts that held a panel in place below the monitor. After looking inside with a flashlight, his face tightened.

"Bastard cut the power," Kapp said, turning to Jesse. "Think you can fix this?"

"Could take a while."

"We can't spend that much time on *maybe* getting in," Kapp said. "We need to get Eli out."

Kapp's body stayed still, but his mind paced. He looked at Mara, who still shuddered from the cold of outer space that constantly crept through the walls of Starling II. The heating system onboard wasn't quite powerful enough to make the ship warm—just less cold than death.

"J"—Kapp turned to his friend—"can you cut the heat to just the cockpit?"

Jesse offered Kapp a grim and silent affirmative.

7

HYPOTHERMIA

Eli could see his own breath. Pumped out by his massive lungs, vapor hung in the air between him and the computer screen. After months of preparation, these were the final moments of the mission that would assure his son's safety. Before the long nap, he had sat at that same screen to adjust the wake-time of his stasis chamber by two months. He shuddered to think that Kapp had almost caught him then and there.

Kapp's voice broke the silence. *"Come out Eli—you'll freeze to death."*

We're all dead anyway, Eli thought. He rubbed his hands together and continued with his work, a last-ditch effort to automate the trajectory of Starling II and the missile attached to it. His own negligence had forced him into a corner. Eli had been so careful breaking the comm system two months earlier and poisoning the only person who could fix it, only to be found out by forgetting to shave. *Stupid.* Pushing away the self-loathing, he focused on the task at hand. If he didn't hit the target, his son would be killed. Numb fingers slowed him down, but he kept writing the program, ignoring the pleas from below.

"You can't do this!"

Violently shivering, Eli struggled to type the last few lines of code. He wouldn't have had to rush through it if he had just shaved a day earlier. *Stupid.* The crew would have been forced to destroy the alien ship the right way. They might have even made it home. Too late for thoughts like that, though. Soon his body would shut down from the cold. At last, satisfied with the program, Eli hit **EXECUTE**. *A fitting word,* he thought.

Mara pleaded through the intercom. *"Eli—think of the rest of us. Think of the world. You're destroying our chance of contact with extraterrestrial—"* Bursts of static interrupted the transmission. *"—always dreamed of. You could start a war! Think of how many lives you might be taking if you destroy that ship."*

Eli pulled the tattered picture of his son out of his pocket, the one that had been taped to the inside of his stasis chamber. He looked at the smile on the young man's face. *What about his life?* He didn't want to hurt anyone, but he saw no other option. A choice between the lives of aliens and the life of his son was no choice at all. The law had been written, and Eli had to obey. By force of will, he justified his actions, leaving no room for doubt.

His muscles ached from the cold. Turning the picture over in his trembling hands, he read the note scrawled on the back, the final reminder of the threat placed against his pride and joy. It had been slipped to him just before launch:

Do it, or he dies.

It won't be quick.

It won't be painless.

The words churned in his brain as he let the cold overtake him. Soon, his body gave up on shivering. Every movement exhausted him, so he stopped moving. Staring at the picture, he couldn't remember his location or his purpose. He only felt the pressure building in his bladder, deep aches in his flesh. Just before the hypothermic amnesia took his brain, his body felt hot. He frantically clawed at his clothes in an attempt to remove them, to stop the burn. The last thought on Eli's mind before the darkness overtook him made him panic.

What if he breaks his promise? What if he kills my son anyway?

8

THREE LEGGED CHAIR

After Lana left with the leaked photos, Asher moved from the booth to the bar to throttle his budding anxiety with a cocktail or five. As he drank, the patronage of the downtown establishment, scant to begin with, shrank until he and the bartender were the only occupants in the dimly lit space. With his forehead in his hands, he slouched forward, staring at the muddled mint leaves floating in the last half of his mojito.

"You okay, hun?"

Asher looked up at the bartender. He couldn't see her baby bump behind the high bar, but he knew it was there. "You can keep serving me. I'm not drunk."

"I meant"—she put a warm hand on his forearm—"are you okay? You seem really low right now."

Asher looked past the woman's external beauty and saw genuine kindness in her eyes. "I just—"

The words got caught in his throat, but not a single hint of impatience interrupted those kind eyes, eyes that Asher couldn't believe he hadn't noticed before. He took a few sips of his drink.

"There's just a lot going on right now," he said.

Maintaining both eye and physical contact, she nodded. "Wanna talk about it?"

He finished his drink. "Like I said, it's a lot."

"I've got time," she said, smiling and gesturing around the empty bar. "What's your name?"

"Asher."

"Good to meet you," she said, reaching her hand out to shake his. "I'm—"

"Emily," Asher said.

Her eyelids narrowed. "How did you know that?"

"Your name tag," Asher said as if it were obvious.

"But—I'm not wearing it."

Asher peered awkwardly at the shelf of bottles behind Emily. "You'll probably think this is weird, but I remember seeing it months ago."

She stared at him for a moment, her eyes narrowing playfully.

"Not weird, just observant." Emily tucked some hair behind her ear. "I like that."

The tension in Asher's shoulders released a bit. "Thanks."

"So, you wanna tell me what's bothering you, or what?"

Asher's tongue probed his front teeth, looking for stuck mint leaves.

"Can I have one more mojito first?" Asher asked, letting his lips curve into something other than an anxious grimace. "Before I spill my guts."

"Of course," she said. "I think I'll have one too."

Asher shot her a look. He peeked over the bar at her pregnant belly.

"Virgin, of course," she said.

When Emily turned to get the rum bottle from the shelf behind her, her open back maternity blouse allowed a glimpse of a tattoo that her previous work getups had never revealed. On the center of her back, Asher saw something that replaced his half smile with a full grin. He saw the unmistakable mark of one of his favorite creations, permanently inked into her skin: the artwork for Coldplay's eighth studio album.

After muddling, pouring, and shaking, Emily came back with the drinks and handed the spiked one to Asher.

"Coldplay, huh?" Asher said.

"Oh, you saw that?" Emily rested her elbows on the bar and leaned forward. "My parents were big fans. Took me to see the band live before they broke up."

Asher's head tilted to the side. "Coldplay didn't break up, they retired."

A burst of laughter escaped Emily's lips. "I meant my parents."

"Oh," Asher said, feeling a bit dumb.

"Anyway, their music changed my life—saved it, really."

Asher nodded. He knew the feeling well. "Favorite song?"

"Fix You," Emily said. "Duh."

"It's so sad, though." Regardless, Asher loved that song.

"Yeah, but"—Emily shrugged, her jewelry and eyes sparkling in the bar light—"I don't know. Sad songs kinda make me feel happy. Does that make sense?"

"It's not weird," Asher said, shaking his head. "Just cathartic."

Emily looked around the empty bar, then back at Asher. "I think I'm gonna close this place early today."

Asher started to rise, but Emily stopped him with a hand on his.

"You can stay," she said with a smile. "If you don't mind talking to me while I do dishes."

•|•

Days later, Asher paced outside of a local music venue, puffing on cannabis-infused vapor. From inside came the discord of a live soundcheck. As he performed the nervous ritual, Asher recalled some painful memories of getting stood up—rare memories, but only because dates were a rarity in his life.

After talking at the bar for hours, Asher had finally gotten the nerve to ask Emily out. Technically, he only asked her to *hang out*, but he considered it a good start. They decided to meet at Container Park to see a local band perform. Emily said she knew the bassist, and Asher saw that the band's bio claimed Brit Rock influences, so it seemed like common ground. At least there wouldn't be a bar between them. He just hoped she would show up.

She entered Asher's vision from behind a sculpture, some heart-shaped piece of metal covered in locks. The locks hung like piercings from every inch of the sculpture, cascading down in various layers of color and size. Chaotic yet organized, grungy yet beautiful—like the woman that stepped from behind it.

Emily wore a black and white Arctic Monkeys tee with frayed shorts. The tattoos on her long legs were still visible through the coin-sized diamonds of her fishnet tights. Multiple chunky bracelets cuffed her wrists. Asher could imagine her blonde hair done up in a mohawk, and the thought was still sexy. Her dark red lips parted into a smile.

"You look good," he said. "Punk rock as hell."

"Thank you." She smiled, and her shoulders bobbed slightly. "Sorry, I'm late."

"Are you?" Asher turned a wrist to look at his watch, but then he remembered he left it at home. He put his arm back down awkwardly, and she laughed.

"Let's go. Three Legged Chair's set starts at—"

"There you are," a voice said from behind Asher. "Hello, love."

The man stepped past him and scooped Emily up into a hug, lifting her off the ground for a few seconds in the process. Tan biceps bulged at the cuff of his tight-fitting tee shirt as he kissed her...on the lips. A spasm of jealousy erupted from somewhere deep inside Asher. He tried to keep it at bay, but it tightened in his chest.

"Ugh, your lips are wet," Emily said when her feet returned to the ground. "Martin, this is Asher.

Martin turned around and flashed a bleached smile. "Nice to meet you."

"Martin," Asher said, trying his best not to look depressed, "like the guitar."

"What?" Martin asked.

Asher cringed at the encounter, but more at himself for never asking Emily about her relationship status. *Someone this beautiful can't stay single long,* he thought.

"Never mind. Nice to meet you."

"Let's go," Emily said, nodding toward the entrance. "I'll buy you guys a drink."

She took each of them by the arm and pulled them toward the ID check, where they scanned their wrists on a panel. Asher went last because he didn't have his e-ticket yet.

"Thank you, Mr. West." The voice came from a mounted speaker.

"Please consent to the fifteen credit charge for entry."

"I consent."

"Voice recognition failure. Please try again."

"I consent," Asher said, annoyed.

"Voice recognition failure. Please try again."

Asher wanted to punch the damn thing, but there was a line forming behind him.

"I consent to the fifteen credit charge for entry," he said, annunciating each word.

"Voice recognized. Your account has been charged fifty credits. Please enter."

"You said fifteen!"

The turnstile unlocked and Asher pushed through it, more stressed about the line of impatient people behind him than the glitchy machine. He found Emily and Martin standing by a short fence surrounding a treehouse. She was laughing at something he said, and Asher's chest spasmed again.

"You gotta buy your ticket online next time," Emily said, winking at Asher. "It could've sold out."

Asher had actually thought about doing just that, but he decided to hold off on the purchase—just in case Emily didn't show up. "What can I say? I like to live life on the edge."

He felt stupid saying it, but she giggled anyway. "What do you two want? It's on me," she said, putting a hand on her growing belly. "And don't forget that you're drinking for me, too."

"The usual," Martin said.

Asher nodded. "Same for me."

Emily went to get the drinks, leaving the pair of men to stand in awkward silence.

"Even when she's not working, she's still serving us drinks," Martin said. An amused noise came from the back of his throat.

Asher faked a laugh. "Old habits."

"I guess. So, Asher, what do you do?"

Asher hated that question. It directly translated to "how do you make money?"

"I'm...between jobs at the moment," Asher said.

Martin nodded, and—not without envy—Asher noticed his

chiseled jawline, his nearly flawless skin. He wondered if the man had received the new nano-vaccine.

"I practice massage therapy," Martin said, even though Asher didn't ask. "You look pretty tense, mate. Want me to fix that?"

Asher nearly scoffed. "I'm okay, man, but I bet the ladies love that."

Martin shrugged just as Emily returned with the drinks: a water bottle for herself, a mojito for Asher, and an appletini for Martin.

"You two and your girly drinks," she said, then the riff of an electric guitar caught her ear. "To the stage!"

•|•

During the show, Asher found it hard to keep his eyes on the band. His gaze kept drifting to Emily, who bounced along to the music and mouthed the words to every song. Martin kept wandering off, but Asher still felt his presence like a dagger in the heart every time he returned. Whenever he came back, he would either put an arm around Emily or pull her into a spin.

Three Legged Chair ended their set with a cover of Mr. Brightside by The Killers, a Vegas staple. The entire crowd sang along in drunken unison. Even Asher found himself loosening up a bit. The final chord rang out to silence, the applause faded, and then the band began to pack up their gear. Martin jogged to the stage to talk to them, but Emily stayed behind.

"Let's give the rockstars some space," she said. "Want another drink?"

"Yeah," Asher said. "I'll go with you."

They walked to the stage-side bar and got in line. Asher didn't know what to do with his arms, so he folded them. He searched his head for something to say.

"Did you like the show?" Emily asked, breaking the silence.

"I did."

She sighed. "It just didn't seem like you were enjoying yourself."

"I was, I just—"

"Usually when you go to a concert with a girl, you're supposed to dance with her." Her lips bunched to one side. "Did you not want to?"

Asher's palms began to sweat. "Of course I wanted to."

"Then why didn't you?"

The line moved forward, and they shifted with it. At that moment, Asher wished that Kapp was there to give him some advice. This was followed by a rush of guilt for having a crush on his best friend's potential baby-mama. After mulling over his thoughts for a painful amount of time, he decided to just admit the truth.

"I like you, Emily. I'm just not very good at dancing, and—"

He paused.

"And what?" she asked.

"And I didn't want to piss off Martin."

The momentary confusion on her face disappeared in a fit of laughter.

"What's so funny?" Asher asked.

"Oh, you thought—" Her laughter became hysterical. "Oh god, you thought that—"

"What?"

"I can't," she said, catching her breath. "I literally can't."

The people at the bar started looking at her, probably confused about whether she was crying or laughing.

"Asher." She wiped happy tears from her eyes and pointed toward the stage. "Just look."

In front of the stage, which was busy with the activity of a quick changeover, Asher saw Martin making out with someone vaguely familiar—the male bass player of Three Legged Chair. Understanding slapped him in the face.

"Oh man, you have the worst gaydar," Emily said, locking her arm around Asher's and resting her head on his shoulder. "Have you tried the spicy pickles at Corduroy?"

An odd change of subject, Asher thought, but he was still relieved. "Can't say I have."

"Oh my god, you *need* to," Emily said, her voice rising in pitch. "Come on. Let's get out of here."

9

SPEED/CAUTION

The three remaining crew members of Starling II floated in grim silence, Mara's soft weeping the only sound louder than the hum of the ship's operational systems. Tears drifted from her face to form silvery constellations around her as she wiped the skin below her spectacles. The gravity of their decision revealed itself in each of their postures. Kapp let his forehead sink into his hands while Jesse tried to massage the sleep out of his legs. His body had trouble adjusting to the pains of Eli's sabotage. Mara still shivered from the cold of space. Just as Jesse worried, Eli had bolted shut the hatch door that led to the cockpit. The immediate threat was out of the way, but Kapp knew they'd have to find a way in at some point.

"We killed him," Mara said.

Jesse put his arm around her. "We had to, Mara."

"What if we did it for nothing?" She wept. "What if the object on Phobos is abandoned? What if it's empty?"

"We didn't have time," Kapp said. Still seething about the betrayal, he only felt the guilt vicariously.

"We could have found another way!" Mara shouted.

"Well, we didn't." Kapp spoke through gritted teeth. "Eli went against orders. There was no other way."

Contemplating the words of their commander, all stayed silent on the lower deck. Soon, Jesse's mouth stretched open against his will, and the yawn spread contagiously among them.

"You two get some rest," Kapp said. "I'll keep trying to break into the cockpit."

"You could try using the—"

WEAPON ARMED. The alert rang out in a robotic female voice that filled the cabin. Mara flinched so violently that her glasses flew off. She started to hyperventilate.

"I—I thought we—stopped him in time," she said between frantic breaths.

"So did I." Kapp's pain and fatigue evaporated from the heat of adrenaline. He pointed to the mess of wires that Eli left behind the auxiliary panel. "J! Let's fix this command station."

Jesse pulled himself toward the open panel. "Soldering iron?"

Kapp moved toward the tool drawer on the opposite wall.

"Mara, can you grab my tablet?" Jesse asked. He used a carabiner to attach himself to his work area so he wouldn't float away in zero Gs. Kapp quickly returned with a small toolkit.

WEAPON ARMED.

"Mara!" Jesse said again, but she didn't respond.

Mara lacked both pigment and alertness, and she couldn't catch her breath. Kapp knew these as signs of shock. He kept having to remind himself that Mara—a scholar, not an adventurer—wasn't suited for the stress of outer space. Beneath his authoritative exterior, he pitied Mara's situation, but he knew that crisis was never the time to shut down.

"Get your shit together, Stone."

Her bottom lip quivered. "I—I'm trying."

WEAPON ARMED. The alert made her flinch once again.

"Do you want them to die?" Kapp asked, pointing to where he imagined Phobos to be. "Do you want us to die?"

"No," she cried. "It's just too late. We—"

"It's too late when we're *dead*," he said, enunciating each word with more passion than the last.

Mara cowered from each verbal blow as her commander scared the fear out of her.

"And last time I checked," he said, "we're still breathing."

•|•

The trio worked together to reassemble the auxiliary command station. A visual disaster, but everything seemed to be plugged in correctly.

"Moment of truth," Jesse said, flipping the switch that would boot up the computer.

The screen stayed blank for a moment before blinking to life. The crew members let out breaths they didn't know they'd been holding. Line upon line of code filled the display, gibberish to everyone but Jesse.

"Eli did a number on the UI," Jesse said, his fingers tap-dancing on the keys. Kapp marveled at his speed and precision. "But I can work around that."

"What now?" Mara asked.

"Hmm…looks like he was an amateur hacker." Jesse coughed. "Or he was in a hurry."

Kapp looked over Jesse's shoulder at the streams of numbers. "What can we do?"

"Nothing for now. I should be able to disarm the weapon once I get past this firewall, but that could take time. You two should rest for a little while. I'll wake you if anything changes."

"Okay," Kapp said, leading Mara toward the sleeping chambers. He knew he wouldn't sleep until he regained control of Starling II, but Mara looked exhausted.

Kapp tucked her into a sleeping bag, then he floated toward the medicine cabinet across the hall. He returned moments later with a pill bottle and a water bag.

Mara sniffled. "I should stay awake and help."

"No, you need to sleep." He handed her a sleeping pill. "We've got this."

"But—"

"After we sort this out, we'll need you awake and alert. Sleep."

He took off her glasses and handed her the bag of water. Reluctantly, she swallowed the downer.

"Everything will be okay, Mars."

Kapp forced his voice to sound more confident than his thoughts.

•|•

Kapp took a swig of scotch on his way back to the auxiliary command station. *Just to take the edge off,* he thought. Before his first interplanetary trip, he had been no stranger to the bottle, but the crash landing and his subsequent back injury gave him an excuse to truly form a habit—his way of coping with the pain. When he arrived at the station, Jesse gave him a severe look.

"Couldn't sleep," Kapp admitted, taking Jesse's steely gaze as some form of judgment.

"Kapp, I disarmed the missile, but—"

Kapp sighed, his excitement immediately shut down by his least favorite coordinating conjunction. "What is it, J?"

"I originally thought the missile had been armed for launch."

"Armed for launch?" Kapp's chest began to tighten. "Wasn't it?"

"No." Jesse's voice dropped into a serious tone. "Eli armed it for detonation."

The taste of alcohol on Kapp's tongue dissipated, washed away by the taste of fear. His knees buckled, and he might have collapsed if it weren't for the lack of gravity. "No," he said.

Jesse soon confirmed what Kapp had already deduced. "We're on a collision course for Phobos."

Kapp closed his eyes and pinched the bridge of his nose between tense thumbs. Behind closed eyelids, his pupils rolled upward. "How many days until impact? Maybe we can drill into the—"

"Hours," Jesse said. "Just under two."

Speechless, Kapp exhaled a sigh.

"Eli programmed the ship to slowly accelerate to max velocity. Besides that first burst, we didn't feel it." Jesse calmly recited the facts. If he was miserable, he didn't show it.

"You can't change our trajectory from here?" By the time the words left his lips, Kapp already knew the answer.

"Not with the time we have. It'd be a close call, even if we had the cockpit back."

Kapp's mind understood the futility of their situation, but his body raged against the idea of death. Desperation formed ideas, notions previously unthinkable because of their magnitude.

"Then we need to take it back."

•|•

Kapp was trained for extravehicular activity, but he had never experienced an actual spacewalk. Inside the airlock, he attached a cable to his suit that would tether him to the ship. He had a toolkit strapped to his chest. Jesse would open the external crew module hatch remotely: Kapp just had to get there. For the two astronauts, the necessity of success displaced all fears of failure.

Jesse's voice sounded through Kapp's headset. *"Airlock depressurizing."*

"Copy." Kapp's voice echoed inside the dome surrounding his head.

"Are you tethered?"

"Yep," Kapp said, too focused on the task at hand to worry about the formalities of radio communication. With a turn of his wrist, he lowered the helmet's sun-protecting visor over his eyes. "Open the doors, J."

The cracking doors hissed as they released the final bit of air into the void beyond. Through the opening, Kapp saw the red tint of iron oxide on the surface of Mars. He was close enough to distinguish valleys from mountain ranges, volcanic fields from vast Martian deserts. Countless stars filled the periphery, threatening to steal his focus with their brilliance. With all the recent chaos, Kapp hadn't gotten a chance to take in the view. It was even more beautiful than he remembered.

"Just follow the handholds."

Kapp pulled his torso out of the airlock and held himself in place. His helmet couldn't rotate with his head, but he could still get a 180° view of his surroundings. He turned his body until he saw the first handhold directly to his right. Beyond Starling's nose, he caught a glimpse of the gray, meteor-dimpled surface of Phobos. The proximity of the moon hastened his glove toward the curved handle.

"Here we go," he said to no one but himself.

Kapp didn't know why they called it a spacewalk. He didn't have to use his legs at all to scale the side of the crew module. Lacking the prehensile anatomy of hands, his lower limbs actually got in the way. If Kapp moved the wrong way, he risked accidentally pushing himself away from the ship, which would threaten his grip and slow him down. Sure, he could be reeled back in by the tether, but there was no time for a mistake like that. Straddling the fine line between speed and caution, Kapp silently performed what he decided to call a space-crawl.

"How's it going out there?" Jesse asked.

"Halfway there," Kapp guessed. Like a focused climber on the face of a cliff, he hadn't looked down to confirm his progress. On Earth, he had a fear of heights, but that probably had something to do with gravity. In space, there was no falling down, only falling away.

Kapp looked ahead at the moon and could see it even better than before. Squinting, he could make out the outline of the massive crater, but not yet the object resting inside it. Crossing the speed/caution line, Kapp picked up his pace. He took handhold after handhold, thinking about the insanity of the mission, marveling at the extraordinary circumstances, and agonizing over everything that had gone wrong.

"Shit," Kapp cursed as an invisible force yanked him back. He retreated to a lower handhold before the inertia could send him spinning off the face Starling II. "J, I think my tether is caught on something."

Jesse's voice came through the static. *"I have eyes on the attachment point. The line is taught."*

"It's supposed to be long en—"

"I think you attached the wrong tether."

Kapp cringed at his rookie mistake.

"Kapp." Jesse's voice stayed positive. *"I'm reeling you back in. We'll try again."*

Kapp could almost feel the moon's presence, like it had eyes on him—a daunting approach. Reaching for the tools strapped to his chest, he looked at the tether, which attached him to the ship like the cord between a baby and its mother. He couldn't recall his own mother's face, but he had distant memories of the comfort of being held. Safe. Attached. The residual feeling warmed him deeply. But the time for safety was over. Without a second thought about his past or his own life, Kapp reached out to cut the cord.

"Just open the hatch," he said. "I'm free-climbing."

"Kapp, no—"

"I have to."

Kapp made the last half of the ascent with haste. Unsure of what drove him, onward his body moved, drowning out the protest of his mind, like a train chugging along in a set direction, indifferent to the voices of the people within. His heart beat audibly between rhythmic steps as handhold after handhold disappeared behind him.

Kapp made swift progress around the trapezoidal curve of the crew module. Looking ahead at the approaching moon, he reached instinctively toward the final hold. He gripped firmly with his bionic arm as he let go of the lower hold. When he tried to pull himself forward, he realized something dreadful, something that made him feel like he had accidentally skipped the final step of a staircase. His hand held nothing. The last handhold was missing.

Before he could react, Kapp's inertia sent him floating slowly along a trajectory misaligned with the open hatch. He had only moments to act, estimating that he'd miss his desired destination by less than a foot. The tiniest amount of thrust was both all he needed and all he couldn't have.

He removed the glove from his right hand. The chill of space seeped through his metallic limb into the flesh surrounding his attachment point. With some struggle, he pressed a small button on the wrist of his prosthetic, twisted it off at the elbow, and pulled the detached limb out of the sleeve of his suit. He locked the forefinger of the limb into a "come hither" gesture. Reaching as far as possible with the arm held in his left hand, he tried not to think about the threatening glare of Phobos. Instead, he focused on the tiny loop of metal that made up the handle of the hatch door.

Not quite close enough, he knew he'd miss it. A half an inch off and he'd end up crashing into the surface of the moon before his ship—if he didn't freeze to death first, which he surely would. He wasn't even confident that the forefinger hook would be strong enough to hold its shape. Reaching desperately and floating silently toward his fate, Kapp closed his eyes and hoped for the best.

•|•

Floating toward certain death, Kapp felt an overwhelming sense of peace. Time seemed to expand and contract, imperceptible. Eons passed in a second. To Kapp, life was the edge of a cliff that he had always walked along, sometimes far too close to the gulf below. This time he had stepped over the edge, eternally falling into the chasm. Galaxies formed and dissolved in his mind. Life evolved and destroyed itself. Stars exploded, only to be reborn from the ashes. Then one day, when Kapp could no longer feel the weightlessness of the endless fall, he opened his ancient eyes to see himself clinging to the edge of life by his fingertips.

10

PANCAKES AND COFFEE

Asher woke up smiling, memories of the night still fresh in his mind. Emily slept beside him, completely still save for the slow rise and fall of her belly, life within life. Slowly, he rolled onto his side and propped himself up to get a better look. The bed creaked beneath his elbow. Her eyelids fluttered and then stilled. Asher could smell the intoxicating aroma of her perfume and felt the heat radiating from her skin. The hint of a smile came to her lips, happiness contagious.

For the first time in months—perhaps for the first time in his life—anxiety released its grip on Asher's heart. He could almost forget about Kapp and the Starling II mission. Almost.

Minutes passed, and the arm supporting his head began to numb. He didn't care. He watched the light of dawn creep from the cracked curtains of Emily's bedroom, across a floor littered with both their clothes and into a bed shared for the first time. The sunlight touched her face, feeding the small smile until it blossomed into something living, powerful, awake.

"Good morning," Asher whispered.

He kissed her cheek, the skin beneath her ear, and then her neck.

"Stop," she said playfully, "you're gonna make my hair grow."

He laughed. "What?"

"Goosebumps," she said, rolling to face him. "They make your hair grow, and I just shaved my legs."

"That's fine," Asher said, inching closer until they shared a single pillow, face to face, eyes lined up with eyes.

"I'm sorry we couldn't—"

He silenced her with a kiss. "Don't be."

The bump of her pregnancy pressed against his bare stomach.

"You're a good man, Ash," Emily said. "Most so-called men would run from someone as pregnant as me."

Asher still hadn't summoned up the courage to ask about the father. He banished all thoughts of Kapp or someone else impregnating his new girlfriend, choosing instead to think about the future.

"What can I say? I've always had a thing for hot moms."

She giggled, which made her stomach move softly against Asher's. It moved again, this time not so softly, even after she stopped laughing. Her eyes widened.

"Did you feel that?" she asked.

"Was that—"

"Oh my god, she kicked." Emily's mouth stretched into the shape of an O. "The first time! That was amazing. She must like you."

Asher smiled. "You know it's a she?"

"Not for sure," Emily said, "but I have a feeling."

They lay silent for a while longer, Asher's thoughts ripe with possibility. He imagined thousands of mornings with Emily, each one getting better with time, and what it might be like to father someone else's child—to form a new family and let the days pass in happiness instead of stress. And even though worries about Kapp still nagged at him, one bright look from Emily sent the dark thoughts fleeing into the recesses of his mind.

"The baby's hungry," Emily said after a time. "Which is just my excuse to have you buy me pancakes."

"I'm always down for breakfast." Asher sat up. "Mind if I go home and get some fresh clothes first?"

"Do you have to?" Emily pouted. "You can just wear some of mine."

Asher's feet touched the carpet. "Believe me, you don't want to see me in fishnets."

"Or do I?" She bit her lip. "You don't know what I like."

Asher came to her side of the bed and kissed her again. He didn't want to leave, but he had accidentally left his phone at home, which made him anxious.

"I'll be back in an hour," Asher said, starting to get dressed, "and then I'll buy however many pancakes it takes to satisfy an unborn child."

"Good, because she's ravenous." Emily pulled the blankets up to her neck and yawned. "And she needs a nap."

Before Asher shut the bedroom door, he almost said, "I love you," but thought it might be too soon, even though he felt such emotions beginning to stir.

•|•

Asher scanned his wrist at the door and entered Kapp's condo, which he had been living in for months. He considered taking Emily there the night before, but her place was closer to Downtown, where they just had their fifth date, dinner at a mob-themed Italian restaurant. He also didn't want to take her back to where she and Kapp—

"Welcome back, sir."

Asher recoiled instinctively. Jax's intrusions still surprised him.

"Shit," he said. "Volume down next time."

"My apologies, sir. You have three new messages. Shall I read them to you?"

"I'll read them myself," Asher said. "Where's my phone?"

A ringing came from the master loft.

"Start some coffee," Asher said as he began to ascend the floating staircase. "And make it hot."

"Maximum coffee temperature is one hundred and eighty-five degrees. Will that suffice?"

"Sure," Asher said. "Sugar, no cream."

Asher's entire wardrobe covered the floor of the loft-style bedroom, remnants of his mad dash to find the perfect outfit for his date. The mess alone was reason enough to not have her over. He chose something else to wear, less of a drastic decision this time because Emily had already agreed to be his girlfriend. Thinking he might spend the night at her apartment again, he quickly packed an overnight bag—more clothes, his tablet, a toothbrush.

"Are you expecting company?" Jax asked. "There's someone at the door."

"Who?" Asher asked.

"I don't know. He's not a registered guest. Shall I politely ask him to—"

"Pull up security cameras."

A video feed filled the mirror in front of Asher. A man dressed in the black guard uniform of the IES approached the front door. Asher heard the knock before he saw it on the screen.

"Deadbolt," he said, and Jax obeyed.

"Your coffee is ready, sir."

"Not the time, Jax."

"I'll keep it hot," Jax said.

Asher grabbed his phone from the counter and swiped to reveal his new messages, all from the night before: one from Emily saying she was ready to be picked up, one from his mom back in Ohio, and one from Lana...

The article will go live at 6 a.m. tomorrow.

Asher's anxiety came back with ferocity. He tugged at his hair and checked the time in the mirror. 9:11 a.m. The man on the screen knocked again, louder this time. Asher paced around the master bathroom. Maybe he could escape from the balcony, but he needed time.

"Intercom," Asher said.

The sound of the man's breathing came through speakers set into the ceiling.

"Hello," Asher said.

"Sorry to interrupt, Mr. West," the man said. "I'm just delivering a check and need you to sign for it. Severance pay."

Asher raised an eyebrow. He recognized the voice. It belonged to Nai, the head of security at Groom Lake.

"Hold on, I'm changing."

Asher pressed an icon on the mirror to mute the intercom, wondering if it was just paranoia getting to him. How could the IES even trace the leaked photo back to him? Could Nai's appearance be a coincidence? An answer came through the video feed as the man began to fiddle with the lock.

Asher shouldered his backpack and hurried down the stairs. "Open the balcony," he said.

Glass doors slid open automatically and disappeared into pockets in the wall. Asher peered over the edge of the balcony. Three stories up, and no way to climb down, unless—

"Jax, how deep is the community pool?"

"Residents of Park House enjoy a suite of resort-style amenities, including a community center with a game room, 24-hour valet parking, and an Olympic lap pool. Would you like to—"

"If I jump into it from the balcony, will I survive?"

"Diving from resident balconies is listed as a prohibited activity in the community guidelines."

The edge of the deep end sat only a few longitudinal feet from the balcony, an easy enough jump forward. It was the height of the fall that dizzied him. Asher stepped closer to the railing, his heart pounding, preparing for the worst. The metallic slide of an opening deadbolt reached his ears, but he couldn't get himself to jump.

"Shit," he said.

Asher raced back into the kitchen, grabbed a knife, and hid in the pantry just as the front door cracked open.

"Asher," Nai taunted, "where are you?"

Hands sweating, squeezing the handle of the knife in one hand and his phone in the other, Asher held his breath. Soft footsteps on the hardwood grew louder, and then quieter once again as Nai passed the kitchen.

"I know you're home," he said. "I can smell the coffee."

Asher heard him approach the balcony, the sound of his boots changing once they hit the concrete. Fumbling, nearly dropping the knife, Asher unlocked his phone, summoned Jax with the press of a button, and whispered, "Lock the balcony doors."

The house obeyed. When Asher came out of the pantry, he saw Nai trying to pry the pocket doors back open with his bare hands.

"Yeah, good luck with that," Asher said.

He dropped the knife on the counter, pocketed his phone, and then thought better of it. Too easy to track. He dropped it down the sink and said, "Garbage disposal."

Sparks flew from the drain, and a terrible shredding sound filled the kitchen. During the ten seconds it took to dispose of his phone, Asher failed to notice that Nai had somehow opened the balcony doors and reentered. He now stood on the opposite side of the kitchen island. Steam rose from the fresh cup of coffee that sat on the counter between them. Asher picked up the knife again.

"Look, man," Nai said, raising his hands. "I'm unarmed. I didn't come here to hurt you. Holden just wants to talk."

He pulled something from his belt, which made Asher flinch.

"About what?" Asher asked, realizing it was just the man's phone.

"You know what." He dialed a number. "Just put down the knife and let me bring you in."

Asher didn't want to give up his advantage, but he couldn't see through the granite to verify that the man was unarmed. He stayed silent until the call went through.

"This is Nai, requesting transport." Nai looked back at Asher's hand. "The knife."

"Okay, fine." Asher put down the weapon and reached for the coffee mug instead. "You want this?" he asked, offering Nai the steaming mug. "It's imported from Africa."

"Sure." Nai smiled. "It does smell pretty—"

A hundred and eighty-five degrees of scalding coffee hit Nai square in the face. He screamed and sank to his knees, wiping at his red and swollen eyes, howling in agony and letting out a steady stream of curses.

"Jax," Asher said, heading to the front door, "call an ambulance."

"Right away, sir."

11

HIGHWAY TO HELL

The change in inertia snapped Kapp back to reality. He opened his eyes to see that the hook had caught. Too shocked to be relieved, he awkwardly pulled himself toward the hatch using his detached prosthetic and grabbed onto something more solid.

Once safely inside the cockpit, Kapp got himself situated. He paid no attention to the dead man strapped in beside him as he re-attached his prosthetic. He only allowed himself glimpses of Eli's hands floating in his periphery, covered in ice crystals that sparkled in the porthole-filtered starlight.

"Come in, J," Kapp said into the radio.

"Well, I'll be damned," Jesse said, his Southern accent slipping out. "Y'all actually made it."

"Barely."

"What happ—"

"Please just seal the hatch. And turn the heat on."

In response, the portal that Kapp had so nearly missed shut itself mechanically, and the cabin began to pressurize. Struggling against the confines of his suit, he strapped himself in beside Eli's corpse. His shoulder was numb from the cold that had seeped through his open sleeve, but he ignored it.

"Wake Mara, and let me know when you're suited up and strapped in."

"Way ahead of you."

"Good," he said, tapping through controls. "We're about to pull some massive Gs. Reversing thrust now." The screen before him beeped its approval. "Hold on."

Front boosters fired on Kapp's command. As the ship's acceleration began to decrease, the straps pressed tightly across his chest. His head rolled forward as far as his space suit would allow. Eli's body made similar motions, but without muscles that could automatically tense against the change in inertia, he looked more like a test crash dummy than a human. Using the purchased time, Kapp had a moment to think. He had serious doubts about his ability to reverse the mutinous acts of the dead man that sat beside him. An eerie silence filled Kapp's helmet as he pondered this conundrum.

Jesse's voice destroyed the quiet. *"Kapp, can you reach the panel under Seat B?"*

He looked to his left, careful to keep his gaze below Eli's neckline. "Affirmative, but the seat is currently occupied."

"What do you m—oh. Well, if you can get to it, patch the aux command cable into the main system, and I'll see if there's a way for us to avoid collision."

The last thing Kapp wanted to do was touch the man. He looked at Eli's hands first, clenched around a crumpled piece of paper. Kapp tried to remove it, but Eli's frozen grip held it tight. Hesitantly, Kapp unfastened the belts that crossed Eli's chest. He accidentally looked up at the frozen grimace drawn across his face—a mixture of pain and fear. Though Eli's murder had seemed necessary at the time, Kapp felt a pang of regret, wondering if there might have been a better way to handle the situation. He swallowed such thoughts, wishing he could wash them down with a bit of whiskey.

When Kapp released the belts, Eli's body lurched forward with the allowance of more slack, but still remained secure. Kapp didn't want the body to float freely through the cabin since it could injure or kill him if he pulled any evasive maneuvers. He opened the panel beneath Eli's seat and followed Jesse's directions to bridge the gap between the cockpit and the auxiliary systems below.

"Alright, I'm in."

Kapp could imagine Jesse on the lower deck, typing furiously in desperate search of a solution. If anyone could save the day, Jesse could. On the screen, Kapp looked at their proximity to Phobos and the trajectory projection, a straight red line between the ship and the Martian moon. Salvation seemed an impossibility.

"Alright, I've got a simulation coming your way." A blue curve appeared on Kapp's screen beside the red line. *"If we pull max Gs, we'll miss the moon by a hair—that is, if the sim is accurate."*

Kapp grunted into his microphone, partly in response and partly from the pain in his thawing shoulder.

"There's only a small margin of error. This path also puts us into a standard orbit around Mars."

"Alright, let's do it."

"We might even have enough fuel left to eventually get out of orbit and start on a trajectory toward home."

Kapp smirked and shook his head at Jesse's optimism. "One thing at a time, J."

Home hadn't even crossed Kapp's mind. He had more immediate problems to address. The simulation showed twenty-three minutes to avoidance or impact. Twenty-three minutes to salvation or doom. The two forces stood in opposition, like the holy notions of heaven and hell. What a thin line they fought over. In less than half an hour the crew would either be alive or dead. If Kapp had to die, he didn't want to do it in the silent company of a dead traitor, so he pulled his tablet off the wall and held the home button until it chimed.

"Jax, play some classic rock on the intercom."

"Right away, sir." The guitar intro of an AC/DC song came through the speakers and filled the cabin before Jax even finished responding.

Mara's voice popped into Kapp's headset. *"Is that Highway to Hell?"*

Kapp looked at the tablet, smirked, and mouthed something that looked a lot like "brother trucker."

•|•

The icon for Starling II closely followed the blue line drawn on the simulation graphic. Coupled with the music, this caused the mood on board to become less dire as the ship approached the Martian moon. The crew remained strapped in, peeling away from the moon at a harsh, but bearable, force of six times the average gravity of Earth. The tight lining in Kapp's suit helped his blood circulate to the important parts of his body, but he still felt like he weighed a literal ton.

He struggled to speak through the pressure. "Almost there—"

A sudden jolt shook the ship. Kapp got butterflies in his stomach, that top-of-the-roller-coaster feeling. The accelerometer wavered and dropped below the 6 G mark, which meant that the ship was losing altitude relative to Phobos.

"Thruster misfire?" he asked J.

"Lost it completely. We're too low."

Nearing the end of the line, the Starling icon started to dip below the sim curve. Alarms went off in the cockpit, flashing red accompanied by piercing beeps. Kapp had to compensate for the loss of thrust, but he had no time.

"Full force to the remaining thrusters!" Kapp yelled, pulling a lever back to increase the ship's altitude.

"We'll hit the G limit and—"

"Override!'"

The accelerometer slowly climbed.

6.25 Gs.

6.5 Gs.

6.75 Gs.

Too slow. Kapp could almost feel the threatening mass of Phobos ahead and below. The lever got stuck until Jesse keyed in the command to override its safe limit. Once he did, the mechanism clicked past its previous barrier.

7 Gs.

7.25 Gs.

The pressure became painful as Starling II dipped into the gravity well of the moon. The compression suit he wore could no longer hold the blood in Kapp's head. He tensed his body in an attempt to remain conscious, his face contorted in a strange frown.

7.5 Gs.

7.75 Gs.

Fuck, he thought, as the proximity sensor of Starling II began to ring out in a chaotic rhythm. *We're still gonna hit.*

8 Gs.

With what little strength remained in his heavy arm, Kapp jerked the lever backward, and the crew of Starling II blacked out.

12

BLADES

Asher stood in the bathroom of a dingy motel room, avoiding his reflection in an age-stained mirror. Locks of his brown hair filled the sink, beneath a pair of scissors he had borrowed from the front desk. Shaking his head, he dared a glance at the mirror. He had trimmed his hair so short that he could see his scalp, a total hack job. He hardly recognized himself, but that was the point.

He touched his cheek, remembering how Emily had done the same thing that very morning. It had only been ten hours, but ten hours of panicked running felt more like ten days. His only stop was to fill his bag with cash on the outskirts of Vegas. It took him forever to find an ATM that far out of the city. If the IES were tracking his bank activity, they'd think he went north, but he turned around after pulling out the cash.

What does Holden want? he wondered, unable to look away from his strange reflection.

It didn't matter, anyway. Soon the world would know the truth about the Starling II mission, and Asher would be safe once again. He just had to wait it out, avoid retribution until Holden's corruption came to light. Then he could return to Emily, communication with Starling could be re-established, and life would go on.

Parallel strips of light moved across the bathroom's peeling wallpaper, gaining Asher's attention. He quickly peeked through the half-open blinds before returning his attention to the next task, one he had been avoiding. Disguising his appearance would mean nothing if he could still be tracked.

He gulped loudly.

Turning his left wrist over in preparation, he felt the slight bump of his identity implant, then drew a line across the area with a permanent market. From the tiled counter, he picked up a razor blade—already sterilized and ready to do its job.

Without overthinking it, he brought the blade to his wrist, ready to make the incision. But then he hesitated. His spine quivered. The scene reminded him too much of his past, something horrible he had once tried.

•|•

Asher sat alone in the dim light of his studio apartment. Graduation had passed, but textbooks and loose paper still littered both the floor and the desk ahead of him. The dank room smelled like dirty laundry and stale coffee. Bitter tears fell on an unfolded piece of paper in Asher's hands as he read the hurtful words once again.

Dear Asher West,

Thank you for your interest in the IES flight training program. After full consideration of your application, we regret to inform you that you have not been selected for this year's class. The Interplanetary Explorers Society received a record number of applications this year, hundreds of which came from Stanford graduates alone. As you know, this is an extremely competitive program. While your academic performance far exceeded those of your classmates, your results on the medical examination were less than optimal. We wish you the best in your future endeavors.

Sincerely,
The IES Board

Asher crumpled the tearstained relic of his failure and tossed it to the ground. Piled on top of everything else going on, the pain of the news bore down ruthlessly upon him, unrelenting. It hurt to breathe, so he held his breath, but that hurt worse. Once again his body had failed him. He dragged it into the bathroom and looked at it in the mirror, cursing the pathetic reflection. He hated what he saw: the body that had not been manly enough to win his father's respect, the body that had been beaten over and over again by bullies, the body that had been systematically rejected by potential lovers. Asher wished nothing more than to leave the wretched thing behind.

With tears burning his face, he reached into the drawer and pulled out a disposable razor. The rigid plastic surrounding the blades splintered under the weight of his boot. Asher rummaged through the mess and pinched a single blade between two fingers, a tool to end his suffering. The edge of the thin metal reflected an ominous light as he held it in front of him. Its sharp edge glistened in the fluorescent light, threatening but somehow inviting. After a moment of hesitation, he pressed it to the inside of his left wrist and inhaled deeply.

The first slice concurred with his exhale. Endorphins rushed through his body, temporarily numbing the pain. He felt the rush before even the first drop of crimson could hit the linoleum at his feet. Looking down at the blood that had betrayed him, all he could think was that there wasn't enough of it. He wanted to fill the sink with it, let his life go down the drain.

A knock reverberated through the walls, which Asher ignored. He pressed the blade down harder for the second cut. Instead of dripping, blood spilled, the new pain alleviating the old with renewed vigor.

"Asher, open up." Apartment walls muffled the voice. "I brought beer and pizza."

The knocking and the cutting continued, each growing bolder with time. Asher felt a pleasant lightheadedness begin to push out his burdened thoughts. Relaxed, he sank to the bloodied floor where he could focus on the pain.

"Come on, I know you're in there."

Time seemed to slow as the yells grew louder, more frantic. If more words were said, he ignored them. Clouding out all else, the relief he had found was too overpowering. The crack of breaking wood barely touched his fading senses. Even the sharp smell of iron and the thump of approaching footsteps couldn't stop Asher's blade from making its final journey across his flesh. With eyes closed, he could not see the panicked face of his friend, but he could feel the touch of arms breaking through the fog, scooping him up—a feeling he would never forget.

13

BASTARD

Kapp's mother screams, and the sound leaves as quickly as it comes—like breaking glass. The explosion blinds him, and a high-pitched ringing mixes with the scream still echoing in his mind. Beneath the growing scent of smoke, he can smell blood. His vision fades back in, and he sees that he's surrounded by flames. He looks down. His right arm is gone—just gone—and he can't move. Blood spills to the floor, sizzling on the hot tile, then the darkness descends.

Kapp woke in a state of confusion, smothered by the darkness coiled around him. His thoughts felt even stickier than the suit that clung to his skin. The pulse that radiated through his head seemed foreign as it beat relentlessly upon his brain. Turning his body, he realized that a headache wasn't the only damage. Kapp's shoulder tingled and stung around the metal of his bionic arm. The pain made him realize he was still alive.

Everything rushed back to him at once, raising his heart rate and pulling him into the present moment. In disbelief of his own survival, he wondered why darkness lived in the cockpit.

Pulling all those Gs probably knocked a cable loose. Nothing J can't fix.

Instinct drove him to check on the wellbeing of his crew. He fought through the pain of unstrapping himself and reached through the biting darkness, accidentally bumping Eli's corpse as he felt around for his tablet. He shuddered from the cold touch before continuing his search. Unable to locate the device in the dark, he thought of a better idea.

"Hey Jax," he said, his voice muffled by the dome surrounding his head.

A ping meant that the device heard him, and the screen sprung to life, awaiting Kapp's next command. The glow momentarily blinded him. Once his eyes adjusted, Kapp located his position in regards to the cabin, but he still struggled with his position in space.

"Where are we, Jax?"

Kapp could barely hear the British accent through the carbo-glass of his helmet. "I'm unable to connect to nav charts at this time."

He exhaled a sigh over his dry tongue. "Can you turn on more lights?"

"I'm unable to connect to anything, sir. My apologies."

"Shit—just keep the screen light on, okay?"

"Roger that," Jax said, the tablet's screen intelligently illuminating to max brightness.

Kapp floated toward the hatch door that led to the lower deck and found the toolkit that Eli had used to seal it. With a battery-powered drill, he made quick work of the bolts surrounding the fixture. A tight squeeze in his bulky suit, but Kapp managed to descend the ladder with the tablet illuminating his path.

He found Jesse and Mara on the lower deck, already equipped with flashlights. Though both of their faces were pale, Kapp couldn't help but grin, happy to see them alive. Before the blackout, he had thought he would never see anything again.

"Are you okay?" they asked in unison.

"I'm fine," he lied, trying to ignore the various aches that were only getting worse. "I just can't believe we avoided collision—that we're alive."

Jesse and Mara looked at each other, and then back to Kapp.

"What?" Kapp asked, turning to each face. "We must have, right? We're in zero grav—"

Kapp stopped speaking when he realized what Jesse and Mara had already concluded, when he remembered that near-zero gravity could feel damn similar to zero gravity. It became clear to Kapp that they weren't floating safely through space; they were shipwrecked on the surface of Phobos.

•|•

Hours later, sunlight began to pour through the portholes of Starling II as Phobos made its rapid orbit around the red planet. The crew surrounded the auxiliary command station, where Jesse began a diagnostic check of the ship using a bank of backup batteries.

"Life support systems are still operational," he said between keyboard clicks. "Atmosphere is standard."

In light of the new information, the crew twisted off their helmets, which had grown foggy from extended use. The fresher air cooled their sweaty faces. A sense of direction had been established from hours of experiencing the nearly nonexistent gravity of the moon, but it was almost negligible with each crew member feeling as if they weighed only a few ounces.

"What now?" Mara asked.

Kapp had no immediate answer for her. He couldn't have imagined the mission going as horribly as it had. Crisis after crisis had beaten him into submission, but still, he resisted. His time spent awake on Starling II felt more like a year than a few days. With nothing imminent to fight against, though, the weight of everything that had happened since waking from stasis threatened to crush him. Jesse and Mara looked to him with a hungry expression, their eagerness to survive, to do something, replacing what should have been misery.

"Now," Kapp said with as much confidence as he could muster. "We'll do our best to fix this mess."

When Mara opened her mouth, she spoke feebly. "How?"

"Well—we can't do anything on no sleep and with empty stomachs, so let's start with that."

•|•

After loading up on freeze-dried food, the crew slept for one orbit around Mars—about eight hours. When Kapp arose, he removed the dressing from his shoulder and inspected the wound underneath. The skin around the prosthetic connection point appeared purple. It stung when he touched it. Frostbite. He snuck a few sips of his favorite painkiller before heading out of his chamber.

"Morning," Jesse said over a steaming bag of coffee.

Kapp raised a single eyebrow. "How'd you heat that up?"

"Oh, I've been awake for a few hours." He handed Kapp an identical bag. "I automated our solar panels to follow the sun."

Kapp beamed at Jesse's resourcefulness and took a sip. "Of course you did."

Mara popped into the room. Like the rest of her, the color of her hair looked faded, but so did the sadness that she had been wearing since Eli's death. Jesse squeezed her hand when she arrived beside him.

With his brain fully alert from a good mix of caffeine and alcohol, Kapp decided the only way to remain sane would be to tackle their problems one at a time. "Today," he said, "we need to go outside."

"Why?" Mara asked.

"We need to see how bad the damage is, we need to get a sense of where we are and what's possible, and"—Kapp sipped his coffee—"we need to get Eli's body out of the cockpit."

The sadness returned to Mara's face.

•|•

The crew stayed silent as they pulled Eli's mass from the crew module to the lower deck. His massive limbs floated freely, bumping into nearly every surface during the descent.

"What are we going to do with him?" Jesse asked.

"Does it matter?" Pulling Eli around a particularly tough corner, Kapp winced through the pain of the exertion. "He's a traitor."

"He was threatened," Jesse said. "You heard, his son—"

Kapp wanted to yell, but he held back. "He would have killed us all."

Mara seemed like she wanted to protest, but she hadn't managed to speak since seeing the body, and that trend continued. To Kapp, she looked like she needed to vomit as she avoided looking at Eli's corpse.

Jesse just shook his head. "Eli wasn't a bad man, Kapp."

"Maybe not," Kapp said, "but he was a coward."

"He was my friend," Jesse said, letting go of Eli's body to look directly at Kapp.

"Friend's don't poison each other, J." Reaching the tightest point in the tunnel, Kapp had to pull harder. "Straighten his legs, will you?"

"I didn't want to kill him," Jesse said, his lips tight, nearly quivering. "I've never done something so bad. I feel terrible."

Finally, Eli's body passed through the opening.

"Well, don't." Kapp touched down on the lower deck first. "We have bigger problems to worry about."

"I'd feel better if we at least had a funeral," Jesse said. "Said a few words, maybe."

"Suit up," Kapp said, impatient to get it over with. "It's not like we can bury him."

•|•

Squeezed into the airlock, the crew members spoke to each other through their radios.

"Alright, Mars," Kapp said, "once we're out there, it's gonna feel like we can jump off the moon—"

"Trust me, we can't," Jesse said. "But if we did jump, it could take over ten minutes to land."

"Right." Kapp turned his attention back to Mara. "You're tethered anyway, so just take the pictures and then reel yourself back in. We'll be back in no time."

Their words did nothing to erase the worry from her countenance. "What about you? You're not tethered."

"The cords aren't long enough for how far we have to go." Jesse consoled her with a smile and a hand on her back. "We'll be fine using the handholds. I promise."

"Let's open it up, J," Kapp said.

Jesse pressed a button on the wall, and the outer doors slid open, revealing the red planet just above a gray horizon. Noticing the irregular curve of the horizon, Kapp got a better sense of the smallness of the moon. The floor of the airlock stood nearly level with the dusty ground.

Mara's eyes grew wide. "Whoa."

"We don't have long before eclipse, so let's go." Kapp took in the view for a brief moment. "I'm sure we'll have plenty of time to sightsee," he added, thinking to himself that their time on Phobos would probably only depend on how much food they had left.

Kapp gripped Eli's arm in his metal hand, indicating their next move. Jesse grabbed the other arm, and Mara retreated to the corner.

"Count of three?" Kapp asked.

Jesse nodded grimly, and Kapp began the countdown. On three, the duo pushed as hard as they could and sent the body flying at an upward angle toward the horizon.

Coward, Kapp thought, looking at the limp silhouette of the big man against the stars. Without knowing who had threatened Eli, he had no one else to direct his anger at, and he doubted that he would ever get the chance to find out. Kapp just knew that if he ever did find the culprit, he would gladly kill him.

Eli floated in a slight arc, like a boat on a still lake. Mara whimpered behind her helmet, and Jesse wore a troubled frown. Kapp remained stoic, lost in his own deflection of grief, slow-simmering anger. The shrinking silhouette reminded him of the ancient Norse funeral practice, and suddenly he wished that he had a flaming arrow to shoot the bastard with.

•│•

After triple-checking the tether, Kapp and Jesse sent Mara flying in a similar fashion, but in an upward direction. She would hover above the ship, snapping photos of it and the surrounding area. The remaining pair decided to circle the ship to assess the damage. Jesse's boots hit the dust first.

"One small step," he joked.

Kapp admired Jesse's ability to stay positive in crisis, especially since his own thoughts, when unoccupied by anger, had been drifting toward the idea of a slow death on the surface of Phobos. Unlike Jesse, Kapp had only one positive thought: *At least there's plenty of scotch.*

"We might not be the first lifeforms to walk here," Kapp said, his boots touching down behind Jesse's and his mind beginning to contemplate the alien ship that must be nearby. Dust flew up around their boots but didn't float back down.

They followed the edge of the crew module toward the nose of Starling II, the same ascent that Kapp had made before the crash landing. With eyes on the parts of the hull that touched the ground, they used the handholds to guide their progress. Attempting to stay perpendicular to the ground, Kapp pushed up on one of the holds, planting his feet. The whole ship budged, rocking back and forth for a moment before settling.

Mara's voice came through their headsets. *"What was that?"*

"I forgot that Starling weighs—what?" He turned to Jesse. "Under a hundred pounds in this gravity?"

Jesse closed his eyes for a moment, apparently crunching the numbers in his head. "About eighty—impossible to notice when we're inside."

Kapp tilted the ship again, but with purpose. "Check underneath."

Hindered by his suit, Jesse awkwardly bent down to take a look. "Scratched up, but intact."

"Quite a landing, Kapp," Mara said through the radio, sounding hopeful for the first time since the crash. *"The skid marks behind the ship are long, but they don't look very deep. Must've barely skimmed the surface."*

Kapp took in the praise, grateful for the light gravity that made the landing possible, even though he had been unconscious for it. If the event had occurred in any other gravity well, the ship would have been toast, and the crew would have been crumbs.

They found a similar amount of damage on the other side of the crew module, so Kapp and Jesse made their way toward the service module to inspect its systems. With tedious motion in the low gravity, Kapp filled the long moments between handholds with memories of cold beer and bikini-clad women. He could almost feel the swelter of late summer Vegas by the time he woke from his daydream to see the object of his and Jesse's pursuit.

The dull metallic sheen of the service module blended in with the gray of the earth and stone that held the machinery, so it took a moment for Kapp to realize the problem with the scene. If his suit weren't so rigid, his shoulders would have shrunk in dismay upon seeing that part of the service module had been pierced by a giant shard of moon rock. Wedged between bent fixtures and shattered sheet metal, the shard barely protruded from the outer surface of the ship. Kapp couldn't tell how deep the thorn had sunk, but it didn't matter. Starling II would fly no more.

•|•

They met on the lower deck after returning to the airlock and shedding their suits. The sun was already setting behind the near horizon, creating an orange glow that barely illuminated the messy room. The first one there, Jesse hovered in front of the computer until the others arrived.

"What are you working on?" Mara asked, gripping his shoulders from behind with her small hands.

"Assessing the damage," he said, typing. A diagram of the service module rotated on the screen.

Kapp listened to the exchange, eyes shut against the panic taking form, head resting in his metallic palm. He cringed from the necrotic pain spreading through his shoulder. Jesse's voice sounded distant, clouded in doubt. Kapp and Mara floated silently, letting the flight engineer do his job, engaging in a grim dialogue with their eyes.

"Doesn't look good," Jesse said. "Not at all."

Kapp didn't expect it to, but the truth still knocked like an unwelcome guest. Mara looked at Jesse expectantly.

"Do y'all want the bad news or the worse news first?"

Kapp couldn't take the suspense any longer. "Just say it."

"Well,"—Jesse paused, which didn't help with the anxiety boiling inside of Kapp—"The reason for the blackout is that our power cells have been, for lack of a better word, completely fucked."

To Kapp, these words felt like those of a lover admitting "we need to talk," the initial stab that always comes before the twist of the knife. Jesse's voice began to speed up.

"When I saw the minimal damage to the hull, well, I started to figure out what it would take to escape this gravity well. I was hopeful that we might be able to get back into orbit, but now—"

The engineer sucked in a big breath, moisture barely beginning to glisten in his blue eyes. Even with a lungful of air, he couldn't finish his sentence. His head just shook back and forth instead. Mara tried to comfort him with a touch.

"What about the comm tower?" Kapp asked, the calmness in his voice beginning to quiver as well.

"I can probably fix it if you want to send a message home, but—" The composure Jesse had regained in order to speak began to slip away once again.

"But what?" Mara asked, her voice as soft as drizzle.

"It won't do much good." Jesse's eyes found the floor. "The tank was breached. We don't have enough oxygen to wait for a rescue."

Mara began to cry quietly, and Kapp became speechless. Jesse's eyes met his with the most serious expression Kapp had ever seen. It held no trace of hope, only guilt and sadness and doom. Jesse took in a sharp breath.

"We don't have enough oxygen to last a week."

14

DOUBLE-TAP

Asher pulled off the dirt road a mile from the Groom Lake Launch Facility, hid his cash-bought junker behind a grove of Joshua trees, and stepped into the moonlight. In place of his long brown locks, he wore a buzz cut and a ball cap, his thin frame almost skeletal from a lack of consistent sleep and nutrition.

Asher had been on the run for weeks, hiding from the IES. They still wanted to bring him in, even though Lana's article had widely been regarded as a hoax. He hadn't been able to contact Emily, and he wouldn't even try until he could assure her safety—until Holden and anyone else involved were behind bars. He just needed more proof of Holden's corruption, which he intended to get that night.

He shrugged on a backpack and checked his shotgun. The black metal felt cool between his bony fingers, radiating a sinister energy. Even so, it comforted him. With a pocket full of ammo, he hiked in a diagonal direction away from the road. He tapped a silver band on his wrist, and the attached device beeped as it projected an array of data directly onto the imperfect canvas of his inner arm.

11:15 p.m.

45 minutes until shift change.

Asher took paranoid glances behind him every few minutes, a habit he had developed since Nai arrived at his door. Though he never caught anyone, he had a constant feeling that someone was watching him.

Even after looking back, he still felt the need to check for any objects that someone could hide behind.

The stars above mocked him, shining too brightly through the unpolluted air of the deep desert. Through the clear night sky, he could even make out the distinct glow of Mars, where he hoped Kapp was safely orbiting. Though he wanted to, Asher couldn't believe that losing contact with Starling II was an accident. He couldn't even subscribe to the idea that contact had been lost in the first place. Things like that just didn't happen.

Asher checked his back, once again clutching the gun, the only thing that made him feel safe. When the chain link horizon came into view, Asher crouched behind a thicket of sagebrush. He pulled a pair of binoculars out of his bag and placed them above the dark circles of skin that barely concealed his skeleton. His augmented gaze followed the fence to the guard post, a small tower to the left of the gate. A single man sat in the tower, his face illuminated by the glow of his device. Asher recognized him as Walker, one of the newest security guards.

Too easy, Asher thought, strapping the shotgun onto his pack and pulling out his tablet. Again, he checked the time.

11:31 p.m.

He pulled up the guard schedule on his tablet. A few gestures later he spoofed a message, which would appear to come from Walker's supervisor. Asher sent the words directly to the guard's screen:

Hey Walker. Jones isn't coming in tonight. You can head home early.

Through his binoculars, Asher thought he saw a look of suspicion flash across Walker's face. The young man typed a response.

Are you sure? I don't mind pulling a double.

Asher started typing his reply before Walker could even hit send.

You've had enough overtime this month. I'll have Nai watch the gates remotely tonight.

The man on the tower stared at his phone, scrunched his eyebrows. Asher shifted nervously. For a moment he thought his ruse had failed. Walker hesitated to reply, turning his head in both directions before returning his attention to the device in his hands.

Ok, thanks.

After gathering his things, Walker descended the ladder and walked lazily toward a small parking lot near the fence. Asher followed him from a decreasingly safe distance. As he walked, Walker scrolled through a feed of videos, giggling dumbly. Asher lessened the space between them, masked by gaps in the silence. Walker made it to his Jeep, unaware of the shadow that lurked behind him. Reaching for his keys with one hand, he tried to double-tap a particularly funny post with the other. Before he could like the video, though, the skin of his neck was pierced with a needle. Asher let him scream. He knew that no one would hear it. Retreating into the safety of darkness, he stowed the tranquilizer in his pack. Walker stumbled around for a moment before dropping his phone and keys in favor of clutching his neck.

Asher silently counted down from ten, blocking out the frenzied, depleting cries. As Walker struggled against impending unconsciousness, Asher's face became stoic.

Right on cue, Walker's head double-tapped the hard ground.

With Walker unconscious in the backseat, Asher overrode autopilot mode and drove the Jeep parallel to the fence and away from the gate. He parked it out of sight before glancing at the time projected between the scars on his wrist, one much fresher than the others—the place where his identity implant had once been.

11:45 p.m.

Looking at the implant-removal scar, Asher dreaded what he had to do next. He crawled into the back of the Jeep and slapped Walker's face. Hard. The young guard offered no response. Confident with the effectiveness of the tranquilizer, Asher grabbed a sharp knife and a pair of rubber gloves from his bag. For a brief moment, he considered leaving Groom Lake to continue hiding out. Instead, he snapped on the gloves and forced himself to continue his rogue mission. He took Walker's forearm, turned it over, inhaled a calming breath, then—careful not to cut too deep—surgically removed the microchip from Walker's wrist. Only a thin ribbon of red leaked from the wound, which Asher hastily bandaged.

Minutes later, he stepped out of the vehicle wearing a stolen uniform and a blank expression. Using Walker's device, he sent a quick message to the man that would be arriving soon to replace him.

Hey Jones, had to leave early. Nai is watching remotely until you get here.

Asher took off in a jog away from the parked Jeep and its occupant. He had no time to let himself feel bad about Walker, who would wake up disoriented and a bit traumatized, but otherwise healthy and, more importantly, alive. He made it back to the guard tower, checking his back frequently with increased paranoia.

A water cooler stood at the base of the tower. Asher drained most of it onto a nearby bush before dissolving several tablets of Rohypnol into the remaining water. Obtaining the date rape drug had been the sketchiest part of his whole plan, but he needed a way out and knew it would do the trick for his escape. *At least I'm taking some of it off the black market,* he thought, justifying the dark alley purchase. Instinctively, he checked behind him while putting the lid back on the cooler.

With the trap in place, Asher opened the door to the left of the locked carport using Walker's wrist implant. He couldn't believe he was actually breaking and entering his old place of employment— and of his own volition. He was finally doing something instead of just hiding and waiting. As the door swung behind him, Asher felt excited, so much so that he failed to notice the door behind him creeping back open before it could shut completely.

15

STRANDED

Kapp tossed and turned in his sleeping bag, unable to get comfortable or quiet his mind. Even the alcohol he had consumed before bed couldn't cure his restlessness. He turned again to Jesse, who was having a similar bout of insomnia. The two had been speaking in whispers every so often throughout the night, careful not to wake Mara.

"What about the stasis chambers?" Kapp asked. "We could fix the comm tower, get in touch with Groom Lake, and then sleep until—"

"There's not enough solar energy to power them," he said. "We barely have enough to run the microwave."

Kapp exhaled a long "um," whiskey fumes biting at his tongue. "How about—"

"Kapp," Jesse said. "I want to get home as much as you do, but—"

"There has to be a way, J. I didn't sign up for—"

"Let me finish." He spoke in a raised whisper, keeping an eye on Mara. "I want to go home, but—listen—it's not gonna happen."

Kapp shook his head slowly, with a hint of outrage, but otherwise didn't respond.

"I reran the numbers, Kapp. Even without all this damage, the systems wouldn't last long enough to wait for a rescue. It's just over a year until the next launch window, not nearly enough time to engineer and build something capable of saving us. You know this."

"I can't die here, J." Kapp sighed. "Not like this."

"You can, and you will." Mara began to stir in her sleep, mumbling in a strange mix of romance languages, which distracted Jesse for just a moment. "It's not a matter of if, it's a matter of when. And all that really matters is what we decide to do *before* it happens."

Before we die—the words that Jesse couldn't get himself to say. Defeated, Kapp considered the implication. His thoughts spun with the room, a tornado of intoxication and fear. "What should we do then, J?" He turned and gripped Jesse's shoulder, looking for answers in his eyes, his voice switching from a whisper to a plea. "I should be strong right now. I should have the solutions to our problems. But I feel helpless."

"You're not alone, Kapp."

"So, what do we do?" His eyes begged. "What do I do?"

"You can drink yourself to death, or"—Jesse put his hand on Kapp's shoulder, matching his friend's gesture—"we can finish what we came here to do."

Kapp began to understand.

"We can try to communicate"—Jesse pointed somewhere in the dark—"with whatever's out there."

•|•

Kapp awoke with a splitting headache and a deep pain in his right shoulder. He used his good arm to unzip his sleeping bag, afraid of moving the other too much. In the vacant chamber, he could see his own breath. He moved into the adjacent room at a zombie's pace, still a little drunk. Not in a good way.

In front of the glowing screen of the auxiliary command station, Kapp saw a heap of blankets with two heads sticking out, turned toward each other—one with pink and one with dirty blonde hair.

"At least some of us are warm," he said, the opportunity to tease overpowering how terrible he felt. Jesse and Mara jumped apart, startled by his intrusion. They looked at Kapp with a sheepish expression, and he laughed. "Hey, don't stop because of me."

"We're just looking at the pictures from yesterday," Mara said.

"Looks like it," Kapp said, turning toward the galley to throw a bag of coffee into the heater.

Inter-crew relationships were technically forbidden, but Kapp couldn't deny Jesse and Mara their last week of humanity. The coupling made perfect sense. He could tell that they just clicked, like two matching puzzle pieces that happened to fall out of the box next to one another. She seemed to soften him, and he seemed to fortify her—until both met at a happy middle ground. Kapp had witnessed this bizarre act of nature many times but had never felt it for himself. The ding of the microwave snapped him out of his third-wheel rumination.

"What'd you find?" he asked, warming his hands with the heated coffee. "Besides each other's tongues."

Mara blushed, her cheeks nearly matching the color of her hair. Natural roots had begun to spring up beneath her artificially-colored locks.

"We analyzed the landmarks in Mara's photos to find our position on the moon." With a few gestures, Jesse pulled up a 3D model of Phobos. A flashing icon appeared near the rim of Stickney, a large impact crater and the defining feature of the roughly potato-shaped moon. "That's where we are now," he said, pointing at the icon.

"And the object?"

"The ship is here." Jesse pointed to the center of the crater. "As long as it hasn't moved since the last Wisdom photo was taken."

Kapp looked at the scale key beside the model. "So we're—what—five kilometers away?"

"Roughly."

Kapp was pleasantly surprised but also frightened of their proximity to the alien craft. "Not too far."

"Maybe on Earth, it's not. The problem is getting there. Walking is nearly impossible in this gravity, and we're not equipped with jetpacks."

"Hmm." Kapp's eyes rolled backward, a natural attempt to see his brain and the thoughts it hid. He could hear Jesse, but his mind wandered.

"Even if we could walk," Jesse said, running a hand through his long hair, "our tanks don't hold enough O2 for the journey."

Kapp looked back at the 3D model, honing in on Stickney. Jesse's voice seemed to grow more distant as Kapp delved into his own thoughts.

"Plus, we have to consider how treacherous the descent would be from the edge of the crater to the bottom."

Leaning over Jesse toward the screen, Kapp focused on a groove that ran in a straight line from the rim to the floor of the crater. He ignored the buzz of Jesse's speech and the throbbing in his own shoulder.

"It's all loose sand and rock. We could get caught in a landslide."

Landslide! The word splintered Kapp's focus, resonating sharply through the drone that surrounded him. He raised his hand to silence Jesse, who was still going on about the dangers of walking to the bottom of the crater, and displayed a mischievous smile.

"I think I know a way to get there."

•|•

Kapp's plan required Jesse's engineering expertise, so he and Mara passed the time in the cockpit while Jesse tinkered on the lower deck, each consumed with their own project. Mara worked on one of her brain puzzles, a three-dimensional jigsaw that looked like good practice for cracking a safe, and Kapp worked on swallowing enough Vicodin to rid himself of the frostbite pain.

"So," Kapp said, beginning to feel the buzz, "Jesse really robbed the cradle."

Mara rested the puzzle on her lap. "He's only eleven years older."

"He was born in a different millennium than you."

Her shoulders rose. "So?"

"I mean—it must be hard to relate. You were still in high school when he started at NASA."

"You don't know how early I graduated."

"Ahh, you're one of those." Kapp tried to stretch his back, but the pain stopped him. "Asher graduated early too."

"I know," Mara said, smiling, "but I beat him by two years."

"Wow," Kapp said. "How long have you and J been hooking up, anyway?"

She shook her head and scoffed. "That's really none of your business, Kapp."

Kapp shrugged. "Just curious."

Mara's attention returned to her puzzle. "No, you're high."

Kapp's eyes narrowed. "You know, you're one to talk. How often do you pop an Adderall?"

"That's different. At least I have a prescription."

Too exhausted to argue, Kapp let the sudden flare of anger drain away. He stayed quiet, and Mara got more involved in the challenging jigsaw. She began to struggle with it, frantically moving the pieces around, trying to find a way to make them interlock. Then she groaned and threw the puzzle at the wall, all of her hard work breaking apart and floating wildly through the cockpit.

"What the hell!" Kapp said. "Are you okay?"

"No, I'm not fucking okay." Mara began to laugh and cry at the same time. "I feel guilty and terrified and so, so sad. Eli—he was just trying to protect his son, and we killed him. What are we doing, Kapp? We're just gonna die here, anyway."

Apparently, Jesse's undying optimism had not yet rubbed off on Mara. Kapp didn't know how to respond at first, but then he began to think about Jesse's pep talk from the night before, how they couldn't just roll over and die.

"What are we doing?" he asked, more to himself than to Mara. "I don't know, but we're doing it together."

•|•

One hour later, Kapp donned his space suit next to the airlock. He wore everything but his helmet, which Mara held in her small hands. Jesse came into the room, holding a small, rectangular object wrapped in black plastic.

"That's it?" Kapp asked, pointing with a metal index finger. The motion caused electric shocks to radiate from the damaged flesh that hid beneath his suit, the pain barely suppressed by the drugs that ran through his blood. "It's kind of small—isn't it?"

"It won't take much," Jesse said, beginning to smirk. "And didn't anyone ever tell you that size don't matter?"

"No one's ever had to," Kapp said, patting Jesse on the back of the arm, the Vicodin heightening his mood despite the severity of the situation. "Has Mara told you that yet?"

Kapp reached for the helmet, and Mara helped him twist it on, her face blushing. He pressed a button that opened the inner door of the airlock. Jesse handed him the package, which he attached to his suit using a strip of velcro. Finally, Kapp retreated through the open door, still grinning.

"At least you guys won't have to worry about me walking in on you for a little while." Kapp pulled down his visor. His laughter continued, even after the airlock doors shut behind him.

•|•

Kapp stood in front of the spacecraft adapter, the bottom part of Starling II that had once been attached to the launch vehicle. He found two holes in the metal that would fit the bulky gloves of his space suit. Bracing himself, he bent into a crouch and inserted his hands into the holes, then rose, lifting the ship with him. It felt strange, even for someone who completely understood how such feats were possible.

"Alright, we're moving now," he said. "Tell me when the angle is right."

"Copy."

The ship rotated as Kapp sidestepped. Even though the load didn't weigh much, the exertion invigorated his deprived muscles. The crew had neglected the daily exercise routine meant to help their bodies recover from 240 days of disuse. Many things got pushed aside, including Kapp's attention to the alien ship that sat only a few kilometers away. With each new emergency stealing his focus, the ship's presence didn't seem real.

Kapp thought he would have plenty of time to worry about the likelihood and repercussions of communicating with extraterrestrials. The encounters he imagined always took place in some distant future: after launch, after stasis, after weeks of research and experimentation from a safe distance. As he walked alone on the Martian moon, Kapp's present finally caught up to his imaginary future, and the worries he had been avoiding followed close behind.

"Looks good on our end," Jesse said once Kapp had rotated Starling II nearly 180 degrees.

He lowered the ship to the ground, and then, careful to use his undamaged shoulder, he began to push against the spacecraft adapter, digging his boots into the lunar soil. The craft began to slide forward. Kapp counted his steps to pass the time, willing himself to treat each as an accomplishment, a small victory against nature. At the two hundred mark his calves began to burn, but he pressed on. His body became a slave to his intentions, obedient without a choice in the matter. The undergarment built to wick away sweat clung to his skin, but he ignored the discomfort. Focusing on the rhythm of his footsteps, Kapp let the exercise wash over him until his mind possessed a single urge: forward. With his left arm pushing against the ship and his eyes shutting out the world, he failed to notice the disobedience beginning to stir in the less human parts of his body.

Jesse signaled the end of Kapp's labor with a short radio call. *"We're here."*

Kapp laid his burden down and took some deep breaths, metal fingers twitching beneath his gloves. He pulled the package from his chest and opened it. He rotated Jesse's handiwork between both hands until he found the adhesive strips that would attach it to the ship. Without warning his right wrist jerked into a flexed position, sending the device spinning through the empty space above. It happened so fast that Kapp barely had time to curse before reaching up to catch it. The momentum sent him upward, where he floated in the low gravity. Upon landing, Kapp stuck the device to the center of the adaptor before it could escape again, cursing his mechanical hand's unruly behavior.

The device, with a small explosive charge, would give Starling II just enough forward momentum to push it over the edge of the crater. Kapp pressed a button to begin the countdown to detonation and noticed a problem.

"J, how long did you set this thing for?"

Kapp's radio hissed in his ear. *"A hundred and twenty minutes. Why?"*

He mentally scratched his head, unable to physically do so in his space suit. He watched the red numbers of the display blink through a few precious seconds. "I think you missed a zero."

•|•

Kapp should have had two hours to re-enter the ship—a leisurely space stroll and a long pressurization—but Jesse's mistake only granted him twelve minutes. He only needed a few minutes to get to safety, but he and the crew had decided to be cautious. Not cautious enough, apparently.

As Kapp fumbled his way from the back of the ship, he realized he had no control of his bionic limb from the elbow down. The hand was locked at a right angle to the wrist, pushing the materials of his space suit to their limit. This made following the handholds to safety much more difficult, but he remained confident that he'd reach the airlock before detonation. He wouldn't have time for the airlock to pressurize completely, which would make for an uncomfortable ride down the hill, but with the clock ticking he decided to take what he could get.

"I'm sorry, Kapp," Jesse said.

"It's fine." Kapp followed along the side of the ship as quickly as possible. "I'm almost there, anyway. Just make sure the outer doors are open."

Facing the hull of the spacecraft, Kapp used his left hand to pull himself forward. The airlock, the floor of which stood just above head level, became visible.

"You've got about six minutes," Mara said.

"Thanks," he said. "I'll make it there eas—"

The clang of metal on metal and a sense of falling away cut off Kapp's speech. His right arm spasmed, pushing away from the ship and taking the rest of him with it. The tank attached to the back of his suit skimmed the gray, Phobian ground. He reached toward the surface with his left hand, but with nothing to grip he kept sliding. Forbidding the panic from overtaking his reason, Kapp forced his body to relax until friction ended the slide naturally. Sand and pebbles floated around him like dust, skirting the edges of the scene above. Martian red nearly filled the entire width of his visor.

"What happened?" Jesse's words pierced Kapp's disoriented state,

barely audible beneath rabid breaths. *"Are you okay?"*

He bent forward as far as his suit would allow and saw the nose of Starling II hanging over the rim of the crater. Taking stock of his position, he estimated that the malfunctioning arm had sent him 10 meters away from the craft. The limb still twitched from the elbow down.

Hindered by the rigid suit, he made vain attempts to become vertical. Unable to bend at the waist, he dug his heels into the dirt, careful to avoid kicking himself into an upside-down position in the low gravity. The suit allowed for a slight bend at the knee, which he used to scoot himself forward—inch by inch.

"Kapp, are you in?"

"That's what she said," he said, giddy from a mix of panic and Vicodin. The ridiculousness of the situation didn't help.

"Where are you?" Jesse asked, his voice distorted from overdriving the microphone.

"Relax," Kapp said, wincing from the sound. He still had at least 6 meters to go. "I'm close."

"Three minutes. Hurry up."

Kapp closed the distance between him and Starling II with as much haste as reason would allow. Even in his altered state, he knew that rushing would not help. Any wrong move had the potential to waste what little time he had.

Mara spoke again the moment his boots reached the ship, her voice shrill. *"Please tell me you're in the airlock."*

The edge of the opening teased Kapp with its proximity. All he had to do was stand up to reach it, but he couldn't. Without time to think it through, he elbowed the ground with his left arm. As he had hoped, the motion sent his torso upward, but it also caused him to spin to the right. He started to become perpendicular to the ground below, and the world spun around him as if in slow motion.

First, he saw the top of Starling II coming closer, then the horizon to his right. Dark earth and flying gravel passed in front of his eyes. The nearer horizon, the edge of the crater, came into view. In preparation, he reached his good arm out as far as possible. Fully expecting the charge to have blown during his seemingly endless rotation, Kapp was surprised by the sight of the airlock. His gloved hand entered the opening at the corner. Powerless to control his momentum, he could only hope that it would find something to grip. The rest of his body continued to rotate forward, which began to pull his arm back out of the airlock. His fingers bent into a claw that scraped along the wall of the airlock. His gloves couldn't hold on, couldn't stick to flat metal, needed something to grab onto. Through the material of his suit, he felt a slight snag and instinctively tightened his grip into a fist, but the clenched glove held neither edge nor handhold. He felt nothing. Kapp's eyes closed in despair as his arm left the airlock.

Starling II immediately jerked forward from the blast, but Kapp did not.

16

SHADOWS

Asher made allies with the shadows, using them to sneak his way toward the alley between Mission Control and the simulation hangar. The roof of the sandstone structure on his right stretched well beyond the walls of the complex, nearly touching the corrugated metal surface of the neighboring building. To the naked eye, this created a tunnel that ran from one side of the two buildings to the other. Shortly after entering the mouth of this industrial cavern, Asher stopped to take stock of the situation and re-assess his plan. Everything up to that point had gone smoothly, but caution had become a paranoid habit. Hunched over his backpack, he stole a quick glance at the pale light that shone through the alley's opening. Something in the distance caught his eye, but he soon dismissed it as trash blowing in the breeze.

Asher packed all of the backpack's loose items into their appropriate positions before turning his attention to the shotgun. Already loaded, but he checked the chamber anyway. Further down the alley stood a door hidden beneath an understated arch, a side entrance to Mission Control that usually functioned as an outdoor break room. Cigarette butts littered the ground beside the arch.

Asher went inside and crept down a long white hallway of offices, clutching his shotgun between sweaty palms. Silently, he paced until he found the placard he was looking for: Director Bryce

Holden. He scanned Walker's implant, but the stolen credentials didn't work. Asher berated himself for wasting time to cut out the implant in the first place. He should have known that Walker wouldn't have clearance for Holden's office.

In one motion, Asher leaned his shotgun against the wall beside the door and shrugged off his pack. Always prepared, a habit he picked up as a Boy Scout, he took a small set of tools from the bag and began to pick the lock. Purposefully, he slowed his rapid breathing in an attempt to narrow his focus. After a few tries, the lock popped open with a satisfying click. As he turned the knob, he allowed his lips to curve into a proud smile, silently appreciating the new skill he learned online.

In Holden's office, Asher set his gun down on the oakwood desk, poured himself a taste of scotch, and got to work. Logging in to the director's computer was easy enough. Holden hadn't bothered to change his password since the first time Asher snuck in, which he thought was not only odd but extremely irresponsible.

The computer held too many files to look through, especially since Asher had no idea what exactly he wanted to find. He just needed something incriminating enough to get the law on his side, to put Holden behind bars, and to replace the director with someone competent and uncorrupt, someone who would help bring Kapp home.

Asher fidgeted while he waited for the hard drive to clone. He began to worry about the hole he had dug himself into and the long climb he'd have to take to get out of it. With no way to cover his tracks, he had only a long night of driving to look forward to. On the road, he knew he'd feel better; it was the waiting that drew out his anxiety. With one hand tapping on his loaded safety blanket, he brought Holden's scotch to his lips and took a pull, an attempt to ease his panicked mind. It tasted horrible, a drink for old men. He spat the dark liquid back into Holden's bottle, then smirked at the small act of defiance, keeping his eyes on the door handle and the sliver of light that poured through the keyhole.

Light? The realization shook him. *The hall was dark when I came in.*

Before dimming the display of Holden's computer, Asher saw

that the cloning process was 80% complete. He crept to the door of the office and pressed his ear against it, holding his breath to listen. He heard only the hum of the AC unit. Beginning to question his own perception, Asher wondered if the light had been there the whole time. He checked the guard schedule on his tablet. With no patrol scheduled, there would be no reason for anyone to wander that part of the building in the middle of the night. Still, he was overwhelmed by the familiar sensation of being watched, even though that sensation had been wrong so many times before. The beep of the hard drive finishing its job was all it took to inspire action. He leveled the barrel of his shotgun, released the safety, and slowly pushed the door open.

He wanted to run but couldn't. Stuck behind an invisible barrier of fear, he pointed his shotgun at the doorway. A single, fluorescent bulb hung from the ceiling, illuminating a portion of the hallway.

"Who's there?" he asked.

No one responded. Logic began to battle with Asher's senses. He could rationalize that everything was alright, but he couldn't get himself to feel that way. If security were after him, they would have had a team of armed guards at Holden's office in minutes. Instead of hiding in the dimly lit building, waiting for him to come out with his hands up, they'd be busting down the door and asking questions later. Through all his reasoning, he still couldn't convince himself that he had somehow turned on the light himself. His gut told him that someone else did it.

He managed to speak again. "I have a gun."

Though true, Asher's threat felt empty. His anxiety held him back at the moment when he most needed courage. He knew Kapp wouldn't have faltered, and this frustrated him. It was like Kapp could stand on the edge of a cliff because he knew he could fly, like he could see in the dark.

With that thought, Asher realized a new way out. Since the situation was what made him anxious, he decided to change the situation altogether—to level the playing field. He pulled the binoculars out of his bag and up to his eyes, flipped a switch on the side, and shattered the menacing bulb above him with the butt of his shotgun.

Through night-vision lenses, the black world turned green.

Carrying the shotgun at his hip and armed with the new advantage of sight, Asher stepped through the invisible barrier as if it had never been there. To his left, he saw only empty halls and dark offices. His anxiety diminished with each new piece of visual information. He began to question why he had been worried in the first place. He turned his head to the right, his augmented gaze sweeping along the tiled floor to the exit beyond. He immediately saw something wrong with the door. Wide open, but that wasn't the shocking part. Inside the frame, a figure stood like a painting, silhouetted by the lights that shone from behind it. Asher's gut had been right after all.

Too far away to do any damage with the short range weapon, but too scared to run, Asher froze. He dropped the binoculars, put both hands on his gun, and aimed roughly ahead. The hall was narrow enough to make accuracy irrelevant. He just had to get in range. Once his eyes adjusted, he noticed that the person in the doorway didn't appear to carry a weapon. Asher began to march forward until he came close enough to see that the silhouette belonged to a man.

He wore no uniform, no emblem of allegiance to any particular power. Instead, he was dressed in plain black, his manner radiating an air of quiet resistance. In the smolder of midnight, his skin appeared quite tan. As Asher approached, the man continued to lean and loaf in the doorway, seemingly unworried about the shotgun pointed at him. When he spoke, the words came through a trimmed beard that hid most of his defining features.

"You can put that down," he said, inclining his head toward the gun. "I'm no threat to you."

"It seems otherwise," Asher said. "Who are you?"

"Name's Felix." The man reached into his pocket, and Asher raised the gun higher in response, his finger on the trigger. "Whoa, slow down buddy. I'm just getting a smoke."

Asher hyperventilated for a moment. He had been so close to pulling the trigger, and that terrified him. "You work for Holden?" he asked through short breaths.

"Hell no." The man took a cigarette out of its case.

Asher raised his voice. "Why are you here?"

"How about you put down the gun and we have a chat?" The sparks of a lighter momentarily illuminated the hallway before the man spoke again. "I actually helped you out, you know?"

Asher noticed something familiar about Felix's eyes, something he couldn't place. Though he wanted to trust the man, he couldn't. "How so?"

"That guard you tried to drug." Felix took a drag of his cigarette. "He noticed that the water had been tampered with—almost called it in, but we took care of him for you."

Asher didn't want to know what Felix meant by that. "But why? Why are you following me?"

"Well—" The man spoke calmly, his casual body language contagious to Asher, who began to relax against his better judgment. "It looks like we may want the same thing."

Asher doubted that. "I just want my friend back," he said.

"So do we."

"We? What do—"

"What you're doing is brave, Asher—fighting the powers that be. But you're acting alone. You need allies. You need someplace safe." Asher felt as if Felix was reading his mind, plucking at his heart's desires as if they were the strings of a guitar. The barrel of his shotgun lowered. "You asked why you were being followed tonight. Well—we came here to take you there—to safety. You can trust us."

Asher considered the notion. The idea tempted him, but something about the way Felix spoke bothered him. "You keep saying *we*."

"Problem is—we don't know if we can trust you yet."

A cool, damp rag covered his mouth as Asher became aware of someone holding him in place from behind. He fought against his body's urge to breathe, rejecting the advances of the chemical scent invading his nostrils. His skinny frame struggled against the embrace but was no match for the arms that held him. Felix stole the gun from the chaos and exited the hallway. Asher felt a hairy face against his neck. He jerked his head back in an attempt to injure the captor, accidentally inhaling some poison in the process.

He heard the crunch of a nose breaking, and, as the man retreated a step or two, Asher spun himself around a half turn. He could feel the drug taking effect and his vision beginning to blur. In a daze, he stumbled toward the man whose nose he had broken and looked up to see the bloodied face and all-too-familiar eyes of—Felix?

Asher's legs and mind betrayed him, and he crumpled to the floor. Before passing out, he heard the beep of a walkie-talkie and the muffled voice of the second Felix.

"Calix to Beacon. We're ready for extraction."

17

SIR

Director Bryce Holden fumed behind the computer monitor on his desk, which displayed the very thing fueling his rage. Scarlet replaced his usual ruddy complexion. The seasoning of his hair had turned more salty than peppery over the preceding months, and the wrinkles in his forehead had deepened from both age and stress. With an angry grunt, he set down his scotch glass when he heard the phone ring. Before it could chime a second time, he put it on speaker.

"This is Holden."

A lukewarm voice answered. *"I have eyes on Eli's boy."*

"Good," Holden said, cracking his knuckles. He glared at the image on the monitor, the latest from the Wisdom rover. Where there should have been a brand new explosion crater, the shimmering metal hull of Starling II sat next to the massive alien ship. "Eli failed. Get it over with."

The sound of gunfire came through the receiver. With the threat against Eli fulfilled, Holden ended the call with a tap. Revenge made him feel no better, so he continued to sip and seethe as he waited for his next task. A knock at the door did nothing to change the expression that bedeviled his face.

"Come in," he barked.

The door creaked open, and a fit young man in a black guard uniform entered. He had a bandage on his neck. "Sir," he said.

Holden gestured toward a chair and waited for the man to sit. "I'm very displeased with your performance Mr.—" Forgetting the guard's name, he peeked at the note on his desk. "Walker."

Walker's mouth fell open. "With all due respect, sir, I was attack—"

"You failed to do your one duty, your one job." Holden stood. Spit flew out of his mouth as he spoke.

Youthful defiance sprang from Walker, whose body rose with his voice. "First you put us on a wage freeze, and now you're firing me for something out of my control? This is bullshit!"

Holden wanted to snap the kid's neck. His hand rose to strike, but he held back. Instead, he forced his fingers to shape into a much calmer gesture.

"Settle down, settle down. You're not getting fired, Mr. Walker." With one hand in his pocket, Holden made his way around the desk. "You've caused me a great deal of trouble, but I suppose I'm being unreasonable. Now, let me see what the bastard did to you— come on."

Walker narrowed his eyes and pursed his lips as he moved forward.

"I woke up in my car." Walker looked like he might cry. "He stole my clothes. And my ID chip."

Walker turned, removed the bandage from his neck, and revealed a purpling puncture wound.

"Big needle," Holden said, "and deep. No, no, I couldn't fire you, Walker." He put a hand on the man's shoulder and showed some teeth in a sick attempt at a smile. The fingers of his other hand tightened around the object in his pocket. "You've made me far too angry for such mercy."

Before Walker could utter a response, a knife slid out of Holden's pocket and into Walker's heart.

•|•

Holden continued his work as if there wasn't blood soaking into the carpet. His mind remained occupied with less petty problems. He had been so close to earning his prize, but then Eli failed to pull the trigger. The taste of success had been robbed from the tongue of Bryce Holden, a man unaccustomed to the receiving end of thievery. This was why he liked taking care of things himself. He knew he couldn't fail.

A handkerchief collected the blood from his knife before Holden stored both in the drawer. The phone rang, and Holden sighed, cowering from the call he had been dreading. To buy time, he answered just before the call could go to voicemail.

"This is—"

"I know who you are, halfwit." The speaker on the other end of the line condescended Holden with practiced ease. *"I called you."*

"Of course, sir." Sweating, Holden loosened the blood-speckled tie from his thick neck. "Congratulations on the new position, sir."

"Did you expect anything else? They worship me." The voice on the other end of the line crept from impatience to aggravation. *"I didn't call for you to stroke my ego, Holden. Tell me some good news."*

The director gulped down his shame. "We've had a slight hiccup. I don't know what happened yet, but Eli must have—"

"Must I remind you that you promised success?" The sinister anger that came through the phone made Holden's recent outburst seem childish. *"And what I promised you in return?"*

"No, I rememb—"

"I'm so close to a breakthrough. I don't have time to focus on doing your job."

"I'm sorry."

"Sorry? I understand that it's only human to make mistakes, Holden." The man's voice calmed down a notch. *"Fix this, and I may forgive you."*

Nervous goosebumps prickled Holden's skin. "I will, I promise."

"You've shown me the worth of your promises. Now I'll have to come up with a new plan."

Unsure of what to say, Holden waited for the man to continue.

"That ship is the one thing that can stop me, Holden. The one thing!"

Holden's hands began to grow clammy. "I know, sir."

"When it comes—and come, it will—I need to take it for myself."

Holden didn't need to jot down a note on his tablet. His prime objective was clear. "Understood, sir."

"And Holden?"

He swallowed his spit. "Yeah?"

"Inject that man you just killed with the new formula. The sooner, the better."

Holden looked at the puddle of blood still spreading out from below Walker, who lay face-down on the carpet. His gaze circled the crimson pool before continuing up the wall behind an empty bookcase, past the pink petals of a plastic chrysanthemum that sat on top. Finally, he locked onto the lens of a surveillance camera in the top corner of the room. As if in response, it swiveled back and forth on its mechanical arm—waving.

Holden took in a sharp breath and spoke to the camera with as much confidence as he could muster. "Yes, sir."

18

TRAPDOOR

Moments after Starling II began to tip over the rim of the crater, some invisible force yanked Kapp forward. The surprising event forced his eyes to open. He saw that two of his fingers had found and attached to the loop at the end of one of the airlock's tether cables. By sheer luck, he had managed to thread a needle in the dark.

Starling II descended the hill, dragging Kapp behind it. As planned, the ship slid along a groove in the side of the crater, picking up speed during the descent. A sled ride with no snow. Kapp's body spun wildly at the end of the line like a hooked fish. He suppressed his body's urge to vomit, silently grateful to experience illness instead of a slow death stranded at the top of the impact crater.

The ship came to a halt as the sunlight disappeared behind Stickney's rim. Kapp's arm continued to malfunction, bending itself at odd times and angles. His body turned from the momentum, and he saw a mountain looming nearby in the twilight. It took his breath away because Kapp knew that no such mountain existed. Sunlight spilled over the crater's edge onto the top of the massive object, reflecting off the surface in strange and glorious patterns. The material seemed familiar, like tarnished silver, but reflected the light in an eerily different way than anything Kapp had seen before. At his proximity, he couldn't determine the shape of the craft. It had neither wing nor tail. The smoothness of the design reminded him of a river-polished stone, something perfected by natural forces. He couldn't make out a single seam or opening.

Jesse's voice sounded through a burst of static. *"Kapp, come in. Are you there?"*

Awestruck by the sight ahead of him, Kapp didn't know what to say. "Retract the tethers, J. I'm on the end of one."

A mechanical winch sprung to life under Jesse's command, reeling Kapp in. While he waited, he stared at the glistening surface ahead until the outer doors of Starling shut, blocking his view. Once the airlock cycled, the inner doors opened, and he found Jesse and Mara waiting in the room beyond. Without a word, they began to strip him of his space suit.

"Careful of my right arm," he said.

The unruly prosthetic had calmed down, but Kapp still worried that it might malfunction and hurt someone. As soon as it came out of his sleeve, he twisted it off from the elbow with his left hand and tossed it aside. The painkillers were beginning to wear off, and his frostbitten shoulder stung worse than before.

"What happened?" Mara asked, staring at the unrobed flesh.

"My prosthetic was acting up, and I almost didn't—"

"I mean"—she cleared her throat—"your shoulder."

"Oh," Kapp said, avoiding eye contact. "Just a little frostbite. I'll be—"

"It looks really bad, Kapp. Necrotic. Why didn't you tell us about this?"

He shrugged and looked at his shoulder, something he had unconsciously been avoiding. The skin that touched the attachment point for his mechanical limb had turned black, and the purple area had spread even further. With his nose turned toward the injury, he also caught a whiff of death.

"It's really infected," Mara said, her eyebrows inching toward each other in worry. She put her hand on his forehead. "You're burning up, Kapp."

"I'm fine."

Kapp couldn't remember the last time he saw a doctor for anything other than the required pre-mission physical exam.

"Just let me bandage—"

"Let's worry about the mission, Mars." Kapp touched her upper back. "We'll run out of oxygen before this thing can kill me."

•|•

Darkness descended upon the crater before the crew could get a decent look at their shadowy neighbor. No lights or sounds came from the strange craft, but its presence couldn't be ignored. Too wired to sleep, the trio surrounded a small table to share a meal and pass the time.

"If there's something in there," Mara said, "it—I mean *they* must know we're here, right?"

"Maybe." Jesse spoke between mouthfuls of freeze-dried peas. "Or maybe we're so insignificant that they don't even notice us. I mean, we don't sense every insect that crosses our path—there's no need to."

"I guess." Mara blinked rapidly behind her glasses.

"It's easy to think of ourselves as the most intelligent life forms— as if we're so important, but that might not be the case."

Mara stayed silent for a while, letting Jesse's words sink in. "I wonder how big the beings are. This ship is colossal."

"They could have evolved on a planet much different than our own." Jesse's expression became vibrant with thought, endless possibility erasing the worry from his face. "This"—he gestured all around him—"this is a microscopic piece of an infinite universe, a grain of sand on an endless beach. I'm not surprised that we're not alone, but I am amazed that we were able to find each other."

"Now we just need to talk to each other."

"Time'll come," Jesse said.

"Except all of my plans for making contact hinged on the use of our comm tower."

Jesse nudged her. "You'll find a way, sugar."

Mara blushed. "Let's just hope they use a linguistic system based on applied logic."

Kapp listened lazily, his attention drifting between the conversation and his own thoughts. At Mara's insistence, he sat with an ice pack resting on his wounded shoulder and a cocktail of penicillin and fever reducers coursing through his blood. He felt slightly better, but he also suspected a placebo effect. The fever had come on fast, burning up his ability to focus and taking away his appetite. His eyes darted around the room behind half-closed lids, and a piece of food hung at the end of his fork, untouched. His body had even rejected the usually welcome relief of alcohol.

Mara finished her meal. "I can't believe we're actually here."

"It does feel strange," Jesse said, fidgeting with a rubber band.

"It's unreal." She wrapped her arms around herself. "I don't know. I feel like I should be more terrified."

Kapp understood exactly what she meant, and he knew the feeling well. He often found himself doing things without worrying about the consequences. "It's because you've got nothing to lose," he said.

Mara nodded firmly, and Kapp wondered if Jesse had given her a similar pep talk to his own. No longer afraid of death, she—at least on the surface—appeared ready for whatever would come. Their collective future, once volatile and unpredictable, had become something concrete and definable. Knowing that they'd all be dead within a week made their remaining moments both more precious and more expendable. The time for mourning their fate had passed, only to be replaced by a distinctly human instinct...a unified desire to explore one last horizon.

When daylight broke, Kapp, Jesse, and Mara wasted no time exiting Starling II to start their investigation of the alien craft. Kapp, though on a stronger dose of painkillers, still had a heightened body temperature as he donned his space suit. He left his bionic arm behind on the lower deck. It didn't work, anyway. When the airlock opened, a Phobian sunrise greeted the crew. Orange sunlight reflected off of the mountain-sized structure ahead of them in brilliant patterns. They had only a couple of hundred meters between themselves and what they had been calling *the ship*.

Mara's eyes glistened. "It's beautiful."

Kapp and Jesse smiled their responses. The crew moved with both purpose and carelessness. Bouncing along the surface of Phobos, they had silently decided to stop worrying about tethers and low gravity. Curiosity drove them toward the craft like children toward a new toy. They carried cameras, short-range radios, and various devices for signal detection. Jesse held one in front of him, peering at the readout.

"Strange—the only radiation I can detect is coming from Starling."

"So, no one's home?" Kapp asked, looking up and ahead at the massive object.

"Either that or the shell is blocking their signature. I've never seen metal that looks like this."

Kapp let the others travel ahead of him. Even with loads of gear, they floated forward effortlessly, bouncing off the surface of Phobos lightly with their toes. Kapp's right sleeve hung rigidly at his side.

Mara pointed to a spot near the bottom of the vessel. "What's that?"

Kapp squinted and saw a break in the perfect symmetry of the object, like a chip out of the stone. "Let's find out," he said.

When they got close enough, they saw a triangular notch in the curvature of the ship's base, as if a citrus-shaped slice had been removed from it. They stopped a few dozen meters from the opening. Uncertainty held them back. Kapp's over-used undergarment clung to his fevered skin, despite the cooling fluid that pumped through it. He took a deep breath in preparation to speak, but Mara beat him to it.

"Symbols," she said, eyes scanning the inside of the opening. "Let's get closer."

The crew slowed their pace as they approached the wedge. Faint markings completely covered the surface of the wall on the left and only partially covered the surface of the adjacent wall. The scene reminded Kapp of abandoned cave paintings, works in progress left behind by their creators. By the time they stopped moving forward, the notch in the ship hung above them like a canopy. The symbols varied in size and shape, some as large as a dinner plate, but most shared a single commonality in composition: a central shape surrounded by protrusions. Lightly imprinted in the flat metal, they reflected the light at various and interesting angles.

"What do you make of this?" Jesse asked, his mouth agape.

"I've never seen anything like it," Mara said, her eyes slowly pouring over the symbols on the fully covered side. "It doesn't have the typical construction of an alphabet. The symbols are too diverse in composition. Maybe multiple languages?" Kapp could hear the excitement in her voice. "I don't know, guys. We should take some pictures for me to study later."

Jesse nodded. He unstrapped a camera from his chest, removed the lens cap, pulled the viewfinder to his helmet, and aimed it at the wall.

"This is incredible," Mara added.

Jesse depressed the camera's shutter button, but the device didn't click. "Battery's dead," he said, frowning.

Kapp watched him try to scratch his head, but Jesse was left with an unsatisfying glove-helmet collision.

"I swear I just charged it. Let me try yours, baby."

Kapp shot Jesse a look. He could practically feel Mara blushing behind her helmet. She handed Jesse the camera strapped to her chest, then he repeated the same steps again. And got the same results.

"This is freaking me out," Mara said, shaking her head behind carbo-glass and spectacles.

Jesse's face went blank in thought, so Kapp took command of the situation.

"Just study this a little longer, then we'll move on." Kapp turned his entire body but still couldn't see the front of the ship. "We've got about an hour of air left before we have to head back. "

The duo nodded. While Mara analyzed the symbols on the left wall and Jesse fiddled with the cameras, Kapp scanned the opposite wall. Sweaty and fatigued, his body craved a cold shower and uninterrupted sleep, two things he didn't expect to ever get. The symbols were arranged in rough rows, so Kapp read the wall like a book, from top to bottom, left to right. For each shape, he came up with a simple name to help him remember it, wishing the whole time that his suit had a built-in voice recorder. Jesse probably could have rigged something if they had thought of it earlier, but memory would suffice.

Oval-with-eight-skinny-lines.

Squiggly-triangle-with-dots.
Circle-with-four-stubs.
Double-hook.

Kapp named them after familiar shapes, though they had imperfect geometry. The symbols filled him with a strange sense of familiarity. Though he couldn't understand what they meant, they seemed to speak to him of life, almost radiating a living energy. When his gaze reached the final line, he did a double take, nearly skipping over a shape that he instantly recognized. Thinking that his eyes must've played a trick on him, he squinted in disbelief, an attempt to discredit what he saw as an illusion, some fever-induced hallucination. Unable to speak, he simply tapped Mara on the back and pointed at the rune.

Palm-with-four-fingers-and-a-thumb.

A human hand.

•|•

A long silence followed, and then a question:

"How is this possible?"

The query hung in the vacuum that surrounded the crew, perplexing them to the depths of their intelligence, an unanswerable conundrum. Finding the imprint of a human hand hundreds of millions of miles from Earth completely shattered their understanding of possibility.

"Maybe they've been watching us," Jesse suggested. "Copying what they see."

Kapp stared at the impression above, willing his mind to make sense of it. He squinted and turned his head to different angles. Maybe he had misread the sign. Misunderstanding the oddity seemed much simpler than coming up with an explanation for it.

A shimmer of light caught his eye. It stood out from the twinkling array of symbols ahead, diverging from the established pattern. The light came from much closer, so Kapp's eyes had to manually adjust their focus to see it.

Ignoring the discomfort of his sticky suit, he moved to the side, changing his perspective. The vision winked into existence. A hexagonal pattern appeared to cross the threshold between the two walls, forming a superficial surface where the exterior of the ship would have been if it continued to cover the wedge-shaped opening. The nearly invisible bubble scintillated, a mild electric glow pulsating across it.

"Do you see that?" he asked. Jesse's and Mara's expressions questioned him without words, so he continued. "Come here."

From Kapp's vantage point, they caught sight of the bubble.

"Some kinda force field." Jesse's statement came out as more of a question.

"Let's find out." Kapp gestured toward Mara's camera with his only arm.

She looked confused. "It's broken, remember?"

"I know."

Kapp's eyebrows rose, and his palm turned upward to receive the device. She handed it over. With an underhand toss, Kapp sent the camera flying toward the middle of the field. He expected it to bounce off or explode, but it did neither. The device passed through with no resistance before falling straight to the floor of the translucent globe.

"Woah," Mara said. Her mouth hung open at the end of the word.

Jesse seemed equally impressed, his quick mind sending deductions to his mouth. "Artificial gravity—impossible."

Kapp repeated the experiment with the other broken camera, which settled next to the first one at the base of the shape. Satisfied, he made a move for the barrier, reaching an arm toward it.

"Stop," Mara squeaked, grabbing at Kapp's suit. "It could hurt you."

"Didn't hurt the cameras," he said, shrugging off her concerned grip. *Or maybe it did,* he thought, considering how the cameras had both stopped working.

Despite Mara's protest, Kapp pushed his gloved hand past the transparent barrier. It gave no evident resistance. Nothing tragic happened, so he left his hand there, rotating his wrist as if he were bathing it in a waterfall. The baffling imprint of the human hand lay out of his reach, just meters above. Kapp had a strong desire to see it up close, maybe to touch it.

"I'm going in," he said, pulling his hand back out and turning toward his crewmates to deliver the sudden decision.

"Kapp, no," Jesse said. "What if you can't get out?"

Kapp pondered the predicament before trying a new experiment. He reached his arm back through the shimmering surface, wrapped his gloved fingers around one of the dud cameras, and removed it. He presented the camera to his companions and raised his eyebrows suggestively at the results.

"Just pull me out," he said.

Jesse and Mara clearly didn't like the rashness of the plan, but they raised no further objections. Kapp braced himself below the opening before kicking gently against the Phobian dust. His head and torso passed the barrier first. He felt no change in momentum as the motion carried his body upward. As soon as the tip of his boot made it through, though, the change came immediately. Kapp crumpled to the floor of the bubble, the surface closest to the ground, disoriented by the instant change in gravity. He instantly felt an increase in temperature as he struggled to his feet on wobbly legs. Curious, he peered at a digital readout that sat below the polycarbonate dome of his helmet. The thermometer showed 24° Celsius, a far cry from the -80° outside. Looking up from the display, he noticed that his visibility was compromised by condensation. Small droplets of water—or something like water—clung to the polycarbonate surface, dripping down under the artificial gravity and streaking the dome with tiny rivers.

Kapp's eyes darted from one side of the helmet to the other. The inside of his visor shouldn't have collected moisture at all. It had a hydrophobic coating to prevent condensation. With the glove of his suit, he wiped across the dome, removing a swarm of droplets and confirming his suspicion in the process. The moisture came from the outside of his suit, which could mean only one thing.

"J, I need the atmosphere sensor," he said into the radio. "Did you bring it?"

"Repeat," Jesse said. Static choked the transmission, making it barely audible.

"Atmosphere sensor," he shouted, enunciating each syllable.

Jesse heard him that time. He unstrapped the small device from his toolkit and handed it through the forcefield to Kapp's eager hand.

He turned a dial on the side of the device, illuminating a small screen. Then he tapped an icon and held the diaphragm of the sensor in front of his torso. After a few moments, a beep reverberated through the alien chamber, and the results of the scan flashed on the screen:

73% Nitrogen
26% Oxygen
0.9% Argon
0.1% Trace Gases

Slightly high in Oxygen, but nearly standard, Kapp thought, marveling at the results. Lightheaded and sweaty from the fever and too many layers of clothing, he looked up at the wall of symbols, absentmindedly dropping the atmosphere sensor to the shimmering floor. He found the shape of the human hand on the wall above and looked down at his own. Someone tried to speak to him through the radio, but the message came as an unintelligible blend of static and fragmented words.

Kapp looked at Mara and Jesse's nervous faces below and held up a single gloved finger. He wedged his entire left hand into his right armpit and flexed the stump of a limb tightly against it. A jolt of pain shot through his injured shoulder from the effort. He knew it was risky, but he didn't care. Some protrusion of his suit found the release button, and he pulled the glove off in a single motion. Less hot and humid than the air inside his suit, the air of the room chilled his exposed skin. The feeling spread up his sleeve until it reached an airtight seam.

Static filled his helmet, the unheard protests of the captain's concerned crew. An empty sleeve dangled at his side, and the discarded glove joined the cameras and atmosphere sensor on the forcefield's floor. He waved at Jesse and Mara, flexing his uninjured digits to show them he was okay. Their faces showed a mixture of bemusement and relief. Kapp brought his hand to the side of his helmet and depressed the button on the side. The suit needed service, so it took extra pressure to make the button click, but once it did, he smiled and lifted the dome.

His sweaty face stayed wet in the tropical atmosphere, but it welcomed the small amount of cooling evaporation that the air allowed. He took a deep breath, immediately intoxicated by the extra oxygen. Kapp's body felt lighter, his muscles looser, his head clearer as the life-giving substance coursed through his blood. Even some of his many pains began to dissolve. He relished several more cavernous breaths, letting the foreign air fill and soothe the innermost parts of him, thinking the whole time that Earth had been suffocating him, that this was what breathing truly meant, what it was supposed to be like.

The hand-shaped indentation now stood at eye level. Up close he could see the intricacies of the design. Dotted with condensation, webs of lines and wrinkles sparkled along the gleaming metal as if it had been molded around an actual hand. The symbols surrounding the imprint looked just as intricate, though less familiar. He held his palm between his face and the handprint, shaking matted hair loose from his sweaty head. His palm inched closer to the symbol, equally afraid and keen to touch it. Ignoring the complaints from below and the muffled protests from within, he took another deep breath of the impossible air and pressed his hand into the concavity. The wet metal emitted a warmth the same temperature as the surrounding air. He flexed his fingers and pressed hard against the surface, rolling the pressure slowly from one side to the other, like a criminal giving his prints to the cops.

Nothing happened.

With his hand still resting in the depression, Kapp peered down at his companions, who spoke to each other in unintelligible bursts. He bent forward slightly, letting his arm drop away from the wall, mildly disappointed that the impression served no purpose, that it was just decorative and not some kind of button. Just as he was about to motion for Jesse to pull him out of the bubble, the bursts of static grew frantic. The pair below looked at each other and then back at Kapp, arms flailing in some semblance of indecisive sign language. They made a nonverbal decision and bounced up toward Kapp with arms outstretched. When their heads passed the force field, Mara's face disappeared behind a bright circle of illumination that reflected off her visor. The artificial gravity broke and then reversed. Weightlessness returned to Kapp's body as he fell upward. He turned his unprotected head and saw a stark white beam coming from above, a shaft of light spilling out of the yawning trapdoor.

19

BEACON

Before his eyes could open, Asher heard water dripping and felt a cool draft across his skin. His mouth tasted like a hungover morning, and his head ached just as badly. Between the drips, Asher heard a conversation that sounded distant but clear. The first words that Asher caught came from a woman.

"What is it?"

"Nothing good."

Asher's eyes shot open at the sound of the second voice, the man—or men—who had captured him at Groom Lake. Despite the poor lighting, he could see a cracked concrete ceiling and a wall of iron bars. He immediately started hyperventilating, which drowned out the conversation until he forced himself to calm down and listen.

"Felix," the woman said. "What did you learn out there?"

The click of Felix's lighter bounced through the corridor.

"He's getting more powerful."

She let out a breath. "We already knew that."

"It's worse." Felix lowered his voice. "Now he can ship the injections abroad."

Asher rolled to a sitting position on his cot, which squeaked loudly under his weight. The conversation stopped. Footsteps replaced the voices, and Asher retreated into a corner of the room as they neared. He scanned the room for a weapon but found nothing useful. Felix came around the corner, followed by a thin woman, and lifted his hands to show empty palms.

"Morning, sunshine," Felix said, smiling through his thick beard.

"Who are you?" Asher asked, stepping closer to the barrier between him and Felix. "What are you do—"

"We've already met, Mr. West." He flicked the ash from his cigarette, took a drag. "We brought you here to keep you safe, remember?"

"Oh, yeah?" Asher said, rattling the bars between him and Felix. "I don't feel very safe."

"It's not locked," Felix said, kicking open the door of the cell. "We just had to make sure we could trust you before—"

"Where am I?" Asher had a million questions swirling through his mind. "What is this place?"

"I'm afraid I can't tell you that. Not yet." Felix dropped his spent cigarette to the floor and crushed it with his boot. "Walk with us."

Asher didn't budge. He couldn't make his feet move.

"We're not gonna hurt you," Felix said. "Come on. We want to show you something."

The woman turned to leave, and Felix followed. "And please," he added, "try not to break any more noses."

Against his better judgment, Asher crept out of the cell and into the dank concrete hallway—if only because he couldn't stand being behind bars. Something about confinement had always bothered him. That's why he hated nightclubs. He preferred places where he could come and go as he pleased.

Felix and the woman looked back to make sure that Asher followed. They turned left, and Asher looked right to see a long, unlit hallway, which had a slight curve to it. He let them lead for a moment, faked a few lazy paces toward them, and then took off in the opposite direction.

The slap of boots on concrete reverberated through the chamber as he sprinted away from his kidnappers. He didn't look back. He just ran into the near-dark, terrified—like he always did—as fast as his feet would allow. After passing a dozen more cells, he ducked into a doorway with a staircase symbol glowing above. Through the door's small window, he saw corrugated steel steps, a way out.

He stole a glance back down the hallway, fumbling with the rusty doorknob.

Locked.

Asher lifted his leg and gave the knob a firm kick. Dead-bolted into its ancient frame, the door didn't move at all.

"Shit," he whispered.

He continued to run until his lungs and legs burned. Groggy and thirsty, he slowed to a jog and followed the curve of the hallway. More locked doors replaced the cells, but none of the doors had an exit sign. He needed to find a place to hide, to plan an escape.

Finally, a door budged, and Asher found himself in complete darkness. After fumbling for the light switch, Asher realized he was in a dirty mop closet. He wedged a mop handle between the door and the wall and sank to the floor. It almost felt like high school, he thought hysterically. Once his breathing slowed, he tried the faucet. Filthy water poured out for minutes before anything looked remotely drinkable. The brackish smell of the water made him recoil, but he brought his lips to the faucet anyway and drank until his stomach could hold no more. His guts ached from the cold liquid, but his thirst vanished. He relieved himself into the drain before pressing his ear against the door.

Silence.

Asher brought the mop handle to the floor and rested its end on the lip of the steel basin. He stomped on it once, twice, three times before it broke in half. Then he picked up the makeshift weapon, clicked off the light, and crept back into the hallway. He walked carefully, listening for signs of life.

The sharp stick gave him no advantage. His captors had the numbers, the knowledge, and most likely the weapons in their favor. At the least, he knew they had his shotgun. No, fighting wouldn't do. He'd have to play along…for now. Just as he was about to turn back, he saw a green sign shining through the darkness.

ELEVATORS

Smiling at his good fortune, Asher picked up his pace and approached the oasis ahead. He stepped through the arch that led to the elevator room, ready to take a lift to his salvation, but a smoky voice brought him to a halt.

"I admire your hustle, but you went the long way." Felix stood in front of the woman, his hand on a pistol that Asher hadn't noticed before. "I told you we're not gonna hurt you. You can leave if you want, but we'll have to knock you out again."

Asher dropped the stick.

"I'm hoping you'll hear us out first," Felix said.

Asher looked at the woman and then back to Felix. "About what?"

"You'll see," Felix said. "Just follow us."

This time Asher had no choice but to oblige. The last thing he wanted was a gunshot wound. The trio stopped at an elevator with a stenciled number six spray painted above it. The woman pressed the down button and offered a hand to Asher, which he refused to accept.

"I'm Genesis," she said. "Leader of this group. We call ourselves—"

"Beacon," Asher said, his eyelids as narrow as his trust for these people. "Felix said it on the radio after—after the other Felix showed me what chloroform smells like."

Felix laughed. "You're talking about my brother, Calix."

So I wasn't hallucinating, Asher thought. "Twins," he said.

"Yeah," Felix said. "Something like that."

Asher decided not to press the issue. The elevator arrived, along with a typical awkward silence. So many questions, but he didn't know which one to ask first. He looked at the elevator buttons, which appeared to be in the wrong order, and thought he understood why the highest floors had the lowest numbers.

"Are we underground?" he asked.

"Yep," Felix said, "but don't bother asking where."

They took the elevator down to level ten, the lowest floor. The doors slid open, revealing a sterile and spacious room. The spitting image of Felix stood like a reflection near the center of the room, identical to his brother in every way except for the white bandage on his broken nose. Asher stifled the urge to apologize.

"At least I can tell you two apart now," Genesis said.

Asher took a closer look at the woman. Genesis wore all black like her comrades and seemed to be in her twenties. In the new light, the tone of her skin looked more like a faded brown than a tan white, a good match for the emerald tint of her eyes.

"Let's eat," Calix said. He and Asher shared a dirty look.

"I'm sorry that we had to drag you here like this," Genesis said, placing a hand on his back. Asher recoiled a bit, but he let the hand stay. "The twins acted under my orders, so if you need to be angry at someone, be angry at me."

When Asher didn't respond, she continued. "I'm hoping we can put this behind us. We need to work together, especially now. How can we make you believe that we're fighting on the same side?"

Asher wanted, even needed, someone to trust, but the circumstances made trust hard to earn. "How'd you find me?"

"Only the guilty run," Genesis said. "We've been tracking you since you leaked the Starling II documents."

"It wasn't easy once you removed your ID chip," Felix added.

Asher looked down at the fresh scar on his wrist. "Why me?"

Genesis tilted her head, came closer. "The enemy of my enemy—"

"What did Holden do to you?" he asked, shuffling his feet.

"Not just Holden," Felix said.

"It's what Holden tried to do," Genesis said, her voice suddenly sharp. "He strapped a bomb to a research vessel and lied about it. He threatened the life of Eli Morgan's son to send your friend on a suicide mission."

"Wait, what?" Asher perked up. "Eli's son?"

Calix joined the conversation. "We've confirmed several threats made against Eli. Holden tried to coerce him into bombing Phobos."

"Holden tried to destroy everything," Genesis said. "But he failed. Our job is to make sure he continues to fail."

Asher looked from face to face. "Failed?"

"It's all on here," Genesis said, pulling an external hard drive from a pocket and handing it to him.

He took it, turned it in his hands, contemplating whether he should put his trust in a bunch of kidnappers hiding out in a bunker. Sure enough, it was his hard drive. *But what if they tampered with it?*

"I want to see for myself," he said.

"Of course."

Felix led them to a desk and gestured for Asher to sit. He plugged his drive into the computer and got to work. First, he ran a quick check to authenticate that the files hadn't been corrupted. The diagnostic came back clean. Fingers moving furiously across the keyboard, he searched through the cloned files until he found the images from the Wisdom rover. The screen displayed a picture of Starling II on the surface of Phobos. Asher's mouth fell open, his posture stiffened.

"They crash landed?" Asher said, resisting the urge to break down. He felt a panic attack coming on. "Kapp's never coming back."

"Next picture," Genesis said.

Asher found and opened the file, which had a timestamp one day later than the previous file. It took a painfully long time to load on the older system. When the picture finally appeared, Starling II was nowhere to be found. Asher glanced around the room, looking for answers.

"Where did they go?" he asked no one in particular.

He knew that launching from the surface of Phobos would be extremely difficult, if not impossible, after a crash landing. Most likely impossible. He scanned the entire photo, searching every wall of the crater surrounding the strange alien craft, every dusty peak and valley. He found no signs of life. Starling II had nowhere to hide, unless—

"Are they inside the ship?" Asher asked.

•|•

When his heart rate slowed enough to have a conversation, Asher asked for a shower and some fresh clothes. Felix led him to a locker room and left him there with a small bundle. After stripping out of the dirty guard's uniform, he let the hot water rush over his skin-covered bones for a long time while he processed his thoughts. Months of worry washed away with his fugitive stench. Relief came knowing that Kapp lived—or that he had been alive recently—but it also created new questions.

He came out of the locker room in a black jumpsuit two sizes too big and walked to a table in the center of the stark white room. A small pile of military grade MREs sat there, half of them open. Genesis smiled her welcome, and Asher sat down.

"Do you feel any better?" she asked, opening one of the pouches.

"A little," he said.

"Eat."

She handed him the imperishable meal and a plastic fork. He couldn't tell what it was, but his hunger didn't care. He took heaping forkfuls of the sustenance and licked the pouch clean once he finished.

"Have as much as you want," Genesis said. "We have a truckload. Literally."

Asher reached for another MRE. "Where are the twins?"

"Looking through more of Holden's files."

"They're kind of assholes," he said between mouthfuls of some kind of pasta.

A giggle fell from her lips. "You'll learn to love them."

"Probably not," he admitted. "Let's see if they found anything."

Genesis led him back to the computer desk, where Felix sat typing. Calix lounged to the side with an ice pack on his face.

"Find anything, boys?"

"An encrypted folder," Felix said, scratching his chin. "I can't get past it though."

"Can I try?" Asher asked.

"Knock yourself out."

"You already did that," Asher said without missing a beat.

Felix rolled away from the desk with a kick, and Asher replaced him. He checked his fingers for pasta sauce before bringing them to the keyboard and getting to work. The encrypted folder that Felix spoke of was unsubtly labeled **PRIVATE**. Hunched over the keyboard, Asher began his attempts to decrypt it. He went through every trick he knew and several methods he had never tried before, but the folder remained uncrackable. As a last ditch effort, he tried Holden's usual password, and—

"God, he's an idiot," Asher said. "In charge of a multi-billion-credit agency and a complete idiot."

Asher sifted through the files, mostly financial documents and some weird porn, looking for the good stuff. Eventually, something caught his eye, a subfolder labeled **ACCOUNTING**. He opened it and double-clicked one of the contained PDFs. A pay stub. When the document loaded, Asher skipped to the bottom, and the name of the payer gained his attention. He shook his head back and forth, seething at the depth of Holden's corruption.

Huddled around the screen, he and his new allies saw that their shared enemy was on the payroll of an extremely powerful man, the tech guru behind the nano-injection health revolution, the man who cured cancer, an industry leader trusted, almost worshipped, by the masses: Doctor Theo Cage.

20

BOTTLED FEAR

The mouth of the chasm swallowed the crew, pulling them up toward a brilliant diamond of white at the end of the tunnel. The comm systems of their suits shut off, which turned panicked radio squelches into helmet-muffled words. The walls surrounding them appeared to reflect little or no light as if the strange metal absorbed it all instead.

The crew floated into an empty whiteness, the tunnel slammed shut, and gravity returned. They fell over each other, a heap of tangled bodies. Kapp could see nothing but the brightly illuminated suits of his companions, struggling to get their bearings on a sterile white floor. With some struggle, they untangled themselves from each other, sprawling out in the infinite glow that surrounded them. Kapp inhaled deeply, unaware that he had been holding his breath, but happy that his lungs still held air.

Jesse and Mara appeared rattled, bottled fear spilling into the expressions they wore. After observing Kapp for a moment, they popped their visors open simultaneously. The walls of the room came into focus, five of them, all white like everything else.

Mara looked around, scanning the blank walls through tiny, spectacled pupils. Her voice came out fast and breathy, then she gulped down moist air and repeated a single word, the mantra of the terrified: "Shit, shit, shit—"

"Quiet," Kapp said, raising a finger to his lips. He didn't want her to go into shock again. Soon, his eyes found the ceiling of the pentagonal room, and his ears followed.

Kapp heard it first. A sound reverberating through the chamber, soft and low, but inching closer. As the tone neared, it crescendoed into a steady hum. Though he couldn't tell for sure, Kapp had a hunch that it came from above. The sound reached its peak just as a black dot no bigger than a quarter appeared in the center of the low ceiling. The grumble turned into a hiss, and the room began to fill with—

"Gas!" Kapp shouted.

Jesse and Mara closed their helmets and locked them into place. Kapp reached for his, but it wouldn't budge. He tried again, slapping his left palm against the side of his helmet. The fog descended unnaturally fast. He held his breath against the thick vapor, still struggling with his helmet, wishing that he had his damn prosthetic. Jesse reached out a gloved hand, tried to help, but the visor just wouldn't move.

"Broken!" Jesse yelled.

The cloud descended relentlessly, brilliant whiteness that blocked out all else. *I'm going to die,* Kapp thought, fear arriving as a strange guest in the tranquil setting. The fluffy clouds of gas, the searing light, everything radiated a heavenly peace that seemed out of place. Soon, the oxygen in the single panicked breath that he held depleted, leaving him with a burning pressure building in his lungs. Carbon dioxide prisoners raged against their captor, rushing the guards with the ferocity of the oppressed. Before the fog reached him, Kapp shut his eyes tightly. Jesse continued to work on the jammed visor. Not fast enough. The need to exhale overpowered Kapp's will, forcing soured air out of his burning lungs. He choked down an involuntary breath. The tainted air tasted fresh, almost citric. It smelled like a cross between an operating room and an orchard.

For a moment, Kapp thought that he had already died, that these were the scents of a paradise he didn't even believe in. Heavenly. But his lungs still hurt, and he could still sense his legs resting on the floor, could still hear Jesse pounding away at the broken helmet. This wasn't death.

He opened his eyes to make sure and saw the fog dissipating.

"I think I'm okay," he said, nearly blinded by the new light.

Breathing heavily, overwhelmed with the constant mood swings of fate, he wished for everything to slow down, for just one minute to think.

Instead of one, he got hundreds.

•|•

Hours later, some level of resigned calmness crept over the crew. The gas had no apparent effect on them, so for the sake of mobility and comfort, they had decided to remove their space suits, which sat in a heap in one of the five corners. Still, the five-walled room held them as prisoners, unsettling their nerves. In the preceding hours, Jesse had studied every inch of the room, unable to find a single imperfection or weakness in the smooth surfaces. The long wait worsened Kapp's fever, but the sweat had stopped coming. Leaning against one wall, Mara wept without tears, Jesse's hand resting gently in hers.

"I'm sorry," Kapp said from the floor, his words crackling like burning wood. "I didn't think—I didn't expect anything to happen."

Mara came to him, touching his forehead for what seemed like the hundredth time. "I'm more worried about you."

"I'll be fine." Cold sweat and shaky hands exposed his lie. "I just need—"

"Water," Jesse said. "Ice. Cold. Water."

"Don't talk about it," Mara said.

"I ain't been this damn thirsty since—"

"J?" Kapp said.

Jesse lowered his brows. "Yeah?"

"Your Alabama's showing again."

He shrugged. "Speech therapy didn't account for scenarios like this one right here."

"You did that?" Mara asked, wiping the sweat off Kapp's forehead with his comm cap.

"Talk dumb, and people think you're dumb," Jesse said. "But I ain't dumb. I don't need to impress y'all. Not here, not—"

A hiss of air cut him off. One of the walls fell away, revealing a blank hallway beyond. Kapp hurried to his feet, dizzy from the effort.

Mara turned back to Jesse. "Did you do something?"

He just shook his head, staring down the hallway. Then something moved in the distance, a dark shadow at the end of the hall. Like smoke, the silhouette crept closer, raising the hairs on Kapp's neck, before disappearing from sight altogether. Mara let out a small shriek and jumped behind Jesse, who held his ground beside Kapp. Neither of them had anything remotely weapon-like. Jesse stepped forward.

"Don't!" Mara said, the terror pulling tears from somewhere deep within her dehydrated body.

He ignored her, taking a few steps toward and then into the opening. "Y'all stay, I'm gonna—"

The fifth wall fell back into place.

·|·

A scream that seemed to last for hours, and then the panic crawled. Minutes stretched on as Mara and Kapp struggled to process Jesse's disappearance. Kapp did his best to banish horrible thoughts about Jesse getting poked and probed. For all he knew, his friend was already dead, and he and Mara were next. Eyes trained on the wall, Mara sat with her knees to her chest, each breath rapid and relentless.

"Mara," Kapp said, "you need to slow down."

"He's, he's—"

Kapp grabbed her shoulder. He blamed himself for getting them into this situation, but he couldn't allow himself to panic. Not yet.

"Take deep breaths, Mara. In. Out."

"Jesse, he's, we have to—"

"In. Out." She looked like she was about to pass out. "Breathe, Mara!"

"I can't." Mara shook her head. "We have to, we have—"

Another wall fell away, and Mara's breathing stopped altogether. She hid behind Kapp, who stared ahead, hoping to find Jesse. Instead, he saw a figure cross the hallway, the same from before, a flash of black in a sea of blinding white. Definitely not human. The thing moved straight toward them, its form coming into focus. It walked with the slow, silent gait of a predator, inching forward cautiously, hesitant to show itself lest it should become the prey of something else. Finally, when Kapp thought both he and Mara would faint from fear, a charcoal-colored creature came forward, revealing bright eyes and a whipping tail.

Kapp squinted. "Is that a—"

Meow.

The approaching feline would have been shocking if it had not been followed by something even more dark and mysterious. Like the charcoal cat, its pursuer moved with the poise of a predator. The being's posture radiated purposeful confidence and a wild grace as it caught up to the cat, who rubbed its fur lovingly against a pair of thin legs. Kapp couldn't believe what he saw. He attempted to wipe away the hallucination, but when his knuckles left his eyelids, the vision remained. The green eyes that looked back into Kapp's were full of questions, full of fear. They were fierce, beautiful...and inarguably human.

The woman wore a skintight black bodysuit that clung to her fit frame from ankle to neck. She stood tall, walked with purpose. The skin of her bare feet and face appeared pale and unblemished. Shiny, dark brown hair hung from her head, curls kissing her shoulders before ending at her collarbone, concealing everything but the slight elvish point of her ears. Her features, symmetrical and captivating, fit her angular face perfectly: big eyes, an understated nose, and pink lips plump with blood.

"Greetings," she said in an unfamiliar accent, beautiful and strange like foreign music. Her words came out slow and clear, as if she had rehearsed them in front of a mirror. "I am Aeva, protector of this vessel. What are your intentions here?"

The room shook, or maybe it was just Kapp's imagination.

"What?" he asked, stepping forward, nearly tripping. The fever made him feel delusional, and his head spun with conspiracies. "How is this—"

"My apologies." Aeva spoke without blinking or breaking eye contact. "It has been many suns since Arca has had guests. I've forgotten my etiquette. Please, let me tend to your hunger and thirst before we—"

"Arca?" Kapp wanted to sit down. His knees buckled slightly, but he managed to stay upright.

"Yes. You are onboard the starship Arca—the last of its class."

"Oh," was all Kapp could say. His head, still spinning, fell into his palm.

"Are you injured?" Aeva contemplated the duo, her gaze lingering for a moment on Kapp's amputation point. "I see you are not in an optimal state for communication at this time. I will take you somewhere to eat, bathe, and sleep."

They followed her out of the pentagonal room through the empty hall, unable to process the odd meeting in their weakened condition. She led them like children, looking back every so often to make sure that no one wandered off. Her cat took up the rear of the procession, swerving back and forth. His motions ignited a predatory fear in Kapp.

"I apologize for the delay," Aeva said. "Several hours of quarantine are required before entering Arca."

The hall led to a larger corridor, not tight and glowing white like the first, but wide and metallic. The wall sealed shut behind them when they stepped past the threshold, into a space much darker and cooler than the cell they had left behind. Mara's eyes darted around at the foreign symbols etched above large arched door frames. Struggling to walk, Kapp fell behind.

"Where's Jesse?" Mara asked.

"I assume you mean the other man," Aeva said.

Their chatter faded out of Kapp's focus as the fever began to overtake him. The corridor spun as if he had taken one too many shots, only without the dopamine rush. His body couldn't compensate for the sensory confusion. Without warning, his vision tunneled until the only thing that remained was a single speck of light surrounded by darkness, an inverted vision of the dark circle that had leaked gas into the quarantine room hours before. The light lingered for a moment, fading in and out of sight like a distant life raft in a blue-black sea. Kapp's head hit the hard floor, and that too disappeared beneath the waves.

21

AEVA'S TALE

Kapp can still hear his mother's scream, even though her mouth is covered. There's someone else there now, a man crouched beside her. A wall of fire rises between them. The man is holding a knife, but Kapp can't see his face. Only the back of his head. The blade nears his mother's belly, as if in slow motion. The licking of the flames slows to a crawl. Kapp wants to call for help, to stop the man from hurting her. He opens his mouth, but no sound comes out. He tries to stand, but can't move a muscle, not even to blink. The knife takes hours to reach her flesh, and he is forced to witness every painful second.

Kapp woke to find himself submerged up to his neck in a clear liquid. Then he noticed the pale nakedness of his skin glowing beneath the bubbling surface. Letting his eyelids shut once more, he didn't react to these comfortable discoveries, for they were far more peaceful than the nightmare he had woken up from.

His aches and pains had left, and his head felt clear. He took in a moment of bliss, but curiosity and a nagging sense of wanting to escape drove him to move on. When he opened his eyes again, he was no longer alone. The woman from earlier stood at the foot of the tub, her expression blank. Kapp's left hand shot down to cover his groin. Unable to remember her name, he sat up in the shallow rectangle of water depressed into the metallic floor.

"Stay," she said. "You need to keep your shoulder submerged in the healing waters."

Kapp looked down at his frostbite wound, but instead of dying flesh, he saw fresh pink skin forming around his prosthetic attachment point. He let his body sink back into the tub. "How long was I out?"

The woman didn't speak immediately, which gave Kapp time to recall her name. *Aeva.* "One half of one solar day," she said.

Kapp nodded, though he didn't know why. The speed at which he had healed, the strange way that Aeva spoke, it all overwhelmed him, but he had more pressing matters to consider. "Where are my friends?"

"Finish healing," she said, her voice slow and calm. "Then we will go to them."

"Take me now."

"Not yet," she said.

Kapp tried to rise but slipped. "Where are they?"

Aeva turned to leave. "Safe."

"Wait," Kapp said, trying once again to sit up.

She halted in the arched doorway and looked directly at him, her emerald gaze so deep it appeared to go straight through him. He peeked at the hand covering his crotch to make sure it hadn't gone transparent.

"I'll bring you something to wear."

Kapp decided he didn't want to argue naked. "Okay, fine."

Aeva took a slight bow, more of a nod, then left him alone with his thoughts. The cat stayed behind, licking his paws, watching Kapp from a cot-like structure that sat in the corner.

"Fuck off," Kapp said.

The cat bared his teeth and hissed.

"Same to you."

Instead of exploring the strange room, Kapp closed his eyes and attempted to relax. The nightmare had left him anxious enough to wish he had a bottle of something to drown the memory in. Conspiracies about Aeva returned, adding foulness to his already bitter thoughts. Questions and their possible answers spun around his mind.

Was this supposed to be some kind of suicide mission to destroy the advanced technology of another spacefaring country? China? Russia?

Holden wouldn't do that to me, he decided. *Maybe the government went over his head to threaten Eli.*

Kapp didn't like feeling like a pawn in someone else's game, but it was the only explanation that made any sense to him. He just knew that Aeva couldn't possibly be an alien.

Or could she? What if she's just disguised as a human?

Aeva came back twenty minutes later to leave behind a small bundle of clothes, and the theories still ran wild in Kapp's head. He looked at her through narrow eyes but didn't say a word. When she left, the cat followed. Kapp couldn't find a towel, so he air dried for a minute before attempting to get dressed. In the early days of his injury, before he had a prosthetic, he had become a master of one-armed dressing. It had been a while since he had garbed himself without the help of a bionic arm, though, so this time he struggled to put on the clothes: a pair of soft black pants and a loose white tunic. The material was thin and airy without being completely see-through. Kapp thought about Aeva's piercing gaze, how it didn't matter what he wore. He knew she could see straight through him, anyway.

•|•

Kapp kept his suspicions to himself as he followed Aeva through Arca. They followed a long hallway lined with doors. Like the outside of the ship, the internal architecture boasted curves instead of straight lines, subtle bends instead of angles. The corridor meandered through the ship, as if the paths through the metal had been carved by erosion.

"How do you feel?" Aeva asked.

To keep steady, Kapp ran his hand along the shimmering wall to his left, which radiated a soft warmth. "Confused."

"I meant your shoulder."

"It feels fine." Kapp looked down at his stump. "How did you do that so fast?"

"I did nothing." Aeva side-stepped to avoid stepping on the cat's tail. "I believe you call them microbes on Earth."

"Right," Kapp said. "So that bath was full of bacteria?"

"Only the friendly kind."

They ran into no one else on the way, which seemed odd to Kapp because they passed so many doors. Anxious to find Jesse and Mara, Kapp sighed each time they rounded a curve only to find another hallway beyond.

"Can't we just teleport there?"

"That's impossible."

Recent events had utterly shattered Kapp's understanding of possibility, so he had no response. Soon they reached a door at the end of the hall, which opened automatically, disappearing seamlessly into the architecture.

They stepped into a dome-shaped room and joined Jesse and Mara at a large five-sided table decorated with concentric circles.

Mara beamed at Kapp. "Your fever?"

"Gone," Kapp said as he took a seat. He lifted the sleeve of his shirt to show her the missing frostbite wound.

"Incredible," Jesse said.

"I'm glad you're alive," Kapp said.

He laughed. "Takes more than a kitty cat to kill me."

In the soft glow that seemed to emanate from everything, Mara and Jesse looked much healthier and happier than Kapp had seen them since leaving Earth. The black cat took the fifth seat at the table for a moment before jumping up onto the wooden surface and making a beeline for Aeva.

"Hi, Lex," she said, letting him rub his whiskers against her cheek. She continued coddling the creature for minutes, seemingly oblivious to everyone else in the room.

Kapp looked to Jesse and Mara, who didn't seem to mind the wait. Perhaps they had already been briefed, but Kapp still needed answers. When he spoke, he couldn't keep the impatience out of his tone. "So, are we gonna talk or what?"

She looked up from her pet, and her lips nearly curved into a smile. "My apologies. I forget that time seems to move much slower for your kind."

"What?" Kapp asked. He took another look at Jesse and Mara before turning his attention back to Aeva. "Our kind?"

"Yes," she said. "Time seems to move much slower for the young—for the mortal."

Kapp stared at the woman, her words somehow sounding crazier than the entire situation. "What are you talking about?"

Again, they awaited her response.

"You have many questions." Aeva lifted Lex into her lap and began to stroke his charcoal fur with careful grace. "I believe I can answer many of them by telling you the story of how and why I am here—a tale that began a very long time ago."

•|•

"In your language, her full name is Arca the Wanderer," Aeva said, opening a palm toward the ceiling. She spoke clear and slow, her face showing nearly no emotion. "Arca is the last of her class, perhaps the only vessel in this system capable of interstellar travel."

A hologram appeared in the middle of the table, tearing Kapp's gaze away from the enchanting woman. Approaching through a field of artificial stars, an image of Arca appeared in the three-dimensional projection.

"The creators of Arca were once a great and noble race. There is no direct translation for their name, so we shall call them the Architects, for that is what they were—wise builders of civilization. Their history is long and complex, so forgive my summary."

Aeva took a sip from a vessel that Kapp hadn't noticed until it met her lips.

"The Architects evolved on a tiny planet, which became overcrowded and war-torn early in their history. One solution to the problem was to control birth rates—the Architect Empire allowed one birth for each death."

"Like China," Kapp muttered, gaining no one's attention. Aeva continued as if the interruption hadn't happened.

"Over the years, the lifespans of the Architects increased dramatically, so the need for new births diminished. The oldest minds grew brilliant with time, ushering in an era of exponential scientific advances."

Simulations of an oceanless planet appeared in the hologram. When the view zoomed in, strange buildings popped out of the ground at various angles. Small crafts buzzed around the cities like scattered swarms of bees.

"All diseases, even death, were cured." Aeva took a silent breath and another sip from her cup. "When the Architects stopped dying, birth halted altogether. Life became stagnant, and one group of immortals grew bored. They had built a legacy, a vault of knowledge, but they had no one left to pass it on to, so they set their focus beyond the limits of their own world."

Kapp stole a glance at Jesse, who had his arm around Mara. Both kept their eyes on Aeva as she continued her story. He wondered if his crew actually believed Aeva, or if they were just playing along too.

"Space exploration came late for the Architects. For most of their existence, they considered their home planet to be the entire universe. A thick fog blocked their view of the stars, preventing their ancestors from dreaming of what might lie beyond the constantly shifting darkness."

Aeva took another sip, her green gaze pouring over the crew like molasses.

"The dawn of space travel must have been an exhilarating time for the Architects. Endless possibility replaced ancient notions, and advances happened rapidly. With a fleet of colony-class ships like Arca, the Architects were finally able to break free from their home planet to colonize the habitable zones of their local solar system—and beyond."

The hologram zoomed back out to a galactic scale, and lines branched out from the central planet, connecting to the nearest stars before expanding beyond even those limits. It reminded Kapp of the IES logo, but on a much larger scale.

"For many thousands of orbital periods, the Architects lived in peace and abundance, exploring every corner of their distant and secluded galaxy. A new generation of fresh minds began to populate the Empire. Alastar, a young captain assigned to Arca, was at the forefront of these explorations."

A tinge of emotion bubbled to the surface of Aeva's stoic face at the mention of his name. Lex rubbed his furry head against her arm before jumping to the floor.

"Alastar's discoveries along the frontier defied his race's preconceived notions of possibility, and this won him much acclaim. You see—scientists of the era theorized life to be a rare occurrence in the universe. They had set their focus on planets very similar to their own, thinking that life could only generate under the same conditions—but they were wrong. Alastar understood that the Architects might not be the rule, but the outlier. On the frontier of the expansion, he discovered alien races, both primitive and technological, flourishing in the most unlikely of places."

The charcoal cat pounced into Mara's lap, and she flinched before beginning to pet it.

"Alastar used the earnings from his research to purchase the Wanderer and to fill its bay with Beacon class ships, which he used to collect, study, and categorize specimens from across the galaxy. Beacons are able to travel much faster than colony ships, so they were often utilized as scouts. Alastar had all he needed to launch explorations on his own terms. He preferred the solitude of space, where he spent the long journeys between stars on his experiments, over the bustle of the Architect Empire. It was on one of these trips that Alastar discovered the first tunnel."

"Tunnel?" Kapp asked. He couldn't believe he was entertaining Aeva's insane story, but the tale had consumed him.

"Like a wormhole?" Jesse said.

"Alastar only called it a tunnel—one between his galaxy and yours. He studied it for a time before moving on, but eventually he had no choice but to return." Her voice dropped lower. "When darkness infected the central system of the empire from within, Alastar only heard about it through the Beacons. The Surge, as it came to be known, sprung to life in a thriving core world. It spread through the galaxy with immense speed, consuming everything possible in an attempt to satisfy its endless hunger."

Kapp nodded, his face tight, his smile bordering condescension.

"The galaxy had become a toxic and dangerous place," Aeva said, "ruled by a growing force of death disguised as life, so Alastar fled through the tunnel with his specimens, his experiments, and a few survivors. When he arrived in what you call the Milky Way, he sent three of the five remaining Beacons in search of a safe planet to call home—somewhere to form a colony."

A depiction of Earth spun in the middle of the pentagonal table.

"When Alastar visited your planet, he found a race much like his own, but with some fatal flaws, problems he knew could be fixed with enough time. He loved Earth—the people, the animals, the landscapes—and he would have stayed, but Arca can't survive in atmosphere for very long, so he decided to orbit the nearest star to your solar system while he worked on his plan."

Alpha Centauri, Kapp thought. He attempted to organize all the questions pelting his mind, but Aeva's story kept them coming. *What did she mean by Arca surviving?*

"One human woman agreed to leave Earth with him," Aeva continued. "With her help and eons of knowledge, Alastar created a new people to inherit the old wisdom. An immortal race without arrogance. A species capable of guiding all other sentient beings away from the doom that his own people had suffered. I, the first of the Skyborn, am the product of a human mother and an Architect father. Alastar later brought forth my brothers and sisters. For hundreds of cycles, we've waited for Alastar to launch an attack on the Surge."

Kapp raised an eyebrow and scratched behind his ear. Aeva couldn't be older than twenty-five. He wondered how long a "cycle" was.

"Forty-eight Earth-years ago, the final Beacon arrived on your planet carrying a group of Skyborn—my brothers and sisters—tasked with preparing Earth for Arca's arrival."

"I don't think they made it," Kapp said.

Aeva's chin trembled just slightly. "I don't think so either, but before contact was lost, Arca received a large data dump from Beacon Five, enough information for me to learn that your kind has already discovered space travel. Shortly after the transmission came in, Alastar launched his attack on the Surge. He left through the same tunnel that brought him here, and I set course for Earth immediately." She shook her head. "The fact that you're sitting before me makes me worry that I am too late."

"Too late for what?" Kapp asked, the questions finally spilling out.

Aeva sighed, a strangely beautiful sound. "When Alastar first visited Earth, disease was rampant. Humans rode animals to get around. There were no global communication systems." She glanced at the metallic implant jutting from the stump of Kapp's right arm, took a deep breath, and continued. "Now you can hop between planets with relative ease. You can walk on moons with no atmosphere. All of these advances have happened in almost no time at all."

"I don't understand," Kapp said. Nothing Aeva said made any sense to him, and the questions kept piling up.

"Kapp of Earth," she said, "the Surge is not an organic force, but a technological one—and your kind is heading toward a similar fate much faster than Alastar's did."

22

UPGRADES

Asher had a message to deliver. He came to the surface in the mountains, high enough for the pines to escape the harsh desert summers below. A dusting of snow cooled his face, drenched from the exertion of multiple staircases that led out of the bunker.

Behind him stood a wireless tower disguised as a pine tree, a new addition to Beacon headquarters—a place that Genesis called the Clearing. Before Asher's abduction and initiation into the club, the underground lair had been like a remote island. News of the outside world had to be delivered by foot. For security purposes, Genesis wouldn't allow a transmitter to be attached to their systems, but she did relent to Asher's pleas to install a receiver.

After that, with the help of a virtual private network and a freelance hacker hired from the darknet, Asher hacked into an array of classified information feeds, which ended Beacon's horse and buggy days of collecting information. They could finally keep an eye on Theo Cage, and although they had access to private information, it was what their nemesis did in the spotlight that worried them most.

In one video that circulated around the net, Theo presented an upgraded strain of his nano-therapy injections and treatments.

"Behold," he had said from behind a podium. *"The golden age of medicine."*

Then he took a knife to his forearm and made three jagged slices, breaking the skin and releasing a stream of blood. Asher had to avert his eyes. The onscreen audience gasped as the camera cut to their horrified expressions. Then another camera zoomed in on the injury.

"The new product I'm releasing runs in my blood today," Theo said, *"protecting and replenishing my vital fluids, my skin, even my bones."*

Then the blood flow stopped, and the camera zoomed in closer. Over the next ten seconds, the color of the injury faded from a dark red to a salmon color.

Doctor Cage took a rag and wiped the blood away, revealing the light pink of new skin. The outline of the injury slowly faded out of contrast until it disappeared completely.

The audience roared their approval.

Beacon's enemy appeared to be invincible, but Asher couldn't worry about that just yet. To keep sane, he had to focus on one task at a time—and that's what brought him to the surface. Despite the upgrades to Beacon's comm systems, outgoing messages still had to be delivered by foot. Genesis and the twins had been reluctant to let Asher go, but he had already proven his worth to the team, so they relented.

He trekked downhill, snow crunching under his feet, cold air refreshing his mind. A few weeks of safety allowed him to regain a sense of clarity. For the first time in a while, he let his mind wander to good memories—his first date with Emily, the warmth of her head on his shoulder, the way her eyes smiled as much as her lips. He missed her.

•|•

The hike to the nearest road took Asher about an hour to complete. He walked until the light layer of snow became a forest floor of pine needles and cones. In the distance, a squirrel, far enough away from civilization to still fear humans, ran up to the safety of a high branch.

As instructed, Asher followed the empty dirt road for another mile until he found what he needed. Because of the thickness of the trees, he almost missed the shack completely. The building, which looked more like an outhouse than a cabin, had a lean to its wooden frame. Wild vines grew up its sides, completing the camouflage effect.

Asher stepped through the brush to the barn door entrance and pulled a key out of his pocket. He fiddled with the padlock until the two sides of the chain came apart. Dust fell from the doorjamb as he parted the two slabs of wood. His eyes adjusted to the dim room. Between two storage shelves sat an object covered in a blue tarp. Dust filled the room as Asher uncovered the vehicle he would ride into the valley.

"That'll work," he said.

He knew nothing about motorcycles, but the one in front of him looked fast enough to get him where he needed to go and plain enough to avoid extra attention. He grabbed a black helmet from the shelf and walked the motorcycle out of the shed to the road.

Nerves tightened as he prepared to mount the unfamiliar beast. He put on his helmet and tightened the straps, which still felt too loose. Images he once saw in a driver's safety class came to mind—dead motorcyclists. Tightening the straps again, he shook off paranoid thoughts of his own body strewn across the road. Finally, he took a few mindful breaths to keep his anxiety at bay, then he swung a leg over the motorcycle and throttled the engine.

Asher had always been a fast learner, but that never helped with the worry of trying something new. After a rough mile or two, he adjusted to some of the intricacies of riding. He experimented with the acceleration and the brakes until he felt comfortable. Halfway out of the mountains, he actually started to enjoy the drive. The hum of the engine and the slap of the wind became almost meditative, and the thoughts of Emily returned.

Though the helmet hid his face from recognition by either man or machine, Asher still avoided as many populated areas as possible. This became impossible once he reached the Las Vegas valley, filled with residential neighborhoods from foothill to distant foothill. Before he reached the denser areas, he stopped at an In-N-Out Burger just off the interstate, where he scarfed down two animal style cheeseburgers before crossing the street to fuel up.

Most gas stations had been refurbished as charging stations for electric cars, but this one still had a single pump. Asher parked beside it and took off his helmet to better read the sign posted just above the heavily-taxed gasoline price.

CHIP ONLY

Asher glanced down at the scar where his implant had once been. "Hmm."

He pulled a neatly folded stack of bills out of his pocket. The new U.S. currency still had the green color and the presidential faces of the currency of Asher's youth, but the outdated religious language and occult imagery had been replaced with a more secular theme. Before he could overthink it, Asher walked into the shop. Behind the counter, a young woman—short, brown-haired, and bored-looking—took a break from her phone to offer Asher a lazy greeting.

"Hi," she said.

Asher smiled at her, happy to see a human instead of a self-service kiosk.

"Hey—um," he said, wishing he would have thought of an excuse before talking. "The chip reader for the gas pump isn't working."

"I can scan you in here. How much do you want?"

Asher peeled a twenty-credit bill from the stack and put it on the counter. The attendant gave him a look before taking the bill. She blew a bubble and smacked her gum.

"Haven't seen cash in a while?" he asked.

She nodded. "I still need ID verification for cash purchases."

"Jesus," he said, more to himself than to the girl. "What happened to liberty?"

In his opinion, the government had become far too involved in the private affairs of citizens.

"I don't know, dude."

He found the girl's name tag.

"Okay, Jackie," he said, preparing to lie his way out of the situation. "The problem is—my wife tracks my spending. If she sees that got scanned at a gas station, she's gonna know that I took the motorcycle out of storage, and that won't go so well. She's out of town, and she never leaves town, so this is my only chance to ride."

"God, she's psycho," Jackie said. "No offense."

"Believe me, I know." Asher rolled his eyes dramatically. "How about this? You buy me twenty credits worth of gas using your account"—he peeled another twenty off the stack and put it on top of the first—"and you keep an extra twenty for yourself."

"I do need to get my nails done." She picked up the money and held it between two fingertips like something gross. "But that's not cheap."

Asher shook his head and slapped a couple more twenties onto the counter.

•|•

After getting swindled by the gas attendant, Asher hit the I-15. Even though he stayed in the fast lane, self-driving cars still zoomed past him with mechanical precision. With their eyes glued to their devices, the passengers paid him no attention. They just tapped and swiped, looking busy, though they probably weren't doing anything important.

As he peeled away from traffic toward his exit, a wall of graffiti caught his eye. The spray paint manifesto, still vibrant with fresh paint, sent a chill down Asher's spine.

THEO CAGE
HEALER OF HUMANITY

Vandalism wasn't the only testament to the man's reach. Billboard after billboard advertised Theo's patented nano-treatments, which were now free for holders of a government-issued ID. That only ruled out illegal immigrants, criminals, and other off-the-grid types. Most citizens, though, had grown so attached to technology that they didn't mind the under-skin intrusion of privacy— especially if it gave them a little extra convenience in life.

Asher could understand why the population had so readily accepted the injection of minuscule robots into their bloodstreams. They loved the biological upgrades—the convenience of it all. He had to admit that if he didn't know the truth about Theo Cage, he probably would have been one of the first people to line up for free superpowers. As if on cue, Theo's voice started playing in his earbuds, a re-run of a speech delivered with the precision of a money-oiled machine. It hit all the right buttons at the right times.

"Your forefathers promised you a certain set of unalienable rights. These are rights that cannot be taken away. Among these are Life, Liberty, and the Pursuit of Happiness. And though they cannot be taken away, they can be given. My fellow Americans—your ancestors fought to secure your Liberty. Their efforts have allowed you to spend your time in the Pursuit of Happiness. But it is an unfathomable affront to your freedom that this time is so often cut short by a disease, an injury, or even a genetic flaw—something completely out of your control. America has given me so much, so I feel the need to give it something in return. To you, and someday to the rest of Earth's citizens, I will give the full rights promised to you so long ago—I will give you Life. Not fragile and fleeting, but Life eternal."

The final phrase swirled around Asher's mind as he drove through the backstreets. The rumination didn't end until he arrived at an apartment complex a few blocks from Fremont Street, where it got replaced by more gut-wrenching emotions. He parked in a covered spot adjacent to the building, took off his helmet, and wiped the sweat from his brow, which cooled quickly in the desert wind.

Asher's heart pumped relentlessly against his ribcage as he ascended the steps to the third floor. With each step, he felt heavier, slower. Finally, he made it to the door. His arm stopped itself completely before it could reach the painted wood.

Hesitation.

He took a deep breath and tried again. This time his body obeyed, and his knuckles made a sound against the door. He heard footsteps and saw the peephole darken.

Then the door opened.

Framed by the doorjamb, visual clutter surrounded her silhouette, but Asher only saw one thing—kind eyes drained of their usual glow. He could only breathe the simplest of greetings.

"Emily."

23

URANIUM

Aeva left to prepare a meal, leaving the crew of Starling II alone with their thoughts. For a while, none of them spoke. The surreal setting, the miraculous healing of his shoulder, the magnitude of Aeva's tale: all of it made Kapp feel like he was in a dream. He didn't know what to believe.

A technological threat? He looked at the attachment point where his bionic arm should've been. Sure, people had grown reluctant on technology, especially over Kapp's lifetime, but he doubted that humanity would destroy itself because of it. This alien—*no, this woman*—was clearly worried, though.

"How does Aeva know English?" Mara said.

Lost in his own questions and doubts, Kapp just shrugged.

Jesse, observant as ever, had at least one answer. "She said that Arca got an upload from Beacon Five before losing contact."

"Oh, that's right." Mara's eyes widened. "She's just so fluent. It's amazing."

"Forty-eight years to practice," Jesse said. "Or something like that."

Mara shook her head. "She just looks so young."

A condescending laugh fell from Kapp's lips. "You guys actually believe that she's some immortal human-alien hybrid sent to save humanity from destroying itself?"

The door slid open, and Aeva entered carrying a large platter.

"If you truly doubt the validity of my tale, I can show you evidence that corroborates it."

Kapp visibly shrunk. "I just—"

"And you shouldn't forget that you came to my home."

"Aeva, I didn't mean—"

"To me, you are the aliens."

Kapp hadn't thought of it that way. "We're just being cautious. This is all so strange."

"That's fair. I am sure you still have many questions." Aeva pushed the platter to the center of the table. "But first, let us eat."

Fruits and vegetables filled the platter, only some of which looked vaguely familiar. Aeva gestured toward the abundant cornucopia.

Mara hesitated. "Is it safe?" she asked Jesse.

"I assure you it is," Aeva said. "I just picked them from the garden."

With his stomach growling, Kapp picked up a vine of orange fruits. A tangy scent wafted off of the grape-like bundle.

"What are these?" he asked.

"Uvuus," Aeva said, plucking one off the vine. "They originally grew on the vast plains of Darqon, one of the first life-bearing planets that Alastar discovered—if you can believe that."

Kapp detected an inkling of sarcasm in Aeva's tone. "And they're edible?" he asked. "For humans?"

"Our stomachs are not so different." Aeva plopped the orb into her mouth, closed her eyes, and her cheeks dimpled in a massive grin. "They're my favorite," she said. "Try one."

Kapp bit down until the skin of the fruit broke, filling his mouth with a sweet tartness unlike anything he had ever tasted before. The involuntary smile that lifted his cheeks somehow made the taste even sweeter. For a moment he stopped thinking about the strange setting, the tales of technological doom, whether any of it was true.

"The Darqoni loved this crop for its jovial effects," Aeva said as Kapp handed the vine to Mara and Jesse. "Unfortunately, only a few specimens survived the Surge."

"A few specimens of this fruit?" Mara asked, beaming from its effects.

"No." The smile on Aeva's face vanished. "A few specimens out of the entire ecosystem."

With full stomachs and cheeks tired from smiling, the group left the pentagonal table to take a tour of the starship Arca. Kapp walked beside Aeva, Jesse and Mara followed close behind, and Lex bounced along at the rear of the procession.

"I have a question," Kapp said.

Aeva simply nodded.

"How old are you?"

The question might've seemed rude on Earth, but Aeva didn't react negatively. She just kept walking forward, her spine straight and her steps soft. She went so long without answering that Kapp couldn't tell whether she had even heard the question.

"I'm not quite sure," she said. "I stopped caring about that long ago. Skyborn do not age past their prime. Alastar gave us that gift."

Kapp looked back over his shoulder at Jesse, who shrugged before raising his own question.

"If y'all were on your way to Earth, why did you stop here?"

Aeva took another of her immortal pauses. "Arca is an extremely efficient vessel. Her propulsion is powered by an engine that manipulates gravitational fields."

Jesse looked like he could drool at the mention of the theoretical propulsion method.

"'To function, the engine requires what you call uranium. There's enough onboard to get to Earth, but not enough to leave. My scans detected deposits beneath this moon's surface, so I stopped here to mine more. Just in case." Aeva ran a hand through her dark brown hair, tucking a few pieces behind the slight point of her ear. "It's taking longer than expected."

Kapp took a few more slow steps. "Aeva, my people—they've been trying to communicate with you for almost a year now. If you speak our language, if you're trying to help us like you claim, why haven't you responded?"

"I could not. Alastar modified the communication systems to prevent the Surge from tracking us. Arca can only communicate with Beacon class ships, specifically the Beacons that Alastar sent out himself."

"So now what?" Kapp noticed that he had fallen a few paces behind, so he jogged back to his original position behind Aeva. "What happens next?"

"In a few months, we should have plenty of Uranium." She stopped walking and turned to the crew. "Then I will bring you to Earth. With no remaining Beacons, I have no option but to make the voyage without the usual preparations. I have waited many suns in hiding, but the time for caution has ended. I intend to stop humanity from reaching the same fate as the Architects, from creating their own Surge. It is my duty. "

"We're going home?" Mara asked, a joyful tear glistening behind her glasses.

Aeva nodded.

"How fast can Arca travel?" Jesse asked, placing a hand on Mara's back.

"Arca's max speed is approximately ten percent the speed of light." Jesse's jaw dropped. "However, it takes quite some time to reach that speed, and it's far too fast for such a short journey."

Kapp had trouble thinking of a couple hundred million kilometers as a short journey.

"Did Alastar make any other modifications?" Jesse asked, clearly geeking out.

"He did," Aeva said. "The shield that surrounds Arca. Her hull is protected by an ancient sentient species called the Artazoa, which grows in colonies similar to the coral of Earth, but in much harsher environments. Alastar discovered a way to communicate with the Artazoa. The colony that surrounds Arca provides a strong, self-healing surface—perfect for space travel. But more importantly, the species is able to reject unfriendly technologies."

"What do you mean?" Mara asked.

"Nothing inorganic may enter Arca without the Artazoa's consent."

Kapp recalled how the cameras stopped working when they got close to the entrance of the ship. He thought of the force field they had wandered past, the sterile quarantine room beyond, and the far-too-empty hallways.

"Aeva—where are the rest of your people?" he asked.

"Come," she said. "I will show you."

•|•

Aeva led them up one level and down a hallway that ended near the nucleus of the ship. At her touch, a door slid open to reveal a dark room beyond. When they passed the threshold, the lights switched on, illuminating several long rows of machines. A dull glow emanated between blinking lights. Walking forward, Kapp squinted at the vertical tubes that shot up from the base of each machine. Beyond the foggy liquid that filled the vessels, the sight of pink flesh made the hairs on his neck rise.

"For now, the rest of the Skyborn sleep," Aeva said, placing a hand on the vessel. "Until we find our new home."

Mara looked squeamish. Her eyes found the floor and stayed there.

"So, you're alone?" Kapp asked. "You've been alone this whole time?"

"Since Alastar left to destroy the Surge, yes." She frowned, a sight that Kapp realized he didn't enjoy. "Arca's gardens cannot support the dietary needs of a large crew. I've thought about waking a few…but they look at peace here."

Looking at the sleeping Skyborn, peace wasn't the first thing to come to Kapp's mind. "What was Alastar like?" he asked.

Aeva stared off into the distance. "Alastar was an incredible being with unmatched wisdom and empathy. This final mission of his is a selfless attempt to save not only our lives but all lives. For this, I will always revere him as the greatest hero."

An unspoken moment of silence descended over the four of them. Mara kept her eyes down, while Jesse studied the pods.

"What did the Architects look like?" Jesse asked.

Aeva's frown disappeared, but her eyes still carried some sadness. "Come with me."

She led them to the last row of pods. Unlike those in the Skyborn rows, each pod varied in size. They walked in silence, save for the low hum of Arca's systems. The same foggy liquid filled these vessels, but the inhabitants of each looked much different.

"Behold," Aeva said. "The last survivors of the Architect galaxy."

Kapp peered past the fog of the first pod to see a grayish figure. A hairless head sat at the top of its long neck. Slitted nostrils gave the beast a reptilian look, but Kapp found no scales on its body. Two thin arms hung at the side of its torso. He looked for its feet but found hooves instead—four of them.

"Wait, you're descended from one of those?" he asked.

Aeva laughed, a sound like gentle raindrops.

"This is a male Darqoni—the growers of the fruit you just ate." Aeva spoke as if she was reading from a textbook. "Their long necks helped them to see over the tall grasses of Darqon to spot approaching predators. Darqoni technology and culture were both primitive when Alastar found them, but their people were wise and peaceful. To the right is a female."

Mouths agape, the crew moved on to the next pod. The female Darqoni looked exactly like the male, but with a central row of nipple-like protrusions along its torso. Kapp felt like a kid touring a natural history museum for the first time. Mara studied the inscriptions etched into the metal below each pod.

"Next are the Kalgrin."

Aeva indicated a smaller pod containing what appeared to be a brown ball of fur. Upon further inspection, Kapp saw that most of the fur hung from the Kalgrin's massive head, covering its small body like a robe. Three-fingered hands shot out from either side, and each finger ended in a claw.

"They evolved on the rocky surface of Nureod, where their talons helped them to climb. Eventually, the atmosphere became toxic, so the species had to move into an underground system of tunnels to survive. How Alastar found them there is a remarkable tale, but one for another time."

Kapp shook his head at the craziness of it all. Not one, but several extraterrestrial beings floated in front of him, suspended in liquid—undeniable evidence of life thriving outside of Earth's minuscule atmosphere. Contemplating the odds of the encounter gave him a headache. Apparently sensing the overwhelming nature of everything, Aeva skipped a few pods.

"There will be time to see the rest," she said, "but here is the answer you seek. The last Architects."

The being in front of Kapp made the rest look like unfinished works of art. The Architect looked more human than any of the other species he had seen. He stood tall and elegant, with nearly transparent skin—pale and powerful like a marble statue. Beyond his thin lids, the being had massive green eyes, windows to the brain that radiated some profound, eternal wisdom. The Architect, perfectly proportional and symmetrical, floated in his pod with a godlike stature.

Kapp only looked away to get a glimpse of the next in line, a being obviously female. Her naked body seemed so human that he averted his eyes, avoiding her breasts and focusing instead on her hands and feet. They had five fingers, five toes, fingernails like his own. Despite how foreign it looked, her face was soft, kind, even beautiful. She had an exotic flair, not unlike Aeva's.

"How long have they been like this?" Kapp asked.

"Hundreds of years, perhaps." Aeva took a breath. Kapp thought she looked rather hopeless. "I have not seen them any other way in my lifetime."

"You will."

Kapp wasn't sure why he said it, only that for some reason he couldn't stand to see Aeva upset. This woman, who he had run into on an alien ship millions of miles from home, who claimed to be born among the stars, an impossible stranger—somehow she made the rest of the incredible beings in the room disappear.

•|•

"I have a gift for you," Aeva said as she led Kapp, Jesse, and Mara down another empty hallway. The final door slid open in front of them. They walked through it, directly onto a raised deck that overlooked a massive room. Light came from the ceiling, illuminating the first half of the cavern.

Unlike the natural curvature found in the rest of the ship, the architecture in this room looked more orderly and angular. Metallic flooring filled the central third of the room, and on either side stood walled-off partitions, lined with strips of lighting, and filled with foreign technologies—odds and ends that Kapp had no name for. The space, though cluttered in places, shone without grease or grime.

"This is the hangar bay," Aeva said. The platform lowered until it was level with the flight deck below. "It's where Beacons are—sorry, where Beacons *were* launched and received."

"Amazing," Jesse said, eying the runway in the center of the room. "I meant to ask you before, but how do you manipulate gravity onboard?"

"It's one of the Architects' most advanced discoveries," she said. "I will give you access to a translated knowledge base if you wish. But first, your gift."

After a few more paces forward, the rest of the bay lit up. At the other end of the hangar sat a beat up hunk of metal that looked out of place in the pristine environment. With an upturned palm, Aeva gestured toward their gift—Starling II.

"How did you do that?" Jesse asked, picking up his pace toward their battered ship.

Aeva let her usually straight lips curve into a minuscule smile. "Gravity."

•|•

Aeva used some of her odd tools to help Kapp and the others enter their ship. Passing through the door from the unknown to the familiar shocked Kapp's system. After exploring the incredible halls of Arca, he felt claustrophobic in the tin can of a spacecraft. The only things he cared to get from the ship were his bionic arm and his last case of Glenlivet, so he and Aeva sat at a makeshift table while Jesse and Mara gathered their belongings. Aeva flinched when Kapp twisted the prosthetic on.

"Shit," he said. "It's still not working."

Aeva sat at the table with perfect posture. "It's the Artazoa defending Arca from anything—unnatural."

"Well, can you make it stop?" Kapp let the dead weight fall to the table, and a loud crack echoed through the cabin. "I kind of need my arm."

"It will be done," she said, staring at the limb like it was something dead. "What happened to your…real arm?"

"An explosion took it off, but I hardly remember," Kapp said. "I was five."

A half-truth—he couldn't remember everything, but he also never tried to get past that mental barrier, though he often had nightmares about the event. With his good arm, Kapp reached into the case beside the table and pulled out a bottle.

"Scotch?" he offered. "It's expensive."

"What is that?" she asked.

"Alcohol," Kapp said. He twisted off the cap and poured a healthy dose straight into his mouth.

"Oh. No, thank you." Aeva made a haughty expression. "Ethanol inhibits brain function."

"That's the point," he said. He took a sip and then inhaled sharply, barely making a face.

Jesse and Mara came back carrying bundles of clothes and a few personal items, mostly Mara's books and puzzles.

"Y'all done?" Jesse asked, dropping his bundle into an empty plastic crate.

"Yep," Kapp said.

Aeva began to rise. "Then I will take you to your new chambers."

"Wait." Jesse sat down at the table. "I've been thinking about your problem—about why you've been on Phobos all this time."

Aeva just looked at him, waiting for him to continue.

"You're mining uranium to power your engines, which will take a while, but you're also in a hurry to get to Earth."

She nodded.

"Well," Jesse said. "I just realized that we have some—some uranium, that is—right here on Starling II."

Kapp, realizing what Jesse was getting at, smiled at the resourcefulness of his flight engineer. But then he frowned, recalling the thing that nearly killed them all. His eyes found the central column of the ship before Jesse could point at it.

"Should be uranium in the missile."

24

CHAOS

Kapp had no idea how long he slept. Disoriented, he awoke in the small room that Aeva had brought him to the night before. Still half asleep, he stared at the ceiling, which radiated a soft, metallic glow similar to the outside of the ship. His bed, a simple pad, made no noise as he rolled off it and looked for his shirt.

"Good morning," a voice said.

Kapp inhaled sharply. Aeva stood in the doorway, her ever-present sidekick Lex rubbing his fur against her heels.

"Morning," he said, cringing at the smell of his own breath.

"We need to talk," Aeva said.

Kapp pulled on his shirt, noticing that his right arm was finally working.

"Thanks for this," he said, flexing metal fingers.

"You're welcome."

She sat down on the bed beside him, and Lex jumped into her lap.

"Where's my crew?" he asked, scratching the charcoal cat between the ears.

"Mara is busy studying the language of the Architects, and Jesse is extracting the uranium from your bomb."

Coated with disgust, the word *bomb* came out of her mouth like a dagger.

"What can I do?" Kapp asked, turning his torso to stretch. The pain in his shoulder was gone, but the nerve damage in his lower back flared up violently.

"Can I trust you, Kapp?"

If Aeva had said his name before, he couldn't remember it. The word touched down on his eardrum like a butterfly. He noticed how close she sat to him, so close he could smell the mild scent of exotic fruit exuding from her skin.

"Why wouldn't you?" he asked.

"You came here with a weapon." Aeva let a drop of anger leak through her usual emotionless facade. "You could have destroyed everything."

"But we didn't." Kapp stared into her green eyes. "We carried the weapon as defense—just in case things went sour."

"I know that," she said. "While you slept, Jesse and Mara recounted the tale of Eli's betrayal and your heroic efforts to stop him. I thank you for that."

"Then why don't you trust me?" Kapp's eyebrows dropped a notch. "I almost died to stop him."

"It's not you exactly," she said, reaching to pet Lex. "It's just—"

She looked away, a few of her fingers grazing over Kapp's hand as the two of them caressed her beloved pet.

"What is it?" he asked. He had to stifle the accidental electricity that had shot from her skin to his.

"I'm afraid," she said.

"Don't be," he said. "Fear is no good."

"You sound like"—her bottom lip quivered before she continued—"you sound like my father."

"How so?" Kapp asked.

A sad smile appeared on Aeva's face. "Alastar used to tell me that love is always stronger than fear."

"Well," Kapp said. A short burst of air escaped his nostrils. "I don't know anything about that."

"Neither do I," Aeva said. "Fear is all I've known. It's clear that someone on Earth wants Arca destroyed."

Kapp hadn't thought about it in a while, but he had an unknown enemy on Earth as well, someone who didn't care about his life or the lives of his crew. The thought boiled his blood.

"I won't let that happen."

Aeva shook her head, just barely, silently staring into the distance. "You are just one man."

Kapp didn't know what to say at first. She wasn't wrong, but his thoughts rose in protest against the assumption that he was powerless.

"One man almost destroyed this place," he said, looking around the strange room. "And one man stopped him."

Aeva smiled, snapped out of her distant gaze, and made eye contact with Kapp. "If most Earthlings have the same courage as you," she said, rising to leave, "humanity might just stand a chance."

•|•

"What's it like?" Aeva asked. "On Earth."

She and Kapp walked through Arca's gardens, an expansive room with high ceilings and rows of plants that grew from holes in the metallic floor. Kapp noticed that despite their exotic origins, most of the plants still had green leaves. Chlorophyll seemed to be a universal pigment. All of the strange plants reached toward the artificial sunlight that filled the entirety of the ceiling.

Kapp brushed a vine out of his way like a curtain. "What do you mean?"

"I've seen pictures," she said, "and I've studied some of your many cultures. I know what your planet looks like. At least what it looked like forty-eight years ago, but what is it like being there?"

Kapp didn't know how to answer. In truth, he always felt like he didn't belong there, like the world was out to get him. But he also had good moments, days when he didn't crave the emptiness of outer space.

"It can be overwhelming." Kapp paused, figuring out how to best phrase what he wanted to say. "It's chaotic. Things happen for no reason. It seems like most people just flail around with no regard for what they're doing, for the consequences of their actions. Sometimes I wish there was more—I don't know, order. Silence."

Aeva plucked a ripe uvuu from the vine. "Chaos is not unique to Earth."

"I know that. I just—" The words got caught in his throat, words that he had never spoken aloud. "I feel stuck when I'm there, caught in the current of everything."

"Most things cannot be controlled." She flicked the small fruit directly at Kapp's forehead.

"What the—what was that for?"

"Chaos," she said. "Could you have stopped the uvuu from colliding with your face?"

He regarded her for a moment. "That wasn't chaos. You planned it."

"One person's plan can be another's chaos. You cannot control the intentions of others, only your own." Aeva plucked another uvuu off the branch but ate it this time. "Could you have stopped it?"

Aeva's question reminded Kapp of stoned conversations with Asher, the kind that went far beyond small talk. "I could have stopped you if I knew you were going to throw it."

"But one cannot see the future," she said. "You're suffering from illusions of control. It's impossible to predict the chaos. You can only react to it."

The debater inside of Kapp rose to the surface. "You're predicting a catastrophic end to humanity. That's what you're trying to prevent."

"Ends are inevitable." Aeva picked another uvuu. "This has been learned from the past. I have seen it. I only aim to delay the end of something very precious and rare. I want to protect life as it is."

"History repeats itself?" he asked, citing the old cliché.

"Precisely," she said, tossing the fruit at his face.

This time he caught it.

•|•

They walked from the garden to the hangar bay and crossed the runway to where Jesse was working. The first time they had visited Starling, nothing onboard worked, so the lights shining out of the ship's portholes surprised Kapp.

As if reading his mind, Aeva said, "Jesse required power to extract the uranium, so I spoke with the Artazoa."

"How do you do that?" he asked.

"I will show you another time."

They walked up a ramp and entered Starling II through the airlock. Surrounded by tools and removed panels, Jesse sat beside the central tube that held the missile.

"How's it coming, J?" Kapp asked, patting his friend on the back.

Sweat dripped from Jesse's mop of hair while he worked. "Almost there."

"Great."

Aeva looked around the room. "You traveled how long to reach Phobos?"

"About eight months," Kapp said. "Why?"

"That is a long time to spend in such close quarters."

Kapp chuckled. "We were asleep for most of it." He turned to Jesse. "Need anything?"

"Negative."

"Wanna see the cockpit?" he asked Aeva.

She nodded. Without thinking, Kapp grabbed her hand to lead her toward the upper deck, and she pulled it out of his grasp.

"Sorry," he said, shrugging off the sudden awkwardness.

Aeva moved gracefully through the tight spaces of the ship, while Kapp fumbled. When they reached the cockpit, a chill dripped down Kapp's spine. He hadn't been up there since he and the crew removed Eli's body. Darkness filled the cabin, except for a few blinking LED lights, including the indicator light on his tablet.

"Jax," he said. The display flashed to life. "Turn on the cockpit lights."

"Right away, sir," the voice of the intelligent assistant chimed.

The cabin lights came on, illuminating Aeva. She stood near the entry, her posture rigid and her face tight.

"Who did you just communicate with?" she asked.

"No one—just a computer."

"I see," she said. Kapp detected a hint of skepticism in her tone.

"Jax," he said. "Introduce yourself."

Jax's British accent came through the intercom speakers. "Hello, miss. I am Jax, the personalized intelligent assistant of Commander Kapp Adams. I am a highly specialized assistant, but my code is a subset of the Transcendent Response Unit system developed by Cage Industries. Feel free to ask me anything, and I'll do my best to answer."

Kapp watched Aeva as she listened. Throughout the introduction, her expression shifted from confusion to fear, and then to anger.

"Turn it off," she said. "Now."

"What?" he asked, but then he remembered her dark tale about technology. "Oh, Jax? He's harmless."

"Harmless?" Aeva asked, raising her voice. "There is nothing harmless about a computer impersonating life."

"It's not like that." Kapp picked up his tablet. "Jax, you're not going to take over the world, right?"

"Not yet, anyway," the machine joked.

Kapp laughed, and Aeva stood like a statue with her arms folded.

"If you can't see why this is dangerous, how can I convince the people of Earth that it is?"

Kapp wanted to argue, but he decided against it. "Look, I'm sorry. I forgot about your little phobia."

She scoffed at him and looked away.

"Jax, power down."

"Gladly, sir," Jax said. "But first, you must acknowledge an important alert. There is one message in your inbox tagged as *URGENT*. Shall I open it?"

Kapp turned to Aeva, who still avoided eye contact.

"Is that okay?" he asked. "It's from Earth."

"I suppose," she said, "but then you must turn it off."

"Okay, fine. Let's get Mara. We should look at it together."

"I'll send for her."

•|•

Escorted by Lex, Mara was the last to arrive in their chosen meeting spot, the same pentagonal table from before. Jesse's face lit up when she stepped into the room. He sat behind a wrapped package and a pile of alien fruit.

"What's going on?" Mara asked.

"We got a message from Groom Lake," Kapp said, pouring some of his scotch into a geometric vessel.

"I thought comm was down."

Jesse cut in. "I fixed our receivers before we left the ship."

"What did it say?" she asked, taking a seat beside Jesse.

"We're about to find out," Kapp said.

He picked up his tablet, and the four of them crowded around one side of the table. Kapp tapped the icon for Mission Control and opened up the message. The video buffered and then began to play, revealing a tight shot of Director Holden behind his desk.

"Groom Lake to the crew of Starling II. The IES is aware of your crash landing on Phobos, and we hope that this message reaches you. Approximately two months ago, contact was lost between Mission Control and Starling II."

"No shit," Kapp said.

Mara elbowed him. "Shhh."

"The IES immediately launched an investigation," Holden continued. *"Our data logs showed that Eli Morgan awoke from stasis just before the comm systems went down. As I'm sure you've found out by now, you have been the victims of an act of sabotage. Our investigation uncovered threats made against Eli Morgan's family, threats that caused him to compromise our entire mission. We also discovered that information about the nature of our mission has been leaked to a radical group just before launch, a group that believes contact with extraterrestrials will lead to the demise of humanity. Upon detainment, leaders of this group admitted to being behind the threats."*

Kapp thought of some of Eli's last words, the cries that came through the intercom: *If I don't do it, they'll hurt him.* Thinking about what they had to do to Eli, Kapp's chest tightened, and his throat began to hurt. He thought of Eli's son growing up without a father, wondered if the kid had a mother in the picture. Kapp had grown up with neither parent, but it was a loss that he couldn't truly remember.

Holden's voice broke Kapp out of his dark thoughts. *"Just before Eli woke from stasis, Asher West provided the media with photos of the object on Phobos."*

Kapp, Jesse, and Mara shared a look at the mention of their friend. Kapp shook his head.

"How he acquired them, we haven't yet found out, but we believe that he is a part of the conspiracy. West is currently on the run from the authorities. They have a lead on his location, so we expect to learn more soon."

"I told him about the photos," Kapp admitted, his voice panicky. "This is so fucked up."

Mara shushed him again as Holden's message continued.

"Commander Adams and the crew of Starling II, when you receive this message, if you're still alive—just know that the whole world now knows your story. Earth is watching, and we'll do everything in our power to bring you home. Just let us know that you're alive."

Jesse and Mara nodded along to the speech, while Aeva listened with little emotional response.

"Finally, if you've made contact with extraterrestrial beings, do your best to share with them the message that you were sent to share—that we welcome them to Earth with open arms."

The screen went blank as the transmission ended, and Kapp immediately shut off the device as he promised. The four of them returned to their seats in silence, individually processing the new information.

Aeva spoke first, her calm voice a contrast to the frenzy building in Kapp's mind. "It comforts me to know that the fiends who wanted to attack Arca have been detained."

"I'm glad they caught the bastards too, but they have Asher all wrong," Kapp said, turning to his friends. "There's no way he was a part of this. He wouldn't do that to me."

"I know," Mara said, reaching for his hand to comfort him. "We'll figure this out."

Kapp took a long sip of his scotch.

Aeva turned to Jesse. "How much fuel were you able to extract?"

"I have no scale to weight it, but here it is," he said, pushing the package across the table.

"Thank you," she said, accepting the gift and standing up. "This looks like quite enough. Tonight I will retract the drills and prepare the gravity engines. Rest well, everyone. The next time the sun sets over the crater's edge—we leave for Earth."

25

THE TRUTH

Though the beauty remained in Emily's eyes, their usual kindness vacated quickly upon recognition of Asher. Where there had once been a clear, blue sea, Asher saw only troubled waters—a slow storm finally raging. Thunderclouds seemed to gather in her irises, sparking and crackling, threatening to release their energy. Her pupils dilated, a tightening and deepening whirlpool. Asher tried to smile, to say something, but he couldn't make his mouth move. Without warning, Emily's open hand—like a flash of lightning—struck his cheek. The door slammed shut, a sound like a thunderclap.

Asher let the pain in his face dull before rapping his knuckles on the door once again. This time he stood a few paces back, bracing himself for another violent outburst.

Silence.

He tried again, but Emily's shoulder remained cold. Resting his forehead against the door, he tried to think of something to say—anything that might quiet the storm.

"Emily," he said, raising his voice so it could carry through the closed door. "I deserved that."

"Go away!" she yelled, her voice muffled by the door.

"Emily, listen—"

"I don't want to talk to you, Ash." Even through the barrier, he could hear her cries. "Please—just leave."

These words hurt him worse than the slap. Asher didn't know what to say. He felt like some vital organ had been beamed out of him.

"If you wanted to break up with me," she continued, "you could have at least been a man about it!"

"Emily, I—"

"Seriously, Ash, how old are you? You can't just disappear like that." Another bout of silence, spoiled only by the sound of tears. "I thought something terrible happened to you."

"I can explain." Asher reached to pull at his own hair, an old habit, but his new cut made it impossible. "Just let me in, and we'll talk."

A palpable silence filled Asher's ears, twisting his stomach into nervous knots. He was definitely missing an organ.

"Emily, I came here"—tears came to his eyes, choking him up against his best efforts to keep his composure—"I just came here to say goodbye."

The peephole darkened.

"Well, you're a little late," Emily said. "Only dumbasses say goodbye *after* they leave."

Asher smiled, despite how terrible he felt. "Then I'm the biggest dumbass of all."

"Yep!" Emily's footsteps started moving away. "Now go home."

"I have no home. Emily, I—"

"What, you're fucking homeless now?"

"No, I mean—I have a home." Asher let out a dramatic sigh. "It's hard to explain. Will you just—"

"I don't care, Ash." Audible tears escaped through cracks in the doorjamb. "You broke my heart."

Asher was about to give up. He turned away in frustration and saw a few people eying him suspiciously. Probably tenants of the apartment complex, but Asher couldn't be sure. His paranoia kicked up a notch.

"Listen, Emily, it's not safe for me out here." He turned back, rested his head against the door. "Five minutes. That's all I need."

Asher waited for her to say something, for the door to open. Instead, he heard her walking away again, further withdrawing from him. An internal door creaked and slammed, and then there was silence. Thoroughly defeated, Asher checked over the rail to see if anyone was still watching him. He planned to make a quick and sad escape from the premises, thinking how stupid he had been to even hope for a positive interaction. Of course, she would be pissed. He had completely ghosted her. Vanished without a word. And even though it hadn't been his fault, he regretted it.

He turned to leave, to descend the stairs back to a sad existence, but the sound of footsteps returned, followed by the hesitant cracking of Emily's door. With more than a frightened second to look at her, Asher saw that she wore a conservative maternity blouse, which hung loosely over her baby bump, so different from the tight, sexy getups she usually wore. In her hand, she held something she might throw at him, but he didn't know how much damage she could do with…a bag of frozen peas?

"I hate myself for this," Emily said, scanning Asher's red face, "but I kind of feel bad about hitting you."

There she was, the Emily that couldn't hurt a fly.

"Here," she said, offering him the makeshift ice pack.

He took it in silent gratitude. Bringing the cold relief to his face, hanging his head in shame, he followed Emily into the safety of her apartment. Wordlessly, they sat at her small dining room table.

"Two minutes," she said coldly.

"I just want you to know the truth, and then I'll leave you alone—forever if that's what you want." Asher drew in a pained breath. "Bad things are happening, and I just want you to be ready for them. I want to keep you safe, Emily. I want to keep you safe because I—"

The words got stuck in his throat. He was too scared to say them—too afraid to put himself out there. His eyes automatically avoided hers.

"Because what?" Emily asked, finally breaking the silence that had built up after Asher's sudden choke.

"You're the last"—Asher forced himself to look her in the eyes, to be a man for once—"You're the only person left on this planet that I truly care about."

"Well, that sucks," she said, her tone not angry, but definitely not pleased. "What happened, Ash?"

Asher swallowed loudly. "Do you remember Kapp Adams?"

Emily looked down at the curve of her pregnancy and scoffed. "How could I forget?"

Under the table, Asher's fingers fidgeted with a hair tie that he still kept on his wrist, even after chopping off all his hair. According to the digital clock in the kitchen, he had already wasted one of his allotted minutes.

"Well, Kapp was in danger—shipwrecked—and the director of our space program lied to the public about it."

Emily narrowed her eyelids and rested her chin in her palm. "And?"

"And I wanted to get Holden fired, so I leaked official documents, proof of"—Asher knew the words sounded crazy, so he hesitated to say them loud, choosing instead to whisper them—"proof of the aliens."

"Oh, god," Emily said, shaking her head in anger. "I thought you came here to seriously apologize, Ash. I need you to—"

"I leaked the photos to Lana, and she ran an article in the—"

"You're talking about that hoax."

"It wasn't a hoax, Emily."

She scoffed. "How gullible do you think I am?"

"The IES came after me for what I did. That's why I didn't come back."

"Okay, I'm done with this."

"Emily, you have to believe me. There's more too, I can prove it."

"Well, I just think you're lying. It's time for you to go."

"I'm not lying, Em. It's not safe here—that's the truth. I want to protect you and your baby—that's the truth." His voice rose with his body, with confidence. "I love you—that's the truth. There's only one lie I told to you today, and it's one you're going to forgive me for, because you mean the world to me, Emily, and I will not lose you."

Then she paused, stopped in her tracks to take a second look at Asher. Slowly, the storm clouds in her gaze dissipated, until all that remained were clear skies. A single drop fell from where the clouds once were, rolled down her cheek.

"So, I lied," Asher said. "I didn't come here to say goodbye, Emily."

He took a chance, reached out to grab her hand.

"I want you to come with me."

26

BLACKOUT

"This is Commander Adams to Groom Lake. I'm recording this brief message to update Earth on our status. As you can see, the crew and I—with the exception of Eli Morgan—are alive and well. We survived the crash-landing on Phobos. Instead of resigning to a slow death here, we suited up to complete our objective. The object on Phobos has been identified as a starship, and the existence of extraterrestrial life has been confirmed."

Kapp imagined the cheering that would erupt in mission control upon receiving this Earth-shattering revelation.

"We've made contact with the ship's inhabitants and communication channels have been established. At the risk of sounding cliché, I'm happy to say that they come in peace. And there's more good news. Since Starling II is out of commission, the beings we've encountered have agreed to take us home."

Kapp stayed purposely vague.

"Our estimated time of arrival at the launch facility is November 20th—just after dark. The captain of this ship has some requests, which we fully expect you to honor. First, our landing is contingent upon you setting up a secure perimeter. She's worried about being attacked so we'll need full defense. I trust you have time to do that. Second, she also requests that you set up a meeting with world leaders to happen upon our arrival. She has an urgent message to share with Earth. For the sake of security, our arrival must remain a secret until

after this meeting. There's no time to tell you everything now, so we will fully debrief upon arrival. Until then, expect no further transmissions from Starling II. Commander Adams out."

Kapp watched the scripted video for a second time before nodding to Jesse.

"I'll set it to automatically uplink in one hour," Jesse said. He turned to Aeva and asked, "That's enough time, right?"

"Yes," she said. "Your ship can be safely ejected by then."

Exiting the hangar bay, Kapp nodded a final goodbye to the vehicle that got them to Phobos.

•|•

Later that day, Aeva took the crew up to a level they'd never been to before and led them toward the front of the ship. A door slid open at the end of the hallway, revealing a crescent-shaped control panel. The sight beyond the panel made Kapp gasp. A star-filled sky appeared before them, completely unobstructed, untainted by the haze of space-proof glass, like a clear pool that they could just dive into. The universal mural stretched out around them like a canopy.

"Are you ready?" Aeva asked.

"Let's go home," Jesse said. He put an arm around Mara and pulled her close.

"Home," she said, smiling. "And I thought we'd be stuck here forever. Thank you, Aeva."

Aeva dipped her head once, and Kapp took a seat in one of the teardrop-shaped chairs that lined the view screen.

"How do I strap in?" he asked.

"It's not necessary."

Aeva took a seat in the center of the console, and the rest of them spread out around her. She placed her hand around a black orb to her right, and then a hologram appeared before her, displaying an array of foreign data. Kapp couldn't decipher any of it, but Mara looked through the symbols, nodding along in recognition at some of them.

With a slide of Aeva's hand, a map overlaid the dome around them, augmenting their reality with live navigational charts. A five-sided icon slowly grew and shrunk near the bottom right corner of the display.

"That's Earth," Aeva said.

The stars shifted down and to the left until the icon was directly in the center, disorienting Kapp because he felt no movement.

"Incredible," Jesse said.

Aeva rolled her fingers backward over the orb. Kapp watched her focus as the holograms around her changed their form, bending and shifting with each of her slight movements. His gaze shifted back and forth between Aeva and the sea of stars. A bottomless pool of beauty sat both beside him and before him. Kapp kept his eyes on one as Arca dove into the other.

On the second day after leaving Phobos and the wreck of Starling II behind, Kapp rose from a nap, his stomach aching with hunger. He exited his simple dwelling and made his way to Arca's onboard gardens, where he hoped to snag a handful of uvuus to snack on. The doors slid apart silently, revealing a forest of alien foliage.

After navigating the lush labyrinth, he found the uvuu plant and snapped a hefty bunch off the vine. Plucking the fruits off one by one, he popped them into his mouth, savoring their delicious flavor and intoxicating effects as he browsed his other options. He strolled through the rows of plants as if they were aisles at a grocery store. After deciding on a melon-sized piece of fruit that looked like a cross between a banana and a grapefruit, Kapp wanted to bring the feast back to his room. He tried to go back the way he came, but he couldn't remember the route he had taken through the maze of plants.

Usually, this would anger him, but since boarding the alien ship, he carried an extra ounce of patience. In fact, his body and mind had never felt better. This feeling was bolstered even further by the uvuu dopamine rush. Instead of stressing about the situation, he decided to wander while he ate, taking in the sights and smells of the garden. Eventually, the sound of water drew him toward a curve in the scenery. He came around the corner and peered ahead to find the cause of the sound.

Kapp almost couldn't see through the steam rising from the floor, but then his eyes adjusted. Streams of water fell like rain from a wide circle of holes set in the ceiling. His gaze followed their path, not to the floor, where the droplets splashed against the smooth surface before draining away, but to the woman bathing herself beneath the downpour.

Aeva stood with her profile facing the gardens, rubbing some kind of spongy plant against the naked flesh of her sides. Kapp's jaw opened a few notches. He hid behind a tall shrub with purple flowers, intending to leave before she could see him—but he couldn't resist. He took another peek through an opening in the foliage and saw the lather forming in her hair, slowly dripping down to trace the curve of her silhouette.

She stood like a goddess carved out of marble, an angel painted on the ceiling of some ancient chapel—a true masterpiece. The beauty of what Kapp saw physically hurt him. It twisted his insides into a tight knot. Aeva—the kind of woman that could break the hearts of men by merely existing—stood before him in her natural form. Bare. Perfect. It shattered Kapp's heart knowing he had no chance with the exotic beauty.

Overwhelmed with longing, his body tensed. He dropped the melon, which rolled out from his hiding place, and fumbled in a futile attempt to catch the runaway fruit. Cupping her breasts, Aeva turned toward the dull thud, looking for the cause of it. Eyes scanning the lush gardens, she stopped the water and wrapped herself in a white cloth. Soon she found the fruit on the floor—but Kapp was long gone.

It took Arca only days to cover the distance that it took Starling II months to travel. Mara and Jesse filled their time consuming whatever information Aeva would give them, while Kapp explored the ship and tried to learn how to fly it by watching Aeva—any excuse to be near her.

On the final day of their journey, she took him down to the lowest level, into a small room filled with dim blue light. Over Aeva's shoulder, a metallic pillar stood in the middle of the room.

Indented symbols covered its entire surface, just like those Kapp had seen when he entered Arca. The imprint of the human hand stood out the most. He thought of the hands of the Architects, how similar they were to his own, and then his mind drifted to the other beings he had witnessed—sleeping in their tubes.

"They're all hands," he said, voicing his realization. "The symbols, I mean."

Aeva nodded her confirmation. "The hands of the sentient races—the known ones, at least."

"Wow," Kapp said, mesmerized by the twinkling reflections that glanced off the pillar. "So many."

"There were." Aeva stared ahead at the glittering column and didn't speak for a long time. "Do you wonder why they were all so similar?"

Kapp let his eyes drift between the symbols. "I don't know," he said. "I guess because survival requires certain traits. It helps to be able to pick things up. Tools."

She ran her fingers across the pillar. "Alastar thought that there might have been some connection between all life, that life sprang forth from seeds scattered by the same gardener ages ago."

Kapp scoffed. "Oh yeah, then where's the gardener?"

Aeva didn't answer.

"You're talking about gods," he continued. "Honestly, I don't believe there are any."

Kapp had always been a skeptic, at least since he developed a full brain. In his opinion, it was impossible to be an astronaut and a theist at the same time.

"Not gods in the sense that you think of them," Aeva said. "Just advanced beings. Alastar thought that the Artazoa might have been the gardeners, that their willingness to protect life might have come from a desire to help their own creations."

"Are they?"

"It's hard to tell," she said, "but they are the most advanced lifeforms that Alastar ever came in contact with. Intelligence with few physical needs. Power without selfish desire."

They circled the pillar as they spoke. "Where did Alastar find them?" Kapp asked.

"He didn't," she said. "They found him. Come."

Aeva gestured toward the indent of the human hand. "Speak to them," she said.

With a bit of hesitance, Kapp placed his hand on the pillar. He had no idea what to do, so he just closed his eyes.

"Hello," he said and instantly felt stupid.

Aeva laughed, a magical sound that echoed off the walls of the chamber.

"Not with your words," she said. "With your mind. Try again."

Kapp closed his eyes once again, but this time he kept his mouth shut. He heard only the sound of his own breathing, the rhythm slowing as scattered thoughts thinned out until only the breaths remained. The soft darkness of his eyelids transformed into an immense darkness, eternally deep and black. He felt as if he could look into it forever and feel nothing, as if time itself had stopped. Kapp heard a click, and the vision before him began to change.

A single spot of white light appeared, drowning in a sea of black. It grew slowly and steadily, but still, the darkness smothered it. A sense of time passing overwhelmed Kapp's senses, and he could no longer feel his body. One light became two—and then four—and their numbers kept multiplying until Kapp thought they might finally eclipse the darkness. But behind each light, he could sense an eternal depth, one that he knew could never be filled.

And the lights gathered together, stronger in number but still hopeless. Kapp heard the sounds of struggle, smelled the blood of billions. And the darkness surrounded, crushing the unified light into a nearly invisible point. That final, soft glow flickered, then vanished. Time stood still before jumping forward. When it returned, the flicker became a flare that burned the shadows back into their depths.

•|•

Kapp woke up soaked in sweat, the vision still vividly fresh in his mind. It took him a moment to recognize the bedchamber he had been assigned to, filled with just a simple pad and his few belongings. Still in the same clothes, he thought he couldn't have been out long. Every time he blinked he saw the lights.

What did it all mean?

Eventually, he crawled out of bed and wandered through Arca's halls, now sensing the life within the shimmering metallic walls. He went to the usual meeting spot, the room with the pentagonal table, but found it empty.

"Jesse," he called. "Mara."

A gentle touch tickled his ankle, and he looked down to see Lex.

"Hey," he said. "Where are they?"

The charcoal cat shot down the hallway. He stopped at the apex of a curve and looked back, checking to see if Kapp followed. The routine continued until they reached Arca's cockpit.

"Finally," Mara said, the first to notice Kapp's entrance. She sat up from the console and stood in front of Kapp, followed shortly after by Jesse. "Are you okay?"

"Yeah—yeah, what happened?"

"I'm not sure." Aeva seemed to appear out of nowhere. Over her tight black clothing, she wore some kind of robe that ended in a point just behind her knees. Her long brown hair was tied back in an intricate, spiraled bun. "You stood at the pillar for a very long time and then—"

"You blacked out," Jesse said.

The phrase meant something entirely new to Kapp after seeing the strange vision of the darkness consuming the light.

"How long?"

"Quite long," Aeva said, gesturing toward the picturesque dome window above the control console. "We've almost arrived."

"You missed atmospheric entry," Jesse said. "It was amazing."

Spots of light filled the lower half of the viewport. What Kapp's peripheral vision had interpreted as a sky full of stars was actually an array of city lights coming from Earth. Ahead, the lights disappeared in the fading twilight of a recent sunset over the curved horizon. The beauty of the landscape and their impending arrival made Kapp forget about the blackout.

"Wow—okay, are you ready?" he asked Aeva.

"I have prepared for this my whole life," she said, peering into the distance.

•|•

Mesmerized by the sights ahead, Kapp sat in one of the teardrop-shaped chairs as Aeva piloted Arca toward their destination. He had never before seen Earth from such a picturesque vantage point. The course they had charted took them on a discreet journey toward the Mojave Desert. Nighttime provided the rest of the cover that they needed.

Avoiding the bright coast and dense population of Southern California, Arca crossed the line between black sea and dry land near the Oregon-California border. Aeva flew the ship over vast national forests, avoiding as many residential areas as possible as they arced south toward Death Valley. In the clear of the desert, she began to lower their altitude and straighten out their route.

"We're now on a direct course to the rendezvous point," Aeva said. She hadn't spoken during the entire descent. "It won't be long now."

"Are you nervous?" Mara asked.

"I feel a strange emotion," she said. "But I will be alright."

"I didn't think of this before," Kapp said, "but do you have any way to prove what you're gonna tell them—about where Arca came from?"

"You have seen the proof."

Kapp considered her answer. By then—especially after communicating with the Artazoa—he completely believed her story, but he worried that the world might not. Within minutes they reached their destination, a landing strip in the center of the Groom Lake complex. Trenches lined the fences of the complex, a recent addition.

"Secure enough?" Kapp asked, and Aeva nodded.

Soon, Arca came to a stop over the landing pad, where it hovered for a moment before dropping in altitude. The ship landed so gently that Kapp didn't even feel a bump when they touched down on the asphalt.

"Let's do this," he said.

Once Arca settled onto the hard ground, Aeva, Kapp, Jesse, and Mara made their way to the lower deck. As always, the cat bounced along close behind. They entered the white quarantine chamber where the crew had spent their first hours on the ship.

When the door sealed, Aeva turned to the crew.

"I've put not only my life but a treasure of life in your hands," she said. "Promise me you'll protect Arca at all costs."

The group nodded.

"We promise," Kapp said.

"Thank you."

The floor opened up, and gravity shifted. Slowly, they sank down the stark white tunnel until they stood on the forcefield below. Surrounded by the handprints of the sentient races, they watched as a robotic dolly wheeled a wide ramp to their location. Shut down by the Artazoa, the bulbs that lit the edges of the ramp dimmed when they reached a certain threshold.

Kapp's metal fingers tapped a nervous rhythm on the side of his leg. He wondered what everyone would think of the woman born in space—half human, half something else entirely. To his side, Aeva placed her hand on one of the shimmering symbols and spoke a single word in her native language. Kapp didn't know what it meant, but the sound waves seemed to radiate a powerful energy.

The ramp arrived just beneath them, and the forcefield that they stood upon grew to encompass its upper edge. Floodlights came on, illuminating a set of armed guards marching through the dust toward the ramp. Lex hissed at the approaching strangers. They stopped at the bottom of the ramp, where Kapp saw the familiar shape of Bryce Holden among them. The months had aged him quite a bit.

"Why do they carry weapons?" Aeva asked.

"To protect us," Kapp said. "I'll go first."

He stepped through the wall of energy, out of the warm and humid ship, into the biting cold of the wintertime desert, the wind howling and nipping at his ears. The others followed, and Mara started shivering. With her elegant robes and her haughty posture, Aeva approached the other party like royalty. Kapp could see the goosebumps rising on her neck.

"The air is so—empty," she said, walking beside Kapp. "And dry."

"You'll adjust," Kapp said.

"Commander Adams," Holden said. "Welcome home."

Kapp nodded his greeting. "Thank you," he said.

"Introduce me to your friend," Holden said, ignoring Jesse and Mara as he eyed Aeva. Something about the way he looked at her bothered Kapp.

"She'll introduce herself at—"

"I am Aeva," she said. "Thank you for welcoming us to Earth."

"Ahh," Holden said, "so she speaks English."

"I speak many tongues," Aeva said. "Learning is the greatest pastime, and I've had a lot of time to pass."

A laugh boomed in Holden's chest, shaking the folds of skin around his neck. Kapp had never heard Aeva attempt a joke before. When the group reached the bottom of the ramp, the guards got into an escort formation around them.

Holden led the procession. "Everyone is waiting inside Building C—come. We must debrief immediately."

The group got into a pair of Humvees and made their way to one of the warehouses near the edge of the complex. Visibly worried, Aeva kept looking back at her ship, which could still be seen over all of the buildings. When the cars stopped, they stepped out, into the dust and the cold. Holden rose his voice over the wind as they walked from the vehicles to the door.

"The President has gathered as many world leaders as possible," he said, "but many couldn't make it due to the short notice. The absentees will join us over an encrypted video feed. Your language study should come in handy tonight, Aeva."

"Indeed," she said.

Holden tapped his identity implant on a pillar by the door. It slid open, and the group walked into a spacious room much like the hangar that held the Starling II flight simulator, but strangely different. The space was large, clean, and overwhelmingly empty.

"What is this?" Kapp asked, turning to Holden. "Are we in the right building?"

"Yes," he said, a savage attempt at a smile twisting his ruddy jaw. "You're just where you're meant to be."

"What are you—"

"Guards," Holden said, the heavy door hanging on its hinges behind them. "Lock them up."

Joined by the rising protests of the crew, Lex hissed again. Kapp looked to his left, where he saw the shine of new steel bars in front of a row of cells. His mind barely had time to process this. He turned back to see the guards pulling out handcuffs, Jesse's fist colliding with one of their faces, the trust draining from Aeva's face. Everything happened at once, and fast. Finally, Kapp felt the sting of a taser—then everything went black.

27

OUT COLD

Though Kapp's body went limp and his vision faded to black, his mind remained aware of the cold concrete cracking against his face, the clink of cuffs on his bionic wrist, the feral sounds of a one-sided struggle. He spat the metallic taste of blood out of his mouth, but it returned instantly. Just as his tunnel vision began to fade, a guard dragged him to his feet in one strong pull. Kapp returned the favor with a forehead to the man's nose.

"Let go!" Kapp screamed through the madness around him.

A flood of red came out of the guard's broken nose and poured over a painless smile on his face. Kapp tried to jerk his torso away from the grip of a second guard, but he missed the opportunity. To his right he saw Holden leaning against a corrugated steel wall, watching from a safe distance, his jawline hard and his foot tapping.

"I'll take Aeva first," he yelled over the fray. "Put the rest in the cells. Walker, be careful with that one."

A trio of guards, who had already subdued Jesse and Mara, dragged the pair toward the steel bars. Kapp looked back at the face of the first guard, Walker, whose blood had stopped coming.

"Follow me," Walker said, turning away.

Kapp took another lunge toward him. "Fuck you."

Walker turned back, gripped Kapp's shirt with both hands, and lifted him a few inches off the ground. Besides the crooked nose, he seemed to have a perfectly symmetrical face. Kapp wanted to break more of the symmetry. Walker looked young, clueless—and batshit crazy. He cocked his head to the side like he was cracking his neck, and the bridge of his nose popped back into place by itself as if the nasal fracture had never occurred.

"Holy shit," Kapp said, a thought turned verbal.

"Follow me," Walker said as he set Kapp back down.

Kapp decided to obey this time. Except for the cat, he was the last one struggling against his captor. Lex scratched at a guard that tried and failed to hold him at arm's length. Stripes of bloodied flesh covered his arms, neck, and face. Lex twisted his way out of the man's grip and shot off toward the exit. Holden raised a hand halfway up his torso as if to say "let it be," and Lex ran out of the cracked door.

Walker and the other guards followed Kapp to his cell, took off his handcuffs, and locked him in. With his hands around the bars, Kapp saw Holden gloating from a distance.

"You're dead," Kapp said, nearly snarling at the traitor. "When I get out of here, you're fucking dead."

"We'll see about that."

"Why are you doing this?" Kapp tightened his grip around the bars. "Aeva came here in peace. You don't understand. This is bigger than any—"

"Strange how she looks so human." Holden's calmness only made Kapp angrier. "Isn't it?"

"Where is she?"

"Don't worry, Adams." He turned to leave. "We'll take care of her. And we'll take care of you too if you comply."

"I trusted you." Kapp raised his voice as Holden went further and further away. "We were friends. I've been to your house for Christ's sake!"

Holden kept walking until he reached a door at the far end of the building. Kapp's yells became enraged screams, bloody saliva flying from his mouth.

"COME BACK HERE!"

The door slammed shut.

•|•

Kapp didn't know how long he was in the cell for, but he watched the guards leave in shifts. With every prisoner subdued, only two guards stayed behind, including Walker. Still seething, Kapp paced around the small room for quite a while before taking a seat.

"J! Mara!" The croak of his voice bounced off concrete walls. "Are you hurt?"

"I'm okay," Mara managed to say.

"Me too," Jesse added.

The concrete walls between cells blocked them from sight, but to Kapp, they sounded scared.

"Why did this happen?" Mara asked.

"I don't know," Kapp said, "but we'll fix it. I've dealt with men that bite harder than Holden."

"Do you think he had something to do with the sabotage?" Jesse asked. "With Eli?"

The mention of the two treacherous men made Kapp want to punch something. "I'm sure he did. That pathetic son of a—"

The door at the other end of the warehouse creaked open. Aeva stepped out, escorted by the cat-scratched guard. The red wounds on the man's neck and arms had already turned into the pink of new flesh, and Kapp knew he couldn't have been in there *that* long. Aeva looked unhurt, except for the deep ache in her eyes. This was still enough to make Kapp's fists clench around the cell's bars.

The guard took Mara next. Like Aeva, she went quietly, though she visibly quivered from fear. With furrowed eyebrows, Kapp shook his head.

"Kapp," Aeva whispered once Mara and the guard were out of sight.

"What happened in there?" Kapp couldn't stomach the thought of Holden laying a hand on her. "Are you alright?"

"I'm fine, but Kapp?"

"Yeah," he said.

"They want access to Arca," she said, her voice stern, "but that must never happen."

"I know. But we might be too late."

"We're not too late." Her voice got even softer. "Do you remember the word I spoke when we departed Arca?"

"Wasn't it—"

A violent shush stopped his speech. "Don't say it. They might be listening."

"Sorry," he said, tasting for the first time the strangeness of the word on his lips. He had never been one to apologize, but he found himself saying sorry to Aeva quite often.

"Arca is impenetrable until the word is spoken—at least by any Earth technology that I know of." Kapp could imagine the look on Aeva's face as she spoke, the traces of worried sadness bleeding through a facade of emotionless courage. "I don't know how Holden knows about it, but they want the word. He will try to convince you to give it to him, but you must not."

"I won't," Kapp said, already planning to spit in Holden's face. "I promise."

"Thank you," Aeva said. "One more thing."

"Yeah?"

"If anything happens to me," Aeva said, "you have to get back to Arca—and leave this place."

•|•

Sooner than Kapp expected, Mara came back, this time escorted by Walker. Her tears looked small without the magnification of her glasses, which sat broken in the middle of the warehouse, stomped to pieces in the scuffle. Walker pushed Mara, blind and visibly terrified, past the door of her cell, locked it shut, and turned to Kapp, who returned the look with a one-finger salute. Walker's face betrayed no reaction as he stepped toward Kapp's cell.

"You better not touch me," Kapp said, rising from his corner.

When Walker spoke, his voice came as a gravelly monotone. "It's your turn."

The cell clicked open, and Walker took rhythmic, unrelenting steps toward Kapp, who turned his body away. He wedged himself tighter into the corner and brought a nervous hand to the attachment point of his prosthetic.

"I said—"

The voice sounded closer than before, so Kapp braced himself. "It's your turn."

When Kapp guessed Walker to be two paces behind him, he swung his body to the left, pushing off the wall for momentum and stretching his arm to its full length. In his left hand, he held his entire prosthetic arm. A clenched metal fist collided with Walker's temple, and the crack of breaking skull reverberated through the concrete and steel structure. Walker crumpled to the floor with a thump.

Mara squeaked her concern, and Kapp said, "I'm okay. Stay quiet."

Twisting his arm back on, Kapp stepped around Walker, thought better of it, and returned to raid the body. Blood pooled around the man's downturned face, and his fingers twitched like he was playing an invisible piano. Kapp found the taser on his belt, unclipped it. He tapped the pockets and found a phone, a multitool—no keys.

Kapp went to the door, checked the locking mechanism, and returned to the corpse. He became overwhelmed by an intrusive thought: *I've killed two men now.* But the thought of Holden's smug face made him want to increase that number to three.

He shook off the strange feeling, pulled the stolen multitool out of his pocket, then he grabbed Walker's left arm and found the bump on the inside of his limp wrist, right beside a curious pair of scars. A blade came out of the multitool with a flick of the thumb. Never-before-used. Sharp. Kapp made an incision beside the bump, and blood came like a waterfall. He pushed his thumb against the small mound of flesh, felt a pop, and heard a clink when the pill-shaped chip hit the bloodied concrete.

With the ID chip in one hand and the open knife in the other, Kapp exited the cell. Encouraged by the lack of extra security in the warehouse, he rushed to the next cell and unlocked it by holding the chip against the exterior panel for five seconds.

"What did you do?" Jesse asked as Kapp waited for the door to unlock. "Is that blood?"

"No time," he said, handing Jesse the chip and the open multitool.

"What did you do, Kapp?"

Kapp started to turn away. "Get the others out."

"Out where?" Jesse tried to stop him. "Where are you going?"

Kapp pulled the taser out of his back pocket. "Holden is expecting me."

·|·

On his way to the office, Kapp dialed the only phone number he had memorized and held the guard's phone to his ear. After a brief moment of uplink silence, he heard a beep and a realistic female voice.

The number you dialed is not in service. Please hang up and try again.

With everything going on, he had forgotten that Asher was an outlaw. At least—after witnessing Holden's treachery—he knew that his friend chose the right side. He considered dialing 911, but he decided that the police would be useless in his situation. The IES had top-shelf authority. Instead of trying to look up a phone number for the feds, he pocketed the phone and marched toward Holden's door.

During his last ten paces, Kapp slowed down. He put his ear against the door and listened. After a minute or so, Holden's voice came through the cheap wood.

"Damn it, what's taking him so long?" he said, accompanied by the impatient sound of fists hitting a desk. "Well, don't just stand there. Go out and check."

Kapp backed away as footsteps came toward him. As the door opened, he hid behind it. He let the guard pass, the one that Lex had attacked earlier. Somehow, the damage had healed entirely, but Kapp had no time to consider the strangeness of this. When the door shut behind the guard, Kapp took a few quick steps and brought the taser to the man's neck. He pulled the trigger, and his target collapsed without even a cry of pain. *Perfect.* Jesse and the others were huddled together near Kapp's cell. He waved them over, and they met in the middle of the warehouse floor.

"I think it's just us and Holden left," Kapp said. "Tie this one up in a cell before he wakes up, and I'll take care of Holden. Jesse, try to find the guard schedule on one of their phones. I need to know how much time we have."

Jesse nodded, holding a pale Mara under his arm. It looked like he was supporting her entire weight. Aeva was already beginning to tie the sleeping guard up with his own belt.

"Alright, I'm going," Kapp said. "Meet me—"

"Wait," Mara said, snapping out of her panic for a moment. "Holden, he—"

She gulped down some air.

"What is it, Mara?"

"He has a gun on his desk."

Kapp nodded his understanding, but it didn't change his mind. "When you're done, meet me outside of Holden's door. This shouldn't take long."

•|•

As he approached the door, Kapp shouted at himself. He had to be convincing.

"Let go of me," he yelled. "I'll go in myself!"

"Follow me," he said, mimicking Walker's low monotone.

Kapp kicked against the door, trying to create the sound of a struggle. He hoped Holden would rise, would come to see what the commotion was, would get further from his gun and closer to Kapp's taser.

"Just send him in," Holden yelled from within, clearly irritated. Kapp had underestimated the lazy bastard. Of course, he wouldn't use his own legs more than he had to. "We need to talk alone, anyway."

Kapp came into the room with his hands behind his back, pretending to stumble. The office was darker than the fluorescent warehouse, dusty like it hadn't been used in ten years. Holden looked up from his tablet and smiled.

"They had to cuff you?" Holden asked, smiling. "Seems about right."

"Fuck off."

The gun sat on the desk between them, an old-school Beretta revolver. Six rounds. Already cocked.

"Commander Adams," Holden said. White stubble coated his usually well-groomed face. "I need you to compromise with me."

"You look like shit," Kapp said.

Holden just laughed. "Tough words for someone tied up."

"I don't negotiate in handcuffs," Kapp said, faking a fight against the non-existent chains behind his back. He took a small step toward the desk.

"You're gonna have to." Seeing Holden's smirk, Kapp didn't even need to fake his anger. "Walker has the key."

Kapp took another step forward, gauging Holden's reaction. The thick man didn't reach for the gun, didn't seem worried at all. Kapp just needed to get close enough to pounce. A liquor bottle sat on the shelf behind Holden.

"I need a drink," Kapp said, inching forward again. "I can't talk with this headache."

"Ahh, I forgot how to reason with an alcoholic."

Kapp recoiled from the word. "What's this about?"

"I'm the one asking questions here." Holden loosened his necktie, undid his top button. He pulled a different bottle and one glass out of a drawer. "Is that clear?"

"Okay," Kapp said.

Holden poured a glass of scotch. "And I'm the only one drinking—unless you give us what we want. If you do that, you can have all the booze your heart desires. You'll be free. You'll be"—He turned a palm up and rubbed his thumb against his forefingers—"well-compensated for your compliance."

Kapp pretended to mull things over. "I'm listening."

"I know how much you like your money," Holden said. "How does a private island sound? I can make that happen. I can get you far away from all this bullshit."

"What do you want?" Kapp asked, forcing his voice to sweeten a bit.

Holden took a drag from his rocks glass. "We need to get on the ship. On Arca. It's for the safety of—"

"Should've asked nicely." Despite his best efforts, Kapp couldn't pretend to entertain Holden's offer any longer. "You probably scared the shit out of Aeva. It's her trust you need."

"Adams," Holden said. "You think I had a choice? I didn't want to. I had to lock you up." He took another sip, slurping the scotch into his maw obnoxiously. "I got direct orders from the President. This is a matter of not only national but global security."

"Holden, we had terms." The man's name came out of Kapp's mouth like "bad dog" from an angry pet owner.

"And you never waited for a response," Holden spat. "Are you this blind? You act like I broke your trust—but we had no agreement."

Kapp had to admit that Holden's logic stood. "Still, you lied to us. Made us believe we were safe."

"We had to be sure that you were you, and not some alien impression of you. Especially after seeing how human Aeva looks. You're a smart man, Kapp. Smart enough to understand protocol."

The words exited Holden's mouth like a rumbling shit, and Kapp could smell the lies.

"Okay, okay—I get it. It was out of your control. Protocol."

"Right."

"I'd like to speak to the President to confirm that—since this is above your payroll."

Holden's face distorted ever so slightly. Kapp took a slow step forward until the two of them were equidistant from the revolver. His finger found the trigger on the taser held behind his back.

"You will soon enough." Holden leaned forward in his chair, placed five fat fingers on the desk. "For now our priority is protecting Earth. Help me get on the ship."

"What was it you said before?" Kapp asked, stealing another inch toward the revolver.

"Huh?"

"Your message for the aliens," Kapp said, his voice beginning to mock Holden. "Tell them that we welcome them to Earth with—"

Open arms flew from behind Kapp's back. His metallic hand reached the Beretta before Holden could even blink a reaction, knocking it out of the way as he lunged forward with the charged taser. The director slid back in his rolling chair, a futile attempt to avoid Kapp's attack.

Pain shot from Kapp's knees as they collided with the desk. He toppled over the obstacle and reached the sizzling weapon toward

Holden, honing in on the wrinkles and stubble below his chin.

He missed, and they both tumbled to the floor, a riot of limbs. Holden pushed Kapp off of him, keeping the taser at bay. With his muscles hidden under a layer of fat, Holden was stronger than he looked. Kapp dropped the weapon and brought a metal fist to Holden's face—and another one. A knee hit Kapp's crotch, and the deep ache bent his body into the fetal position.

With his cheap-shot advantage, Holden rolled over and put his weight on Kapp—all 350 pounds of it—struggling and then succeeding to hold down Kapp's flailing limbs.

"Yield," Holden yelled.

Kapp spat in his face—the satisfying realization of his jail cell daydream. He twisted and turned in an attempt to free himself, but Holden's weight remained inescapable. Holden shifted one hand from Kapp's wrist to his neck. Kapp tried to bite the intruder as he slapped against Holden's side with his freed hand.

"Tell me how to get on the ship," Holden said, tightening his grip around Kapp's neck. The look in his eyes became wild, ferocious like a starved wolf.

Kapp couldn't respond, couldn't even breathe. Another set of fingers found his neck, and he heard a click, a sound that Holden seemed to ignore. The hands relented for a second, just long enough for Kapp to choke down some air before the weight came down again.

"Tell me," Holden yelled.

Stars filled the periphery of Kapp's tear-glazed vision as precious oxygen departed, swallowed up by his starved brain. His windpipe threatened to collapse, and his neck flexed against the inevitable. Vision tunneled. Exhausted limbs began to give up the fight.

"Let him go," a voice said, cool with an Alabama twang.

Kapp's focus shifted beyond the traitor holding him down, to the already-cocked Beretta, and then to the man who held it. Jesse fired the gun into the drywall and cocked it again.

"Bless your heart." He smacked the smoking barrel against Holden's skull for good measure, and a drop of blood fell on Kapp's face. "Hands to yourself. On your knees."

Holden's grip loosened, and he brought his fat fingers behind his head. With some struggle, he rose to a kneeling position and looked at Jesse with visible contempt.

"Oh boy," Jesse said, the words riddled with high-pitched Southern joy. "Someone looks madder than a wet hen."

Kapp choked down a few breaths and got up. Just as Holden began to open his mouth to speak, Kapp delivered another bionic punch to the man's head.

Out cold.

28

PICKLES

Asher descended the steps into the bunker, careful not to use the rickety handrails of the second flight. The fragile cargo in his pack made clanking noises that reverberated through the depths of the stairwell. He had only been away from the safety of the bunker for half a day, but the hours since then seemed to stretch.

Calix loped behind him, identical to Felix in every way but his temperament—that and the crook of his broken nose. Without a word, they entered the elevator and took it down to level six, where Asher got off.

"Thanks for driving," Asher said.

"No trouble." Calix inclined his head and smirked. "Good luck."

The doors shut before Asher could respond. Calix had barely spoken the entire trip, but Asher didn't mind. He understood introversion, and he had an appreciation for people who listened more than they talked.

He tapped his pocket to make sure he didn't lose anything during the descent, then made his way down the concrete hallway. He stopped at his bedroom, where he checked his reflection in the glass of a windowed door, then smiled at himself—a trick he had learned to inspire confidence.

You've got this.

Satisfied, he continued to Emily's door. Beacon's bunker only contained twin sized beds, which made cohabitation hard—

especially with one person pregnant—so the pair had settled for two rooms down the hall from each other.

"God, what took you so long?" Emily asked when he entered.

"It's not like we're walking distance from a Walmart," Asher said.

"Sorry, I'm just—"

"Just extremely pregnant?" Asher said as he sat on the foot of the bed.

Her eyes smiled. "How could you tell?"

Instead of answering, Asher kissed her belly through the thin cotton blanket. He pulled a glass jar from his backpack and handed it over.

"Bread and butter, are you serious? I asked for dill."

"Oops, those are for me," Asher said, reaching into his bag once again. "I thought these cravings were a myth, but I guess—"

"Give me the damn pickles, Ash."

He obliged, opened the jar for her, then waited for her to eat some. Even in the fluorescent light, wearing no makeup, she looked beautiful.

"How do you feel?" he asked

She brought a hand to her belly and frowned. "Close, I think."

"What's wrong?"

"I'm nervous," Emily said. "These people, they're—"

"They're fine."

"They kidnapped you!"

"Yeah," he said, scooting up to sit beside her, "but it all worked out. And Genesis is a really good doctor, so you don't have to worry."

Her lips bunched to one side. "How do you know?"

"She told me," Asher said, unprepared for the negative direction of the conversation.

Emily sighed. "When did you get so trusting?"

Exhausted from the excursion, Asher yawned and let his body sink deeper into the mattress. "Probably since I met you."

They stayed quiet for a while. Emily ate dill pickles, and Asher settled into a position where he could caress the nape of her neck, the curve of her body. It was something he never tired of, the act of loving.

"How long do we have to stay here?" she asked. "I miss the sunlight."

Truthfully, Asher had no idea. Emily had been underground for weeks, and so had Asher—except for the few excursions he and Calix made to get supplies.

"Just until we know we're safe," Asher said.

"But how long will that be?"

The world was changing, and Asher knew it. The effects of the nano-vaccine revolution had gone global, and only a few people on Earth understood the true repercussions.

"As long as it takes," Asher said.

Emily stayed quiet, shifting her weight to stay comfortable. Finally, she rested her head on Asher's thin shoulder.

"Did you bring me anything else?" she asked.

"I did." Asher put a hand in his pocket, squeezed his fist around the diamond ring within it. "But it's a surprise."

Emily kissed his cheek and left her lips there long enough for him to feel her smile. "You know, you shouldn't keep a girl waiting."

Asher nearly pulled the ring out of his pocket, but he wanted to wait for the perfect moment. There would be time, after all.

"As long as it takes," he said.

•|•

The day passed as many days did in the bunker—silent, uneventful, and often filled with sleep. Something about being underground sapped Asher of all his energy. Still suffering from paranoia, he often woke with a start, terrified that he'd find someone looming over him, ready to take him. But no one was ever there. In the middle of the night, he woke to the sound of a knock at the door, which rushed the rhythm of his heart.

"Come in," he said, after checking that Emily was decent.

A light came on, and Genesis stepped into the room, her posture rigid. "Sorry to wake you, but it's urgent."

Asher rose quickly, his head nearly hitting a bulb that hung from the ceiling. "What happened?"

"You got a call."

Though Asher's phone had long been destroyed by the garbage

disposal, Beacon still monitored calls made to his number.

"And?" Asher asked.

"It came from Groom Lake."

Asher became vaguely aware of Emily's hand on his back, a comforting touch. "It's time?" he asked.

"Our video feeds confirm their arrival," Genesis said. "Felix is preparing for departure."

Asher pulled on his pants and started to walk toward the door, but Emily's hand gripped his wrist.

"Wait," she said, "what if it's a trap?"

Unwilling to feel fear, Asher just shrugged.

"You have to come back, Ash," Emily said, bringing her other hand to the curve of her abdomen. "I can't do this without you."

"You won't have to." Once again, Asher's hand found the ring in his pocket, then he leaned down to kiss her, his lips lingering as long as urgency would allow. "I'll be back in a few hours."

29

IDENTITY

The captive and the free gathered by the cells with their roles reversed. Holden and the living guard were held behind bars, gagged with their own clothes, bound with their own cuffs. In the next cell, Walker still lay in a pool of blood.

"Man, you went full-on Alabama in there," Kapp said to Jesse. "Thanks."

"Any time," Jesse said, too busy swiping through one of the guard's phones to look up.

Shaking his head, Kapp turned to Mara. "Did you know you're dating a badass?"

"Found it," Jesse said.

Kapp peered over his shoulder at the spreadsheet, but Jesse beat him at number-crunching.

"We've got less than two hours until shift change," Jesse said.

The four of them took a collective breath. *Enough time to make a plan,* Kapp thought. Just as they all started to have a discussion about who in the world they could trust, the screen in Jesse's hand changed. The guard schedule got knocked away by an incoming call.

UNKNOWN NUMBER.

"Answer it," Kapp said. "Speakerphone."

Jesse tapped the answer icon, and sound erupted from the phone in static overtones.

"Hello," Kapp said.

"Who is this?" a distorted voice at the other end asked, drowned by the static.

"You called me. Who is this?"

Another roar of static and then *"—West. You dialed my—"* came through the speakers.

Kapp looked to the others before returning to the call. Aeva paced back and forth, patrolling the entrances with fierce eyes. Jesse and Mara shrugged simultaneously.

"Repeat," Kapp said. "You're breaking up."

"I said this is Asher West. You dialed my number."

Then Kapp remembered. He had tried to call Asher on the way to Holden's office.

"Asher, it's me—Kapp."

Static reigned for a moment, and Kapp thought the call had dropped.

"I need you to prove it."

It wasn't the response Kapp expected, but he understood. It only took a second for him to conjure up a private memory to prove his identity. The thought made him grin.

"Asher," he said. "Remember that one time in college when I walked in on you jerking off into a—"

"Okay, I believe you," Asher said, his voice rising an octave. *"Kapp, where are you?"*

"Groom Lake," Kapp said, regaining his composure. "We're in a warehouse."

"Building C," Jesse added.

Kapp quickly recounted their capture and the matter of their pending escape.

"Bastard," Asher said, mimicking Kapp's thoughts about Holden.

"What's going on, Ash?" Speaking to his best friend felt surreal. "Holden said that you—"

"There's no time to explain everything now."

"Then when?" Kapp asked. "Where are you?"

"Coming to you—can you get to the helipad?"

Kapp tried to picture the complex but came up short. "I think so."

Jesse nodded. "I know how to get there."

"Okay, good. We'll be there in an hour."

"We?" Kapp asked, but his mind had moved on. Aeva continued to pace, her face solemn. Standing on his toes, Jesse looked ready to move. Crippled by her lack of eyewear, Mara scanned the room uselessly.

Beneath the gagged moans of their waking prisoners, none of them could hear the slow crackling in the next cell, a sound like a distant campfire. Busy preparing for their escape, they missed the sound of cracked skull bone snapping back into place.

•|•

Kapp let Jesse wield the revolver, knowing it would be more useful in the hands of someone who had learned to shoot as a child. Jesse checked the cylinder. Five bullets left. He replaced the depleted round with ammo they had pilfered from Holden's desk. Kapp and Aeva each held a taser, and Mara held the back of Jesse's shirt for guidance. They huddled near the exit.

"Ready?" Kapp asked.

They nodded, and Jesse pulled Walker's ID chip out of his pocket. He held it to the panel by the door, which flashed green after five seconds.

"Wait," he said, peering at the blood-crusted device in his palm—that tiny chip that held so much information. "We should take ours out—so they can't track us."

Kapp cringed at the thought, but he agreed. He checked the time on one of the stolen phones. "Forty-five minutes. It'll have to be quick."

They found a first aid kit and got to work. Kapp sterilized the blade of the multi-tool and laid it beside a pair of tweezers, gauze, and tape. He brought the blade to the inside of his left wrist. Although he had performed the same procedure on Walker, it felt much different trying to cut into his own flesh. An invisible barrier of self-preservation stopped him. Like stepping into a freezing river—he knew he could do it, but his body wouldn't let him.

"I'll do it," Aeva said, the first words to leave her lips since their escape.

She held Kapp's wrist in her soft, strong hand. Electricity again. Kapp wondered if she felt the connection too, but one look at her face made him doubt it.

"How are you so calm?" he asked, handing her the knife.

She took a breath, but her eyes didn't drift from the task at hand. "For now, at least, I know that Arca is safe."

Always the ship, Kapp thought.

"I know that help is on the way," she continued. "These are good things. I'm trying not to focus on the bad. Unlike some, I don't suffer from illusions of control."

Her words calmed him, distracted him. Kapp didn't even notice the blade until it had completed its trip across his skin. Then came the sting, the heat of blood. Aeva plucked the chip from the open wound as easily as a stray hair.

"Next," she said, already beginning to clean the surgical tools.

As Kapp wrapped the now aching wound, he looked at the ID chip on the concrete and visualized some of the data it contained.

> *Name: Kapp Adams*
> *DOB: January 9, 2005*
> *Hair: Brown*
> *Eyes: Green*
> *Occupation: IES Astronaut*
> *Current Address: 326 Deer Walk Cir.*
> *Mother: Isabella Marie Adams*
> *Father: Unknown*

None of that seemed to matter anymore. Kapp's world had grown much larger and his priorities more narrow. The family he was born into had been replaced by the few who stood with him. They all could have died on Phobos, but somehow they got a second chance. Kapp could not go home. He didn't want to go home. If he was honest with himself, he never really considered it home, anyway. The things that identified him could no longer be contained in a pill-sized bundle of circuits. So, without an ounce of hesitation, he shattered his old identity with the stomp of a boot.

•|•

The blue glow of dawn approaching provided just enough light to illuminate the path of their escape. Half the trip would be through a narrow alley between warehouses, the rest a straight shot across an open field to the helicopter pad. Easy enough.

The defensive perimeter had tightened around Arca. Trenches surrounded the ship, hosting guns that aimed outward in all directions. The sight, along with the chill of the wind, made Kapp shiver.

With Mara on his tail, Jesse looked around a corner into the alley.

"All clear," he said, signaling with the barrel of Holden's pistol.

The band of fugitives ducked between the buildings in an untrained formation. Kapp took up the rear of the procession, while Aeva walked soundlessly in front of him, her fit silhouette sneaking like a predator in the growing light. To Kapp, she looked dangerous—untouchable. This only made him want to do just that.

Something touched his ankle, and his body flinched violently against it. His wandering thoughts retreated as every inch of his skin responded to the attack with frightened gooseflesh. He let out a high grunt, kicked the intruder, and lit up the alley with his taser.

In the electric glow, his eyes saw a demon before his mind could rule out the impossible. A pair of vertical pupils surrounded by reflective green looked back at him above a set of bared teeth—razor sharp. When Kapp realized what stood before him, he let go of the trigger, and his tense skin began to relax.

"Shit, Lex. I almost killed you."

The cat found Aeva's heels and looked back at Kapp with an expression full of contempt. He could have sworn that the animal shook its head back and forth.

Aeva bent down to scratch her pet between the ears, Kapp took a few deep breaths to calm himself down, and the group continued on.

They made quick work of the alley—too quick. Jesse crept ahead to peek around the corner.

"Chopper's not here yet," he said. "I say we wait here until we see it coming, then we'll make a run for it."

"Good plan," Kapp said.

"Uh oh," Jesse said, his eyes still trained on their destination. "There's someone patrolling the pad."

"Can we take him out?"

Jesse shrugged. "He's packing heat—AR and a sidearm."

"I don't like this," Mara said.

"Any blind spots? If we can get close—"

"Not really," Jesse said. "We're outranged, anyway."

Just then, Lex's ears swiveled toward the mountains, and Aeva's followed. The cat's eyes found the helicopter pad, and then he shot out of the alley like a bullet. Kapp took a few steps forward, almost into the danger zone.

"He'll blow our cover," Kapp said.

Aeva put an arm out in front of him and said, "Wait."

Then the humans heard what Aeva and the cat had already picked up moments earlier. From the mountains came the sound of their salvation, the air-splitting drone of an approaching helicopter—a signal to act, and Lex was the first to heed it.

Out in the field, the cat's gait adjusted to the slightest movements of the guard, who paced lazily in the opposite direction. A blur of fur, Lex picked up speed as he neared the clueless man. And then he leaped.

The guard turned toward the sound of paws hitting asphalt, but was too late to dodge the attack. With claws outstretched, Lex flew through the air from a nearly impossible distance, following the trajectory of a perfect arc that would culminate at head-level. The man was only able to turn around halfway before the claws hit his throat. One set of claws only broke the surface, but the other found purchase deep in his flesh, tearing life away with the ease of its intended purpose. As fast as the claws came, they left, ripe with stolen skin and blood.

Moments after Lex touched back down to the ground, the guard clutched the shreds of his flayed neck and began to stumble. Lex coldly watched the gurgling mess of a man spin, fall, and thump to the ground, licking the gore from his paws the whole time.

When the motion stopped, Lex turned toward Aeva and tilted his head. She nodded at the animal. Jesse faced Mara with a mix of disbelief and horror on his face. Unseen by the rest, Kapp grinned.

The sound of blades cutting air grew louder, and Aeva's eyes found the sky.

"I see it," she said.

Kapp followed her gaze to the top of a sandstone ridge in the distance, where a black helicopter made its glorious ascent from the depths of the horizon.

"We're clear ahead," Jesse said. He turned to Mara. "The ground is flat. Can you jog behind me?"

"I think so," she said, her eyes wide.

"We're almost out of here." Jesse brought his hands to the sides of her arms and pulled her closer. "We're gonna make it. But just in case we don't—"

Then he hunched down, just a few inches lower—and she turned her face to his and smiled a gentle smile, one that was more eyes than mouth. When the distance between them became magnetic, Mara inched ever closer, her heels rising from the ground with the stealth of sprouting flowers.

"I love you, Mara Stone," Jesse said, grinning from ear to ear despite the surrounding situation.

Mara inhaled a slow breath and then whispered, "I love you too."

Then their lips met, perhaps for the first time—perhaps for the last time. Kapp watched the kiss, and to him, the kiss seemed more foreign than an alien craft. He had kissed plenty of women, but never like that. He could almost see the passion exuding from them like a cloud of mist. A pang of jealousy hit his heart with its unwelcome swelling.

The lovers parted, and Kapp realized that the mist he had seen wasn't in his imagination. A cloud of dust floated beside him. At first, he thought it came from the approaching chopper, but the direction it came from didn't make sense. He turned his head toward the open space between the roofs of the two buildings. More dust fell from above—followed by the man who caused it to fall.

Pain shot from Kapp's ankle as he collapsed to the ground under the weight of a surprise tackle. The man dropped down on Kapp like a bag of bricks and knocked the wind out of him. When he came to his senses, Kapp delivered a metal elbow to the man's stomach.

Jesse joined the fight. After a swift kick to his ribs, he shouldered all of his weight against the attacker's side. The man tipped like a cow. With the weight gone, Kapp rolled away and shuffled to his feet. The group backed away in unison. Then Jesse aimed his Beretta at the man, who was also getting up.

"Not one step closer," Jesse said.

He ignored the warning, and Jesse had no choice but to fire his weapon into the shadows. The crack of exploding gunpowder created a strange echo between the two buildings. The shot couldn't have missed his chest, but the man kept pacing forward. He stepped into the light with fresh blood seeping from just above his stomach. In the new light, Kapp recognized the blood-soaked but otherwise perfectly intact face. Before him stood Walker—completely alive.

Jesse cocked the weapon and fired again, taking off a chunk of Walker's shoulder in the process, but the man continued forward, his expression unchanged. Behind them, the drone of the chopper grew ever louder.

"Run," Kapp yelled, ears momentarily deaf from the gunshots.

Jesse fired two shots in rapid succession, then they booked it out of the alley. Undeterred by four bullets, Walker began to run after them. Aeva wasted no time sprinting ahead of everyone, but Kapp and Jesse stayed between Walker and Mara, who was the slowest of the group thanks to her short legs and lack of eyewear.

Jesse aimed behind him and shot again. Less than a hundred feet ahead, a circle of dust began to surround the helicopter as it touched down. Another gunshot rang through the complex, followed by a series of clicks, then Jesse threw the empty revolver at Walker, who was still gaining on the group.

This is impossible, Kapp thought. Then he stopped running. Jesse came to a halt as well.

"Get to the chopper," Kapp yelled, cocking back his right fist. Waves of pain came from his sprained ankle.

Walker caught up, his tattered clothes soaked in the blood of six bullet wounds. A scattered path of red led all the way to the alley behind him. His face lacked both pigment and any semblance of emotion.

"Why won't you die?!" Kapp yelled.

Instead of waiting for a response, he knocked some of Walker's teeth out with metal knuckles. The attack only slowed the guard down for a moment before he began kicking at Kapp's weakened ankle. Kapp lost his balance and fell to the dusty ground on his back. He felt a kick to the ribs, then he saw the tread of a shoe raising high above his head, preparing to stomp his lights out for good.

Kapp turned his head to the left, an attempt to avoid certain death if his face got crushed from the front. Through the rising dust, he saw something round hit the dirt a few meters away. It bounced twice, then it popped open and emitted a high pitched sound that crescendoed rapidly.

As soon as the sound reached Kapp's ears, Walker dropped to the ground beside him.

"Come on," someone yelled above the roar of the helicopter. "There's more coming!"

A pair of scrawny arms helped Kapp to his feet, then he saw a face that took him a moment to recognize. The buzzcut was new, but the smile was unmistakable.

"Ash," he said.

"Let's go, Kapp." Asher supported some of Kapp's weight as he began to lead him to the chopper. "You're safe now."

30

REUNION

Packed with runaways and rescuers alike, the six-seat chopper sprung from the complex as soon as the last shoe left the ground. Summoned by Jesse's gunfire, men ran toward the helipad and raised their rifles to the sky. Semi-automatic gunfire peppered the bulletproof glass, creating an array of star-shaped white marks on its surface. Kapp ducked down until the blasts stopped coming, then someone handed him a headset.

A voice broke through the chaos. *"Anyone hit?"*

Kapp would have recognized the voice anywhere. It belonged to Oliver, the man who had flown him to Groom Lake four times a week for months before the Starling launch. From the middle seat, Kapp checked the rest of the passengers.

"Negative," he said. "Good to see you, Oli."

"Aye, mate."

Clearly too focused on the task at hand to offer more of a greeting, Oliver tilted the stick forward. The chopper picked up speed in an easterly direction. Kapp didn't recognize the man that sat in the co-pilot seat, but Aeva kept glancing at him. Like Oliver, the man up front kept his attention outside of the cabin. Both men watched the chopper's tail in the rearview mirrors.

For a brief time, everything stayed calm. The purr of the engine, the sight of his friends still living, the pink sunrise over the sandy hills—it all allowed Kapp to relax for a moment. His adrenaline dropped to a level that made his aches and pains more apparent, but he didn't feel overwhelmingly amped up anymore. Pump by pump, his heart rate slowed.

"Drones," Oliver yelled.

Without hesitation, the man to Oliver's right unstrapped himself from the seat. Cool air hit Kapp's face as the front passenger door popped open, then the man leaned out. He clung to the craft with one hand and held out a long-barreled pistol with the other. A shot rang out, dulled by the headset and the engine noise. Kapp's heart rate began to climb once again.

"One down," the shooter said. *"Let 'em get closer."*

The helicopter slowed down a notch, and the man leveled the barrel of his gun once more. He waited for another drone to catch up, then he fired two quick shots. The flash of an explosion lit up his face, which was suntanned and bearded.

"Two down."

The man, who almost seemed bored by the task, chambered another bullet and peered back at the empty sky behind them. Kapp itched to help but didn't know where to begin.

"Should be three, Felix," Asher said.

"Copy."

Kapp looked around at his tired and dirty friends. To his left, Mara shrunk under the arm of Jesse, whose torn shirt was decorated by a medley of blood, some of it his own—most of it not. Asher, the cleanest of the bunch, sat beside Kapp. Something seemed different about Asher, something that Kapp couldn't quite place. Not the haircut, but the way he carried himself. Kapp thought he saw some level of confidence that wasn't there before. Beyond Asher, Aeva sat by the bullet-bruised window, comforting the cat in her lap. Lex was a certified badass, but he didn't seem to like heights.

Without warning, the stranger named Felix fired the pistol again. The third drone, which followed much closer than the first two, veered downward just in time to avoid immediate destruction. Another shot missed the retreating drone, which swerved until it flew directly behind them and out of sight.

"Damn machine learning," Asher said.

The drone came around to the opposite side, where it caught up and kept pace with the chopper. In the faint light, Kapp saw its camera swivel toward them.

"Everyone strapped in?" Oliver asked

Felix responded first. *"Affirmative."*

Oliver pulled a lever, and the door closest to the drone popped open. Icy wind blew across the cabin through the new opening.

"I don't have a shot from here," Felix said.

Mechanical eyes honed in on Kapp. He imagined Holden watching from the ground—probably with a sour look and bag of ice on his swelling face. He remembered the satisfying sound of his metal fist hitting treacherous flesh—a dull, squishy thud.

"I got this," Kapp said, reaching into his pocket. "Can you get closer to it, Oli?"

"Aye," he said, and the distance between the two crafts started to close.

With computational precision, the drone automatically steered away to keep a safe distance. Kapp mouthed some profanities at the camera. *Not close enough,* he thought. As if in response to Kapp's thoughts, Oliver sped up the turn. He outpaced the machine's reaction time, but not quite enough. It veered away before Kapp could make his shot.

Oliver took a quick turn in the opposite direction. As soon as the drone began to follow, he swerved back toward it. Kapp felt the butterflies of weightlessness for a moment, but this time he was prepared for the maneuver, unlike the machine that flew beside them.

The two crafts reached the apex of their proximity, and the bloodied multi-tool flew from Kapp's false hand before the drone could retreat again. It soared over Mara and Jesse out of the chopper, where it hung in the open air for a split second before colliding with a single propeller blade, causing the only damage necessary. The mechanical bird spun wildly and crashed to the earth below.

•|•

Oliver took the group east until they reached a high mountain pass. Kapp thought they must have crossed the border into Utah, but after the fight, he had been too tired to ask. Eyelids heavy with incoming sleep, he had to keep them open by force of will alone. Oli had the advantage of caffeine, but everyone else onboard began to succumb to the fatigue of their recent experiences. Yawns spread like contagion through the cabin. Mara and the cat passed out completely, both in the laps of their chosen companions.

The journey through the winding pass awakened Kapp's senses. As they climbed in elevation, the pines grew thicker, and the pass more narrow. They followed the path of a one-lane dirt road for a while, but that too disappeared beneath the trees, which grew increasingly covered in winter white as they neared their destination.

Kapp barely saw the clearing before they reached it, but Oliver touched down on the white earth with practiced grace. Flurries of fresh snow flew up from the ground surrounding the craft. Though the pilot landed softly, their arrival still woke up Mara and Lex, who yawned simultaneously and began to investigate their new surroundings. A circle of tall pines stood around them, protecting them from sight in all directions.

Oliver cut the engine, and the propellers began to slow. The sound of headsets hitting hooks and buckles coming undone replaced the hum of the engine. One by one, everyone placed their feet onto solid ground.

Aeva approached the man named Felix. She kept her distance at first, like someone running into an old acquaintance at the grocery store. Then she started shaking her head back and forth.

"Felix—I can't believe this," she said, her eyes darting around the man's mostly hidden features, taking in his face. A tear sprouted from the corner of one eye, and her lower lip trembled. "It's really you."

A smile, not quite as white as the snow, shone through his beard. "It is."

Felix reached out his right hand, and Aeva gripped his wrist with both of hers. He brought his other hand to her wrist, and they held the strange greeting as they continued the conversation.

"Felix," she said, "for many cycles, I've convinced myself that you were dead."

"Like you said, it's really me."

"How?" Aeva didn't lose composure often, but strong emotions began to show themselves. "What happened?"

"We both have stories to tell, but now is not the time."

If the forest seemed alien to Aeva, she didn't show it. She kept her eyes trained on Felix.

"Um, excuse me," Kapp said to the two of them. "I'm kind of confused."

Aeva turned to the group. A few tears still glistened in her smiling eyes.

"I did not expect this meeting to ever occur, but I'm glad that it has. Felix, this is the brave crew of Starling II that saved Arca from destruction."

"I've heard all about you," Felix said, sharing a look with Asher.

"Everyone," she said, "this is Felix—my brother."

•|•

Asher led them through the forest, while Felix walked behind and guarded their rear. His leather jacket hung loosely around Mara's tiny frame. Even with the extra layer, she still shivered. Hungry wind blew from ahead, nipping at their ears, carrying their voices back through the pines.

"We're almost there," Asher said.

Kapp walked with a limp. Aches and pains blossomed in his body, payback for the torture he had put it through since leaving Earth. *How long has it been? Nine months?* He made a mental note to ask someone.

The sun approached the middle of the sky, reminding Kapp of how long he had gone without sleep. The last slumber he remembered was when the Artazoa knocked him out and showed him a vision of the darkness consuming the light. His head pounded and his throat burned. Though he hadn't had a drink in over a day, this feeling rivaled his worst Vegas hangovers.

The group reached another small clearing and approached a pile of branches coated with a fresh dusting of snow. On top of a nearby hill, Kapp saw a tree that looked suspiciously like an antenna. Felix jogged ahead and began to pull logs from the pile. By the time everyone arrived, he had cleared the cover to reveal a small hatch door, much like the one on the crew module of Starling II. Grunting from the effort, Felix twisted it open.

"Ladies first," he said to Asher.

"I hate you," Asher said, then turned to the rest of the group. "It's not a long ladder, but it's dark down there, so be careful."

Asher mounted the narrow ladder and began his descent, followed by Jesse, who insisted on staying below Mara to help her. Everyone else followed, but Felix stayed behind to close the hatch and to patrol the other entrances. The journey downward ended on a cracked concrete floor. Asher pulled a flashlight from his pack and lit up the hallway. Leaky pipes ran across the low ceiling, dripping their waste to the floor below.

"What is this place?" Jesse asked.

"An old bunker."

"Military?"

"It was privately owned by some rich nut job who thought the world was ending—watch your step." Asher shuffled sideways to avoid a pothole. "Genesis paid a pretty penny to buy the place from the guy's kids when he died. I guess they had no interest in dad's crazy survival pad."

"Genesis?" Mara asked.

"Another Beacon survivor. You'll meet her. Anyway—turns out the old nut's paranoia wasn't far from the truth. Things are getting pretty bad out there, but down here"—he changed course to avoid another hole—"we're safe."

A door appeared before them, framed by Asher's circle of light.

"Just a few more staircases, and then you all can get some rest."

They filed through the door one by one and began to climb deeper into the mountain. Before they reached the second flight of stairs, Asher stopped everyone.

"Don't grab the rail on the right," Asher said. "It's coming loose, and I haven't fixed it yet. Still on my to-do list."

He shined his flashlight on the tricky rail. An immense darkness stretched out below the metal bar.

"It's a long way down," Asher continued, guiding everyone past the obstacle one by one.

Kapp stole a glance over the edge of the concrete steps. Impossible to tell how deep the shaft went, but he figured that no one could survive the fall.

"Good place to kill yourself," Kapp said.

No one responded to his observation. The group continued their descent into the bunker. A plague of yawns returned. Kapp, curious enough to fight the fatigue, decided to end the sleepy silence. His words, directed at Aeva, struggled to exit his dry mouth.

"I didn't know you had a brother."

"A few, actually," she said from in front of him. "Felix is not my genetic brother, but we were children together."

Kapp tried to imagine Aeva as a child, but his imagination faltered. He opened his mouth to ask more questions about her space-bound childhood, but Asher cut into the conversation.

"So, I've been asking Felix, but he won't tell me. Are he and Calix—"

"Clones?" Aeva asked. "Well, technically—Felix is the original and Calix is the clone."

"I knew it," Asher said, raising his voice.

Kapp just shook his head.

Aliens, self-healing guards, clones—things just keep getting stranger and stranger.

Deeper down the rabbit hole they went.

The lower the group climbed, the warmer it got. By the time they exited the elevator on level six, everyone was sweating. They followed the curve of a concrete-floored hallway until they reached a row of rooms that looked more like cells. Kapp shivered at the fresh memory of his last experience behind bars. Water fell from various points on the ceiling, creating a syncopated rhythm of drips. Asher gave the first room to Jesse and Mara, who said a quick goodnight before literally falling into bed.

"About time those two hooked up," Asher said, but Kapp was too tired to respond.

They brought Aeva to the second door.

"I wish to speak to Genesis," she said.

"She won't be back at base until after sundown," Asher said, "so you might as well get some rest."

She nodded and entered the second room. "Rest well, Asher of Earth. Thank you."

Lex hopped in after Aeva to claim a spot on the bed, then she shut the door.

"Asher of Earth?" Asher turned to Kapp and let out a small laugh. "I like that."

They continued walking until they reached the third door.

"I guess this one's mine," Kapp said.

"Yep. Should be everything you need in there. Clothes, water, MREs."

The sight of the bed made Kapp yawn. "Thanks, Asher. I don't know how you pulled this off, but thanks."

"Of course." For a moment, Asher seemed like he didn't have any more words, but then he spoke up. "Kapp—I know you're tired, but can we talk for a little while? Catch up?"

As much as Kapp missed his friend, he didn't think he could keep his eyes open for another minute. His body raged against the idea of staying up any longer than he had to. Everything hurt. As he opened his mouth to say this, Asher, who must've seen the hesitation in Kapp's expression, spoke again—three magic words that gave Kapp a little boost of energy.

"I have beer."

"Lead the way," Kapp said without missing a beat.

They went to Asher's room just around the corner. Unlike the other chambers, his space had a lived-in messiness to it. Clothes and loose pieces of paper littered the floor. A black and silver mini-fridge sat in the corner.

The whole scene reminded Kapp of their freshman dorm, where he always had to clean up Asher's shit and banish him to the common room whenever he had female company. Kapp sat on the bed, the only piece of furniture in the room, while Asher pulled two bottles from the fridge.

"Shit," Asher said, "I forgot to get a bottle opener."

"Have you forgotten about my skills already?" Kapp asked, reaching for one of the bottles.

He held it in his bionic hand and put a thumb against the neck of the bottle, directly under the cap. With a quick flick, the bottle cap flew off the top and jangled to the concrete floor.

"I remember when you mastered that," Asher said, smiling.

"I wasted far too much beer shattering those bottles," Kapp said. "It took me a while to learn not to squeeze so hard."

"That's what she said."

They both laughed. Kapp opened Asher's bottle before taking a slow sip out of his own. The hops bit his tongue like a feisty lover, that old familiar mistress. He welcomed her with a secondary gulp.

"Ahh," he breathed. "Maybe I'll stay for two of these."

"I thought you might."

Asher reached under the bed and pulled out a pre-rolled joint and a lighter. Kapp could already feel the hop-induced relaxation setting in.

Weed would only improve that feeling.

"So," Kapp said, "crazy shit, right?"

Asher nodded. "I guess I've come to terms with it."

"How did you end up with"—he couldn't think what to call them at first—"these outlaws?"

Asher recounted the story of his discovery of the nuclear weapon onboard Starling II, his leak to the media, and Nai coming for him. Then he moved on to his abduction and initiation into the group known as Beacon. Kapp listened intently but struggled to keep his eyes open, especially after hitting Asher's joint a few times during the conversation.

"Wow," Kapp said, his high thoughts beginning to wander. "It's strange, you know? So much has happened to you, so much time has passed—but to me, it feels like I saw you a couple weeks ago."

"Yeah, buddy." Asher smoked the ass-end of his joint and tossed the butt to the ground. "Kapp—there's something I need to tell you."

"You're gay?" Kapp giggled as he popped the top off of another beer. "Everyone already knew that."

Asher groaned. "2040 and you're still making gay jokes?""

"Okay, okay." Kapp took a long draw from his beer. "What's going on?"

"You remember Emily, right?" Asher asked.

Kapp yawned. "Remind me."

"The woman you had—you had sex with her the night before the Starling launch."

"Oh," he said, twisting his lips into a smile of recollection. He recalled a blur of tattooed skin and pierced body parts. "Yeah, I remember. What about her?"

"Well," Asher said, avoiding eye contact, "first of all, we're kind of dating."

Kapp wondered why Asher considered this information relevant, but he humored the man's genuine concern. "If you thought that I'd be mad or something, I'm definitely—"

"No, that's not it," Asher said.

"Well, what is it?"

"She's here—at Beacon headquarters." Asher's heel tap-tap-tapped on the concrete floor. "I brought her here to keep her safe."

"That's good," Kapp said. "It is kinda hard to have a relationship when only one of you lives underground."

"And to keep her child safe." Asher rubbed his fingers together as he spoke. "I told you she was pregnant, right? Did you see that message?"

"I did," he said, beginning to tire of the conversation. He was honestly proud of Asher for scoring such a hot girlfriend, but he really needed sleep.

"Kapp?" Asher's nervous motions stopped, and he looked his friend straight in the eye.

"Yeah."

"Emily only had one partner during the time that she could have gotten pregnant—one encounter, actually."

"And?" Kapp asked, preparing to call it a night. He took in one last mouthful of beer before he could process what Asher was so obviously implying. But just as Asher responded, understanding lit up his brain like a flashlight in the darkness.

"It was you, Kapp—you're the father."

Beer shot out of Kapp's mouth.

31

A BETTER WORLD

His mother's scream rings out in Kapp's mind as the blade nears her abdomen. Flames lick at the ceiling, an impenetrable barrier. Walls of fire rise and fall, blocking his view of the man hunched over her. With each fleeting glimpse, Kapp sees more blood pooling beneath her body. Suddenly, the man is standing, saying something that Kapp can't hear. He can't see his face, but somehow he looks familiar. Water begins to fall from the ceiling, destroying the flames. The man leaves… carrying…something.

Sirens break through the high-pitched ringing in Kapp's ears. He tries to yell for help, but the smoke chokes him. The flames are gone now. He forces his body to move, to scoot across the glass-littered floor toward her. Blood spills from where his arm had once been, and even though it's hot, he feels a rush of coldness creeping from the wound. Tears burn in his eyes by the time he reaches her. She looks like she's sleeping. He struggles to pull her closer, to pull her back, but none of his efforts work. The sirens grow louder. He can't wake her, and he's so, so tired. Crying, he rests his head on her lap and falls asleep.

•|•

"Kapp—are you okay?"

Kapp's body jerked to life. It took a moment for his waking brain to recognize Aeva. Even though the grime of battle still clung her clothes, Kapp thought she looked like an angel sent to save him from the depths of hell. He struggled to slow his heavy breathing. Droplets of cold sweat clung to his forehead.

"You were screaming," she continued.

Kapp wiped his forehead with the corner of his bedsheets. "I'm fine. I just had a—"

"Nightmare?" Aeva sat down on the edge of the bed. "I have them too from time to time. In the dream—what did you run from?"

Kapp sat up and leaned against the headboard. His body ached everywhere, especially his lower back and ankle. He considered Aeva's question for a minute, a strange way to ask what the dream was about.

"I ran from—I don't know. Death, I guess."

"As we all do," Aeva said. "You seem to dodge death everywhere you turn. It's no wonder you dream about it."

Kapp yawned. "What are your nightmares about?"

Aeva looked restless for once. She stared off dreamily as she spoke. "All through my life, Alastar told me tales about the Surge. Entire planets devastated—so much life lost. It must have been terrible to witness."

Kapp tried to find similarities between his fears and hers, but he couldn't. "Hasn't Alastar gone to destroy it? The Surge, I mean."

"Yes," she said, tucking a piece of hair behind the slight point of her ear. "But even he may fail. And though the threat would take many generations to reach this system, I still fear for the safety of Arca. It appears that threats against life are not unique in this universe."

Regret washed over Kapp, and Aeva began to stir like an ADD child in class. Some distant problem seemed to have her attention.

"Aeva," Kapp said, "I'm sorry for getting you into this—for trusting Holden. I should've been more careful."

Aeva rose to leave and took another of her immortal pauses, this time making direct eye contact with Kapp. "I forgive you, Kapp Adams. You could not have known the true intentions of your leaders. I just hope that it is not too late to save Arca."

Kapp nodded. "We'll fix this."

"I hope so. But for now, let us wash the blood from our skin and gather everyone together." She lingered in the doorframe for a moment, an angelic silhouette—beautiful without trying, probably without even knowing it herself. "I am eager to hear about the current state of Earth and the fate that befell Beacon Five."

•|•

Asher led the band of filthy survivors to the showers. He brought towels and fresh clothes for everyone, and a new pair of glasses for Mara. They didn't match her style, but they matched her prescription, and that was enough.

Kapp stripped down in the locker room and turned a knob in the shower. He stepped into the high-pressure stream and forced his tense muscles to relax. The white tile darkened beneath him as the water poured over him, lukewarm but still refreshing. Underneath the dirt and dried blood, he found a plethora of fresh bruises, including a hand-shaped one on his neck. Their color approached a yellow-brown, somewhere between the color of mustard and wet sand. He pushed on one of the bruises and cringed from the immediate ache.

After Kapp and the crew washed up, they took the elevator down to level ten. The stainless steel doors opened into a large room with a table in the middle. Unlike the dingy interior of the rest of the complex, the floors and walls in this room shone with spotless white cleanliness. The sterile chamber reminded Kapp of Arca's quarantine room.

Felix and his clone sat at the table, indistinguishable from one another except for one broken feature. Kapp didn't recognize the caramel-skinned woman that sat beside them but thought she might be Genesis. The perfection of her posture rivaled Aeva's.

The sight of Emily and her baby bump made Kapp squirm. The two of them made fast, fleeting eye contact. He pulled out a chair and opened his mouth, summoning up the nerve to greet her, but he had no idea what to say.

"Hello, Kapp," Emily said.

Kapp gulped loudly. "Nice to see you again."

"Mm-hmm."

He avoided her gaze, looking instead to Asher. "Should we—"

"You two should talk," Asher said. "Go."

Kapp could practically feel the eyes on him. "You think now is the time?"

"Let's just get it over with," Emily said.

Standing up revealed the true state of her pregnancy, and Kapp wondered if there was such thing a fourth trimester. He followed her to a sitting area, a semi-private place to talk. On the way over, he mentally rehearsed a half-assed apology: *Sorry for knocking you up before I left the atmosphere.* Emily sank into an old couch, and Kapp sat across from her. He took a deep, painful breath.

"Look, Emily, I'm sorry for—"

"Funny how you remember my name now." Her eyes narrowed, an effect amplified by winged eyeliner. "You know, I should have gone home with Asher that night."

Kapp's shoulders and head dropped. "You know I was drunk when we met."

"An excuse that can only work so many times."

His head found his palms, and he groaned. "What do you want?"

"If it were up to me, I'd never see you again." She leaned in closer, her anger softening into something more like acceptance. "But I love Asher, and Asher loves you."

Across the room, the elevator opened and Aeva entered the room, stealing Kapp's focus for just a second. Emily continued.

"You have no idea how much he's done to try to help you, the risks he's taken to get you home." She shook her head firmly, her voice slowing. "Now that you're here. Now that we're both here."

"Look, I'm sorry," Kapp said. "If you need money, I have—"

"Oh my god," Emily said. "I don't need your credits. Honestly, money will probably be useless sooner than later."

"I meant I can help take care of the baby."

"Stop," Emily said. "Asher's in an awkward enough situation as it is. Let's just agree to be civil with each other. You don't need to be a father, Kapp. I don't want you to father my baby, anyway. Asher can do that."

Kapp didn't want to father the baby either, but her words still stung. "Okay," he said. "That's fine."

"I know what you've done for him," she said, placing a soft hand on his wrist. "How you saved his life."

"And he just saved mine," Kapp said, remembering their mad flight from Groom Lake, Walker's dead eyes. "Guess we're even."

"Asher's a lot stronger than you think," she said. "But he still needs us."

Kapp nodded, finally summoning up the nerve to look at her directly.

"Are we good, Emily?"

A deep breath and a sigh.

"It's a start, Kapp."

•|•

Dressed in fresh clothes, wet hair tied back in a tight ponytail, Aeva stood to address the small conference gathered on level ten.

"I never hoped for such a meeting to occur, but I'm glad that we lived long enough to gather together. We—the surviving crews of Starling II, Beacon Five, and new friends from Earth—have been formed into an alliance by the combination of our fates. It is my belief that we fight for the same side. For Arca."

"For Arca," a few said in unison.

"You do not yet all know each other, but I feel that all of your intentions are true. There will be time for more formal introductions. There will be time to make a plan. But first, let us begin with the sharing of tales." Aeva looked at their faces as she spoke, lingering for a second on each. "Genesis, I have lived far too long in the darkness. I am eager to hear what happened to Beacon Five."

Aeva took a seat, and all eyes turned to the woman across from her.

"We woke from stasis one Earth year before our arrival," Genesis said, rising from her seat. She had a similar accent to Aeva's, but far more muted, like that of a second generation immigrant. "That's when Beacon Five began to collect data from Earth's satellites to stream back to Arca."

Asher put an arm around Emily. Neither looked even slightly concerned by the alien tale. Kapp wondered how long they had been underground together.

"Our cloaking shield powered on with no issues—we followed every protocol." Unblinking, Aeva stared into the distance as Genesis spoke. "Felix analyzed the data and planned our descent. During that year, we studied the language and culture surrounding our point of arrival. We were going to land in a large desert, not far from where we are now. On the day of our descent, conditions were perfect, but when we broke through the atmosphere—"

Genesis took in a sharp breath, and a gang of drifting eyes returned to her face.

"When we broke through the atmosphere," she continued, shaking her head. "I don't know for certain what happened, Aeva. We followed protocol, we scanned for obstacles, and we should have arrived without issue. Like I said, conditions were perfect, but somehow our entry failed, and Beacon Five fell from the sky."

Kapp recalled his crash landing on Phobos, and the fear that it had ignited in him—fear extinguished by his will to survive.

"When our systems began to fail, there was only enough time to adjust our course slightly," Genesis said. "We aimed for the nearest body of water, a deep lake, knowing that it would not save the ship, but that it would at least conceal it. The cloaking shield held until the very end, and then the five of us ejected. We watched the demise of Beacon Five from above as we drifted to the Earth."

Kapp only counted three people—Genesis, Felix, and Calix. He was tempted to ask about the location of the others, but he didn't want to interrupt the story.

"We couldn't find each other until the sun rose, and by that time there was no trace of Beacon Five. Through the night, her remains sank into the depths of the water."

A moment of silence, and then Genesis spoke again.

"We built a camp by the waterside, but the changing weather forced us to leave that place." The memory seemed to visit the mind of Genesis like an unwelcome guest. "We wandered for days until we found a road, which we followed. Taelyr nearly died of thirst, and all of us were hungry. But the first humans we encountered were very kind. They asked where we were going and offered us a ride, but we didn't know how to answer. Ramses saved us with a clever lie, and we were brought to the nearest town."

Aeva leaned in closer, revealing more emotion than Kapp had ever seen her display.

"We knew only two things: that one day, hopefully, Arca would come to Earth and that we had to be ready for it. We decided to integrate into society, to stock up on resources so that we might better prepare for your arrival." Though everyone gathered to hear the story, Genesis seemed to speak directly to Aeva. "At that time, securing a false identity was not difficult. We acquired new names—new lives. The five of us split up and spread out to avoid detection. We only gathered once per year."

Kapp tried to recall how many years earlier Beacon Five had left Arca. *Forty-something?*

"Over time we worked to amass a sizable amount of resources. I trained to be a doctor. Taelyr built a farm. Felix and Calix began working in government intelligence. They shared a single identity, which allowed them to pull off some impressive feats and to earn the trust of some very important people over the years. We kept our eyes on the sky."

"And Ramses?" Aeva asked.

"We were all successful in our chosen paths, but Ramses found the most success. One year, he brought a piece of Beacon Five to our yearly rendezvous. By diving down to the wreckage, he recovered the crystal, which held all of the ship's data. His goal was to build a new Beacon, or something similar, so that we might send you updates as you approached Earth." Genesis looked to both Felix and Calix. "We all thought that it was a great plan, so we poured our earnings into his pursuits. For years he tinkered with the crystal, trying to reverse-engineer it, and over time he did make small breakthroughs."

"Where is he now?" Aeva asked.

Genesis seemed to expect the interruption. "Eventually, Ramses brought someone to our yearly gathering—a woman named Bella. He had told her everything about where we came from, what we were doing on Earth. We were angry at first, but during Bella's visit, we grew to trust her, to love her even. All seemed well, and we accepted their union. Ramses told us that he had made a breakthrough on the crystal, that within a year he'd have schematics ready for a new Beacon. But after that week, we never saw him or Bella again."

"What happened?" Aeva asked.

"A few years later, Bella sent Felix a letter." Genesis shook her head back and forth deliberately. "It said that Ramses had changed, that he had secluded himself in his lab, that he was planning something bad. She didn't know what his plan was, but she was worried about her safety—and the safety of her child. We went to help her, but—"

Genesis took in a sharp breath, her eyes watering.

"When we got there Bella was dead," Felix said, "and Ramses was gone."

"And the child?" Aeva asked.

Felix shrugged. "We don't know. The place was destroyed."

"Where's Taelyr?" Aeva asked, her gaze frantically darting between Genesis and the twins.

"Taelyr is gone too—killed by Ramses." Genesis reached across the table to grab Aeva's hand. "He's been hunting us ever since. That's why we live here."

"Do you know where he is now?" Aeva asked, her voice shaking. Kapp had never seen her so angry. "We have to—"

"Should we just show them?" Felix suggested.

"Yes," Genesis said. "They should see for themselves."

Felix jogged over to the opposite side of the room and came back with a remote control. He pushed a button on the device, and a projector lowered from the ceiling. Its bulb warmed up until a rectangle of light appeared on a nearby wall. Felix pushed a few more buttons on the remote, the room lights dimmed, and a video began to play. Audio crackled from speakers in the ceiling.

"Imagine a better world," the voiceover began.

Kapp thought the voice sounded familiar. A visual of Earth spun slowly in the center of the black screen.

"A world free of disease."

The onscreen globe morphed into the head of a woman, clearly plagued with some disease. As a post-rock soundtrack faded in, the illness began to drain from her face. Yellow eyes turned white and her ruddy skin cleared.

"A world without pain, without suffering."

The music steadily grew more epic, the pauses between statements more dramatic. A video of a child falling off his bicycle played in slow motion. The child stood up, smiled, and brushed the gravel from his skinned knees. The camera zoomed in on his wounds, which had already started healing. Kapp trembled at the memory of Walker's nose popping back into place.

"Imagine a world without death," the voice continued, *"one where you can stay young forever."*

Attractive twenty-somethings danced on the screen, their skin, hair, and teeth more perfect than those in any cosmetics commercial Kapp had ever seen. Then the music reached a climax before stopping completely. The last note echoed out beneath the narrator's final words.

"Welcome to that world."

The video faded to black, and text appeared in the center, bold and shiny propaganda.

CAGE INDUSTRIES
BUILDING A BETTER WORLD

"Not long ago," Genesis said, "Ramses began to appear in the media. With unnatural means, he cured a multitude of diseases, and now he uses those same means to control the masses. You've seen for yourself the capabilities of his nano-injected soldiers. He infiltrated the IES in an attempt to destroy Arca, and every day he grows more powerful. Aeva—he has since changed his name to Theo Cage, but the enemy we face is our own brother."

32

GOOD BOY

Hesitantly, Holden approached the arched entrance of Theo Cage's private Southern California residence. His roundish shadow darkened the marble floor below his feet as he made his way up the wide staircase. At the top, two armed guards stood beside a pair of adjacent white pillars. They scanned him with their dead eyes and nodded their nonverbal permission to pass.

You poor, mindless servants, Holden thought. *More machine than man.*

Before the doors could part automatically, Holden caught a glimpse of his reflection. Blackened skin surrounded his right eye, and a bandage covered the pistol-whip wound on the side of his head. His entire body still hurt like hell from the beating, but he feared that his upcoming meeting would hurt even more. After a deep sigh, he stepped into the foyer, a circular room skirted by a pair of spiral staircases.

"Holden." The voice of his master boomed through the intercom, more jovial than usual. *"Come join me in the lab."*

Holden relaxed a little. He walked down a long hallway to his right, scanned his wrist at the door, and entered the lab. Fluorescent light spilled from every inch of the ceiling, giving the room an unnatural glow.

Ahead, Theo stood beside a long stainless steel table covered in beakers, petri dishes, and other pieces of equipment that Holden didn't understand. His skin had a plastic shine to it—like a wax statue. When he saw Holden, he set down a syringe he was holding, removed his protective goggles, and placed them in a pocket of his white lab coat.

"Sit," Theo said, gesturing to a nearby seat that resembled a dentist chair.

"I'm alright, sir," Holden said. "I sat for a long time on the way here."

Holden thought he saw rage flash like fire across Theo's eyes, but the flame disappeared as fast as it came.

"You came from Groom Lake, yes?"

Holden knew that the question was just a formality. His implant ensured that Theo always knew his location, but he had to oblige.

"Correct, sir."

"I see he did a number on you," Theo said, taking a closer look at Holden's injuries. "You're still living in the stone age, Holden. Why won't you let me heal you?"

Holden swallowed loudly. "That wasn't part of the deal, sir."

In truth, he didn't want the nano-bots anywhere near him. Though the tiny machines were invisible to the naked eye, Holden imagined them as ants or termites or other crawly things.

"Kapp Adams. Kapp—Adams," Theo said, enunciating each syllable as if he could taste the words. "The name rolls off the tongue, doesn't it?"

The mention of Kapp sent waves of heat through Holden's body. "I suppose, sir."

"You've failed to take care of him and his friends one too many times. First on Phobos, and now this."

"I know, but—"

"Holden, Holden, Holden," Theo said, his voice thick with condescension. "I need you to get a better handle on things. Or should I find someone more capable?"

Panic gripped Holden's mind. "You didn't tell me about the rebels. How were my men supposed to expect a rescue party?"

"These sound like excuses, Holden," Theo said, the anger in his tone flaring up like gasoline in a fire. "Stop acting like a child, and take responsibility for your actions. My work consumes me."

He took a step toward Holden, who cowered like a kicked puppy.

"I'm sorry, sir. It's just—my daughter is getting sicker. I've done everything in my power to uphold my end of the deal, but you keep—"

"For the love of science, Holden, please stop this torrential sniveling." Doctor Cage flashed a menacing grin. "In a couple of days, all of this will be over. You need to learn patience."

"What do you mean—over?" Holden asked.

"That's for bigger brains to worry about, Holdy." Theo came closer to Holden and gripped his shoulder tightly. "Consider this your final chance. Keep an eye on Arca while I finish my work, and I'll make sure your daughter gets her cure. I'll administer the antidote myself if that's what it takes. I'm just far too busy to babysit you."

Holden didn't know why, but Theo's words soothed his worries about the whole ordeal.

"Thank you, sir."

"You've always been loyal to me." Theo ran a hand over the smooth, shiny skin of his bald head. "Like a good dog."

Theo squeezed Holden's shoulder, igniting a pressure point of pain. With ease, he forced the big man down into the chair.

"But good dogs sit when they are told. Do you understand?"

"Yes, I—"

"You've bitten the hand that feeds," Theo said, raising his voice between clenched teeth.

Cold shackles sprung from below Holden's seat and wrapped themselves around his wrists and ankles, tightening like boa constrictors.

"Please," Holden begged, "don't."

"It's my turn to speak." Theo took a few steps toward the lab table. "When a dog bites, its owner can do one of two things."

Holden squirmed against his restraints, but they held like vice grips.

"He can tame it"—Rubber gloves snapped against Theo's wrists as he spoke—"or he can put it down."

Theo picked up a syringe from the table, took off its cap, and started toward Holden, who felt a stream of urine heating his pants.

"Please, sir—I'll do whatever you want. Just give me—"

"You whine. You beg." Theo let out a deep, guttural laugh. "You even piss on the furniture like a bad, bad dog."

"I know I've let you down," Holden cried. "I'm sorry. Please, just—"

Theo silenced the begging by shoving a handful of rubber gloves into Holden's mouth. Then he stepped behind the chair until it blocked him from sight.

"In this new world of mine—there is no room for untamed animals."

Holden was too scared to feel the needle penetrating his neck, but he did feel an odd sensation immediately after Theo depressed the plunger of the syringe. Numbness spread from the needle's entry point until it reached the injuries on his head. Then the burning began—a crawling sensation under the skin surrounding his eye. The wound on his scalp sizzled like Pop Rocks, not audibly but somehow he still heard it. He soon found that he could no longer move his body.

This is it, he thought. *I'm dying.*

The burning sensation faded, and Holden found that he didn't actually care if he died. He didn't want to live. He didn't *want* anything. The numbness spread until it consumed everything: his thoughts, his feelings, his memories—his desires, especially. The things that made up Bryce Holden were still there, buried deep in the recesses of his mind, but the wants and needs in his head were no longer his own.

Theo released the shackles and removed his gloves. He took the gag out of Holden's mouth and studied the man's transformation closely. Holden's black eye had healed completely, and the gash on his head was about halfway there. The anti-aging had already begun; Holden looked about ten years younger and counting. The excess fat would fade in time.

Excellent.

The word entered Holden's mind in Theo's voice, which would have been surprising if Holden had any emotions left.

Stand.

Holden's body rose from the seat and stood erect. Droplets of urine fell from his pants and splashed into the puddle below.

You've made quite a mess. Theo flashed a malicious grin. *Go on, clean it up.*

Holden automatically searched the room for a rag. After finding one, he got on his hands and knees and began to soak up the puddle.

Dogs don't use towels. The voice in Holden's head grew louder. *Lap it up, Holden.*

Deep in his mind, Holden's own voice screamed out in protest. He tried to fight it, but his body moved against his diminished will. His hands tossed the wet rag to the side. His eyes found his own reflection on the wet floor, and the selfish desire to stop almost showed itself in that deadened gaze—almost. But there was no stopping himself. Holden, or what was left of him, lowered his tongue to the wet tile.

Good boy.

33

LOST IN THE SAUCE

Silence reigned as everyone in the room processed the news about their enemy.

"Death disguised as life," Aeva said, shaking her head back and forth with iron steadiness. "I should never have come. There is no refuge here. Earth is on the brink of its own Surge, and we're likely too late to stop it."

She stood up and began to pace back and forth along one side of the conference table. Her expression became dark, worried.

"We must return to Arca before Ramses—before Theo destroys her."

Genesis spoke next. "If he wanted to destroy her, he could have done that by now. I believe his objectives changed once Arca escaped the first trap."

"How do you know that he hasn't done it already?" Aeva asked.

"We've got eyes everywhere," Asher said. "I checked the video feed of Groom Lake less than an hour ago."

"Yes," Genesis said, "We know that Arca is safe for now."

"Perhaps you're right." Aeva spoke calmly, but without any hint of reassurance in her voice. "I hope."

"Holden did interrogate us for the password." Kapp felt the need to stand up during the conversation, but his sprained ankle was still throbbing. "Maybe they just want something that's inside—is there something we can bargain with?"

"Arca holds many treasures," Aeva said, "some that a despot might desire, but nothing we can part with."

Felix joined the conversation. "What password do you speak of, Aeva?"

Emily raised a hand to say something, but everyone ignored her.

"I've put Arca on lockdown. Only Kapp and I hold the key." Aeva stopped pacing, and her eyes widened. "Oh no. We've only days before the Artazoa perish in this environment. After that, the lockdown will fail."

"How many days?" Jesse asked, always trying his best to be prepared for all outcomes.

"Guys," Emily said, squirming in her chair.

Aeva spoke quickly. "It depends on the oxygen levels in the atmosphere—I will have to calculate it. Someone give me the numbers, please."

Emily whispered something to Asher, the only person paying her any attention.

"We need to find out what Theo wants," Aeva said, her mind clearly spinning.

Kapp found his moment to speak up. "Maybe he just wants to leave Earth."

Aeva didn't seem to like the thought. "We can't let that—"

Asher slammed something on the table.

"Excuse me. Um—I don't mean to interrupt." He had an uncomfortable expression on his face. "But I think Emily's water just broke."

•|•

A flurry of activity followed the news. Genesis and the twins rushed around to various supply rooms until they found everything they needed to complete their makeshift maternity ward. Asher kept a comforting hand on Emily, who began to hyperventilate from the pain growing inside her. Kapp stood awkwardly while they waited, suddenly craving a drink. No one was prepared for the premature labor, especially not him.

When everything was ready, Genesis and Asher helped Emily to her feet and walked her into the sterilized birth room. Mara silently cleaned up the mess that they left behind, and everyone else stood in a circle.

"Don't worry." Felix spoke with an unlit cigarette between his lips. "Emily's in good hands. Even before our arrival, Genesis used to deliver new lives on Arca."

"Yeah," Calix said, "animal lives."

"We're all animals." Felix sparked his lighter and brought the flame to his cigarette. "Gen is a great doctor."

Before Felix could take a puff, Aeva plucked the freshly lit smoke from his mouth.

"Hey," he said.

"Why are you doing that?" Aeva asked, haughty as ever. "You're poisoning yourself."

Kapp recalled the time when Mara took his scotch bottle away on Starling II, just before he uncovered Eli's betrayal.

"You're a fucking drunk," she had said.

But if he hadn't been drinking, he would have never found the evidence in the trash, and they might have all died, not just Eli. An unwanted image of the big man's frozen corpse—floating toward the Phobian horizon—flashed across Kapp's memory. At that moment, he had felt only anger at Eli, but as he thought more about the man's situation, regret began to seep through Kapp's rough exterior, tightening his stomach into a knot. With all the new revelations, he now understood that Eli was just a pawn.

A pained yell came from the maternity ward, pulling Kapp back into the present moment. He wanted to get away from the sound, away from the memories, away from the pain that nipped relentlessly at his body like a vulture.

"Hey, Felix," Kapp said. "You got any liquid poison?"

Felix took the cigarette back from Aeva, who looked at both men with an expression that bordered annoyance. "I think we have some vodka in storage."

"Great," Kapp said. "Not my first choice, but I'll take it."

"Follow me." Felix turned toward the elevator shaft. "I want to show you guys something, anyway."

•|•

Mara stayed behind to help Genesis, while the twins led Kapp, Jesse, and Aeva to the storage room on level nine. The group walked between rows of high shelves filled mostly with imperishable food. At the end of one row, Felix grabbed a plastic bottle and handed it to Kapp. He took a closer look at the faded paper label and found that the vodka had been bottled in 2017.

"Vintage," he said, twisting off the lid with his bionic hand. "I haven't had bottom shelf vodka since college."

"You couldn't pay me to drink that stuff," Jesse said, shaking his head back and forth. "We used to call that a hangover in a bottle."

Kapp took a nasty swig, and the muscles in his cheek tightened. "Tastes like nail polish—with undertones of rubber."

That didn't stop him from killing a third of the bottle by the time they reached their next stop, the room that Felix wanted to show them. Beyond the storage room, the group came to a steel door. The spray-painted sign above it had too many faded letters to remain legible, but Kapp could make out an A and a couple of Rs. Felix typed in a code, then the locking mechanism groaned and clicked. He shouldered the door open, and they stepped into the room.

When the fluorescent bulbs came on, Kapp saw a stainless steel table with a couple of black plastic cases on top of it. White mesh grids covered two of the walls from floor to ceiling. Dozens of weapons, organized by size and purpose, hung from hooks on the mesh: long rifles, assault rifles, handguns, and a few specialty weapons. A shelf of ammo filled the third wall.

"Welcome to the armory," Felix said. He leaned against the high table and grabbed his chin.

In a daze from the booze, Kapp looked around the room dreamily. A large spider crept along a crack in the concrete ceiling. He imagined the creature with Holden's face and considered shooting it with one of the handguns. The thought made him smile.

"Damn," Jesse said. "Y'all are packin' heat."

Aeva walked along one wall, examining the weapons as if they could jump out at her. "I will need to learn how to use these," she said.

"It's pretty simple. Just point and shoot," Calix said, his voice slightly more nasal than Felix's. "You'll learn fast."

"You've all seen what we're up against." Felix moved to the opposite side of the table and put a hand on one of the cases. "Gunfire doesn't do much to Theo's minions."

That's an understatement, Kapp thought. He still vividly remembered Walker, who should've died, jumping on him from the warehouse roof and not giving up the chase, even after Jesse put six bullets in him.

"They have tiny robots in their blood that block their pain receptors and heal their cells." Felix popped the latch on the black case in front of him. "One of the only ways to take them out for good—is with one of these bad boys."

Felix opened the case and lifted a piece of foam egg carton from the top, revealing a set of round metallic objects with seams around their circumference.

"These are electromagnetic pulse grenades," Felix said, picking one up carefully. "When they're activated, they release a short burst of energy that disrupts all kinds of technology—bad news for the little bots."

Jesse looked at the grenades like a nerd at a comic book store. "I'll be damned."

Kapp nodded in recognition. "Ash saved my life with one of those."

"Cal," Felix said, handing the weapon to his clone. "Wanna show them how it's done?"

Calix accepted the orb and nodded. Everyone else followed him out of the door and down the hallway. Kapp stumbled on the raised doorjamb on the way out. The pain returned to his ankle, and he limped behind the others. He tried not to think about the child being born one level below—his child.

"To activate the grenades, all you have to do is twist the two halves in opposite directions." Calix stopped walking forward. "You'll hear a click when you do it. The timing is variable. One click is equal to one second, so if you want to delay the activation by three seconds, just twist for three clicks and then throw."

"What's the max delay?" Jesse asked.

"Fifteen clicks."

Without warning, Calix held the grenade between his hands and began to twist it like a wet washcloth. The device clicked five times, and then he rolled it down the hallway. If there were ten pins at the end of the hall, Calix would have had a strike. The grenade came to a halt and popped open, emitting a high pitched sound, then all the fluorescent bulbs within several meters of the weapon flickered out in unison.

"Nice," Aeva said. "I like those."

Jesse turned to Calix. "Did you design them?"

"Kind of," Calix said. "We stole the schematics and tweaked the design with our own improvements. We also have an EMP shotgun. It's just a prototype, but it works well."

"Can I see it?" Jesse asked.

"See it?" Felix stomped out his cigarette and started back toward the armory. "You can shoot it if you want."

"To the range?" Calix said.

The hallway—and everyone walking in it—began to spin around Kapp.

•|•

Kapp made the angry walk of the denied drunk. Though he kept saying he was fine, no one would let him anywhere near the gun range to watch Jesse play with his new toy. Aeva volunteered to take him away, so he followed her to the elevator. As he stumbled down the hall, his anger soon faded, dissolved by the low-grade alcohol in his blood.

Aeva walked silently ahead of him, and Kapp's gaze drifted to the tight fit of her leggings. His drunk mind paid careful attention to the way the fabric stretched and shifted, the way its transparency changed with each motion. From pure experience, he could tell that she wore no underwear.

They stepped into the elevator without a word. Kapp stabilized himself on the elevator rail with both hands, an old trick to stop the spins. It didn't really work. Shamelessly, he looked over his shoulder at Aeva, who seemed to barely notice he was there. She pressed a button to start their ascent.

Kapp wanted to tell her that she was beautiful, not just her body, but her mind as well. He wanted to say that he loved spending time with her, that he felt more connected to her than any human he had ever met. More than anything, he desired to have another of their rare, but insightful, philosophical talks—to have any conversation with the exotic woman would have done the trick. But his intentions, buried deep beneath layers of pain and intoxication, did not align with his actions. Before he could stop himself, the animal side of Kapp emerged.

"Aeva." Kapp paused and hiccuped loudly before letting go of the elevator rail and turning around. "Can I be honest?"

"I'm sure you will be," she said, still not looking at him.

He scanned her up and down—mostly down. "I've always thought you're so sexy. Like really, really, ridiculously good looking."

Her green eyes turned to his. Where his fried brain expected to see gratitude, he only saw disgust. This still didn't deter him. He stumbled closer and put a metal hand on her waist. She shrunk from the touch, and Kapp's irrational anger returned.

"Why do you hate me?" he mumbled, lost in the sauce. "Don't like my false arm?"

Kapp shook his prosthetic. The elevator slowed down and came to a halt. The doors slid open, and Aeva stepped off. She waited for Kapp to exit, and then she looked at him with hard, piercing eyes.

"Kapp," she said sternly. "Do not confuse my fear with loathing. Do not mistake my preoccupation with contempt. We have a war to prepare for, and meanwhile, you are getting drunk. Entire planets have been wiped out by similar negligence to what I've seen here on Earth, our enemy has all the power, and his soldiers are almost invincible. But you seem to worry only about yourself."

Kapp shrunk from the verbal blows. Part of him wanted to argue, but he kept his mouth shut for once and let her continue.

"As far as my hate for you…if you've paid any attention to our interactions, you'd understand that I quite like you, Kapp. I think you can be a brave and selfless man at times. You saved many lives on Phobos. You got us out of prison, and for that, I am extremely grateful. However, I could do without your drunken advances. If I despise any part of you, it is this part."

•|•

When he made it to his room, Kapp vomited out the poison and crashed into the bed. He fell asleep before his head even hit the pillow. The night seemed to pass in a single blink. For a while, he tried to go back to sleep, but shame, amplified by a toxic headache, nagged him like a worried mother. It knock-knock-knocked at the door of his mind, a constant reminder of his drunken mistakes. Before meeting Aeva, he had never been one to regret his actions. Usually, he forgave himself quickly, often with the help of more alcohol—but disappointing Aeva felt much worse than disappointing himself.

The need to apologize overpowered his desire to hide in bed all day. He forced himself up and winced at the sharp pain in his head. The rest of his body still hurt, but not as badly as the day before. Nausea returned when he tried to stand up, so he took a few deep breaths.

After a short mental pep talk, Kapp made it to a sink around the corner from his bedroom. He drank directly from the faucet until his stomach could handle no more, then he splashed cold water on his sweaty face and slapped his cheeks a few times. He didn't bother changing out of yesterday's clothes before limping to the elevator.

By the time he reached level ten, he could feel a pounding in his head, as if his brain was trying to escape. The fluorescent glow of the sterile room ahead widened as the elevator doors opened, stabbing the prisoner in his skull like a jagged knife. He squeezed his temples but found no relief.

As he stepped into the room, something much sharper than the shaft of light pierced his mind, reminding him of what he had forced himself to forget the night before—a sound that temporarily displaced his quest for Aeva's forgiveness. From somewhere ahead, Kapp heard the high-pitched noise of a baby crying…his baby.

34

NEW LIFE

Mara sat outside of the maternity room, rocking the crying child in her arms. She looked up from the bundle when Kapp got close, but he kept his eyes on the baby. It had the generic, fetal look of every other newborn he had seen—impossible to tell the gender. Still, some of its features looked overwhelmingly familiar. The green eyes were definitely his, but the wispy tufts of light hair looked nothing like his dark locks. The newborn seemed bigger than it should in Mara's tiny arms, but that's not what caught Kapp's attention. Behind her thick lenses, Mara was crying too.

"It's a girl," she said, her lip trembling.

"Mara, what's wrong?"

He wondered if all women cried when they held newborns, but the tears streaming down her face didn't look even slightly happy.

"I'm so sorry," she whispered to the baby between frantic breaths.

"Mara," Kapp said, with as much patience as he had in him. "Where is everyone?"

Too hysteric to continue the conversation, Mara transferred the bundle to one arm and pointed at the nearest door. An odd sense of protectiveness overtook Kapp. He suddenly doubted Mara's ability to care for a newborn in her state of mind.

"Can I?" he asked, reaching toward the child.

Kapp took the baby from Mara and cradled her soft head in his left palm, afraid that he might damage her. The child radiated a soft, calming heat. He couldn't remember the last time he held a baby.

He couldn't quite place the feeling, only that it was new to him. A pair of fresh eyes found his face and lingered there for a moment before closing. Just as his daughter stopped crying, tears started welling in Kapp's eyes.

Kapp didn't bother knocking before entering the maternity room. He expected to find everyone in there, gathered to congratulate the new mother, but the space was fairly empty. The sight of Aeva sent a wave of shame through him. She looked at the baby girl in his arms, and her lips tightened into a straight line. Genesis stood on the opposite side of the bed, cleaning up a tray of medical equipment. She moved with an equally solemn energy.

Then Kapp's attention turned to the third woman in the room. Emily lay under fresh white sheets that covered her to the neck. Multiple piercings hung from her ears, shining between strands of golden hair, reflecting the sterile light. Her eyelids hung peacefully over her eyes, and the relaxed skin of her face had a soft glow to it. They were both in the same room, but he looked at Emily as if some unexplainable fog floated between them.

He took a step closer, and the child squirmed in his arms. He didn't have to check for the rise and fall of Emily's chest to realize what had happened. Aeva and Genesis bowed their heads in unison.

"There were complications with the pregnancy." Genesis spoke softly, as if she could disturb the dead. "I did all that I could, but it wasn't enough."

Kapp's guts wrenched when he looked down at the now motherless baby—then at Emily. He knew almost nothing about the mother of his child. If Asher hadn't kept in contact with her, Kapp wouldn't have even known her name. Because of the long nap, it only felt like weeks since they met, but so much had changed in that time. He tried to speak, but the words wouldn't come.

"Jesse and the twins have gone to prepare a grave," Aeva said.

The words echoed in Kapp's head for what felt like a long time before he could open his mouth again.

"Where?" Kapp asked. "I can help."

"They went to find a nice spot on the surface," Aeva said. "I'm sure they're almost done by now."

On the outside, he remained calm, but panic began to set in. Kapp needed to get out of the room, to pass the tragedy in his arms to someone else—anyone more capable. Emily didn't want him to father the baby, anyway, she wanted—

"Asher? Where is he?"

"I'm not sure," Aeva said. "He left just before you came here. He said he needed to be alone."

Kapp asked the question in a practical way, but the words sparked darker thoughts in his mind. No one in the complex knew the Asher that Kapp knew. No one had been there to see Asher's usual reaction to tragedy. But Kapp could vividly remember finding his best friend bleeding out in an apartment bathroom from self-inflicted wounds. He remembered driving a hundred miles per hour on the shoulder of the freeway to get Asher to the emergency room. He had stayed up all night in the hospital's waiting room, unsure of whether Asher would live or die—and *that* suicide attempt was about not getting into flight school. Asher had never lost a loved one, not even a grandparent—not even a pet as far as Kapp knew. He shuddered to think what his friend might try in the face of a real tragedy.

"We have to go," Kapp roared, too focused on saving the living to worry about disturbing the dead. He handed his tragic child to Genesis and started toward the exit. "I think Asher's gonna hurt himself."

•|•

They left the child with Mara so that Genesis could help with the search. She knew the underground complex better than anyone, so she offered to do a sweep of all the unused floors while Kapp and Aeva went to the areas they had already explored. Since those areas were few, they decided not to split up. Kapp didn't remember the elevator being so slow, but a single floor felt like it took minutes to ascend. He even tried to squeeze himself through the doors before they could open completely. Aeva came out behind him, and they jogged down the hallway of level nine, leaving Genesis behind.

"Check that end of the hall," Kapp said. "Meet me back here."

When Kapp went into the storage room, the fluorescent lights turned on automatically. The brightness sent a sharp wave of pain through his head. As fast as he could, he limped past shelves of cleaning supplies and chemicals. He saw the plastic vodka bottles and stifled a gag. Ironically, the liquor wasn't stored far from the rat poison. The room held plenty of things that Asher could hurt himself with—but no Asher.

Where are you?

On the way out, Kapp grabbed a bottle of Aspirin with a faded label off the medicine shelf and swallowed three of the dry, white pills. No chaser. He wanted to take something stronger, but he needed to keep his wits about him.

"Any luck?" he asked when he saw Aeva again.

"No guns are missing from the armory," she said. "The range is also empty."

Kapp hadn't even considered the possibility of Asher shooting himself. The thought made him shiver. Gravely, he wondered if Asher had his own gun stowed away somewhere.

"Let's go."

•|•

Their next intended stop was level six, but the elevator slowed to a stop one level too soon. Kapp twitched impatiently as the doors slid open.

"Seven and eight are clear," Genesis said, stepping onto the lift.

Aeva nodded. "Nine is clear as well."

"I instructed Mara to check level ten while she's down there."

Kapp tried not to think of Mara alone with a newborn and a dead body, but the thought invaded his mind relentlessly. The elevator moved slowly toward level six, swelling his anxiety with each painful inch of its ascent. Finally, they reached the curved hallway that led to the living quarters.

"I'll go to the left and meet you on the other side," Genesis said.

The other two went to the right. Ignoring the protests of his hurt ankle, Kapp turned his limping jog into a full on sprint. Without even breaking a sweat, Aeva matched his pace. When they reached the row of doors that marked their temporary home, she peeled off to check the first few rooms. Kapp continued straight to Asher's.

Panels with nine-digit keyboards adorned the wall to the left of each door in the hallway. Kapp had no doubt that these locks were originally intended to keep people in, not out. Unlike all the others, Asher's door was shut. Kapp tried the doorknob, but it wouldn't budge.

"Ash," he yelled, pounding on the door. "Ash, come out!"

He couldn't help but recall the Friday night after college graduation, when he brought pizza and beer to Asher's studio apartment, intending to blow off some steam with his best friend. Instead, he found Asher bleeding out in the bathroom—hiding behind a locked front door. In his mind, he could see visions of that wooden door overlaid on the metal door in front of him.

"Ash, open up." Kapp leaned against the portal with all his weight, testing its strength. "I'm not letting you try this again."

"The other rooms are clear." Aeva appeared beside Kapp like a ghost. "Is he in there?"

Kapp nodded. "We need to get this door open."

He considered kicking in the knob, but he didn't think he could manage the task—not with his sprained ankle. He took a few steps back and rammed the door with his shoulder, but the integrity of the entrance didn't falter. It stood like a mountain against his pathetic attempts to knock it down.

"Kapp, stop." Aeva put a hand on his back. "You'll hurt yourself."

He ignored her. Frantically, he began to punch the knob with his bionic hand, which dented the metal but not much else.

"Asher," he yelled. "Open this fucking door right now!"

Then Genesis came from the other direction. She moved like Aeva—a sly, graceful predator, but a predator out of her element, like a cheetah stolen from the plains and placed in a cave. Kapp continued his assault on the door, sweat dripping from his face, until she reached his side and typed in a code on the panel. The lock clicked, and Kapp rushed into the dark room.

His entrance triggered the automatic lights, which illuminated the organized chaos of Asher's bedroom. Clothes, dirty and clean, covered much of the floor. Balled up blankets and sheets drooped off the side of an unmade bed. On top of a dusty mini fridge, which served as a nightstand, sat a single sheet of paper. Kapp picked it up and squinted at the message scrawled on it in handwriting even messier than the room.

To-Do: Bunker Upgrades
Install wireless tower
Disguise entrances
Motion sensor alarms
Fix rail on staircase B2

Kapp barely glanced at the document once he realized that it wasn't a suicide note, but the final list item caught his attention. He thought about the crew's long, tired journey into the mountain after their rescue—the forest, the ladder, the tunnel. He remembered looking over the broken rail of a staircase into what looked like a bottomless pit. Finally, his observation about that treacherous part of the path came to mind.

"Good place to kill yourself," he had said after peering into that immense darkness.

It had been a brainless remark, just another one of Kapp's many verbal blunders, but the weight of those words resonated deep in his mind. *Good place to kill yourself.* He dropped the note to the concrete floor and turned to Aeva and Genesis, who both regarded him with worried expressions.

"What is it?" Aeva asked.

Kapp started toward the exit. "I think I know where Asher is."

•|•

Kapp's clothes clung to his skin by the time he reached staircase B4. He fought with all his might against his weakening pace, but ultimately he had to slow down on the last few flights.

"Ash!" he yelled for the hundredth time, his voice still booming despite the strain.

Quiet as mice, Genesis and Aeva ascended the steps behind him in the dark. They had one flashlight between the three of them, and Kapp held it.

A circle of light found the spray-painted marker for staircase B3. "Ash!"

The three of them began to ascend the next set of steps. B2 sat just around a corner at the top of B3. With each pump of his leg muscles, Kapp felt more and more hopeless. *He easily could have ended it by now,* he thought. Behind him, Aeva and Genesis whispered to each other.

"Did you hear that?" one of them asked.

Kapp had heard it too, a sound like a drop in a distant bucket. He made it to the landing at the top of B3, took a deep breath, and held it. He didn't know how he'd react if Asher wasn't up there—either he'd continue his frantic search, or he'd go grab another bottle of vodka to drown in. After a slow exhale, he rounded the corner and aimed his flashlight upward.

For a moment, Kapp's heart sank, but then the beam of light hit his target. Asher sat below the loose rail with his legs hanging over the edge, one hand on an adjacent step and the other clenched into a tight fist. There he was, half of a sad silhouette. He had a dead look in his one visible eye—like all of his tears had been depleted.

"Ash. I know you're hurting right now." Kapp had to concentrate on what he'd say next, knowing that the wrong words might force Asher's hand. He settled on an old cliché. "But what you're trying to do is a permanent solution to a temporary problem."

Asher didn't turn to Kapp. He just sat still, peering over the edge, his head beginning to shake slowly from side to side.

"A temporary problem?" The anger in Asher's voice surprised Kapp, but despair coated it nonetheless. "I know Emily was just some conquest to you, maybe not even that, but—"

"But you loved her." Kapp ascended another step. "I know that, Asher."

"I didn't love her in the past, Kapp. I still love her"—Asher took in a sharp breath—"and she was the only person to ever love me back."

"That's not true," Kapp said, beginning to choke up himself. "Your friends, your family—they all love you."

Kapp braved a step forward, scared to get too close.

"Not like she did." Asher sniffled. "And even if people do care for me, it doesn't matter. We're all gonna die, anyway. Don't you see that the world's ending? It's pointless. Don't you see?"

Asher was probably right, but Kapp couldn't feed his hopelessness.

"That might be true, Ash, but we haven't died yet. For now, we're still alive. And besides, I—" The words, which felt strange on Kapp's tongue, were an act of desperation, but even before he said them, he knew that they were true. "I love you, man. You're my best friend. Please don't do this."

Then Asher looked at Kapp. Even though he didn't open his mouth, his bloodshot eyes spoke volumes.

"I can't do this without you, man," Kapp continued. "You're right, everything is fucked up. But if the world's ending, why leave early? Why kill yourself?"

Genesis stepped up beside Kapp. "Asher of Earth—you might be right. Perhaps all is lost, but I refuse to go down without a fight. You have proven yourself as a powerful ally in this war, and for that I thank you. If your wish is to die, will you at least die fighting for those that want to live?"

Asher stayed quiet for what felt like a long time. He kept glancing over the edge, which made Kapp nervous.

"I can't do it. I can't—"

"There's something else you should know," Genesis said. "I started analyzing Emily's blood before she—before she perished. I found trace amounts of the nano-injection compound."

Her words momentarily gained Asher's attention, but then his gaze drifted back into the abyss below.

"I doubt she was injected," Genesis said, "but the bots could have spread through contact with someone who is."

Kapp had trouble understanding why the information was relevant, but the thought of contagious nano-bots worried him.

"We've already seen the bots used by Theo to heal and control his subjects—but today I discovered something else."

Get to the point, Kapp thought. He considered running up to Asher while Genesis distracted him.

"The nano-bots have the ability to synthesize a powerful sterilant."

Kapp wasn't immediately sure what that meant, but the words

sparked something in Aeva. She seemed more alert.

"I believe that Theo is attempting to not only control but to sterilize humanity." Genesis spoke with a sad sense of confidence. "And I—it's just a theory, but I truly believe that this sterilant caused the complications that killed Emily."

"Asher," Aeva added. "If you won't fight for the living, perhaps you'll fight for revenge."

The despair on Asher's face turned to pure anger. He leaned forward, precariously close to slipping off the edge.

"I can't—"

Kapp bounded up a few steps to grab him, to stop his friend from jumping, but his sprained ankle gave out, and he stumbled to the concrete. He watched Asher's movements helplessly.

"I was going to say"—Asher rose to stand—"I can't kill myself. Not here, anyway."

Asher reached his clenched fist over the edge and opened it. From below came the same sound that Kapp had heard from staircase B3…a drop in a distant bucket.

"There's water at the bottom," Asher continued. "If I jump, I might survive."

For once, Kapp was grateful for Asher's over-analytical brain.

"And besides," Asher said as he made his way down the steps to join his saviors. "If what you're saying is true, I can't leave this world yet."

Then Asher wiped his tear-stained cheeks with the back of his hands, swallowed hard, and said, "There's someone I need to kill first."

35

SMART COOKIE

Everyone gathered in the forest around a shallow grave. Jesse and the twins had done their best, but the frozen ground proved nearly impossible to work with their limited tools. Flurries of snow drifted slowly through the thin mountain air, adding to the crust around the feet of the mourners and sticking to their black clothes. The pines rustled above, creating a blanket of soft sound, an undertone for the eulogy. Asher spoke to the sky.

"Emily," he said. "You were the kindest person I've ever met. Everyone could just see it in your eyes."

Tears leaked from Mara, creating waterfalls below her spectacles. Jesse held a comforting arm around her thin shoulder. He had a pistol strapped to his belt, right next to three EMP grenades. Everyone else was armed too—just in case.

Asher recounted some of his favorite memories of Emily, a history that seemed far too short. He mentioned the day that they met—how beautiful she looked. Then he talked about the first time that he truly saw her. He shared a funny story about their first date, how he thought she wouldn't show up, how happy he was when she did, and how he had mistaken her gay friend for her lover. Tears filled his eyes, but his voice didn't falter. Finally, Asher told everyone that he had been planning to propose to Emily. He pulled the ring out of his pocket and showed them.

"You picked me up when I was at my lowest," Asher said. "You filled the emptiness in my heart, and now that you're gone—I realize just how deep that pit had gotten. I love you, Emily. I always will."

Kapp choked up as Asher finished his speech, then Felix and Calix lifted the makeshift gurney. They walked Emily's cloth-wrapped body over the grave and lowered it carefully into the cold ground. A pair of shovels hit a pile of snow-dusted earth beside the grave. Just as the twins started their work, Aeva and Genesis began to sing.

The song was unlike anything Kapp had ever heard. A strange melody filled the air, layered with a perfect harmony. The pair of alien women synchronized their voices so perfectly, it was impossible to tell who sang which part. Kapp couldn't pick up on the rhythm or the words. It sounded like the ancient language of the Architects, but he couldn't be sure. He just knew that it was beautiful. The final note echoed through the Clearing as the twins finished filling the hole.

Asher placed a diamond ring on the dirt. "May the lights guide you home, my love."

The funeral attendees returned to the bunker to get out of the cold, but Asher stayed behind until snow covered the shallow grave, erasing it from his sight—but never from his mind.

•|•

A day and a night passed quickly. Everyone knew that the time to act was fast approaching, but no one could come up with a solid plan. Aeva grew more impatient every time that they met to discuss tactics.

"Perhaps I can speak to Theo," she said at one of their many meetings. "Reason with him."

"We've already been over this," Genesis said. "He'll just torture you until you give up the password—or worse."

"I would never give him the password," Aeva said, clearly disgusted at the notion.

"You don't know that." Felix put out his cigarette. "You might say anything once you're injected."

"Besides," Genesis said. "Theo is not the Ramses of our youth.

He's a different person now. There is no reasoning with a lunatic."

Kapp, Jesse, and Mara sat on the sidelines of the group meetings. Asher didn't even attend half of them. He spent most of his time at the gun range, where he had taped a photo of Theo's face over one of the targets.

Aeva paced back and forth along one side of the conference table. "If only there were a way to level the playing field."

Mara fiddled with one of her puzzles while everyone else talked. Kapp rocked the child, still unnamed, in the crook of his real arm.

"We could recruit people," Kapp suggested. "There have to be some off-the-grid, anti-tech groups that might fight for us."

"Not enough time," Aeva said. "We have days, not weeks."

"Even if we do make it to Arca by force," Genesis said, "there's still the matter of what to do with Theo and the mess he's made."

The mess she referred to had been brought up in an earlier meeting. According to the data, Doctor Cage's nano-vaccine had already spread to China, Europe, and Australia, and shipments of the compound were on their way to Russia. The majority of Americans had already been injected. Even worse—Genesis was able to confirm that the bots could spread through blood, sexual contact, and sometimes even saliva. The world belonged to Theo Cage.

"We can worry about that later." Aeva raised her voice. "Right now, I'm worried about getting Arca out of this atmosphere before the Artazoa die."

The baby in Kapp's arms began to cry, so Kapp stepped away from the meeting. Mara, who had been acting like a surrogate mother, followed him. Kapp checked the child's diaper. Still clean.

"She must be hungry," he said.

Mara reached out for the child. "I don't think so."

"I wish I spoke baby," Kapp said, handing the bundle over. "I never know what she's thinking."

Mara grabbed a rag from the diaper bag slung over Kapp's shoulder.

"I actually did my thesis on language acquisition in infants. Listen closely to the cries, and you'll see that her verbal reflexes are slightly different based on her needs."

"Huh?" Kapp muttered. "In English, please?"

"Even across cultures, the sounds are the same," she said. "It's a way that babies communicate before they acquire the language of their parents. Listen. Right now the cry sounds like *eh*. The cry for hunger sounds more like *neh*."

He couldn't really hear the difference with the voices loudening in the next room.

"What does *eh* mean, then?"

"It means"—Mara placed the rag and the baby's head over her shoulder and began patting on her tiny back—"she needs to be burped."

A bubble of trapped gas parted her small lips, accompanied by spittle, and the crying stopped immediately. Kapp shook his head back and forth, smiling in disbelief.

"In six months," Mara said, "we can start teaching her sign language."

"You're one smart cookie, Mars."

He could only hope that they'd still be alive in six months.

•|•

When they returned to the meeting, Aeva was gone. Everyone else sat silently around the table. Kapp felt like he could swim through the tension thickening the underground air.

"What happened?" Kapp asked

"Aeva stormed out," Genesis said. "She's frustrated with our lack of progress on the plan."

Kapp sympathized with both sides. He had always been a planner, but he couldn't help those urges to act—to do anything other than sit and wait. *Aeva just needs some reassurance,* he thought. *Maybe I should talk to her.* Thinking about their last private conversation deterred him from that idea. He still hadn't gotten the nerve to apologize.

A piercing sound interrupted his thoughts. It startled the baby, who began to cry once again. The shrieking alarm came from horns on the ceiling. Felix ran over to one of the computer monitors, followed by everyone else.

"There's a hatch breach on level zero," he yelled over the alarm.

"Did they find us?" Mara asked. "Did someone get inside?"

Felix typed something into the computer, and the sound stopped. He drew a pistol from his waist, checked the magazine, and pulled the slide back. A bullet clicked into the chamber.

"One way to find out."

•|•

The level zero tunnel, usually a dark and treacherous expanse, glowed a dull red under the emergency lights. Plumbing ran along the ceiling, dripping its under-maintained mess into puddles on the floor. Potholes sank into the concrete every few meters. Felix peeked over the final step of staircase B1 and scanned the space from behind his gun.

"Clear," he said, stepping over the threshold.

The others followed, except for Mara, who stayed behind with the baby. Even Asher came out of his seclusion to lend a hand. They had run into him in the elevator, but they didn't bother looking for Aeva.

"How many entrances are there?" Kapp asked, growing uncomfortable in the oppressive silence.

"In this tunnel?" Genesis paused for a moment. "Four or five—they're spread out though."

"Hmm…why so many?"

"The original owner of this place intended to build houses on the surface. Inhabitants would have access to the bunker in case of emergency."

"One big basement," Kapp said, staring ahead. "Not a bad idea."

"We're lucky to have this place," Genesis said. "Our original hideout was in a warehouse."

Felix silenced the conversation by stopping in his tracks. He augmented his weapon with a flashlight and pointed it at a ladder that led to the ceiling. At the top, nestled between a pair of pipes, a small hatch door hung on its hinges—open.

"I think this is the one." He got closer until his eyes were level with one of the ladder's rungs and pointed. "See?"

Kapp took a look until his eyes adjusted and found the pattern. A layer of grime was missing from each rung on alternating sides, exposing dryer rust. *Footprints*. He followed Felix's flashlight to a small pile of dirt on the floor and then to the hole in the ceiling.

"Uh oh," Felix said, scratching his neck.

"What's wrong?" Asher asked, finally speaking up.

"It looks like"—Felix put down the light, shook his head, and let out a short sigh—"It looks like this hatch was opened from the inside."

All the necessary questions began to bombard Kapp's mind. *How? Why? Who?* Especially who.

It didn't take long, however, for the answer to present itself. The chaos in his head found order, and certainty hit him like a brick. Like a frustrated curse, he spoke the only logical answer under his breath.

"Aeva."

•|•

Calix went to track Aeva through the forest, and everyone else returned to level nine. They found Mara and the child locked up in the armory—as planned.

"Is everything alright?" she asked as soon as they entered.

"Aeva's gone rogue," Genesis said.

"What?"

"I think she's gunning for Arca herself." Frustration filled the tone of the exotic woman's voice. "I've never seen her this impatient before. Alone—on an alien planet. She's going to get herself killed."

"We have to go after her," Kapp said, reaching for one of the guns hung on the armory wall.

"And get ourselves killed? We have no plan—and no time to make one."

"We can't just let her do this alone," Kapp said, raising his voice.

"Guys," Mara squeaked.

"Well, what do you propose we do?" Genesis raised her voice to match Kapp's. "It's not like we can just walk into Groom Lake, guns blazing."

Kapp thought he heard an "excuse me," but his anger was beginning to come to a head, eliminating his listening skills in favor of formulating a response to bite Genesis with. A torrent of arguments came from everyone at once, but one voice broke through the downpour.

"Shut up, and fucking listen to me for once!"

Kapp did a double take at Mara. He didn't know she could get that loud, but it definitely silenced him. When the other voices faded out, Mara spoke again, this time at her normal volume.

"I have an idea," she said, her confidence rising. "I know I'm probably the least qualified to make a battle plan. I'm just a linguist. I've lived my life in books. I'm not an astronaut, or a solider, or a doctor. I wasn't born in the stars."

Mara turned to each person as she spoke.

"I'm completely unremarkable, but if there's one thing I do understand—it's fear." Her voice cracked slightly as she spoke. "I've been scared this whole time."

No one responded. Mara had their full attention.

"I think that our enemy doesn't seem fearful enough," Mara continued. "We've all been focused on Theo's strength compared to ours, on his numbers compared to ours. He wants us to be intimidated. He thinks we'll do nothing. But fear—his lack of fear. That's his weakness."

Everyone nodded along.

"I say we use that against him."

"I'm listening," Kapp said, setting his gun down.

Gathered around a table, surrounded by weapons, hidden beneath a mountain—the misfit band of rebels listened closely to Mara's plan. She laid out every detail with clarity and finesse. Not a single person critiqued her ideas. Even the child in Mara's arms stayed quiet for the presentation. By the time she finished, Kapp couldn't erase the grin from his face.

Now that's one smart-ass cookie.

36

NOW WHAT?

Short on vehicles because of Aeva's rogue mission, Kapp and Felix had to share a motorcycle. With the winding mountain roads behind them, they made quick work of the interstate. It took only a couple hours to reach their destination, a fulfillment center at the south end of the Las Vegas valley. They parked the bike in a small lot, around the corner from a row of loading docks, and took off their helmets. Behind them, the lights of the Strip shone like a beacon in the pre-dawn darkness.

"Are you sure that's it?" Kapp asked, raising his head in a quick gesture. "They all look the same."

"One of those three," Felix said. "Let's get closer."

They snuck to the next concrete outcrop and hid behind a dumpster. Kapp's limp had vanished, but his ankle still felt tight. Felix pulled out a pair of night vision binoculars he had borrowed from Asher. Just as he put them to his eyes, red taillights lit up the wide alley, followed by the repetitive beep of an eighteen-wheeler backing up. They ducked back down and watched the truck complete it's J-turn before its back end passed the dumpster. Felix squinted at the license plate.

"That's the one," he said, stowing the binoculars in his messenger bag. "We're late."

"No," Kapp said, looking at his watch. "He's just early."

Once the truck rounded the corner, they ran back to the

motorcycle and hopped on.

"Now what?" Kapp said between heavy breaths. "How do we stow away on a moving truck?"

"Now"—Felix revved the engine—"we improvise."

Kapp held on tight, Felix revved the engine, and they shot out of the parking lot.

•|•

Loose clothing slapped against Kapp's skin, a monotonous and unfamiliar experience for him. It felt wrong to travel so slowly by motorcycle, but they couldn't risk blowing their cover. They followed the truck from a safe distance on a freeway clear of traffic, save for the earliest of commuters and the latest of drunken revelers. Both types snoozed in the backseats of their hired autonomous cars, while Kapp pondered the chaos unfolding around them.

"What are we doing?" Kapp asked for the third time, raising his voice loud enough to be heard above the engine's drone.

"Waiting for the driver to pull over somewhere." Felix switched lanes to avoid a cardboard box. "They may be part machine, but they still have to piss like the rest of us."

"Great," Kapp said. "But what if he already went?"

"I don't want to think about that," Felix yelled over the roar of the engine.

Mountains to their left appeared as silhouettes against the waking sky as they passed Sahara Avenue, then Charleston and the 95. The interstate curved to the east and the Strip disappeared from their rearview mirrors. Twenty minutes later, they passed the Las Vegas Motor Speedway and drove into the desert beyond. Traffic thinned when the truck turned onto the 93 North, so Felix slowed down to put more space between them and the truck.

Kapp knew the route to Groom Lake by heart. Even though he had mostly flown there in the past, he had taken the drive through the desert several times. At every gas station that he and Felix approached, he held his breath and hoped the driver ahead would pull over. The chances for that happening grew slim as the two northbound lanes became one. Soon, the red and yellow sign of the Ash Springs Shell Station pierced the horizon.

"Felix," he yelled. "That's the last gas station before the turnoff."

Felix gave him a gloved thumbs-up and let the motorcycle lose some more speed, even though the truck didn't appear to slow down. It approached their last chance for a bathroom-break miracle with the same cruise-control speed as before. The truck rolled relentlessly across the asphalt, and Kapp imagined the GPS navigation countdowns of his youth, back when people still drove cars.

Half a mile.
A quarter mile.
700 feet.
500 feet.
300 feet.
200 feet.
100 feet.

Then, just as Kapp began to lose hope, before he could curse in frustration, he caught a glimpse of their salvation—red lights illuminating the back of the truck.

•|•

Stepping off the bike with practiced grace, Felix took off his helmet in the parking lot of the gas station. Kapp reached up to do the same, but Felix hit his arm.

"Don't," he said sternly, his eyes darting to a wall of the building. "Facial recognition."

Kapp looked up at the camera mounted above the glass doorway. The gas station appeared old, but its surveillance technology looked brand new. The eye of the camera swiveled toward him.

"If you're flagged, we're toast," Felix said.

The driver of the truck stepped down from his mechanical beast and crossed the parking lot. The man was short but fit. His face, which wore no expression whatsoever, had the plastic sheen of the nano-injected.

"Morning," Felix said as the man passed him.

The driver nodded an awkward greeting and walked straight into the glass doors. He didn't wince from pain, but he did look slightly embarrassed.

"Sorry," he said, reaching a hand toward the door's push bar. "I'm used to automatic doors."

"Aren't we all?" Felix said, grinning sarcastically.

As soon as the man left their sight, Felix and Kapp sprinted to the cargo door of his truck and tried the latch. Locked.

"Damn," Felix said. He scratched his head. "I didn't bring tools for this."

"Guess we'll have to ride up front," Kapp said.

Felix looked straight at him, something the man rarely did. "Not a bad idea."

"I was joking."

The driver-side door opened without issue, and the duo peered inside. Kapp hoped the truck would have a spacious backseat, maybe with a bed to hide under—but it was clearly designed for shorter trips. Instead, he found one row of cracked leather seats and a center console with an oversized cup holder.

"New plan," Felix said, pulling a pistol from some hidden place in his coat. "Fall back."

They retreated a few paces along the side of the truck, which blocked their view of the building. Kapp originally thought that Mara's plan was foolproof, that it would provide him and Felix with a fast and safe entrance into Groom Lake. He braced himself for the upcoming shit show. After a minute or two of waiting, he heard footsteps. Felix released the safety of his pistol, and when the driver came around the front end, he aimed the gun at the center of his shiny forehead.

"Morning," he said again.

The man said nothing. He didn't even appear to process the threat of a pistol aimed at his brain. He just continued forward, a little bit faster than before—just quick enough to slap the gun out of Felix's hands with uncanny power. It hit the asphalt and made a dull clank.

Kapp pounced on the man. The first strike of his metallic fist hit the driver's chin, forcing his head to turn ninety degrees. When it turned back, Kapp saw a dislocated jaw but no other sign of suffering. The jaw bone popped back into place by itself. Felix punched him in the gut, which forced a grunt out of the man's twisted mouth, but nothing else. The driver fought like two or three men, using all of his limbs in unison to defend and attack. Kapp brought a boot to his crotch. It did nothing to help their cause.

Felix reached for his fallen pistol, but it got kicked under the truck. Then, while the man was busy assaulting Felix, Kapp got his bionic hand around his throat and squeezed. He held the man at arm's length and watched his short limbs flail desperately. He heard the click of his hand's gripping mechanism as it reached its safety limit—hard enough to squeeze the juice out of a lemon, but not hard enough to accidentally break a coffee mug. If he was angry enough, Kapp could push far past this barrier, like when he crushed the bottle of scotch on Starling II. Luckily, he had plenty of anger left.

He could hear, but could barely feel, metallic fingers ripping through flesh. Looking away from the carnage, he crushed the truck driver's trachea with the force of a trash compactor. The man crumpled to the ground and twitched a little as Kapp wiped the tainted blood off his hand onto his pants.

"I don't think he'll be healing from that," Felix said, shaking his head back and forth.

Adrenaline pounded in Kapp's veins. He looked at the man's crushed throat, the blood pooling around his neck, and stifled the urge to vomit. He had killed before, twice now, but never so violently.

"What the fuck do we do now, Felix?"

•|•

Kapp could feel the rumble of eighteen tires on a dirt road and could smell the stench of dropped food and drying blood. The swell of an uneven rubber floor mat dug into his back, right at the point on his spine that caused him the most trouble. He tried to adjust his position for comfort, but he had limited space under the truck's high seats.

"Are we almost there?" he asked.

"Yep," Felix said.

"Won't they recognize you at the gate?"

"I'm not in anyone's database," Felix said from behind the steering wheel. "Unless Theo is working the door, I think we're fine."

Kapp had to give him that. "Okay—but how do you know the credentials will work?"

He couldn't see his comrade, but he could almost feel him shrug. The leather seats squeaked.

"I don't," Felix admitted. "But do you have a better plan?"

Kapp stayed quiet. He didn't have a better plan. Their new plan seemed pretty far-fetched, but it was the best they could come up with under pressure. At least Felix had a knack for improvising. After killing the driver, stealing his keys, and cutting out his identity implant, they had stowed his body in the back with the rest of the food shipment. Then they had taped the microchip to the inside of Felix's wrist, underneath his jacket. The beep of a walkie-talkie disrupted Kapp's worried thoughts about the ordeal.

"We're ready for you," Felix said. "Let's make it rain."

"Copy."

Minutes later, the brakes of the eighteen-wheeler squealed, and the vehicle came to a halt. Kapp began to sweat from both nerves and heat. He heard the driver side window roll down.

"Wrist," a monotone voice said.

After a couple of seconds, Kapp heard three short beeps.

"Let me try again," the voice continued. "Your credentials aren't scanning."

Another three beeps, and Kapp's nerves tripled. Their entrance into Groom Lake would require even more blood.

"I don't know what's wrong," Felix said. "It worked at the gas station an hour ago."

"This happens sometimes," the guard said. "Thicker jackets like yours can block the sensor."

Felix didn't respond. Kapp heard him reaching for his gun.

"Go on, then," the gate guard continued. "Roll up your sleeve."

37

MAKE IT RAIN

Emily.

With her name on his lips, Asher woke from one nightmare into the next—the worst of all, a world grown cold from the extinguished flame that had been Emily. A world where the taste of her tongue, the smell of her neck, the touch of her fingers were all just memories. Shivering in the dark, Asher used every ounce of strength in him to greet this dark world, to force his eyes open. With that impossible task accomplished, he focused on the red glow of his alarm clock.

His bare feet hit the concrete. Win or lose, he thought, this would be the last time he woke up in the chambers of the bunker. He never wanted to see the place where he had spent his final days with Emily again. They had been scary, but good times. When he showed up at her doorstep, Emily had been reluctant to join him underground. If he didn't have proof of everything, she probably wouldn't have come with him—but she did, and in those weeks she had filled the dank cavern with her warm energy. But the space was now quiet, devoid of her warmth, and everything in it seemed to know she was gone.

Slowly, mechanically, Asher got dressed, grabbed his things, and left the wretched place behind.

Frozen winds howled their greeting when he reached the surface, taunting him with their pathetic attempts at causing him pain. The ice crystallizing around his heart had already left him numb. He crunched through the snow until he made it to the helicopter in the center of the Clearing. Oliver stood beside it, wearing a thick winter coat.

"Asher," he said, his accent less defined when he talked slowly. "I'm very sorry for your loss. If there's anything I can—"

"You can fly me to Groom Lake," Asher said. He knew that Oliver meant well, but the words helped nothing. "I'll take it from there."

"Alright, then," Oliver said after an awkward pause. "Hop on."

Asher took a seat in the back of the chopper and waited for the others. Jesse and Calix came out of the ground, followed by a pair of ropes tossed up by someone in the tunnel. Together they hoisted their cargo out of the hatch. Genesis and Mara came up next, the latter of which resembled a marshmallow in her fluffy white coat.

Jesse set down the load and scooped Mara into an embrace that lifted her feet several inches off the ground. They held each other, speaking words that Asher couldn't hear—a painful farewell, but possibly not a permanent one. He gulped down the sadness gathering in his throat and tried not to think about his parting with Emily. That final, permanent goodbye...he couldn't shake it.

After a moment, Mara disappeared back into the ground. Someone had to stay behind with the child, and she was the obvious choice—a great caregiver, but not much of a fighter. If all went according to plan, they would see her again soon. Asher stepped out of the helicopter when the others arrived.

"Is this it?" he asked, helping them load a particularly heavy duffle bag.

"Yep," Jesse said. "I didn't have time to run all the tests, but it should work just fine."

"Let's hope so," Genesis said. "Our lives depend on it."

•|•

The sun began to rise as they flew across the vast emptiness to the west of their mountain home. Oliver piloted the craft in a straight line, without any attempt to avoid detection by either man or machine. In fact, they wanted their enemy to know they were coming—just not right away. Mara's plan relied on it.

The passengers rode in silence, and Asher could almost hear his heart pumping in anticipation. He wondered if it was the same feeling that soldiers on all fronts had experienced throughout history. Swords, guns, drones, nano-bots—the weapon had never mattered. War was war.

He looked at the EMP shotgun in Jesse's lap. He had an appreciation for the clever weapon. A slide on the bottom allowed the wielder to adjust both the range and scatter radius of the EMP pulses. You could push the slide forward to shoot a narrow pulse at long distance targets or back to widen the pulse, shortening the range of the weapon, but giving its wielder the ability to take out multiple enemies at once.

"Drones!"

Oliver's voice squelched in Asher's headset. Only days before, he had yelled the same thing during their wild flight from Groom Lake. This time, though, they were ready. Jesse leveled the barrel of his gun through the open window and pushed the slide forward to its halfway point. The weapon made almost no sound when he pulled the trigger, and for a moment Asher thought that something had gone wrong, that the weapon had stopped working—but then the drone began to fall out of the sky, accelerating toward the ground.

Jesse hollered and said, "Just like duck huntin'."

The mechanical beast crashed into the earth below them and erupted in a burst of spark and flame. Jesse took out three more drones before they stopped coming. After another bout of radio silence, Oliver landed the helicopter in a dusty outcrop to await Felix's call. Just beyond the next plateau stood the Groom Lake Launch Facility—and the battle to come.

•|•

Calix unpacked one of the duffle bags and outfitted everyone with lightweight body armor. They loaded the guns, prepped the grenades, and attached everything to their belts.

Asher helped Jesse take the heaviest piece of equipment out of its case, an EMP bomb the size of a watermelon. A larger version of their special grenades, it would pack a much bigger punch.

The plan was simple: they would cause a commotion from the sky, Felix and Kapp would find and free Aeva, then they would all rendezvous at Arca. From watching their hidden surveillance feeds, they already knew that Aeva had been captured and which building she was held in. Asher had his own plan, of course…find and kill Theo, whose arrival they had recently witnessed as well. Accompanied by a squeal of static, Felix's voice came through their headsets, signaling the time to act.

"We're ready for you," he said. *"Let's make it rain."*

Calix pushed a button on the dash and said "copy."

As Oliver lifted off, and the tumbleweeds moved around them, Asher pulled out a tablet to do his part. The hack was already in place, a masterpiece of code that he and Jesse had teamed up to create. He just had to hit execute.

"Ready?" he asked.

Genesis nodded, and Asher pulled the trigger. After a short buffer, the program began its work.

"Anti-air turrets are"—he paused for a moment, awaiting the final confirmation screen—"down."

Jesse put a triumphant fist in the air and patted Asher on the back.

"Good work, boys," Genesis said.

In another life, Asher might have been proud of the accomplishment, but the fight that he craved was far from over. Not so deep down, he hoped that the bomb wouldn't reach Theo Cage, because he didn't just want the man to die. He wanted him to suffer.

•|•

When the helicopter reached the lip of the plateau, the group saw that Mara had been right about Theo's lack of fear. He hadn't anticipated the attack, and it showed. The men on the ground scrambled toward the perimeter like the ants of a disrupted colony, looking minuscule next to the massive starship that towered behind them.

Oliver flew low, adjacent to the dirt road, and Calix readied the newly-mounted machine gun. Jesse sat behind him with a handheld version of the same weapon. The chopper veered to the left as it approached the chainlink fence, exposing their vulnerable side.

"Here comes the rain," Calix said.

Gunfire exploded from both guns, peppering the first guard tower. Calix shot high, and Jesse shot low, the full monty. Men fell from the platforms and the ladders, and the dust rose around them. Bullets wouldn't kill the men, not for long at least. But if Mara was right—and she usually was—they would flock toward the creator of their temporary injuries, not due to anger, for they had none, but because of some automatic response. They experienced the phenomena during their escape from Groom Lake, but they could only hope that it hadn't been an anomaly.

They hit a few more towers in the same fashion, then they flew over an alley heavy with foot traffic. Jesse leaned out of the door and showered the masses below with bullets. When he came back inside, a stream of blood flowed down the side of his scalp, dripping from a missing chunk of his dirty blonde hair.

"Are you hit?" Genesis yelled over the fray.

"Just grazed." Jesse handed Asher the hot machine gun and put a hand over his wound. "Hot damn, it stings."

Genesis staunched the bleeding while Asher took over Jesse's position. After reloading, he helped Calix attack the final guard tower. The kick of the weapon almost knocked the wind out of him, but it felt good to release some anger in the form of flying lead. He kept a sharp eye out for Theo as Oliver turned toward the helicopter pad. They gained enough altitude to protect them from the guns below before hovering in place.

Then they waited.

•|•

Slowly but surely, the injured rallied and the dead rose, their mortal wounds healed by the bots in their blood. Like moths to a flame, they crowded below the helicopter, some firing at the sky, most just reaching hopelessly upward.

Every once in a while a bullet would get lucky and ricochet off of the bottom of the helicopter, but chances of bullet penetration were slight, if not impossible. Asher wondered how long it might take for backup to arrive. *Not before I get my revenge,* he thought as he helped Jesse arm the weapon.

Unlike some bombs, the EMP bomb wasn't designed to detonate on impact. Instead, it had a timer like the grenades. If it hit the ground before detonation, it would just shatter. It might crush one person, but not all of them.

"Altitude?" Jesse asked

Oliver's voice came through the static.

"One thousand, two hundred, and twenty meters."

"Accounting for drag"—Jesse typed the figures into a calculator app—"we have just under sixteen seconds to impact. Ash, let's set it for thirteen."

Asher turned the dial until the display flashed the correct number, then Jesse double-checked it. With some struggle, they moved the bomb to the edge of the open doorway.

"Ready when you are, Oli."

"Hold on," he said, making micro-adjustments to their position. "Alright, we're right on top of the fuckers."

"On two, you arm it. On three, I'll push," Jesse said to Asher.

"Copy."

"One," Jesse said.

"Two," they said together as Asher pressed the button.

The display on the device changed from thirteen to twelve just as Jesse said "three" and pushed. It took a second heave to get the thing out of the door, costing them some precious time. With the job done, both men put their eyes over the edge and looked down. Fifty or so guards huddled in the middle of the helicopter pad, and a few stragglers were just catching up to the group. Just before the bomb reached the crowd, they all tumbled to the ground like dominoes. A couple more lucky bullets hit the chopper.

"Oh no," Oliver said.

"No, we're fine," Jesse yelled. "It worked!"

"Not that," Oliver said as their vehicle began a slow spin. "I lost a tail rotor. Hold tight—we're goin' down, mates."

38

OUR WAR

Kapp braced himself for the coming gunshot, knowing that Felix wouldn't let the gate guard see the stolen credentials on his wrist and get out of it alive.

"Roll up your sleeve," the man said again.

His tone of voice conveyed no impatience or irritation, only persistence, like a software update notification ignored one too many times—only there would be no clicking *remind me later.* Something had to happen next, and Kapp just knew it would involve Felix putting a bullet through the guard's skull. Maybe several bullets.

"Sorry," Felix said, trying to buy some time. "Hard of hearing. I used to—"

The crack of gunfire reached Kapp's ears, but not as loudly as he expected. It didn't sound like it came from Felix's pistol. It didn't sound like it came from inside the truck at all. The shots continued in short bursts, and then the guard's radio emitted some static.

"All units report to emergency stations immediately."

The gate guard didn't respond to the call. After a minute or two of silence, Kapp sensed the truck backing up and heard that faint, repetitive beeping.

"You're good," Felix said.

"About time," Kapp said, crawling out from under the seat. "Smells like shit down there."

"You might wanna buckle up."

"Why's that?" Kapp asked as he settled into the passenger seat.

Instead of responding, Felix floored the gas pedal. By then, he had backed the truck up a couple hundred feet from the gate, which was now clear of guards, but still locked shut. Kapp fumbled with his seatbelt until it clicked. The truck didn't have much acceleration, but it had plenty of mass. It crashed into the chainlink with enough force to rip fence posts straight out of the ground. Chunks of safety glass showered the dashboard, and the metal mesh of the fence surrounded them like a cage—but the truck didn't slow. It rolled forward until the seams of the fence split, freeing them at last.

"Turn left," Kapp yelled.

Their front end clipped an unsuspecting guard, who got pummeled and then crushed by two sets of wheels. The human speed bump rocked the truck sideways, but just barely. Kapp continued his directions until they reached Building C, where Holden had kept him and the crew as prisoners after disembarking Arca. Their guns locked and loaded, Kapp and Felix exited the truck and wiped the safety glass off their clothes. They each held an EMP grenade in one hand and a pistol in the other.

"You know, you could've warned me about—"

"Shh!"

A small gang of people came around the back of the truck and rose their weapons. Before they could pull their triggers, though, Kapp twisted his grenade one click and chucked it at them. Just before clipping one of them in the face, the device emitted its high pitched squeal, and the attackers fell to the ground in a heap.

"Nice," Felix said. "Let's go inside."

Before entering the warehouse, Felix pulled something out of his pack and stuck it to the wall beside the door.

"What's that?"

"Proximity mine—should take out anyone that comes in after us."

Kapp nodded. "Good thinking."

Felix tried the stolen credentials on the scanner.

Access denied.

He tried one more time but got the same result. Shaking his head in impatience, he jogged over to the pile of downed guards. After dragging one of them to the door like a sack of potatoes, he brought the man's wrist to the panel and held it there for five seconds.

Access granted.

Felix dropped the guard carelessly, cracked the door, and peeked in.

"Clear," he said.

They stepped in quietly. Fluorescent lights illuminated the prison warehouse, where Mara's shattered glasses still sat on the concrete floor among scattered stains of dried blood. Kapp sped up his pace as he approached the holding cells, and Felix came up behind him. They both stopped at the first cell, where Kapp had pummeled Walker's skull. Looking through the window, he saw the large blood stain left behind by that machine of a man, but he didn't see Aeva.

He yelled her name, growing impatient.

They checked the next cell, the one where Kapp and the crew had left Holden bound and gagged during their escape. *Should've killed him then and there,* he thought. That cell was empty as well, so they checked the next, and the next…and the next. Kapp groaned. Though there were much bigger things at stake, a single, intrusive thought bit at him like a mosquito.

What if I never get to apologize to Aeva?

"Aeva," he yelled again, remembering the moment they arrived on Earth together.

"Promise me you'll protect Arca at all costs," Aeva had said.

When he agreed to that promise, he never thought that her life would be one of those costs.

•|•

After a fruitless search, Kapp and Felix took the long way around the warehouse to avoid as much conflict as possible. Felix kept watch for enemies while Kapp scanned the skies. Apparently, the herding of the hostiles had worked—no one crossed their path.

"I don't see the chopper," Kapp said.

"Worse." Felix spat into the sand under his feet. "I don't hear it."

Kapp shook his head. "Maybe they're already at the ship?"

Felix scanned the horizon briefly. "Maybe."

Kapp didn't want to imagine Asher and the others failing. He couldn't fathom the notion. Surely, it was important to save Arca, but saving the ship would mean nothing if no one remained to take care of it. He had to find Aeva.

"Where else could she be?" he asked.

Kapp took his eyes off the sky for a moment and stole a glance at Felix. The man looked physically upset. The hairs of his beard changed angles from the scowl growing on his face.

"Something's wrong," Felix said. "I can feel it."

"What do you mean?"

"Calix and I share a connection." Felix sidestepped around a tumbleweed. "I think he's hurt."

Kapp stopped in his tracks. "Like—telekinesis?"

"You mean telepathy?"

"Yeah, whatever."

"Not exactly like that." Felix peered ahead. "Let's go."

They cleared a few more warehouses, the simulation hangar, and a large portion of the launch facility. The steel skeleton that held Starling II up before its launch still stood in the middle of the complex, at about half the height of the alien ship that towered behind it and everything else. At every building they searched, Kapp grew more restless, the mission more hopeless. In the distance, a pillar of smoke crawled into the sky like an angry centipede, twisting and writhing in the desert's winter winds.

"Is that—"

"Not good," Felix said, shaking his head. "I think it's time to go."

Kapp knew he meant *to the ship*.

"No," Kapp said with more ferocity than he intended. "Not until we find Aeva."

"Kapp." Felix stopped at the corner of the building they had just searched. With the effortlessness of habit, he pulled out and lit a cigarette while he spoke. "I know how you feel about Aeva."

Kapp thought that his feelings had been private. He wondered if Aeva had told Felix about his drunken advances in the elevator.

They rounded the corner of the building, freeing up their field of vision.

"I see the way you look at her. But this"—Felix turned and gestured toward Arca with the lit cigarette in his hand—"this is bigger than any one person...or their feelings."

"This is her war, though. She's the reason we're all here. We can't just leave her behind."

"This is our war"—Felix glanced at the pillar of smoke—"and you and I might be the only ones left to fight it. Do you understand that?"

Felix kept walking toward Arca, despite Kapp's protests.

"Felix," Kapp said, grabbing the man's shoulder. "Please, just help me find her? I'm not going with you—not without her."

Then Felix stopped walking. With a curious expression on his face, he pulled the binoculars out of his bag and honed in on the massive ship ahead of them. Arca's metallic surface glimmered like it had on Phobos, only with much more brilliance. Probably due to the proximity of the sun. The ramp that led to Arca's entrance looked tiny in comparison.

Felix dropped the binoculars from his eyes. "Aeva's on the ramp." He turned to Kapp and dropped his cigarette to the ground. "But she's not alone."

39

FOR ARCA

As the helicopter began to spin, fear did not consume Asher's mind. Instead, a much stronger emotion took its place—rage. With every meter of lost altitude, his anger seemed to double, burning his chest with its unstoppable heat. The thought of dying did not cause this vexation, though, only the thought of dying before getting the chance to avenge Emily's death.

"Hold on," Oliver yelled, his voice crackling through the headsets.

Hearing Oli granted Asher some level of hope. He knew that if anyone could land the flailing bird, Oliver could. Alarms blared through the cabin, a redundant signal of their current catastrophe.

Crossed seat belts and closed doors protected both Oliver and Genesis. Calix stabilized himself by gripping the mounted machine gun, but Jesse and Asher were still vulnerable to the centrifugal force pulling them toward the open door.

Time seemed to slow. The chopper jerked, and both men slid even closer to the danger zone. Where the horizon should have been, Asher saw the dead horde of Theo's minions directly below. His shoulders crossed the edge of the threshold, where his headset fell off and out of the craft. The alarms and the sound of blades cutting through air got louder. Just before Asher's center of gravity could cross over, someone grabbed his ankle.

Genesis pulled him closer to the center of the chopper, where he wedged his legs between the back and front seats, but Jesse still continued his slow slide toward certain death. One of his hands held tight to the doorframe, while the other moved wildly, fighting for purchase in the open air. The vehicle lurched again, more violently this time, and Jesse's legs left the safety of the cabin. Dangling out of the helicopter, he clung to life with a single hand. Asher had never seen the man so terrified. He reached out and clutched his sweaty fingers around Jesse's wrist.

"I got you," he yelled, squeezing with all his might. "Hold my arm!"

Jesse hesitated for a moment, but then, in one motion, he let go of the edge, turned his wrist over, and grabbed onto Asher's wrist. Asher's lateral muscles stretched to their max, burning from the newfound weight. Jesse's fingernails dug into his wrist, but he ignored the pain. Through the open door, the desert floor grew ever closer.

Jesse's body twisted, wrenching Asher's arm into an extremely painful angle, but he wouldn't let go. Calix worked his way around the front seat. Gripping the headrest with one hand, he reached out and clutched Jesse's wrist as well. With some of the weight gone, Asher began to pull. Together, he and Calix drew Jesse inch by inch to safety. Just as his knees crossed the threshold, the horizon reappeared, and with it—the crash.

Dust and debris sprung from below like droplets of disturbed water as the legs of the chopper bounced and bent from the force of the impact. The unstrapped inhabitants of the craft ricocheted off every surface. Shielding his head, Asher's elbows hit the floor, sending a wave of pain up both arms. The helicopter slid forward before beginning to tip over.

Blades and hard ground collided, breaking each other in a cacophonous barrage. Shattered metal flew through the clouds of dust at odd angles. The engines began to slow from the friction, whining their protests. But almost as soon as they began, the aggressive sounds faded, leaving behind only the screams of the alarm and the yells of Asher's comrades. Beneath the rising dust, even with the wind knocked out of him, he smiled.

•|•

Calix crawled out of the wreckage first. He situated himself in the skyward doorframe and reached down to heave the others out. Jesse put a gun in his outstretched hand before letting the man pull him up. Now armed and freed, they both took watch at the exit while the others got themselves together.

"Are you okay?" Genesis asked, reaching for the tactical knife on her belt.

"I think so," Asher said.

In truth, he couldn't tell if he had been injured in the crash. The adrenaline rush kept his pain at bay. Gunfire sounds sent another surge of the stuff through his body. His lungs still rose and fell, he could move his arms and legs, and that was enough.

"Oli, are you hurt?" Genesis asked, cutting her seatbelt with the knife. "Oli?"

When he didn't respond to the second call, she shot over the center console like a startled cat. As she bent her torso forward, blood seeped through a hole in her pant leg.

"What's wrong?" Asher asked.

"Shrapnel," she said, shaking her head. "Oli, talk to me. Wake up!"

She took off his helmet and slapped his face. Though Asher couldn't see the pilot from his vantage point, the cough that came out of Oliver's mouth sounded wet. He cleared his throat.

"Gen," he said, his voice weak, almost inaudible under the alarms and gunfire. "Did we make it?"

"We did, Oli." She put a hand on his shoulder and nodded, tears barely glistening in her eyes. "You did great. You—you saved us."

"Best damn helicopter pilot in the world," Asher added, overcome with gratitude for the man.

"The very best," Genesis said, now running her fingers through Oliver's hair. "What an adventure we've had."

Asher swore that he could feel the pilot's final smile.

"It's time, mates," Oliver said, his voice fading to a whisper. "Go on, then."

Then Oliver exhaled, and his body relaxed. He greeted death—

that final adventure—not with fear, but with acceptance. His job was done, but Asher's had only just begun. Then and there, Asher decided he would fight not only for revenge but for redemption. He would face the enemy not just for Emily, or Oliver, or any other person slain, but for those who could still suffer—for the living.

And for life's best shot at surviving the coming darkness.

For Arca.

•|•

The wreckage burned behind them, the smoke of which rose and shifted with the wind, creating the twisted semblance of a headstone above the carnage. Not far from the crash site, they passed the field of fallen soldiers. Under the light of the early morning sun, Asher saw that the men and women had lost their glossy sheen. They looked human once again. He retched.

"You're bleeding, Gen," Jesse said.

The group ducked into an alleyway, the same one Kapp and the crew fled through on the night of their escape. Calix had already cleared the field of leftover enemies with his long-range rifle, which made for an easy trip. Even without EMPs, a high-caliber bullet through the head seemed to do the trick.

Genesis tore a bigger hole in her pants to survey her wound, then she pulled out her knife.

"I need a flame," she said.

Asher tapped his pockets while the others kept watch.

"Here," he said.

Genesis sparked the lighter and held the flame below the tip of her knife until it became red hot. She took a deep breath and brought the heated metal to her shrapnel wound, which began to sizzle. Her face tightened in a wince until she completed the cauterization.

"Let's go," she said, shrugging off the pain. "Do you have the radio?"

"Lost it in the crash," Calix said. "But Felix is alive."

"What?" Asher asked. "How do you know—"

Jesse cut him off with a loud shush.

"Y'all hear that?" he whispered, pulling the slide on his weapon to the close-range setting.

Asher perked his ears up to listen. At first, he heard nothing but the desert wind, but then came the faint sound of footsteps—not the slap of boots on concrete, or the thud of feet on hardened earth, but the clank and squeak of rubber soles on a metal roof. Jesse put a finger to his lips and motioned for everyone to follow him. Wordlessly, they snuck to the side of the building that had an overhanging roof. As they crept forward, distancing themselves from the lip of the alley, the footsteps faded away until silence reigned once more.

"That was close," Genesis whispered.

But then the footsteps returned, not with the careful pace of a single patrolman, but with the frantic gait of an approaching pack. The silence returned for a split second as three men jumped from the roof, landing on all fours in the alley before rising and drawing their weapons.

"Drop your—"

Calix put a bullet through the speaker's forehead, silencing him forever. Jesse took out the man to his right with a quick shotgun pulse. Both enemies crumpled to the ground like rag dolls. The third man charged toward Genesis and tackled her to the ground while Asher struggled to draw a grenade. His EMP gun recharging, Jesse kicked the man, and the crack of breaking ribs echoed through the alley.

The man, who rose to attack Jesse, had Gen's knife sticking out of his stomach, but it didn't seem to bother him. He knocked the barrel of the shotgun out of the way and put his hands around Jesse's throat. Calix was also in a fist fight with two more guards that had come from above, and Asher could hear more coming. Finally, Asher managed to free the tricky EMP grenade from his belt. He twisted it one click, thought better of it, and twisted it two more.

After the longest three seconds of his life, the device emitted its signature sound, taking down not only the men surrounding them but also two more that had jumped from above. Their nano-bots failed them before their bodies could even reach the ground.

Calix helped Genesis to her feet while Jesse watched their rear. Asher pulled another grenade from his belt and listened for more footsteps. When none came, they let down their weapons and surveyed each other for wounds. Nothing serious. They continued down the alleyway, creeping along, careful to listen for visitors from the rooftop.

Asher knew that Theo had to be somewhere in the complex. He hoped to encounter him on the way to the ship, but as they neared the end of the alley and the vessel that loomed beyond, thoughts of leaving the others to find and kill Doctor Cage intruded his mind once again. *I'll at least help them get there,* he thought. The others had told him about Arca's wonders, and somewhere beneath his obsession with revenge, he did have a desire to explore the alien ship.

Motion at the end of the passage caught Asher's eye. He and the others raised their guns, but something stopped them from firing. The thing crossed the exit too low to the ground and too quickly to be human. It was followed by another—and another.

"Dogs?" Calix asked.

Genesis nodded. One after another, the dogs continued to cross, sniffing the air, oblivious to the fact that they were being watched. Asher counted nine of them before they stopped coming. Just after the final dog passed, he exhaled, unaware that he had been holding his breath the whole time. They crept further forward, inching along with the most careful of intentions—and then the tenth dog appeared.

Asher came to a stop, thinking this dog would cross like the others, but it stopped in the middle of the threshold, pointing its nose higher into the air. Its ears perked up and turned toward the group, followed by its head. A deep, guttural growl came from the dog's throat. It took a few steps into the alley, and then the rest of the pack came up behind it. Above the chorus of growls, a voice rose.

"Don't bother trying to outrun them," it said from around the corner. "They're extremely fast."

The voice sounded familiar, yet foreign—like an old recording of a new acquaintance. Asher hoped that he recognized the voice because it came from Theo Cage, but he couldn't be sure.

The dogs came closer, flashing their teeth, and then a man in a suit stepped up behind them. He had a bulky, muscular frame, a rigid jawline, and a buzzcut of shiny, black hair. Asher thought he had never seen the man before, but something told him that he had. He looked and sounded so familiar, almost like he could be the son of—

"Holden?" Asher asked, his eyes narrowing to focus. "What happened to you?"

Holden stepped forward, and the hounds began to howl.

40

DOMINANT TRAITS

Kapp didn't bother looking through the binoculars to see what Felix saw. Without much direction from his mind, his body moved forward. He strode toward the ramp, unconcerned with who stood on it with Aeva or who he'd have to kill on the way. It didn't matter. Looking at the plume of smoke at the other end of the complex, he realized that all of his friends were probably dead, and the world would fare no better in the future. *This is our war now.* Win or lose, he just wanted it to be over.

The sense of calm purpose that had slowed both his breathing and his heart rate began to fade as Aeva came into focus. She stood near the top the ramp, facing the forcefield of Arca's entrance with her arms cuffed behind her back and her ankles bound together by something that looked like a metallic snake. The immortal and beautiful Aeva, pilot of the starship Arca, protector of all of its harbored treasures, first of the Skyborn people—and, if Kapp didn't do something about it, one of the last. His legs began to run.

Theo Cage stood a few paces behind Aeva, his bald head reflecting the sunlight with a plastic shine. Unsuited for a fight, he wore a white button-up and slacks. Felix and Kapp slowed their pace as they approached the bottom of the ramp. Speaking to Aeva, Theo didn't seem to notice their arrival. Guns drawn, they crept up the aluminum structure until Theo's words became audible. He spoke in the tongue of the Architects, spitting the words out in a way that betrayed the usual beauty and elegance of the language. Midway through his rant, though, his tone and language switched.

"Welcome, Kapp Adams." Theo didn't turn around to speak. "Felix, my old friend—good to see you."

Felix spat onto the ramp. "I wish I could say the same."

Theo turned around slowly, revealing a face as smooth as his bald head. He looked like a wax statue, some poor imitation of a human. His irises, once a vibrant green, had turned a dark gray, and a white film had clouded over his pupils. He flashed a set of perfect teeth.

"I was just telling Aeva how—"

"Let her go," Kapp said, raising his sidearm.

Aeva turned away from Arca, and Kapp caught a glimpse of her face. He had never seen her look so defeated. Her mouth, though undamaged as far as he could tell, had become a pale, thin line— not happy or sad, just numb.

"What did you do to her?" Kapp demanded. The sight of his pistol aligned with Theo's heart, or where his heart should be. Kapp's hands shook with rage.

"Now, there's no need to—"

Kapp put a pair of bullets in the man's torso. Gripping his stomach, Theo hunched forward. Slowly, he fell to his knees, and then he looked down at the wound, blood pooling in a circle on his cotton shirt.

"No," he screamed at the top of his lungs. "No, no, no!"

A gurgling sound came from deep within his throat, and he started to twitch violently, clutching the entry wounds on his gut. Just when Kapp thought he would keel over, the retching turned into hysterical laughter. He looked up at Kapp and Felix, moving his tongue around his mouth like he had food stuck in his teeth. Then he flashed those pearly whites again—but this time he held a pair of bullets in their grasp. He spat them out, and before they could hit the ramp, he was up and beside Aeva with one hand around the back of her neck.

"You really thought that bullets could harm me?" he asked, barely suppressing a sickening snicker. "I'm more powerful than you can even imagine."

Felix touched a grenade on his belt.

"I wouldn't do that," Theo said, staring through Felix with those dead eyes, tightening his grip around the back of Aeva's neck. "All I have to do is squeeze hard enough, and our beloved sister is dead. Besides—my nanites are shielded against electromagnetic pulses."

Kapp thought Theo might be bluffing, but he needed time to figure it out.

Theo continued. "I suppose I should have granted such protections to my devotees, but you know what they say about hindsight. I didn't think you'd show up."

"Devotees?" Kapp asked, trying to buy time. "You mean slaves?"

Theo's laugh, which came out of his nose as three short bursts of air, angered Kapp with its implied condescension. He wanted nothing more than to clock him in the face with the full force of his metal fist, but he held back. The sight of Aeva in the psychopath's grasp enraged him even further.

"Let us not quibble over semantics," Theo said. "Devotees. Slaves. To a god, they are one and the same."

Kapp scoffed. "You think you're a god?"

"Semantics, once again." Theo rolled his neck from side to side. "Of course I'm not a true god. Such things don't exist—but it's hard to not feel like a supreme being when you have the power of one."

Kapp wanted Theo to keep bragging so he could plan what to do next. "Yeah?"

"I can see everything—through their eyes. Billions of pairs of eyes...and counting." As he spoke, Theo stared off into the distance with his milky gaze. "But that's not all. I can also hear their thoughts, trapped in the recesses of their minds, screaming out in protest of my control."

Kapp shook his head at the sick, twisted fuck in front of him, but he let the man continue his rant.

"For instance—right now, I can see that Holden is hunting your friends."

Kapp's eyes narrowed, his breath quickened.

"Oh," Theo said. "You didn't know they survived the crash?" His maniacal laugh returned. "It looks quite hopeless for them. Soon enough, I will see through their eyes as well."

"What do you want?" Kapp asked.

"You know what I want."

"I know that you wanted Arca destroyed."

Kapp glanced at Aeva, then the shimmering ship in the background.

"It was never about destroying Arca—just its inhabitants. In the wrong hands, this ship could spoil everything I've worked for." Theo held Aeva out like a trophy. "It was a risk I wasn't willing to take. Now that I've weeded out the true problem, I can take Arca for myself. And then the true work can begin."

Kapp recalled the story Genesis had told about Theo recovering data from Beacon Five after it crashed. The man had built an empire from a single shard of alien information. Kapp shuddered to think what he could do with Arca's trove of knowledge and tech at his disposal.

"Kill me, Ramses," Aeva said. The ferocity in her voice countered how sullen she looked. "You will not take Arca."

"In due time, dear sister." Theo pulled Aeva closer, and Kapp just knew that he had done something horrible to her.

"Let go of her," Kapp said, jolting forward but stopping himself. "She's not gonna—"

"Aeva has always been so stubborn—so righteous. An advocate of organic life. But organic life is weak. It's far too fragile for my liking." Theo smiled at Kapp. "Like a chicken egg."

Theo tightened his grip around Aeva's neck. Her eyes bulged as she tried to free herself from the building pressure.

"Stop!" Kapp yelled.

"Speak the word, Kapp," Theo said, his smiling lips tight like stretched leather, "and I'll let her live."

"Don't," Aeva said, her voice cracking, her eyes begging. "Please."

"I'll find a way in someday, one way or another." Theo sidestepped toward the edge of the ramp, forcing Aeva to move with him. "And when I do, you'll regret letting her die."

Kapp wondered if Theo knew that the protective Artazoa would soon perish in Earth's atmosphere, leaving Arca vulnerable to his attacks.

"You might as well help me, Kapp. What is it that you want?" Theo asked. "I can give you anything you desire. A house, no—a mansion in the tropics. You can live out your days unbothered by me, drinking tequila on the beach with your beautiful bride."

A flash of confusion crossed Kapp's face.

"Oh yes," Theo said, shaking Aeva's spine from side to side, "I can even make her love you."

Kapp imagined what it would be like to hold Aeva close, for her to look at him with something other than disinterest or disgust—to feel the same way he felt.

"I can give the two of you an entire continent if that's what it takes. Just give me Arca. That's all I need to continue my research."

Kapp opened his mouth to tell Theo to stop, but he faltered. What if Theo could actually give him everything he wanted? A carefree life. A life with Aeva in it. They could leave the whole mess behind and start again.

"Well...what do you say, Kapp?"

Kapp's breathing slowed, and he began to nod.

"Tempting," he said.

Aeva stared him down with her piercing, pleading eyes, deeper than any ocean. Could Theo really make her love him?

"Yes," Theo said, his malicious grin doubling in magnitude. "What will it be, then? Wedding bells?"

"Your offer is tempting," Kapp said, knowing that his next words might mean Aeva's death, as well as his own. In truth, he didn't care much about Earth or Arca—but Aeva did, and that was the problem. "But a life on your terms is no life at all. I don't want to be granted some false love. I want to earn it. The real thing."

The despot scoffed.

"A foolish choice," he said. "I know you think I'm a bad man, but I'm just an architect. I'm trying to build something here, Kapp. An interstellar empire. Humanity is creeping toward this inevitability, and I'm just trying to speed up the process."

"At what cost?" Kapp asked.

"The cost doesn't matter, only the outcome." Theo cracked his neck. "You don't know this, but I've made the most important discovery in the universe. Curing death—that's been done before.

My ancestors did that tens of thousands of years ago. Not even the Surge could invent the technology that I have, even though it would solve its biggest weakness."

Even in the growing sunlight, Kapp could see that just beyond Theo and Aeva, the lights that ran along the edges of the ramp were all out. Too close to the tech-resistant Artazoa, the bulbs no longer did their job. The idea hit Kapp like a falling comet, igniting his mind with its brilliance. He knew that Theo must have not crossed that border for a reason. If Kapp could just push him past it, then maybe—just maybe—the tiny bots coursing through him would malfunction, and he'd no longer be so invulnerable. While Kapp plotted, Theo continued his rant.

"It's a shame that the only people on Earth who can open this ship are the kind I can't control. Although—"

Theo smirked as his glazed eyes found Kapp's prosthetic.

"Your arm. It's not the newest model anymore, but still a powerful upgrade. I considered similar upgrades for myself, but I find my current form the most aesthetically pleasing."

Looking for a chance to strike, Kapp ignored the cocksure comment. Unbeknownst to him, his metal fingers began to twitch.

"In fact, the interface that links the bionic prosthetic to your mind is an early version of the one that links my mind"—Theo tapped his temple—"to everything."

Kapp prepared to pounce, but the sight of Aeva so close to the edge of the ramp held him back. His false arm crept up his torso.

"And although my nano-injections do not work on blood like ours," Theo said, flashing an evil grin. "I do still have some measure of control."

Two things happened in the same instant, one of which took all of Kapp's attention. Without the slightest hesitation, Theo shoved Aeva to his side. Instinctively, Kapp began to run forward as soon as he detected the motion, but he was too late to help. Hands and feet bound, Aeva could do nothing to stop herself from tumbling over the edge of the ramp to the cold, hard earth below.

"No!" Kapp tried to yell, but his voice was gagged by the second incident.

Against his will, Kapp's bionic hand squeezed like a vice around his own throat. He heard the thud of flesh hitting the ground, a scream of pain, and the stomp of Felix running back down the ramp. With unnatural force, Theo kicked Kapp's legs out from under him, and he fell on his back. He began to choke from the pressure around his throat. Theo held down his other three limbs. But even through the chaos and the pain, something that Theo had said overwhelmed Kapp's senses.

"Bluuuliikkurs," he murmured.

"What was that?" Theo asked, releasing some of the tension.

"Blood"—Kapp erupted in a fit of coughs—"Blood like ours?"

"Really?" Theo asked, beginning to laugh. "I assumed you already knew at least some of the truth."

Kapp struggled hopelessly against the weight on top of him before beginning to truly listen.

"Have you never wondered why you look so young? Or why your eyes are so green?"

In truth, he had wondered those things, but with the painful weight bearing down on him he failed to see the relevance.

"You probably like this planet even less than I do," Theo continued. "That's why you became an astronaut, isn't it? Escapism. You have some instinctual urge to leave, like a migratory bird heading south. It's in your blood."

Nothing the man said made any sense, but Kapp stopped fighting for a moment to listen to the rest of it.

"You were not born in the stars like the rest of us, Kapp Adams," Theo said, "but the Skyborn traits are dominant. You're one of us."

Kapp stared into the plastic face that hovered so near to his own. As the impossible words collided with his mind, he realized that he recognized the face—not from the TV or the internet or the day he got his new bionic arm, but from deep in some crevice of his distant memory. Some morsel of thought that he could barely grasp—as if it slipped through the fingers of his mind like dry sand.

"If you won't unlock Arca for your enemy," Theo said, "perhaps you'll do it for your father."

41

HOLDEN'S HOUNDS

The ten hounds at the end of the alley crept closer to the group until their forms became clear. They had thin bodies and long legs built for sprinting, but Asher couldn't place the breed. Their black fur looked exactly like young Holden's hair, sleek and shiny. Growling in unison, the feral monstrosities pulled their lips back and flashed their razor-sharp teeth. Asher looked to his comrades for direction, but everyone stood in a frozen stupor—cornered prey.

"Holden," Genesis said, putting her hands in the air. "Theo wouldn't want us dead. We know the password."

Asher thought she might be bluffing. Aeva hadn't told anyone the password before leaving on her rogue mission, but maybe Kapp had?

"My hounds won't kill you," Holden said, his voice devoid of any emotion. "They'll only change you."

Holden stood far behind his wall of creatures, one more obstacle between Asher and his revenge. He wanted to end Holden's life, to destroy all the microscopic robots that could bring him back. Favoring the smooth metal of an EMP grenade, Asher holstered his pistol, and the others leveled their guns at the approaching pack—an uneven standoff.

"Get ready to run," Jesse whispered, setting his weapon to short-range mode.

Dogs pounced, guns fired, and the group began a mad sprint

back down the alleyway. Several paces into their retreat, Asher stole a glance over his shoulder. Roughly half of the pack, those in the front, had been taken out by a mix of pulses and bullets. The rest made their way over the fallen carcasses, approaching Asher and the others much faster than they could run away. Calix took up the rear of the group, firing behind him with uncanny accuracy. He took out another hound, leveling the playing field.

Before the remaining dogs could catch up to Calix, he stopped and turned to face them. He kicked one to the side, hard enough to knock it out, but another pounced, bringing its paws to his chest. The force of the blow knocked Calix to the ground, where he wrestled against claws and gnashing teeth.

"No!" Genesis screamed.

Two of the dogs continued their sprint past him. One locked onto Genesis, and the other onto Asher, who zigzagged to the left and changed directions. The dog missed by a hair, claws scratching against the concrete to follow his motion. Jesse took it out with an EMP blast.

Asher ran back to help Calix. When he got there, the man was punching his attacker in the head, trying to get it to let go of his arm. Droplets of blood covered his torso, but none of the wounds looked fatal. Asher twisted a grenade one click and tossed it forward. At the sound of the pulse, the dog collapsed onto Calix.

"You okay?" Asher asked.

Carefully, he peeled the creature's jaws apart, trying to free Calix's arm.

"I've been better," he said, wincing.

Blood gushed from the wound as Asher pulled the teeth from it. Up close, he could see that the hound's sharp, anterior canines weren't teeth at all—their middles had been hollowed out and replaced with mechanical syringes.

"*They'll only change you,*" Holden had said.

Asher shuddered. He tore the bottom of his shirt off to wrap the mangled flesh of Calix's arm. He looked pale. Somewhere beyond them both, Jesse and Genesis continued their battle with the final hound, but Asher only focused on the sounds coming from behind him—footsteps, heavy breathing, the cocking of a revolver. He slowly pulled a grenade from his belt. *If Holden was going to kill me, he would have fired by now.*

Calix perked up. "What are you—"

"Shhh," Asher hissed, turning the device in his hand to its max before setting it on the ground.

Asher's life had been a series of countdowns. Kneeling over his injured friend, he remembered counting down the months to high school graduation so he could get out of that hellhole. For years he had counted down the weeks to his eighteenth birthday—the day he could free himself from his oppressive father. More recently, he had counted down shuttle launches for mission control. But none of these countdowns had been as important as the current set of reverse numbers.

15 seconds, he thought.

"Put your hands up and stand," Holden said from behind him.

Asher did as he was told. By the time he rose from the ground, the timer in his head had reached 10 seconds. The sound of Genesis and Jesse fighting their final enemy had ceased, but they were too far away to do anything about Holden. *He won't shoot, anyway.*

"Theo wants you alive so he can punish you for all the problems you've caused."

6 seconds.

With his back still facing Holden, Asher put his foot on top of the grenade.

"Come with me," Holden continued, his voice closer than before. "What are you waiting for?"

3 seconds.

2 seconds.

On two, Asher pushed his foot back. The spherical grenade rolled across the dusty concrete toward Holden. Asher couldn't see it, but he imagined the look of confusion on the idiot's face as the weapon came to a stop at his feet. The final number came out of Asher's mouth as a satisfied whisper.

"One."

The high-pitched squeal of the EMP sounded, and like his hounds, Holden collapsed to the hard ground. Still breathing heavily from the fight, Asher looked around to confirm the kills.

He remembered that Calix had only knocked out, not killed, one of his two attackers.

Before Asher could find the missing creature, the feeling of victory at defeating Holden was replaced with a sharp pain. A guttural growl reached his ears as rows of mechanical teeth sank into his leg, tearing him to the ground. His head smacked the concrete, and he heard the retort of gunfire. Blood sprayed. The grip on his ankle loosened after the blast, but the syringes still pumped. An itching, crawling sensation began to creep up from the bite wound—followed by a wave of numbness and then someone else's voice in his head.

Go to sleep, Asher.

42

ARTAZOR

Understanding sprang forth from somewhere deep in Kapp's mind like water from an underground well. The growing flood washed up memories long since forgotten, mental impressions repressed by the ebb and flow of years and years—dusty relics of the past finally unearthed and polished by the deluge. In the fresh light, he saw that his recurring nightmare—the scream, the fire—while apparently true, had not told the whole truth.

Like the final piece in a jigsaw puzzle, the word *father* completed the picture of what had happened to him and his mother over thirty years earlier.

"I loved her," Theo said, still holding Kapp underneath him. "She was the one good thing about this world."

Kapp stared up at the man, but he kept his mouth shut—not that he could speak, anyway. With the treacherous bionic hand gripping his throat and the significance of this epiphany, speech became nearly impossible. From over the edge of the ramp, he could hear Aeva's pained moans—sounds that meant she was still alive, that Kapp had something to fight for.

"We could have ruled together. It's a shame what happened to her—*my* Bella."

Theo spoke in a way that made Kapp's mother sound more like a belonging than a loved one. The mention of her name, though Kapp had only known her on paper as Isabella, erased any doubt about who Theo claimed to be. He remembered what Felix had said: *When we got there Bella was dead, and Ramses was gone.*

"You and I," Theo said, "we could bring her back, you know?" He leaned in closer, and Kapp tried to find a resemblance between himself and his father. "The cloning technology on Arca is much better than Earth's—and faster too. I still have her genetic material."

In Kapp's nightmares, the man hovering over his mother always held a knife, but that hadn't been the case. Through the flames, he had actually seen Theo with a bloodied scalpel.

"You," Kapp spat. "You cut her open."

"Ahh, so you remember?"

"I do now," Kapp said through a clenched throat. He forced his eyes open, avoiding the memory he knew he'd see if he closed them. "Why did you—"

"I was simply taking back what she tried to steal from me," Theo said, shifting his weight onto Kapp's legs and sitting up. "For years I thought that you died in the fire. When I escaped through the flames, you were unconscious—and missing an arm. There was so much blood."

Kapp rested his left arm, now free of Theo's grasp, on the ground beside him.

"Imagine my surprise when I saw you in my office the day I installed your prosthetic."

"You—you knew?"

"Of course I knew who you were," Theo said. "You look just like her."

Theo leaned in closer once again as if to get a better look. Though he often saw her in his nightmares, Kapp had only vague memories of what his mother looked like.

"For us to meet again," Theo continued, "after all these years—under these circumstances. What a small world we live in. And what poetic justice? I mean, what are the chances?" Theo let out a short snicker. "My own son, the instrument of Arca's destruction."

"She found out what you were doing." Kapp coughed the words out with as much vigor as he could. "She knew. That's why you killed—"

"She knew nothing!" The hands around Kapp's throat squeezed

violently and then released. "She only thought she knew. And I'm not the one who made you an orphan."

"Bullshit!"

"Bella did it," Theo said, shaking his head back and forth. "Your mother tried to kill herself—and you. She left the gas on and went to bed."

"You're lying!" The words burned Kapp's throat with their venom. "You wanted us dead."

"Nonsense." Theo's eyes bore into Kapp's. "You were my firstborn—the closest thing to a miracle I've ever seen. By the time I found you and Bella, it was too late."

For the first time in his life, Kapp could remember almost everything that happened before and after the explosion, but he had to tell the story to himself to make it true. As he struggled to speak, his free hand crept toward his weapon belt. Hot tears poured from his eyes, down his cheeks.

"Why did you do it? Why did you—"

Kapp couldn't keep his eyes open any longer. When they shut, he remembered in vivid detail the blade of Theo's scalpel making its voyage across his mother's swollen abdomen, the blood spilling from her womb to pool on the floor below, where it sizzled on the hot tile. The unearthed memory brought more tears.

"You killed your own child." Kapp could barely speak the words. "You're a—"

"I didn't kill your brother."

Brother, Kapp thought. *I had a baby brother.* The tension increased around Kapp's throat, but Theo's voice revealed no anger when he spoke again.

"But someday, you'll wish I had."

Tears stung Kapp's eyes. "What?"

"I told you—I was simply taking back what Bella tried to steal from me. She wanted to terminate the pregnancy, and I stopped her. You think I'm a bad person for that?"

"No," Kapp said, remembering the blood—so much blood. "Not just for that."

Theo laughed once again—as if Kapp's words were some hysterical joke. "I could have killed everyone on this planet. It would have been easy. Synthesizing an airborne pathogen?" Theo licked his teeth. "That's child's play compared to what I've done. But I didn't kill them. No, I healed their diseases. I took away their pain. Now, these people—all people—they serve a greater cause."

"And you're the greater cause?"

While Kapp spoke, his fingers found the last EMP grenade on his belt.

"I always hated the others. How their lives were governed by fear. How they wasted time running from the Surge, hoping for a brighter future, instead of making it happen themselves."

Theo leaned forward again, his face hovering just above Kapp's, close enough for Kapp to see every detail of the man's synthetic-looking skin. He seemed to have no pores, no external imperfections whatsoever, only a sickness of the mind that radiated from his clouded eyes.

"Artificial intelligence has its limits. But I have something the Surge does not." Theo raised his voice. "I have something Aeva does not. Soon, I'll be much stronger than both."

"You can't fight fire with—"

Under Theo's control, Kapp's metal fingers tightened again, drawing blood from his neck and silencing him.

"I'm prepared to fight fire with an inferno," Theo said through clenched teeth, his face contorting in another spasm of rage. "This is your last chance to give me the password, Kapp. Choose your next words wisely."

The fingers around Kapp's neck loosened. With practiced ease, he formed an insult sure to keep Theo distracted.

"You're a hideous, hypocritical sack of shit in human clothes." Kapp could taste the hatred on his tongue. While he spoke, he twisted the grenade in his left a hand a few notches. "Fuck you."

Theo raised a fist, preparing to strike, then his lips curved into a smile. "Poor choice."

His fist came down like a hammer, fast enough to crush Kapp's face in. Before the collision, though, the activated grenade on Kapp's belt squealed and flashed. Close enough to the blast, Kapp's bionic arm went limp. With the newfound freedom, he simultaneously ducked to the side and delivered a heavy blow to

Theo's torso. He heard, but could not feel, the snapping of a finger bone.

Kapp rolled with the man's shifting weight, bringing himself to his knees just as Theo's enhanced body tumbled to the metal floor. He struck twice more, which kept Theo down but did nothing to move him toward the forcefield. From behind, footsteps faded into the fray, barely audible under the chaotic sounds of the scuffle. The crack of gunfire and then a voice entered the soundscape.

"Hands up, Theo."

Kapp, who had risen to a standing position, stole a glance at his comrade. Jesse looked bruised and bloody, but otherwise intact. His sweaty hair, which clung to the sides of his face, looked more dirty than blonde. Blood—impossible to tell whose—dotted his mangled clothes. He stood like an outlaw with Calix's high-caliber rifle, still smoking, trained on the center of Theo's forehead.

"Fools," Theo said, standing up only feet away from the forcefield behind him. "You're all making a mistake. The world will be a much worse place without me, I assure you."

Kapp looked again to see that the rest of the crew had made their way up the ramp behind Jesse. Calix, with a blood-soaked bandage on his arm and a sickly pallor, struggled to stand. He wobbled like a windblown leaf beside Genesis, who looked more tired than hurt. On her back, she carried the dead weight of Asher. The sight made Kapp draw in a quick, nervous breath

"Is he—"

"He's alive," Genesis said, her tone grim.

Kapp, only slightly relieved by her words, still had worries about Aeva's fall over the edge of the ramp. She and Felix still hadn't returned.

"Surrender," Jesse said. "It's over."

The battered group made a semi-circle around Theo, who flashed a grin. "This is only the beginning."

"Holden's dead, and you're outnumbered." Jesse looked at Theo with cold eyes. "We've killed every last one of your men, and you're fixin' to join them if you don't cooperate."

"You're wrong." Theo's grin doubled in magnitude. "You haven't killed all my men."

Asher sprang to life, knocking Genesis to the metallic floor with incredible strength for his size. In the same motion, he snatched a dirty knife from her belt. Before Kapp could react, Asher was on him like a parasite. One arm grabbed the back of his head, and the other pressed a blade against his throat.

"Kapp," Theo said. "Don't lose your reason."

The knife felt cool against Kapp's neck. *What's going on? Why would Asher—*

"I don't even have to say the word to make him kill you," Theo said, the cockiness returning to his voice. "I just have to think it. And my thoughts tend to wander."

Kapp's prosthetic arm still hung uselessly at his side. He looked into Asher's eyes and understood what had happened. His friend had the same vacant stare, the same flawless skin as the rest of Theo's minions. Behind them both, Calix sank to the ground, finally losing the fight against his blood loss. Genesis caught him before his head could hit the ramp, but collapsed under his weight. Without missing a beat, Jesse pulled the rifle's trigger. The bullet only grazed the side of Theo's bald head. Theo wiped the blood away and turned his attention back to the group.

"You try that again," Theo said, "and my thoughts might wander dangerously close to snapping Kapp's neck."

"Kill me," Kapp said. A new kind of tear came to his eyes, not from dryness but from a true and deep sadness. Asher stood before him—moving, breathing—but Kapp knew that his friend was as good as dead. "I'm not opening the ship."

Theo sighed dramatically, the released air hissing through his perfect teeth.

"I can't read your thoughts, Kapp," Theo said, "but I know you. I know you because I used to be just like you—restless, dissatisfied. Your whole life you've felt like this world is a prison cell, am I right?"

Kapp wouldn't admit it out loud, but Theo had hit the nail on the head. Instead of responding, though, he focused all of his energy on Asher.

"Asher," he whispered. "It's me."

"Because of this, I've decided not to offer you the satisfaction of death," Theo said, inching closer. "Bribery and death threats didn't work, but perhaps this will: If you don't give me the password, I'll imprison you for rest of your days, and those days will stretch on. One by one, I'll slaughter what's left of your friends—slowly, of course. We'll have plenty of time." Theo chanced a step forward. "Perhaps I'll even make you do it. The world you hate so much will look like a paradise compared to what I have in store for you."

"Asher, please," Kapp begged. "I know you're in there."

"He is," Theo said. "His memories and emotions are buried far too deep for you to reach, though."

Instead of resisting, Kapp put his working arm around Asher's back and pulled him closer. The edge of the knife dug into his throat, splitting skin and spilling a small stream of blood.

"I can feel Asher's hate for you—his jealousy. He's already tried to end his own life because of it. Maybe I should just make him do it right now."

Kapp tried to ignore Theo, but the words stung.

"I'm sorry, Ash." Tears streamed down his face as he pressed his forehead against Asher's. "I'm so sorry."

"What a miserable life he's led compared to yours."

Kapp was ready for it to end. The remorse he had bottled up for so long began to seep through its container—a hot, painful flow. His neck craved the blade, the sweet release of death. He felt like a mouse in the jaws of a cruel cat, like he was just being played with.

"You even fucked his girlfriend before he did. Got her pregnant, didn't you?"

Through his burning eyes, Kapp thought he saw Asher's stoic face twitch. He just hoped that his final apology would pierce through the facade and into Asher's mind.

"I'm sorry, Asher." Kapp swallowed hot tears. "If I could have taken her place—If I could have died instead, I would have. Emily was—"

"From the look of her in Asher's memories," Theo said, his voice dripping acid, "Emily was a low-class whore."

A grunt escaped Asher's mouth as he pulled away from the embrace, just far enough for Kapp to see that his expression had shifted from silent resignation to intense anger. His face still had the plastic shine of the nano-injected, but the rage there looked far from manufactured.

Theo Cage opened his mouth to speak more vulgarities. He was about to say something either persuasive or menacing—perhaps another threat that would have fallen on deaf ears. His tone would have had that practiced mix of arrogance and hostility, and his perfect teeth would have glistened in the desert sunlight. Even his waxen face would have been painted with a shit-eating grin. An inferno might have flashed across his dead eyes as he spoke…but Theo never got the chance to speak again.

At the mention of his beloved Emily, something inside of Asher broke free. Some powerful courage that had always been there, buried deep by society or self-doubt, finally clawed its way to the surface. To greet the day—to make his body move through a world that often seemed hopeless—had once been nearly impossible for Asher. But Kapp had changed all of that. Emily had changed it. Humanity had changed it.

So at that moment, even with the world's most powerful man dominating both his body and his mind, nothing could stop Asher. No weight could hold him down. Theo's control over Asher only faltered for a couple seconds, but that was enough.

Without a word, Asher released his hold on Kapp. Before the bloody knife in his hand could hit the tilted floor below, he crossed the distance between himself and Theo, plowing into the enemy with the force of a hurricane.

As his body crossed the nearly invisible barrier of Arca's forcefield, the parts that made up Theo Cage faced an even more powerful foe. The technology in his blood, though shielded from EMPs, stood no chance against the ancient life form encasing Arca—and the mysterious tech-resistant energy that it emitted. Like the cameras Kapp had thrown through the forcefield on Phobos, Theo's nanites stopped doing their job. Silently, without triumphant celebration, the Artazoa conquered the conqueror. As soon as it crossed the threshold, Theo's heart stopped beating.

But so did Asher's.

43

FRAGMENTS

What happened next would later appear as fragments in Kapp's memory, nightmares far worse than childhood trauma, crash landings, or attempted suicide…

A sudden silence.
Falling on hands and knees.
Genesis checking a pair of pulses.
The grim shake of her head.
Screams of no no no.
This isn't happening.
Hurry!
Dropping guns, lifting each other.
Arms under shoulders.
"To the ship!"
Felix carrying Aeva, then Calix.
So pale.
"Put pressure on it."
The glow of a forcefield.
Handprints embedded in Arca's hull.
A word that Kapp could no longer remember.
Gravity reversed.
Falling up.
A white room.
Skip the quarantine.

"Someone radio Mara!"

Floating, obeying orders.

Strange medical supplies.

"It's broken."

Count and pump.

Count and pump.

How many compressions?

"This isn't working."

Try harder.

"I'm sorry, Kapp."

Tears depleted.

Vomit and blood and sweat, but no tears.

"We have to go!"

So tired.

"Try again!"

Adrenaline losing the fight against sleep and blood loss.

44

INTO THE FUTURE

2 Days Later

Kapp set down his pen and folded the piece of paper in his hands into thirds. He flexed his metallic fingers one by one in front of his face, testing their mobility. Jesse had done a good job rewiring the busted circuits and calibrating the prosthetic, so Kapp had sharper motor skills than ever. He was even able to roll a joint, which he now held between chapped lips. In Asher's messy bedroom, the smoke rose up to the ceiling, but not even the cannabinoids could make the pain go away—or the terrible memories. Time seemed to stand still as he sat in despondent silence. His mind revolved around the same few words: *father, mother, brother, friend*. Words that all meant the same thing to him. *Gone*. When the sound of crutches on concrete reached his ears, Kapp didn't have to turn his head to know who stood in the doorway.

"It's almost time," Aeva said, her voice as gentle as drizzle. "You're not having second thoughts, are you?"

She limped closer, one leg wrapped in a cast. Even though Arca's waters had healed their scrapes and bruises, the deeper aches and injuries remained.

"No," he said, stifling the hesitation that crept into his tone. "I think I'm ready now."

Kapp would have offered Aeva a hit of the joint, but he knew she wouldn't accept it. Taking a drag for himself, he rose a lonely, internal toast.

To Asher.

"You know, you don't have to—"

"I know I don't have to," Kapp said. "I want to."

And he did want to. He wanted to be near her forever, and with the knowledge about his true identity—the Skyborn bastard—he knew that forever was now a possibility. Too ashamed, he still hadn't told her the truth about his heritage.

"I've always wanted to."

"Thank you," Aeva said. "Shall we go, then?"

Her eyes widened, infinite pools of green, and Kapp's doubt diminished. In his mind, hers was the only name that didn't translate to *gone*.

"I'll meet you there." Kapp stood up from the edge of Asher's bed. "I just want to say goodbye first."

Aeva dipped her head and exited. Kapp stretched his neck muscles, shouldered his duffle bag, and took a few lazy steps around the room. On the way to the door, something caught his eye. He bent over and picked up a shirt from a small pile of Asher's clothes. Holding the wrinkled Coldplay merchandise between his hands, he smiled at the memory of the concert where he'd gotten it. Asher knew every lyric, and he sang them out of key with a goofy grin on his face. It was probably the happiest Kapp had ever seen his friend, except for when he saw her with Emily—those fleeting moments. After shaking off the nostalgia, he stomped out his joint, folded the keepsake into his duffle, and made his way to the elevator.

•|•

When the lift stopped on level nine, Kapp stepped out with his eyes down and collided with the muscled chest of Calix, whose brother stood beyond. Kapp had pressed the button for level ten, but apparently, the twins had some business to attend to in either the storage room or the armory.

"Sorry," he said, re-entering the elevator. "Going down?"

They nodded simultaneously. Both men looked healthier than

they had two days earlier, but Kapp knew that Calix had a nasty scar under his shirt sleeve from one of Holden's hounds.

"Feeling any better?" Kapp asked.

"Yeah," Calix said, stepping through the double doors. "Thanks to my own personal blood donor here."

"Believe it or not," Felix said, slapping his clone on the back, "our blood is a perfect match."

Kapp smiled. The weed had done wonders for his mood and pain levels.

"I heard you two are staying behind. Is it true?"

"We figured we have to," Calix said. "Genesis will need us for what's to come."

"That and the storage room still has plenty of cigarettes left," Felix added. "Which reminds me—"

He reached into his pocket and pulled out a pack and a lighter just as the doors opened on level ten. The walls of the room they stepped into, once sterile and empty, were now filled with other-worldly equipment unloaded from Arca.

Genesis stood in the middle of it all, surveying her new lab with a tablet in hand. She had traded her all-black battle gear for a white lab coat.

"Wow," Kapp said, peering around at the impressive exhibit of alien tech. "You guys did this in two days?"

"That's all the time we had," Genesis said. "It wasn't easy, but I think we have all that we need."

"Well, it looks great."

"Thank you," Genesis said, beaming. "Have you come to say goodbye? I was just about to head up."

"I was hoping for more of a *see you later*," Kapp said.

"I like that." Smiling, Genesis set down her tablet. "I was expecting to meet you in the Clearing. Is it not time?"

"It is, but first"—Kapp touched the side of her arm, looking over her shoulder at the door beyond—"can I?"

"Of course." Genesis walked toward what had once been the makeshift maternity room. "Follow me."

•|•

The only light in the room came from the machine that stood vertically, directly across from the doorway. An array of blinking lights surrounded the tube-shaped contraption, which emitted a dull and familiar glow from its center. Kapp set down his bag and stepped closer, focusing beyond the cloudy liquid that filled the vessel. When his pupils adjusted, the sight ahead made his stomach clench into knots. Suspended in the strange fluid rested the body of Asher West—pale, thin, and nude.

"Thank you for choosing to leave him behind," Genesis said. "I know it wasn't an easy decision."

Kapp put his hand on the transparent barrier between him and his friend's body, disrupting a thin layer of condensation on its cold surface.

"It's his best chance of survival, right?"

Kapp could vividly remember kneeling beside Asher at the top of the ramp, Genesis desperately searching for a pulse, but finding none. After a mad dash to open up the ship and get him onboard Arca, Genesis had been able to restore his heartbeat—but not much else. For no apparent reason, he remained catatonic.

"His best chance—and ours."

"What do you mean?"

Kapp wiped away some of the condensation to get a better look at Asher's face. His eyelids and thin lips were sealed shut.

"Asher is very important," Genesis said, now standing beside Kapp. "He is proof that humans can survive the destruction of Theo's nanites in their bloodstream."

"But"—Kapp didn't want to ask, but he had to—"Is he still in there?"

"My scans show no visible brain or nerve damage, which is why his paralysis is so baffling." With a quick gesture, Genesis pulled up an image of Asher's brain scan on a freshly-mounted display. "It may take a lifetime, but I intend to find a cure for Asher's ailment. If I can fix him, then I can fix others—and maybe this world stands a chance."

Her confidence granted Kapp with some level of reassurance. Still, it was hard leaving Asher in the care of someone else. Since the day that they met each other in the halls of Stanford, Kapp had been Asher's only protector. Genesis would now take that role for the foreseeable future.

"Did killing Theo do nothing?" Kapp asked after a moment contemplative silence. "I thought that the world might get better with him gone—that everyone under his control might, I don't know, snap out of it?"

"We all hoped that," Genesis said. "But I've been watching a few of our video feeds, and it looks like the injected have been displaying odd behavior since Theo's death. It's as if we slaughtered a chicken—we've cut off the head, but the body still moves. The unrest in Moscow is not a good sign either. Fights are already breaking out. This world has grown far too treacherous, but at least we're safe in here."

Kapp wondered how long Beacon's food supply would last if they had to stay underground for a while. He stared ahead at the ghostly form of his friend. Asher looked like death itself, but Kapp could see the living blood beneath his pale skin. Kapp turned away. He didn't want to remember Asher in such a weakened state.

"Can you hold onto something for him?" Kapp asked, reaching into his duffle bag. "Give it to him if he wakes up."

"Of course," Genesis said, her eyes warm. "When he wakes up. Not if."

Kapp smiled and handed her the sealed letter he had written the night before, the words of which had not come easily. He stayed up all night drafting and revising this final *see you later*. The process drained his energy, but he was unbothered by the drowsiness clawing at his heavy eyelids—he knew that a long slumber would come soon enough.

When Kapp made his way to the surface, the weather surprised him. A warm, dry night in the mountains had melted the snow, leaving behind a fresh layer of damp earth. In the distance, Arca towered over even the tallest pines. Genesis and the twins had already gone ahead to meet the others, making Kapp the ultimate procrastinator, but he felt no obligation to hurry—he just wanted to enjoy his last moments on Earth.

He took in a lungful of the cold mountain air, unsure whether he would ever taste it again. Probably not, he thought, but the notion didn't bother him too much. His cherished memories weren't stored in places or things, they were stored in the few people he had grown to love—and those people, besides the one sleeping ten levels below, were all gathered in the Clearing, waiting for Kapp to join them.

On the way to Arca, he stopped at the makeshift graveyard, which had the recent addition of two stones—not traditional gravestones, but smooth river rocks with engraved inscriptions. Kapp read the laser-etched words of the first memorial.

Oliver Wilson
Aug 1st 1999 - Dec 2nd 2040
"The best damn helicopter pilot in the world."
Died in the fight for humanity.

Kapp closed his eyes and bowed his head in solemn gratitude. His memories with Oliver, though relatively few, were good. He wondered how the man had been recruited into Beacon but knew that he wouldn't get the chance to ask. The next stone read:

Emily
May 18th 2014 - Nov 30th 2040
"May the lights guide you home, my love."
Died bringing new life to the world.

Both inscriptions were beautifully done, but something about the second one bothered Kapp. It had no last name. Whoever made and placed the stones apparently didn't know it. The vision of Asher gently setting a diamond ring on her grave came to mind. Kapp didn't know Emily's last name either, but he knew how he could fix the stone.

He rifled through his duffle bag until he found the knife stored at the bottom, and then he knelt down and got to work, chipping away at the stone with the strength and dexterity of his bionic limb. After several focused minutes, his addition to the design looked sloppy but complete. He stood up to take in the big picture.

Emily West
May 18th 2014 - Nov 30th 2040
"May the lights guide you home, my love."
Died bringing new life to the world.

Satisfied with his work, Kapp continued his hike through the forest, leaving the past behind to make his plunge into the future.

45

FAREWELL

Kapp followed a thin trail through the trees until he saw Jesse and Mara ahead. Mara, who wore a puffy winter coat a few two sizes too big, held a tightly-wrapped bundle in her arms. Smiling widely, she lifted the baby to her lips and kissed her forehead. The trio stepped into a patch of sunlit Earth, where Jesse pulled his tiny lover and the little one in her arms into a long embrace. They held each other with intention, savoring the moment as only survivors do.

Kapp knew he had made the right decision.

Jesse, Mara, and the unnamed child looked like a proper family, a concept equally foreign and enticing to Kapp. After his mom was killed—he still couldn't accept that she had taken her own life—he spent his entire childhood in the foster system, bouncing from house to house, from parent to parent, but never to home. Never to family. More than anything, he wanted that sense of stability for his own progeny, but he knew that he could never provide it. Not with what had to be done.

To solve the problem, he had asked of his friends a simple question, but one with life-altering consequences. It wasn't an easy conversation to have, but a necessary one. Although the parting would be bittersweet, Kapp was happy that Jesse and Mara agreed to adopt his daughter.

"Hey, J." Kapp jogged closer. "Wait up."

"Kapp," Mara said warmly when he approached them. "You're a little late. I thought you might have chickened out."

"Who, me?" Kapp asked. "Don't you know by now that I'm incredibly brave and selfless?"

Mara and Jesse laughed, and the baby mimicked their joyous expressions, blowing bubbles of spit between her tender lips.

"Not to mention good-looking," Kapp added, grabbing the child's tiny fingers. He suppressed a twinge of guilt about leaving her behind.

"You're preachin' to the choir, Kapp," Jesse said, slapping his friend on the back. "It's not really fair though—what with your superior DNA and all."

Kapp had nothing to say to that. He was still processing the information about his heritage, something he did with reluctance and in short bursts of contemplation. He had decided to tell the adopted parents of his child the truth, figuring that someone on Earth had to know.

"You sure about this?" Jesse asked, holding the baby's tiny hand.

"I think it's what Emily would have wanted," Kapp said. "Didn't you say you wanted to settle down, anyway?"

"Find a nice lady," Jesse said. He grinned and winked at Mara. "Check."

Mara blushed, rocking the baby from side to side.

"But some more land?" Jesse peered through the forest. "This'll do."

Together, the group walked in silence, taking in the sunlight where they could, just enjoying the peace and quiet of nature.

"We're gonna miss you, Kapp," Mara said. "All of us."

"Ain't that the truth," Jesse added.

"Well," Kapp said as they came out of the forest into the Clearing, where Arca's massive shadow darkened the path ahead. "Maybe I still have time to change your minds."

•|•

Everyone gathered beneath the glimmering concavity that marked Arca's entrance. Hand imprints of the sentient races filled both walls above them. Most of those civilizations had been wiped out by the Surge, that great technological threat, the only survivors of which were kept in suspended animation onboard the massive colony-class ship. Kapp thought he would have felt some sense of accomplishment for doing his part to save those unique lives. Having slain an immortal despot, he and those that stood around him had done the impossible—but instead of triumph, a deep and immediate sadness overcame Kapp. He might not miss Earth, but he would miss his friends.

No, not friends, he thought. *Family.*

The people surrounding Kapp were not the family he had been born with, or even the family he chose, but the family that had chosen him—those few that believed in him when he didn't believe in himself. They had offered him forgiveness time and time again, even when it felt undeserved. The tears welling in Kapp's eyes came not from thinking about leaving them behind, but from knowing that he could never repay them even if he stayed.

Kapp's time with Genesis, Felix, and Calix had been short, but he had grown to love them just the same—not only for their intelligence and bravery but for their company. Even in the high-stress environment, they treated him with kindness and respect. He wondered if his connection to them had anything to do with their shared ancestry. Pondering this, he realized that the first of the Skyborn was absent.

"Where's Aeva?" Kapp asked the group.

"She has something she wants to leave us," Genesis said, "and she's gone to get it."

They passed the time waiting for Aeva's return in idle chitchat, putting off the inevitable farewell for as long as possible. Kapp took this opportunity to hold the baby close, smelling the sweetness of her scalp and letting her wrap her tiny fingers around one of his own. He took a mental snapshot of the moment. He knew that leaving her with Jesse and Mara was the right choice, but that didn't make it any easier.

"Kapp, you haven't named her yet," Mara said, running her fingers across the child's fuzzy head. "I think you should."

Kapp smiled. He had already decided on a name, but he worried that saying it out loud would make it harder to leave the child behind. The time to procrastinate had come to an end, though, so Kapp had to share the news.

"Isabella," Kapp said out loud for the first time. "After my mom."

"It's a beautiful name," Genesis said. "And you never need to worry about her safety, Kapp. She has all of us to protect her. We will care for her as our own."

Felix and Calix nodded their agreement, and Mara wrapped her tiny arms around Kapp's torso. Jesse squeezed his shoulder.

"I know you will," Kapp said, and he meant it. "Thank you."

•|•

Aeva returned bearing gifts. She descended from the stark tunnel above like an angel from heaven. Though normally she'd be able to jump down from the invisible platform, her injury prevented her from doing so. Instead, Felix and Calix helped her through the forcefield with their burly arms and lowered her to the ground. Since the morning, she had changed into an elegant robe and had her long dark hair pulled up into two messy buns, which revealed the slight point of her ears. In her delicate hands, she held a small assortment of objects, two of which she offered to Jesse and Mara.

"Jesse McCall and Mara Stone of Earth," she said in a formal tone. "Both of you were dragged into a war that you didn't ask for, but you joined our cause fearlessly and without hesitation. You've fought for Arca. You've fought for life. You've proven yourselves as indispensable allies of the Skyborn."

Aeva dropped the gift, two angular vials filled with an iridescent liquid, into Jesse's outstretched hands.

"But I see you as more than allies. For your bravery, I offer you the gift that Alastar wished to offer the human race—the chance to become like us."

Jesse shook his head back and forth, stealing a glance at Mara, who looked equally shocked. Kapp didn't know that what Aeva spoke of was even possible.

"I—we don't know what to say," Jesse said after a moment of silence.

"The choice is yours, Jesse and Mara, but do not make it lightly. Should you choose to use this gift, Genesis can show you how."

"Thank you, Aeva," Mara said.

"You are quite welcome," Aeva said, bowing her head before turning to Genesis. "I have something for you too, sister."

"You've already given us so much, Aeva. We have everything that we need."

"I'll admit that my gift is rather selfish," Aeva said, offering up a hand-sized shard of clear crystal. "In Alastar's records, I discovered something interesting that I want you to look into."

"What did you find?" Genesis asked as she accepted the perfectly symmetrical object.

"Alastar kept the location records for Beacon One."

"Beacon One?" Kapp had to ask. He couldn't remember hearing about it—not that he could keep track of Arca's insane history anyway.

"It was the first Beacon to arrive on Earth. Alastar hid it before returning to the stars." She turned her attention back to Genesis. "If you can find it and fix it, we may be able to stay in touch after all."

"This is great news," Genesis said.

"But why did he hide it?" Calix asked.

"Prying eyes," Felix offered.

"No," Genesis said. "I know why he hid Beacon One from humanity, but why did he hide it from us?"

"A worthy question," Aeva said, "but one that is unanswerable until you go and see for yourself."

"We'll find it," Genesis said, nodding firmly. "I promise."

Aeva pulled her sister into the traditional embrace of the Skyborn, holding one of her wrists with both hands—but she abandoned the greeting in favor of a hug.

"And we will await the good news."

•|•

Jesse and Mara didn't change their mind about staying behind, but Kapp never expected them to. After her adventures on Phobos, Mara had sworn to never let her feet leave the ground again. The pair had their own things to accomplish, anyway—and a child to raise.

Kapp held back the tears as he hugged and kissed these last remnants of his past. He almost couldn't let go.

"Take care of yourself," Jesse said.

"Love you, Kapp," Mara added, her tears magnified by her spectacles.

"Love you too," he admitted, breaking contact before he could lose his composure.

He and Aeva offered their farewells to Genesis and the twins. Before making the final steps toward their shared fate, they faced the entirety of the group.

"Farewell, everyone." Aeva spoke with poise and dignity. "I wish you good fortune as you attempt to save this planet from itself. May we meet again someday."

"In other words," Kapp added, "we'll see you later."

They were the last words to leave his mouth before crossing the threshold of the forcefield, and deep down, no matter how much he wanted it to be true, he knew the statement was a lie. With the help of Felix and Calix, Aeva stepped up beside him, her skin already glistening from the muggy air inside the translucent bubble.

"Do you want to do the honors?" she asked.

Kapp nodded, turning to look once more at the people he was about to leave behind. Jesse had his arm around Mara, the usual smirk on his face replaced with something more heartfelt. Mara's hair desperately needed a dye job, but Kapp thought she had never looked more beautiful. Mimicking her teary-eyed adoptive mother, the child in Mara's arms began to cry, the muffled sound of which released a deep ache in Kapp's heart. *Isabella.*

Wordlessly, he brought his left hand to the appropriate imprint on the shimmering wall, remembering how he had once risked his life taking off his glove to do the same thing on the surface of Phobos. His fingers aligned perfectly with the symbol, and at that moment, he realized that the human handprint didn't come from a human at all—it came from the Skyborn. *My people,* he thought for the first time. With a slight shiver of realization, he thought that Arca might not have opened up on Phobos if Jesse or Mara had tried using their hands instead. *What would have happened if we just turned around and went back to Starling?* The light in the portal shifted under his touch. This time he could feel the Artazoa reading his thoughts. Gravity reversed as light began to spill from the opening above, lifting him and Aeva away from the beat-up band of heroes below—into the safety of Arca's womb.

•|•

By the time Arca left the atmosphere, the pent-up emotions nipping at Kapp's mind had begun to attack with full force. His only friends in the universe, except for Aeva and her cat (if Lex could be called a friend), had decided to stay on Earth, a planet on the brink of massive change. The place crawled with the mindless servants of the once-great Theo Cage—Kapp's monstrosity of a father. The thought of being related to such an evil person made his stomach turn. To add insult to misery, Kapp berated himself for not being able to save his best friend from the catatonic state Theo had left him in. He was already starting to doubt his decision to leave his daughter behind, wondering if the choice had actually been more cowardly than noble. This cocktail of bad thoughts left a strange taste in his mouth. Lost and a bit depressed, he wandered to his old quarters to see if he had any booze left to wash the bad taste away.

Luckily, he did. After taking a swig of the aged scotch, he carried the bottle with him down the long, winding hallway to the cockpit. He walked past the gardens, where fruits both familiar and alien bursted to life in a vivid display of color. The liquor burned in his throat and mind as he passed the pod-filled rooms where the ancient lifeforms—those last survivors—basked in their eternal sleep. As Kapp approached the end of the hall, he thought he could hear weeping.

Aeva stared ahead at the picturesque display. The blue curve of Kapp's home planet filled the bottom half of it. He stepped closer, confirming that the sounds of sorrow came from the beautiful woman ahead.

"What's wrong?" Kapp asked, stepping up beside her.

He didn't need an answer. From his new vantage point, he could see what caused the weeping. The curve of the globe below had been interrupted by an abnormal growth in its center, something that resembled a living organism but reeked of death and destruction. Kapp had seen similar images in history class growing up, and even more recently on the news, but never from an aerial viewpoint.

A mushroom cloud rose into the sky like a succulent reaching for the sun, but it didn't take root in Russia or Europe or China. From their vantage point in the sky, Kapp and Aeva watched in horror as this mushroom cloud sprouted from the ground in North America.

Kapp sank into one of the teardrop-shaped chairs, unable to process the new information. He took a long draw out of the bottle, a futile attempt to burn away his rising anxiety. On a cosmic scale, all of his previous concerns seemed so petty. When millions could be wiped out in a single blow, the trials of one man were insignificant at best. He would have asked to go back—to save his friends or to die trying—but he knew what the answer would be. Arca's journey to find a safer world had to continue, regardless of the consequences.

"I cry not for the fate of our friends," Aeva said, wiping the tears away and coming closer to Kapp. "I know that they can survive this. It just seems like life, that beautiful and unique existence, is constantly bound to destroy itself. It happened to Alastar's home, and it's happening here. I fear for the future."

"I know," Kapp said, taking her hand in his.

This time she didn't withdraw from the touch.

"What if it happens again?" she asked. "Is everything we've fought for hopeless?"

"There's no way to know that," Kapp said, rubbing his thumb back and forth over her knuckles. "But I've felt hopeless so many times—and look at me. I'm still here."

"Well, I'd like to not feel like this." Without warning, she plopped into the large chair beside Kapp. "Let me have some."

"What?"

She took the bottle from his hand.

"I want to try it," she said.

"But—you don't drink." Kapp raised an eyebrow. "Ethanol inhibits brain function, or whatever."

"That's the point," she said, not smiling but not crying anymore either. "Besides, there's a first time for everything. If I'm going to drink alcohol, now is the perfect time."

He couldn't argue with that.

"Okay, but I gotta warn you. Your first time drinking—"

Before he could finish his thought, she brought the bottle to her lips and took two long sips. She shivered a little, her shoulders raising from the shock of the foreign substance. After a quiet moment, though, she relaxed a bit. They sat quietly, hiding in the safety of the small space to avoid looking at the destruction below.

"I like this," Aeva said. "It's like eating many uvuus at once."

"Chaos," Kapp said, remembering their walk through the garden.

"I suppose it's what makes life interesting," she said.

"Alcohol or chaos?"

Aeva's laugh came like music to Kapp's ears. Sinking deeper into the chair, she rested her head on Kapp's shoulder and began to run her fingers across the curve of his bionic forearm.

"I think you might be drunk," Kapp said.

"Why's that?" she asked.

"Lowered inhibitions," Kapp said. "I mean, you've never—"

"I've never what?" she asked, sitting up to look him in the face.

"I guess I always thought you were—I don't know—afraid of this."

He rotated his bionic wrist in indication. Suddenly, he worried what would happen without Jesse there to recalibrate it every once in a while.

"Well," Aeva said, her face level with his—so close he could almost taste her breath. "I was."

"But not anymore?" he asked.

"No." She shook her head back and forth, releasing a few strands of hair from her updo. "Not anymore."

Kapp let out a small laugh. "And why is that?"

Aeva explored Kapp's face with piercing eyes, which lingered on his lips a little bit longer with each passing. Her hand left his arm and wrapped around his neck instead. He let the bottle fall to the floor and spill, completely unworried about it being the last one onboard. The time for escapism had passed. Another of her immortal pauses, then Aeva pulled herself closer to Kapp and brought her mouth to his ear.

"I'm not afraid of it," she whispered, her breath tickling skin. "Because it's part of you."

High above a world growing darker by the minute, beneath the twinkling of countless stars, the lights of which would appear dim if compared to the electricity coursing through Kapp and Aeva, their lips met for the first time.

EPILOGUE

Earth became a pale blue dot behind Arca as Kapp and Aeva flew the ship onward. The emptiness of space stretched out before them like an empty canvas, waiting for them to leave their mark on it. Kapp turned to his co-pilot. His head ached from the time spent without alcohol, but the sight of Aeva eased the pain.

"You still haven't told me where we're going."

"I couldn't risk anyone else knowing," she said, staring ahead at her displays.

"Well," Kapp said, gesturing at the emptiness surrounding them. "I think we're out of earshot by now."

Aeva scoffed and rolled her eyes, then she rotated the black orb that sat below her palm. The display before them became overlaid with a map of the known universe.

"This," she said, "is our final destination."

Under her command, the display zoomed in on a simulation of a gigantic planet orbiting a distant sun. Kapp, who still couldn't read the language of the Architects, had trouble deciphering the label attached to it.

"What is it?"

"Oh," Aeva said, fiddling with the controls once again. "I almost forgot."

Kapp squinted at the strange symbols before him. After a few of Aeva's quick gestures, the alien letters flickered and vanished, leaving behind only a blank map.

"Wait for it," Aeva said.

When the letters and numbers came back, Kapp found he could read them.

"I thought I'd make things more familiar for you," Aeva said.

"More like home."

Kapp nodded enthusiastically, letting his eyes dart from corner to corner of the display.

"I've even uploaded Earth's star charts, though I found them quite inaccurate."

"This is amazing," Kapp said. "Really—thank you."

"You're welcome," she said, visibly pleased about the gift.

"So"—Kapp looked at the label attached to the planet of their pursuit—"Gliese 667 Cc? Why there?"

Aeva took in a slow breath. "It's the resting place of Beacon Three, one of the few known planets in this galaxy capable of supporting life."

"Then why didn't you go there instead of Earth?"

"I almost did," she said. "But Earth seemed better at the time. And I couldn't go on without knowing what fate befell my brothers and sisters."

Kapp didn't want to think about the planet they had left behind. Those wounds were still too fresh. With his eyes on the future, he raised an important question.

"How far away is it?"

Aeva turned to Kapp, offered a mischievous smile, and rose her voice. "Jax?" she said.

Almost instantly, Jax's posh voice rang through the cockpit. It seemed to come from everywhere on the ship at once.

"Gliese 667 Cc is twenty-three-and-a-half lightyears from our current location. At Arca's max velocity, it will take approximately two hundred and thirty-five years to get there."

"We'll have to sleep in shifts," Aeva said before Kapp could even begin to process what such a long time meant. "To keep our minds fresh and our ears open for the good news."

"I hope you packed a few books," Jax said.

Aeva laughed, a hopeful sound, one that meant better days were ahead. Far ahead, but still there. Kapp—with his own mouth shut in an attempt to simply listen—reached across the space between them, and placed Aeva's free hand in his own.

"The planet has a lot of problems—unique challenges that we'll need to overcome." Aeva removed the simulation with a gesture, and the emptiness returned. She faced Kapp and squeezed his hand in return. "But there's nowhere else that we can go. Unless our friends undo Theo's damage, Beacon Three is the last safe place that I know of—possibly the last safe place out there."

THE END

or is it?

THANK YOU!

In an age where attention spans are short, and content is consumed in bite-sized pieces, just making it to this page is an accomplishment worthy of praise. Thank you for spending a few hours of your life reading *The Last Safe Place*. I hope you enjoyed it!

Q: Will there be a sequel?
A: My goal is to write 2-3 more books in this universe, which I'm currently referring to as *The Arca Saga*. Be the first to know about them by joining my mailing list. You'll also get a **free short story**! Just go to www.AuthorAndyGorman.com/ArcaSagaBook2 to sign up.

Q: Can I tell you how much I liked the book?
A: Of course! I would prefer you did it with Amazon reviews. I read every single one of them, I promise. Writers—especially independent authors—rely on readers like you leaving kind reviews. It's the best way to help other people discover our books.

Q: How can I keep up with your writing?
A: I'm glad you asked. Pick your poison...

• **Twitter: @_AndyGorman**
• **Instagram: @_AndyGorman**
• **My Website: www.AuthorAndyGorman.com**
• **Email: Andy@AuthorAndyGorman.com**

I try to respond to all emails, and I love receiving them...even hate mail because it keeps me humble.

ACKNOWLEDGMENTS

I owe my gratitude to a long list of people who have helped, supported, or inspired me during the creation of *The Last Safe Place*...

To my fiancé Lawren for always supporting my creative pursuits. Every time I felt like lighting my manuscript on fire, you were there with words of encouragement (and a metaphorical fire extinguisher). Everyone needs someone to believe in them, and you've always been that person for me. You're the Aeva to my Kapp, the Emily to my Asher, and the Mara to my Jesse. My love for you is infinite.

To my family for their patience. I've spent a lot of time at my desk, which meant time away from you. I hope to find a better balance moving forward. I love you all!

To Larry, Lisa, and Logan for sharing their home with me, feeding me gourmet meals, and taking me on some great adventures over the years. I consider you my second family. Thanks for taking me in!

To Josiah Schotborgh for taking the time during his summer vacation to edit my novel. I've always trusted and respected your feedback. I promise to pay you more on the next one, buddy.

To Jarret Keene, the creative writing professor of my first workshop, for encouraging me during the writing of my early chapters.

To my good friends and first readers, Brandee, Cierra, and Ian, for offering valuable and encouraging feedback before publication.

To all my friends, near and far, for inspiring my work. Writing can get lonely, but you're in my thoughts every time I sit down to put words on the page. I've used your names, your characteristics, and your experiences as bricks to build this story. I wish I could list all of you, but the printing company I use charges by the page, and I'm a cheap bastard. Also, I'd probably forget someone, and then I'd never hear the end of it. You know who you are.

Finally, to the voice in my head that told me I'd never finish this book, that everything I create sucks, and that I'd be better off spending my time doing anything else...well, as Kapp Adams might say, fuck you!

Andy Gorman
October 2018

SPONSORS

Ian Maltzman
www.ThePerceptionEngine.com

Jennifer Priester
www.ammoonlightcreations.com

Rob Jensen Company
www.RobJensen.com

Lawren Linehan
@LawrenLinehan on Instagram

Larry, Lisa, & Logan Linehan

Meghan Thomas

Edward Gorman

Thank you so much for your support!